D0094097

Dear Target Guest,

I think of Target as a place where a person can run in and pick up just about anything, and I'm glad to know that books are included on that list. Not every town has a bookstore anymore, and I think it's great that Target takes an interest in providing and promoting books, especially in the places where people might not be able to easily find them otherwise. I remember when I was a child there was always a book section in department stores, and whenever I'm in a Target store now, I'm reminded of that wonderful time when books were more a part of our everyday shopping experience.

I am honored to be a Target Club Pick. It's a wonderful thing when I meet someone who is reading a book that I just finished and loved, or when someone recommends a book to me that they loved. I can hardly wait to read it so that we can talk about it. Reading is, of course, a solitary act (one of the many things I love about reading), but it's also a great way to come together with other people and exchange ideas—that's what makes the Club Pick so exciting. We'll never all agree on what we like, and a character that one person loves can drive another person crazy, but the magic comes from the conversations that ensue. Books open the door to ideas and opinions—they get us thinking about what is important to us and help us challenge our ideas and forge our opinions.

I also believe that books foster concentration. In this world of constant interruptions and distractions, it's a beautiful thing to fall into a single story that can last for days or weeks, depending on how much time you have to read. I hope the world I've created in *State of Wonder* is one you can lose yourself in for a while. If you enjoy it, please pass it on to a friend, and then get another book for yourself. For me, having a good book and the time to read it is the greatest gift in the world.

I hope you enjoy it.

Ann Patchett

Dear Target Guest,

[illegible] place where [illegible] can [illegible] and [illegible] [illegible] the place where people [illegible] [illegible] [illegible] [illegible]

[illegible] Target Club Pick [illegible] [illegible] a book [illegible] [illegible]

[illegible] [illegible]

[illegible] the world.

Thank you [illegible]

[illegible]

Praise for

State of Wonder

"Is there nothing the prodigiously talented Ann Patchett can't do? . . . Patchett's last knockout pages proceed full speed ahead, with more twists and turns and treachery than the Amazon River. Nothing is as it seems, and the ending is as shocking as it's satisfying. . . . [*State of Wonder* is] extraordinary." —*Boston Globe*

"*State of Wonder* is an engaging, consummately told tale." —*New York Times*

"This is surely the smartest, most exciting novel of the summer."
—*Washington Post*

"This is a masterpiece of a novel." —NPR

"Her sixth and best novel. . . . These pages have a pulsing, seductive rhythm. . . . The wonder of *State of Wonder* is that Patchett poses essential philosophical and bioethical arguments in a story that still speeds along like a literary thriller, reaching a tremendous, deeply emotional crescendo. *Bella scrittura.*" —*Time*

"Ann Patchett's *State of Wonder* . . . [packs] a textbook's worth of ethical conundrums into a smart and tidily delivered story. . . . Ms. Patchett presents an alluring interplay between civilization and wilderness, between aid and exploitation."
—*Wall Street Journal*

"In her most incisive work yet, Patchett achieves alchemy, creating complex, compelling characters, packing a Ph.D.'s worth of scientific knowledge into a nail-biting narrative, setting stark human dilemmas against a lush, exotic backdrop. . . . Reading this book will cause you to call in sick, cancel all plans, and return to page one upon completion." —*People* (four stars)

"Emotionally lucid. . . . Patchett is at her lyrical best when she catalogues the jungle"
—*The New Yorker*

"[*State of Wonder* is] outlandishly entertaining . . . [with] a brilliantly constructed plot. . . . [Her] prose is always astute." —*Elle*

"A gripping new novel. . . . Patchett has an uncanny knack for writing stories about complex characters to whom things *actually happen*. True to form, she manages to braid questions of medical and social ethics alongside encounters with cannibals, anacondas, even an opera house, making this a bubbling stew of a novel."

—*Marie Claire*

"Patchett infuses her characters with fascinating emotional depth."

—*Miami Herald*

"The large canvas of sweeping moral issues, both personal and global, comes to life through careful attention to details, however seemingly mundane—from ill-fitting shoes and mosquito bites to a woman tenderly braiding another woman's hair."

—*O, The Oprah Magazine*

"An expansive page-turner. . . . Patchett's fluid prose dissolves in the suspense of this out-there adventure . . . that readers will hate to see end."

—*Publishers Weekly* (starred review)

"A superbly rendered novel. . . . Patchett's portrayal is as wonderful as it is frightening and foreign. Patchett exhibits an extraordinary ability to bring the horrors and the wonders of the Amazon jungle to life, and her singular characters are wonderfully drawn. . . . Powerful and captivating." —*Library Journal* (starred review)

"In fluid and remarkably atmospheric prose, Patchett captures not only the sights and sounds of the chaotic jungle environment but also the struggles and sacrifice of dedicated scientists."

—*Booklist*

"A thrilling new novel. . . . The world imagined in this novel is unusually vivid. . . . Reading *State of Wonder* is a sensory experience, and even after it's over you'll keep hearing the sounds of insects, and your own head will still be hot." —*More*

"The book's dreamlike claustrophobia weaves a spell. . . . It's a trip well worth taking."

—*Entertainment Weekly*

State of Wonder

ALSO BY ANN PATCHETT

What now?

Run

Truth & Beauty

Bel Canto

The Magician's Assistant

Taft

The Patron Saint of Liars

State of Wonder

Ann Patchett

HARPER PERENNIAL

NEW YORK • LONDON • TORONTO • SYDNEY • NEW DELHI • AUCKLAND

HARPER PERENNIAL

A hardcover edition of this book
was published in 2011 by HarperCollins Publishers.

P.S.™ is a trademark of HarperCollins Publishers.

FIRST HARPER PERENNIAL EDITION PUBLISHED 2012.

Designed by Jennifer Ann Daddio / Bookmark Design & Media Inc.

The Library of Congress has catalogued the hardcover edition as follows:
Patchett, Ann.
State of wonder / Ann Patchett.—1st ed.
353 p. ; 24 cm.
ISBN 978-0-06-204980-3
1. Scientists—Fiction. 2. Medicine—Research—Fiction.
3. Jungles—Amazon River Region—Fiction. I. Title.
PS3566.A7756 S76 2011
813'.54 2010029229

ISBN 978-0-06-220725-8 (Target edition)

12 13 14 15 16 OV/RRD 10 9 8 7 6 5 4 3 2 1

To my friend Jo VanDevender

One

The news of Anders Eckman's death came by way of Aerogram, a piece of bright blue airmail paper that served as both the stationery and, when folded over and sealed along the edges, the envelope. Who even knew they still made such things? This single sheet had traveled from Brazil to Minnesota to mark the passing of a man, a breath of tissue so insubstantial that only the stamp seemed to anchor it to this world. Mr. Fox had the letter in his hand when he came to the lab to tell Marina the news. When she saw him there at the door she smiled at him and in the light of that smile he faltered.

"What?" she said finally.

He opened his mouth and then closed it. When he tried again all he could say was, "It's snowing."

"I heard on the radio it was going to." The window in the lab where she worked faced out into the hall and so she never saw the weather until lunchtime. She waited for a minute for Mr. Fox to say what he had come to say. She didn't think he had come all the way from his office in the snow, a good ten buildings away, to give her a weather report, but he only stood there in the frame of the open door, unable either to enter the room or step out of it. "Are you all right?"

"Eckman's dead," he managed to say before his voice broke, and then with no more explanation he gave her the letter to show just how little about this awful fact he knew.

There were more than thirty buildings on the Vogel campus, labs and office buildings of various sizes and functions. There were labs with stations for twenty technicians and scientists to work at the same time. Others had walls and walls of mice or monkeys or dogs. This particular lab Marina had shared for seven years with Dr. Eckman. It was small enough that all Mr. Fox had to do was reach a hand towards her, and when he did she took the letter from him and sat down slowly in the gray plastic chair beside the separator. At that moment she understood why people say *You might want to sit down*. There was inside of her a very modest physical collapse, not a faint but a sort of folding, as if she were an extension ruler and her ankles and knees and hips were all being brought together at closer angles. Anders Eckman, tall in his white lab coat, his hair a thick graying blond. Anders bringing her a cup of coffee because he'd picked one up for himself. Anders giving her the files she'd asked for, half sitting down on the edge of her desk while he went over her data on proteins. Anders father of three. Anders not yet fifty. Her eyes went to the dates—March 15th on the letter, March 18th on the postmark, and today was April 1st. Not only was he dead, he was two weeks dead. They had accepted the fact that they wouldn't hear from him often and now she realized he had been gone so long that at times he would slip from her mind for most of a day. The obscurity of the Amazonian tributary where Dr. Swenson did her research had been repeatedly underscored to the folks back in Minnesota (*Tomorrow this letter will be handed over to a child floating downriver in a dugout log,* Anders had written her. *I cannot call it a canoe. There never were statistics written to cover the probability of its arrival.*), but still, it was in a country, it was in the world. Surely someone down there had an Internet connection. Had they never bothered to find it? "Wouldn't she call you? There has to be some sort of global satellite—"

"She won't use the phone, or she says it doesn't work there." As close as they were in this quiet room she could scarcely hear his voice.

"But for this—" She stopped herself. He didn't know. "Where is he now?" Marina asked. She could not bring herself to say *his body*. Anders was not a body. Vogel was full of doctors, doctors working, doctors in their offices drinking coffee. The cabinets and storage rooms and desk drawers were full of drugs, pills of every conceivable stripe. They were a pharmaceutical company; what they didn't have they figured out how to make. Surely if they knew where he was they could find something to do for him, and with that thought her desire for the impossible eclipsed every piece of science she had ever known. The dead were dead were dead were dead and still Marina Singh did not have to shut her eyes to see Anders Eckman eating an egg salad sandwich in the employee cafeteria as he had done with great enthusiasm every day she had known him.

"Don't you read the reports on cholesterol?" she would ask, always willing to play the straight man.

"I write the reports on cholesterol," Anders said, running his finger around the edge of his plate.

Mr. Fox lifted his glasses, pressed his folded handkerchief against the corners of his eyes. "Read the letter," he said.

She did not read it aloud.

Jim Fox,

The rain has been torrential here, not unseasonable yet year after year it never ceases to surprise me. It does not change our work except to make it more time-consuming and if we have been slowed we have not been deterred. We move steadily towards the same excellent results.

But for now this business is not our primary concern. I write with unfortunate news of Dr. Eckman, who died of a fever two nights ago. Given our location, this rain, the petty bureaucracies of government (both this one and your own), and the time sensitive nature of our project, we chose to bury him here in a manner in keeping with his Christian traditions. I must tell you it was no small task. As for the purpose of Dr. Eckman's mission, I assure you we are making strides. I will keep what little he had here for his wife, to whom I trust you will extend this news along with my sympathy. Despite any setbacks, we persevere.

Annick Swenson

Marina started over at the top. When she had read it through again she still could not imagine what to say. "Is she calling Anders a setback?"

She held the letter by its slightest edges as if it were a document still to be submitted into evidence. Clearly the paper had been wet at some point and then dried again. She could tell by the way it was puckered in places, it had been carried out in the rain. Dr. Swenson knew all about the relationship of paper and ink and rain and so she cut in her letters with a pencil of hard, dark lead, while on the other side of Eden Prairie, Minnesota, Karen Eckman sat in a two-story brick colonial thinking her husband was in Brazil and would be coming home as soon as he could make Dr. Swenson listen to reason.

Marina looked at the clock. They should go soon, before it was time for Karen to pick the children up from school. Every now and then, if Anders happened to look at his watch at two-thirty, he would say to himself in a quiet voice, *School's out.* Three little Eckmans, three boys, who, like their mother, did not know enough to picture their father dead. For all that loss Dr. Swenson had managed to use just over half the sheet of paper, and in the half a sheet she used she had twice thought to mention the weather. The rest of it simply sat there, a great blue sea of emptiness. How much could have been said in those remaining inches, how much explained, was beyond scientific measure.

Mr. Fox closed the door and came to stand beside Marina's chair. He put his hand on her shoulder and squeezed, and because the blinds on the windows that faced the hall were down she dropped her cheek against the top of his hand and for a while they stayed like this, washed over in the palest blue fluorescent light. It was a comfort to them both. Mr. Fox and Marina had never discussed how they would conduct their relationship at work. They had no relationship at work, or not one that was different from anyone else's. Mr. Fox was the CEO of Vogel. Marina was a doctor who worked in statin development. They had met, really met, for the first time late the summer before at a company softball game, doctors vs. administration. Mr. Fox came over to compliment her pitching, and that compliment led to a discussion of their mutual fondness for baseball. Mr. Fox was not a doctor. He had been the first CEO to come from the manufacturing side. When she spoke of him to other people she spoke of Mr. Fox. When she spoke to him in front of other people she addressed him as Mr. Fox. The problem was calling him Jim when they were alone. That, it turned out, was a much more difficult habit to adopt.

"I shouldn't have sent him," Mr. Fox said.

She raised her head then and took his hand in her hands. Mr. Fox had no reason to wear a lab coat. Today he wore a dark gray suit and striped navy tie, and while it was a dignified uniform for a man of sixty, he looked out of place whenever he strayed from the administrative offices. Today it occurred to Marina that he looked like he was on his way to a funeral. "You didn't make him go."

"I asked him to go. I suppose he could have turned me down but it wasn't very likely."

"But you never thought something like this would happen. You didn't send him someplace dangerous." Marina wondered if she knew this to be true. Of course there were poisonous snakes and razor-toothed fish but she pictured them safely away from the places where doctors conducted scientific research. Anyway, the letter had said he died of a fever, not a snake bite. There were plenty of fevers to be had right here in Minnesota. "Dr. Swenson's been down there for five years now. Nothing's happened to her."

"It wouldn't happen to her," Mr. Fox said without kindness in his voice.

Anders had wanted to go to the Amazon. That was the truth. What are the chances a doctor who worked in statin development would be asked to go to Brazil just as winter was becoming unendurable? He was a serious birder. Every summer he put the boys in a canoe and paddled them through the Boundary Waters with binoculars and notepads looking for ruddy ducks and pileated woodpeckers. The first thing he did when he got word about the trip was order field guides to the rain forest, and when they came he abandoned all pretense of work. He put the blood samples back in the refrigerator and pored over the slick, heavy pages of the guides. He showed Marina the birds he hoped to see, wattled jacanas with toes as long as his hand, guira cuckoos with downy scrub brushes attached to the tops of their heads. A person could wash out the inside of a pickle jar with such a bird. He bought a new camera with a lens that could zoom straight into a nest from fifty feet away. It was not the kind of luxury Anders would have afforded himself under normal circumstances.

"But these are not normal circumstances," he said, and took a picture of his coworker at her desk.

At the bright burst of the flash, Marina raised her head from a black-necked red cotinga, a bird the size of a thumb who lived in a cone-shaped daub of mud attached to the tip of a leaf. "It's an ambitious lot of birds." She studied every picture carefully, marveling at the splendors of biodiversity. When she saw the hyacinth macaws she experienced one split second of regret that she wasn't the one Mr. Fox had tapped for the job. It was a singularly ridiculous thought. "You'll be too busy with birds to ever find the time to talk to Dr. Swenson."

"I imagine I'll find a lot of birds before I find Dr. Swenson, and when I do find her I doubt she'll pack up on the first day and rush back to Johns Hopkins. These things take finesse. Mr. Fox said that himself. That leaves me with a lot of daylight hours."

Finding Dr. Swenson was an issue. There was an address in Manaus but apparently it was nowhere near the station where she did her field research; that location, she believed, needed to be protected with the highest level of secrecy in order to preserve both the unspoiled nature of her subjects and the value of the drug she was developing. She had made the case so convincingly that not even Mr. Fox knew where she was exactly, other than somewhere on a tributary off the Rio Negro. How far away from Manaus that tributary might begin and in which direction it ran no one could say. Worse than that was the sense that finding her was going to be the easy part. Marina looked at Anders straight on and again he raised his camera. "Stop that," she said, and turned her palm to the lens. "What if you can't get her to come back at all?"

"Of course I can," Anders said. "She likes me. Why do you think I'm the one Mr. Fox decided to send?"

It was possible that Dr. Swenson had liked him on the one day she spent at Vogel seven years ago, when she had sat at a conference table with Anders and four other doctors and five executives who made up the Probability Assessment Group to discuss the preliminary budget for the development of a program in Brazil. Marina could have told him Dr. Swenson had no idea who he was, but why would she have said that? Surely he knew.

Mr. Fox didn't know Karen Eckman. He had met her at company parties but he told Marina he could not remember her face, a fact that seemed unforgivable now in light of what had happened. Marina saw the look of gratitude when she took down her coat that was hanging by itself on the rack by the door, but she would never have sent him there alone. The task was one for military chaplains, police officers, people who knew something about knocking on doors to deliver the news that would forever derail the world of the people who lived inside the house. *Anders is dead.*

"She'll be glad you're there," Mr. Fox said.

"Glad doesn't figure into this," Marina said.

Marina was going along to help Mr. Fox, and she went out of respect for her dead friend, but she had no illusions that she was the person Karen Eckman would want to break the news. It was true that she knew Karen, but only as well as a forty-two-year-old woman with no children knows a forty-three-year-old woman with three, as well as any single woman who works with the husband ever knows the wife who stays at home. Marina understood that Karen had made a point of knowing her even if Karen had not consciously mistrusted her. Karen engaged her in conversation when it was Marina who answered the phone in the lab. She invited her to their Christmas open house and the Fourth of July barbeque, where she got Marina a glass of tea and asked her thoughtful questions about protein research and said she really liked her shoes, a vaguely exotic pair of yellow satin flats a cousin had sent her from Calcutta years ago, shoes she loved herself and saved for special occasions. When Marina in turn asked about the boys, what they were doing in school, whether or not they were going to camp, Karen answered the questions offhandedly, offering up very few details. She was not the sort of mother to bombard her husband's polite colleague with the endless talk of Scout meetings. Marina knew that Karen was not afraid of her. Marina was, after all, overly tall and bony with impenetrable eyes and heavy black hair that set her apart from all the Swedes; it was only that Karen didn't want Marina to forget her. And Marina did not forget her, but what was important between them was so deeply unspoken that there was never the chance to defend herself from that of which she had never been accused and was not guilty. Marina was not the kind of woman who fell in love with another woman's husband, any more than she was the kind of woman who would break into the house at night and steal the grandmother's engagement ring, the laptop, the child. In truth, after two glasses of rummy punch at the last Christmas party, she had wanted very much to lean against Karen Eckman in the kitchen, put an arm around her little shoulders, bend her head down until their heads were almost touching. She had wanted to whisper in her ear, "I'm in love with Mr. Fox," just to see Karen's pale blue eyes go round in that collision of pleasure and surprise. How she wished now that she had been drunk enough to confide. Had she ever done that, Marina Singh and Karen Eckman would be very good friends indeed.

Outside the snow had been falling in wet clumps long enough to bury every blade of new spring grass. The crocuses she had seen only that morning, their yellow and purple heads straight up from the dirt, were now frozen as solid as carp in the lake. The tiny blooms of redbud made burdened shelves of snow. Mr. Fox and Marina pushed forward through the icy slush without a thought that they were for the very first time in their relationship leaving the building together. They made the long walk from the southern quadrant of the Vogel campus to the parking lot nearly a quarter mile away. Marina hadn't brought her snow boots. It hadn't been snowing when she left for work.

"I'll tell you something else," Mr. Fox said once they were in his car, the snow brushed off and the defroster turned to high. "I never thought he'd be gone so long. I told him when he left to take his time, to get the point across, but I had thought we were talking about a week, maybe two at the outside. I never considered him staying for more than two weeks."

"He had a hard time finding her, that threw his schedule off to start."

Anders had left the day after Christmas. The company had wanted him to go sooner but Christmas was nonnegotiable for the Eckmans. She had shown Mr. Fox the few letters she'd had from Anders because they confided nothing. He had mostly talked about Manaus and then about the birding trips he had taken in the jungle with a guide. To her, Anders had spoken mostly of rain. If Mr. Fox had also received letters from Anders, and she was sure he had, he never mentioned them.

"So two weeks then. Not three months. I would have told him to come back—"

"You couldn't get a hold of him then."

"Exactly." Mr. Fox let his eyes trail off across the whitened landscape that smeared beneath the windshield wipers. "I would have told him there's a message to deliver and once he gave it to her he should have gotten on a plane himself, with or without her. That was his only job."

"It never would have been as simple as that," she said, as much to herself as to him. No one seriously thought the outcome of telling Dr. Swenson she needed to bring her research back to Minnesota would be Dr. Swenson packing her lab into boxes and coming home—not Anders, not Mr. Fox, not Marina. In truth, it wasn't even essential that she come back. Had she been willing to reopen lines of communication, to prove that the drug was nearly completed, to let the company install a coterie of its own doctors who would give regular and accurate reports of the drug's progress, Vogel would have left her in her research station for years, pouring in cash from an opened vein. But now Anders was dead and the notion of success was reduced to sickening folly. Just the thought of Dr. Swenson gave Marina the sensation of a cold hand groping for her heart. It is fifteen years ago and she is in the lecture hall at Johns Hopkins in a seat safely on the aisle of a middle row, and there is Dr. Swenson pacing in front of the podium, talking about the cervix, *the cervix*, with a level of intensity that elevates to such ferocity that none of them dare to look at their watches. No one in the crowd of a hundred will suggest that class is long over, class should be dismissed, there are other classes they are now in the process of missing. Even though Marina is a second-year resident she is attending a lecture for third-year medical students because Dr. Swenson has made it clear to residents and medical students alike that when she is speaking they should be in attendance. But Marina would not dream of missing a lecture or leaving a lecture over a matter as inconsequential as time. She is riveted in place while the slide show of atypical cells on the high wall before her flicks past so quickly they nearly make a moving picture. Dr. Swenson knows everything Marina needs to know, answers the questions Marina has not yet formulated in her mind. A tiny woman made tinier by distance fixes one hundred people to their seats with a voice that never troubles itself to be raised, and because they are all afraid of her and because they are afraid of missing anything she might say, they stay as long as she chooses to keep them. Marina believes the entire room exists as she exists, at the intersection of terror and exaltation, a place that keeps the mind exceedingly alert. Her hand sweeps over page after page as she writes down every syllable Dr. Swenson speaks. It is the class in which Marina learns to take notes like a court reporter, a skill that will serve her for the rest of her life.

It strikes Marina as odd that all these years later she still remembers Dr. Swenson in the lecture hall. In her mind's eye she never sees her in surgery or on the floor making rounds, but at a safe, physical distance.

Karen and Anders Eckman lived on a cul-de-sac where the neighbors drove slowly knowing that boys could come sledding down a hill or shooting out between the shrubbery on a bike. "That one," Marina said, pointing to the red brick, and Mr. Fox pulled the car to the curb. Marina and Anders must have made about the same amount of money. They never talked about it but they did the same work;

Anders had been at the company a few years longer than Marina so he could have made a little more. But Marina's house, which was quite small and still too big for her, was paid for. She made regular contributions to charity and let the rest of her money languish in the bank while Anders paid for this house, piano lessons, teeth straightening, summer camp, college accounts. How had he managed, three sons and a wife, and who would pay for this life now that he was dead? For a while she sat there, imagining the various birthday parties and Christmases, endless pictures of boys with presents, knotted ribbon and torn-up gift-wrap in piles of red and silver and green, until finally the snow laid a blanket over the windshield and cut off the view.

"Now this is a surprise," Karen Eckman said when she opened the door, both hands grasping the choke chain of an enormous golden retriever; she was a small woman, and it didn't look like a battle she would win. "No!" she said loudly. "Sit!" She was wearing a white knit stocking cap pulled down over her ears and her coat was just behind her, thrown across a chair in the front hall. Marina was blanking on the dog's name, though there was a picture of him on Anders' desk along with pictures of Karen and the boys. He pushed his mallet head against Karen's hip and gave two sharp barks at the unimaginable good fortune of guests in the middle of the day.

"You're leaving," Mr. Fox said, as if this meant maybe they should leave as well.

Karen shook her head. "No, no, you're fine. I've got plenty of time. I was going to swing by the store on the way to pick up the boys but I can do that later. Come inside. It's freezing." The dog lunged forward when they entered, hoping for the chance to jump up, but Karen, who had at best twenty pounds on the animal, managed to drag him to the side of the entry hall. "You get back, Pickles," she said. "You sit."

Pickles did not sit, and when she let him go she rubbed her hands to work out the indentations the chain-link collar had left. In the kitchen everything was neat: no cups on the countertop, no toys on the floor. Marina had been to the house before but only for parties when every room and hallway was pressed full of people. Empty she could see how big the place was. It would take a lot of children to fill in the open spaces. "Would you like some coffee?" Karen said.

Marina turned to put the question to Mr. Fox and found that he was standing almost directly behind her. Mr. Fox was not taller than Marina. It was something he joked about when they were alone. "No coffee," Marina said. "Thank you." It wasn't a bright day but what light there was reflected off the snow and cast a wide silvery band across the breakfast table. Through the big picture window Marina saw a jungle gym standing on a low hill in the backyard, a rough fort gathering snow on its slanted roof. Pickles leaned up against Marina now and he batted her hand with his head until she reached down to rub the limp chamois of his ears.

"I can put him up," Karen said. "He's a lot of dog."

Pickles stared at her, his vision unfocused by the ecstasy in his ears. "I like dogs," Marina said, thinking it was vital that he stay. The dog would have to stand in for their minister if they had one. The dog would be Karen's mother, her sister, whoever it was she wished was standing next to her when everything came down. The dog would have to be Anders.

She glanced back at Mr. Fox again. Every second they were in the house without telling her what had happened was a lie. But Mr. Fox had turned towards the refrigerator now. He was looking at pictures of the boys: the two youngest ones a couple of washed-out towheads, the older one only slightly darker. He was looking at a picture of Anders with his arms around his wife and in that photo they were not much older than children themselves. There were pictures of birds, too, a group of prairie chickens standing in a field, an eastern bluebird so vibrant it appeared to have been Photoshopped. Anders took a lot of pictures of birds.

Karen pulled off her hat and pushed her straight pale hair behind her ears. The flush that had been in her cheeks from the momentary burst of cold had faded. "This isn't good news, right?" she said, twisting the rings on her finger, the modest diamond and the platinum band. "I'm glad to see you but I can't imagine you're just dropping by to say hello."

And for a split second Marina felt the slightest surge of relief. Of course she would know. Even if she hadn't heard she would know in that way a soul knows. Marina wanted so badly to put her arms around Karen then, to give her condolences. She was ready for that if nothing else. The words for how sorry she was ached in the back of her throat.

"It's not good news," Marina said, hearing the catch in her own voice. This was the moment for Mr. Fox to tell the story, to explain it in a way Marina herself did not fully understand, but nothing came. Mr. Fox had given himself over to the refrigerator photos. He had his back to the two women, his arms locked behind, his head tilted forward to a picture of a common loon.

Karen turned her eyes up, shook her head slightly. "The letters have been crazy," she said. "I'll get two in a day and then nothing all week. They don't come in any sort of order. I got one a couple of days ago that didn't have a date on it but it must have been pretty recent. He sounded like he was half out of his mind. He's definitely writing to me less now. I think he doesn't want to tell me he has to stay longer."

"Karen, listen."

Pickles lifted his head as if *listen* was his command. He sat.

"It isn't his job," Karen said, and while she looked at Marina she pointed her finger at Mr. Fox's back. "He doesn't like the jungle. I mean, the birds, he says the birds are spectacular, but the rest of it is making him crazy, the leaves and the vines and all of that. In one of his letters he said he felt like they were choking him at night. Where Anders grew up in Crookston there are hardly any trees at all. Have you ever been to Crookston? It's nothing but prairie up there. He used to say that trees made him nervous, and he was joking, but still. He isn't cut out for this. He isn't some mediator who's been trained to talk down the difficult cases. I understand why you sent him. Everybody likes Anders. But if Vogel has inflated its stock price then that's Vogel's problem. It's not his job to fix it. He can't fix it, and you can't just leave him out there to try."

Marina imagined that Karen had been making this speech in her head every morning and night while she brushed her teeth, never thinking she'd have the opportunity to deliver it to Mr. Fox himself.

"He's never going to say this to you but even if he hasn't been able to bring this nutcase back it's time for him to come home. We've got three boys here, Mr. Fox. You can't expect them to finish out the school year without their father."

This time Marina recognized the sensation at the onset, the helpless buckling of joints, and was able to reach for the tall chair at the kitchen island. Surely it was Mr. Fox's part to give Karen the letter, but then with a fresh wave of grief, Marina remembered that the letter was in her own pocket. She pulled out the chair beside her. "Sit down, Karen," she said. "Sit next to me."

The moment did not bring to mind her own losses. What rushed before Marina was the inherent cruelty of telling. It didn't matter how gently the news was delivered, with how much sorrow and compassion, it was a blow to cut Karen Eckman in two.

"Anders?" Karen said, and then she said it again, louder, as if he were in the other room, as if she both believed what she had been told and denied it. All the cold that swept through Minnesota came into Karen Eckman and she stammered and shook. Her fingers began to rake at the outside of her arms. She asked to see the letter but then she refused to touch the thing, so thin and blue, half unfolded. She told Marina to read it aloud.

There was no way to say she wouldn't do it but still, no matter how much Marina tried to edit the words as they came out of her mouth she couldn't make them into sympathy. "Given our location, this rain," she said tentatively, leaving out the part about governments and their petty bureaucracies. "We chose to bury him here." She could not bring herself to say that this burial was no small task. She should have read the first paragraph, as banal as it was. Without it what was left didn't even sound like a letter. It sounded like some thrifty telegram.

"She buried him there?" Karen said. The bellows of her lungs strained for nothing. There was no air in the kitchen. "Jesus, what are you saying to me? He's in the ground?"

"Tell me who I can call for you. Someone needs to be here." Marina tried to hold her hands but Karen shook her off.

"Get him out of there! You can't just leave him. He isn't going to stay there."

It was the moment to promise everything, but as hard as she tried she could not assemble a single sentence of comfort. "I can't get him out," Marina said, and it was a terrible admission because now she could see very clearly the mud and the leaves, the ground closing in the rain, growing over immediately in tender saplings and tough grasses until it was impossible to find the place where he was. She could feel Anders' strangling panic in all those leaves and the panic became her own. "I don't know how. Karen, look at me, you have to tell me who to call. You have to let me call someone."

But Karen couldn't understand or couldn't hear or didn't care what might have made things easier for Marina. The two of them were alone in this. Mr. Fox had been driven from the room by the sound, the keening of Karen Eckman's despair. She slipped down from her chair and sank to the floor to cry against the retriever, wrapping her grief around his sturdy torso while the poor animal shivered and licked at her arm. She cried there until she'd dampened the dog's fur.

What idiots they were thinking they knew what they were doing! Marina had had to announce deaths to family members in the hospital when she had been a resident, not often, only if the attending was too busy or too imperious to be bothered. No matter how hard these daughters and fathers and brothers and wives had cried, how tightly they clung to her, it had never been that difficult to extricate herself. She simply had to raise her head and there was a nurse who knew more about how to hold them and what to say. Behind her there were charts full of phone numbers that had been compiled in advance. Available clergy were listed for any denomination, grief counselors and support groups that met on Wednesdays. The most she had been asked to do was write an order for a sedative. Marina had made the announcement of Anders' death while giving no thought to death's infrastructure. What about those boys standing in front of the school now, the snow growing into piles on their shoulders while they waited for their mother? How could Marina have forgotten to account for them? Why didn't they know to find somebody first, a dozen somebodies standing ready around Karen while she absorbed the violence of the news? All of those people at the Christmas party, the women in reindeer sweaters, the men in red ties, the people Marina had seen laughing in this kitchen only a few months ago, leaning against each other with their whiskeyed eggnog, they were desperately needed now! And if they hadn't been smart enough to bring family and friends, could they not have thought at least to slip a few sample cards of Xanax into their pockets? There was no waiting out the situation. Giving it time would only mean the Eckman boys would start to panic as a teacher led them back into the school building and told them to wait inside. They would think that their mother was dead; that's where a child's mind goes—always to the loss of the mother.

Marina stood up from the floor, though in her memory she had never sat down on it. She went to the phone, looking for an address book, a Rolodex, anything with numbers. What she found were two copies of the *Minneapolis Star Tribune,* a scratch pad with a clean sheet of paper on top, a coffee mug that said "I Love My Library" jumbled full of pens and crayons, a piece of paper tacked to a cork board that said "Babysitter Emergency": Karen's cell phone, Anders' cell phone,

Anders' office, poison control center, ambulance, Dr. Johnson, Linn Hilder. This is what it feels like when the house is burning down, Marina thought. This is why they give you a number as simple as 911 for the emergencies that will surely come, because when the flames are racing up the curtains and hurtling towards you over the floorboards you won't know any numbers. As much as she wanted to help the wife of her dead friend, she wanted to get out of that house. She picked up the phone and dialed the name on the bottom of the list. She had to take the phone out of the kitchen in order to hear the woman on the other end. Linn Hilder was the neighbor down the street who happened to have two boys who were friends with the Eckman boys. Why, Linn Hilder had leaned out her car window not twenty minutes ago and asked them if they needed a ride home and they had said no, Mrs. Hilder, our mother's coming. Linn Hilder was herself now crying as convulsively as Karen.

"Call someone," Marina said in a low voice. "Call anyone you can think of and send them over here. Call the school. Go to the school and get the boys."

When she came back to the kitchen she saw that Pickles was lying out on the floor to the right of his owner, his sodden head resting at the joint of Karen's hip, and to her left sat Mr. Fox, who had miraculously stepped forward in her brief absence. He was petting Karen's head with a slow and rhythmical assurance. "It's all right," he said quietly. "It's going to be all right." Her head was against his chest and her tears had darkened the stripes on his tie from blue to black. And while it wasn't all right, nothing close to it, she seemed able to hear the steady repetition of the words and was trying to breathe regularly.

Marina and Mr. Fox left the house an hour later, after Karen's mother had been located, after her sister came in with her husband, bringing word that their brother was driving up from Iowa, after Linn Hilder had collected the Eckman boys from school and taken them to her own house until a sensible plan for breaking the news to them could be devised. From the moment Mr. Fox had first stood in the door of the lab with that blue envelope in his hand it had never occurred to Marina that there might be guilt where Anders' death was concerned. It was an accident as much as being pulled under by the current in the Amazon River would have been an accident. But as they stepped into the smack of frigid wind with only Pickles there to see them out, she wondered if the people inside thought of Mr. Fox as culpable. The days were still short and the sun was already low. Certainly without Mr. Fox in the picture, the Eckman boys would be doing their homework or rolling up a snowman in the backyard. Anders would be looking at the clock in their office, saying he was hungry, his body already leaning towards the door in their thriving, living world. She thought it was possible that even if Karen Eckman and her people didn't blame Mr. Fox in the greatest hour of their grief, the blame might still come to them later on, after time and sleep had untangled their thinking. She certainly blamed him for leaving her alone to tell Karen, and for not holding her arm as she carefully maneuvered her way down the unshoveled walk to the car. Did she blame him for sending Anders to his death in Brazil? She struggled with the handle on the passenger-side door that was half frozen down while Mr. Fox slipped into the driver's side. She brushed the snow off the window with her hand and then rapped her bare knuckles against the glass. He had been staring straight ahead and now he turned in her direction and looked startled to see her, as if he had forgotten he hadn't come alone. He leaned over and pushed the door open.

She fell onto the leather seat just as she might have fallen out on the pavement in front of the house had she been forced to wait there another minute. "Just take me back to my car," Marina said. Her hands were shaking and she pinned them between her knees. She had spent most of her life in Minnesota and yet she had never been so cold. All she wanted in the world was to go home and sit in a hot bath.

It had stopped snowing but the sky hanging over the prairie was swollen and gray. The interstate, once they found it, was nothing but a beaten strip of badly plowed blacktop between two flat expanses of white. Mr. Fox did not take Marina back to her car. He was driving instead to St. Paul, and once in St. Paul to a restaurant where in the past they had had remarkable luck not running into anyone they knew. When she saw where he was going she said nothing. She could understand in some dim way that after all they'd been through it was better for them to be together. It was well after five when they slid into a booth in the back of the room. When Marina ordered a glass of red wine, she realized she wanted it even more than the bath. The waitress brought her two and put them side by side on the table in front of her as if she might be expecting a friend. She brought Mr. Fox two glasses of scotch over piles of ice.

"Happy Hour," she said with no particular happiness. "You folks have a good time."

Marina waited until the woman had walked away and then without preamble she repeated to Mr. Fox the single sentence from Karen's monologue that had stuck in her head so clearly after all the others began to melt together. "If Vogel has inflated its stock price then that's Vogel's problem."

He looked at her with what might have been called a wan smile except there wasn't quite enough smile in it. "I can't ever remember being this tired."

She nodded her head. She waited. For a long time he waited with her.

"You know the stock price *is* up," he said finally.

"I know it's up. I guess I don't know why it's up or that it has anything to do with Anders."

Mr. Fox drained his first glass easily and then rested his fingers lightly on the rim of the second. He would be sixty-one in a month but the events of the day had put him safely beyond that. In the dim light of the low-hanging swag lamp with a faux Tiffany shade he could have been seventy. He sat hunched, his shoulders pressing towards one another in the front, and his glasses dug a small red groove into the bridge of his nose. His mouth, which in the past had been generous and kind, now cut across his face in a single straight line. Marina had worked at Vogel for more than six years before they ever came to this restaurant. It was plenty of time to think about Mr. Fox as her employer, her superior. For the last seven months they had made an attempt to redefine their relationship.

"The problem is this," Mr. Fox said, his voice turned sullen. "For some time now there has been . . ." He waited, as if a combination of the cold, the exhaustion, and the scotch had stolen the very word he needed. "There has been a situation in Brazil. It was not a situation that Anders was meant to solve. I didn't ask him to solve it, but I did think he would bring back enough information so that I would be able to handle it myself. I saw Anders as the person who would set things in motion. He would explain to Dr. Swenson that it was essential that she wrap up her research and move directly, with the help of other scientists, into the developmental phase of the drug. Then he would explain to me, based on what he'd seen, what sort of reasonable timetable we should be able to expect. The fact that Anders died in the middle of all this is a terrible thing, I don't need to tell you that, but his death"—and here Mr. Fox paused to consider his words and take a quarter inch off the second glass—"his death does not change the problem."

"And the problem is that this drug which you've been saying for a year now is all but sitting on the doorstep of the FDA doesn't exist? It's not that Dr. Swenson isn't bringing it back from Brazil. You're saying there's nothing to bring back." Mr. Fox was too old for her. He was five years younger than her mother, a point her mother would have been the first person to bring up had Marina been inclined to tell her about the relationship.

"I don't know that. That was the purpose of the trip. We needed more information."

"So you sent Anders out on some sort of reconnaissance mission? Anders Eckman? How was he qualified for that?"

"He was meant to be our ambassador. He wasn't hiding anything, there was nothing to hide. His job was to explain to Dr. Swenson the importance of her finishing her portion of the project. Since she's been down there she's disconnected herself, from—" Mr. Fox stopped and shook his head. The list was too long. "Everything. I'm not entirely sure she possesses a concept of time."

"How long ago did you last hear from her?"

"Not counting today's letter?" He stopped to do the math in his head though Marina suspected he was only stalling. "It's been twenty-six months."

"Nothing? In over two years you've heard nothing? How is that possible?" What she meant was how was it possible he had let this go so far but that was not how he heard the question.

"She doesn't seem to feel she's accountable to the people who have been funding her work. I've given her a kind of latitude that any other drug company would have laughed at, and should laugh at. That's why she agreed to come with us. Her money is deposited monthly into an account in Rio as per our original agreement. I've paid to have a research station built and I don't even know where it is. We sent the whole thing down on a barge, freezers and tin siding, roofs and doors, more generators than you could imagine. We sent everything to set up a fully operating lab and she met the barge in Manaus and got on board and took it down the river herself. None of the workers were ever able to remember where they dropped things off."

"If Anders found it, it wouldn't be impossible to find." Dr. Swenson would never see herself as accountable to Vogel, any more than she would think of herself as working for them. She might develop a drug for the purposes of her own curiosity or the interest of science, but it would never occur to her that her work was the property of the people who signed the checks. Anyone who had spent a thoughtful hour in her presence could have figured that much out. "So pull the plug. Cut the money off and wait until she comes out."

Mr. Fox, who had been holding the remaining and mostly full glass of scotch an inch off the table, now set it down. The look on his face meant to say that she understood none of it. "The project needs to be completed, not abandoned."

"Then it won't be abandoned." Marina closed her eyes. She wanted to sink into the red wine, to swim in it. "The truth is I don't want to talk about Dr. Swenson or Vogel or drug development anymore. I know I'm the one who brought it up but I was wrong. Let's just give the day to Anders."

"You're absolutely right," Mr. Fox said in a tone that was free of concession. "This isn't the time to talk about it, and tomorrow won't be either, nor will the day after that. But since the day is rightfully Anders' I'll tell you this: in finding Dr. Swenson we not only have the chance to solve Vogel's problems, but we could resolve some of the questions about Anders' death as well."

"What questions?"

"Believe me," he said, "there will be questions."

She wondered then if he felt it too, that the blame would come to him eventually. "You're not going to Brazil," she said.

"No," he said.

It was this terrible light that made him look old, the scotch and the heavy weight of the day. She wanted them to leave now, and when they got back to Eden Prairie she would take him home with her. She blamed him for nothing. She leaned across the table of this dark, back booth and took his hand. "The president of the company doesn't go off to Brazil."

"There is nothing inherently dangerous about the Amazon. It's a matter of precautions and good sense."

"I'm sure you're right but that doesn't mean that you should go."

"I promise you, I'm not going. Annick Swenson wouldn't listen to me. I realize now she's never listened to me, not in the meetings, the agreement letters, the contracts. I've been writing to her ever since she left—no e-mail, no texting, she does none of that. I sit down and put it all on paper. I've been very clear about her obligations and our commitment to the project. There's been no indication that she reads my letters."

"So what you need to find is someone she'll listen to."

"Exactly. I didn't think that through when I sent Anders. He was affable and bright, and he seemed to want to go, which counted for a lot. I only thought it needed to be someone from Vogel, someone who wasn't me."

Oh, Anders! To have been sent off on a mission you were never right for. To be regarded after your death as an error of judgment. "So now you'll find the right person."

"You," he said.

Marina felt a small jolt in the hand he was holding, as if something sharp had briefly stabbed through him and into her. She took back her hand and rubbed it quickly.

"She knows you," he said. "She'll listen. I should have asked you in the first place. You were the board's choice, and I made the case against you. I told them I had asked you and you had refused. It was selfishness on my part. This time we've spent together—" He looked up at her now but for both of them it felt almost unbearable and so he dropped his eyes. "It's been important to me. I didn't want you going off. That's my guilt, Marina, sending Anders instead of you, because you would have gotten it done."

"But he *died*," she said. She didn't want to turn back the clock and choose between Anders and herself, to think about which one of them was more expendable in life's greater scheme. She was sure she knew the answer to that one. "You would have rather it had been me?"

"You wouldn't have died." He was utterly clear on this point. "Whatever Anders did, it was careless. He wasn't eaten by a crocodile. He had a fever, he was sick. If you were sick you would have the sense to get on a plane and come home."

Marina didn't approve of the introduction of culpability on Anders's part. It was bad enough that he was dead without it being his fault. "Let's leave poor Anders out of this for a minute if we can." She tried to grab hold of logic. "The flaw in your argument is that you think I know Dr. Swenson. I haven't seen her in—" Marina stopped, had it been that long? "Thirteen years. I know her thoughts on reproductive endocrinology and to a lesser extent gynecological surgery, and not even her current thoughts on either of those things, her thirteen-year-old thoughts. I don't know *her*. And as for her knowing me, she doesn't. She didn't know me then and there is no reason to think she would suddenly know me now. She wouldn't remember my name, my face, my test scores." Would Dr. Swenson know her? She saw Dr. Swenson raise her eyes to the lecture hall, sweep past the faces of all the students, all the residents, year after year after year. There could be hundreds of them in a single class and over the years that quickly added up to thousands, and yet for a brief time Dr. Swenson knew Marina Singh alone.

"You underestimate yourself."

Marina shook her head. "You overestimate Dr. Swenson. And me. We would be strangers to one another." This was halfway true. It was the truth in one direction.

"You were her student, her bright student who went on to do well in her field. It's a connection. It's more of a connection to her than anyone else has."

"Except for her employer."

He raised his eyebrows but it wasn't enough to mock surprise. "So now you think I should go?"

"Are we the only two people available for this mission? I don't think either one of us should go." She could see Anders so clearly now. He had laid it all out for her and yet she had missed his point entirely. "She found a village of people in the Amazon, a tribe," Anders had said, "where the women go on bearing children until the end of their lives."

"Now there's a chilling thought." Marina was inputting numbers and listening to Anders the way she often did, with half of one ear.

"Of course their lives are on average shorter than ours by about a decade but that's true everywhere in the Amazon—poor diet, little or no medical care."

"All those children."

Anders pushed off from his desk in his rolling chair. With his long legs and the short length of floor in the lab he maneuvered around the room easily with his heels. "Their eggs aren't aging, do you get that? The rest of the body goes along its path to destruction while the reproductive system stays daisy fresh. This is the end of IVF. No more expense, no more shots that don't end up working, no more donor eggs and surrogates. This is ovum in perpetuity, menstruation everlasting."

Marina looked up. "Would you stop this?"

He put a thick bound report on her desk, *Reproductive Endocrinology in the Lakashi People*, by Dr. Annick Swenson. "Pretend for a moment that you are a clinical pharmacologist working for a major drug development firm. Imagine someone offering you the equivalent of *Lost Horizon* for American ovaries." He took Marina's hand as if in proposal. "Put off your reproductive decisions for as long as you want. We're not talking forty-five, we're talking fifty, sixty, maybe beyond that. You can always have children."

Marina felt the words pointed directly at her. She was forty-two. She was in love with a man she did not leave the building with, and while she had not broached the subject with Mr. Fox, it wasn't impossible to think that they could have a child. Improbable, maybe, but not out of the question. She picked up the hefty report. "Annick Swenson."

"She's the researcher. She's some famous ethnobotanist in Brazil."

Marina opened to the table of contents. "She's not an ethnobotanist," she said, glancing down the list of chapters: "Onset of Puberty in Lakashi Women," "Birth Rates in Comparable Tribes". . .

Anders looked at the page she was looking at as if this information was printed there. "How do you know that?"

Marina closed the report and slid it back over the desk. From the very start she remembered wanting no part in this. "She was a teacher of mine in medical school."

That had been the conversation in its entirety. The phone rang, someone came in, it was over. Marina had not been asked to sit in on the review board meetings or to meet Dr. Swenson on the occasion of Dr. Swenson's single visit to Vogel. There was no reason she would have been. Obligations on review board committees were rotating and in this particular instance her number had not come up. There was no reason Mr. Fox would have ever known about the connection between herself and the chronicler of the Lakashi people except that clearly at some point Anders must have told him.

"What is she like, anyway?" Anders asked her two or three days before he left.

Marina took a moment. She saw her teacher down in the pit of the lecture hall, observed her at a safe and comfortable distance. "She was an old-style medical school professor."

"The stuff of legends? A suicide in every class?"

Anders was looking at his bird books then, too distracted by tanagers to notice her face. Marina was caught not wanting to make a joke of something that didn't have an ounce of humor in it, and at the same time not wanting to offer up any little crack that could be pried open into a meaningful conversation. All she said then was, "Yes."

In the end neither Marina nor Mr. Fox could face dinner. They finished their drinks, two apiece, and drove back to the parking lot at Vogel, where Marina got in her car to go home. There was no further argument, no plans for the Amazon or the evening ahead. They had both been certain that the answer would be to go to bed together, hold each other through the long night as a means of warding off death, but there in the parking lot they split apart naturally, both of them too tired and too fundamentally alone in their thoughts to stay with the other.

"I'll call to say good night," Mr. Fox said.

Marina nodded and she kissed him, and when she was home and in bed after the bath she had so desperately wanted, he did call and said good night, but only good night, with no discussion of the day. When the phone rang again, five minutes or five hours after she had turned out the light, she did not think it would be Mr. Fox. Her first startled thought was that it was Anders. It had something to do with a dream she was having. Anders was calling to say his car had broken down in the snow and he needed her to come and pick him up.

"Marina, I'm sorry, I'm waking you."

It was a woman's voice, and then she realized it was Karen's voice. Marina reached beneath her to try and straighten out the nightgown that had worked its way into twisted rope around her waist. "It's all right."

"Dr. Johnson brought some sleeping pills over but they didn't do anything."

"Sometimes they don't," Marina said. She picked up the little clock on her bedside table whose tiny hands glowed green in the dark, 3:25.

"They worked for everyone else. Everyone in the house is sound asleep."

"Do you want me to come over?" She could go back now and sit on the kitchen floor with Karen and Pickles. She could lie on Anders' side of the bed and hold Karen's hand in the dark until she fell asleep. This time she would be ready, she would know what to do.

"No, it's okay. I've got my family here, even if they're asleep. It's just that I've been thinking about all this, right? Of course I'm thinking about this." Her voice was remarkably calm on the other end of the line.

"Sure."

"And I've got all these questions now."

"Of course," Marina said, unable to think of a single question she'd be capable of answering.

"Well, why does she say in the letter that she's keeping his few possessions for his wife? Does she think that I'm going to come by and pick up his watch?" Her voice wavered a bit and just as quickly she regained control. "Don't you think she'd mail them?"

His camera, wallet, passport, watch, maybe the field guides and maybe some clothing but she doubted that. Dr. Swenson would return the things that she deemed important, which is to say she would set them aside and forget them. "Maybe she just thought she would give them to the next person who came down there. It would be safer. I imagine a lot of things get lost in the mail." It occurred to her then that this letter could have been lost, or it might have come three days ago, or a month from now. How long would they have waited passively for news of Anders while they went about their lives?

"But what if she isn't sending the things because he still has them?"

Marina rubbed her thumb and index finger into the corners of her eyes. She was trying to pull herself up from sleep by using the bridge of her nose. "I'm sorry. I'm not following you."

"What if he isn't dead?"

Marina pressed her head deep into the pillow. "He's dead, Karen."

"Why? Because we got a letter from some crazy woman in Brazil who nobody's allowed to talk to? I need more than that. This is the worst thing that's ever going to happen to me. It's the worst thing that's going to happen to my boys ever in their entire lives, and I'm supposed to take a stranger's word on it?"

There had to be an equation for probability and proof. At some point probability becomes so great it eclipses the need for proof, although maybe not if it was your husband. "Mr. Fox is going to send someone down there. They're going to find out what happened."

"But say he's not dead. I know you don't believe it but just say. Say that he's sick and he needs me to come and find him. In that case there isn't any time to wait for Mr. Fox to reassemble his committee to find someone else to send to Brazil who has no idea what he's doing."

Slowly Marina's sight adjusted to the darkness. She could make out the shapes in her bedroom, the dresser, the lamp. "I'll talk to him. I promise. I'll make sure he gets this done right."

"I'm going to go down there," Karen said.

"No, you're not." It was all a form of shock, Marina understood that. Maybe tomorrow Karen wouldn't remember this conversation at all.

The phone was quiet for a long time. "I would," she said. "I swear to God if it wasn't for the boys."

"Look," Marina said, "this isn't something that any of us can figure out now. You've got to get some rest. We have to give Mr. Fox a chance to find out what he can."

"I gave Mr. Fox everything I've got," she said.

That afternoon Marina had thought that Karen would never speak to her again, that she would always blame her for bearing the news. The fact that she was the person Karen Eckman called in the middle of the night felt something like forgiveness, and for that forgiveness she was deeply grateful. "What time did you take the sleeping pill?"

Marina waited. She watched the glowing second hand pass the three, the six, the nine.

"Karen?"

"You could go."

So now Marina understood what this conversation was about. When Karen said it, a picture of Anders came very clearly into Marina's mind: his back was against an impenetrable bank of leaves, his feet in the water. He was holding a letter. He was looking down river for the boy in the dugout log. He was dead. Marina might not have a great deal of faith in Dr. Swenson but Dr. Swenson wasn't the sort to announce a death where no death had occurred, that would constitute a frivolous waste of time. "You're the second person to tell me that tonight."

"Anders said you knew her. He said she was a teacher of yours."

"She was," Marina said, not wanting to explain. Marina was from Minnesota. No one ever believed that. At the point when she could have taken a job anywhere she came back because she loved it here. This landscape was the one she understood, all prairie and sky. She and Anders had that in common.

"I know how much I'm asking," Karen said. "And I know how terrible you feel about Anders and about me and the boys. I know that I'm using all of it against you and how unfair it is and I still want you to go."

"I understand."

"I know you understand," Karen said. "But will you go?"

Two

First things first. Marina made an appointment with an epidemiologist in St. Paul and got a ten-year vaccine for yellow fever and a tetanus shot. She got a prescription for an antimalarial, Lariam, and was told to take the first pill immediately. After that she would take one pill a week for the duration of her trip, and then one a week for four weeks after her return home. "Watch this stuff," the doctor told her. "It can make you feel like jumping off a roof."

Marina wasn't worried about jumping off a roof. Her worries were centered around plane tickets, packing, English-Portuguese dictionaries, how much Pepto-Bismol would be enough. From time to time she thought about the upper quadrant of her left arm, which, since those two shots, felt like both needles had broken off their respective hypodermics and were now lodged in her humerus like a pair of hot spears. She allowed these more practical concerns to stand temporarily in place for her thoughts of Anders and Karen and Dr. Swenson, none of whom she could manage at the moment. It wasn't until the third night after she took the first tablet of Lariam that Marina's thoughts swung sharply in the direction of India and her father. In the process of leaving for the Amazon, she had inadvertently solved a mystery that at present was the farthest thing from her mind: *What had been wrong with her childhood?*

And then the unexpected answer: *these pills.*

It came to her in the night when she bolted up from her bed, out of her bed, drenched and shaking, the dream still so alive she wouldn't blink her eyes for fear of calling it back, though really there was no avoiding it. She knew this one by heart. It was the same dream that had marked the entirety of her youth, intensely present and then gone for years, returning at the very moment she was careless enough to forget about it. Standing there beside her bed in the dark, the sheets soaked, her pillow and nightgown soaked, she came to the clear and sudden realization that she had taken Lariam as a child. Her mother never told her but of course she must have, starting the dosage as prescribed, the first pill taken a week before departure, then every week while away, then for four weeks after they returned. Pills meant it was time to see her father as surely as digging through desk drawers to find the passports and dragging the suitcases up from the basement. India pills, her mother had called them. *Come and take your India pills.*

Marina had only the most cursory memories of living in an apartment in Minneapolis with both of her parents but she could summon them back without any effort. Look, there is her father standing at the front door shaking the snow from the black gloss of his hair. There he is at the kitchen table writing on a tablet, a cigarette in the saucer beside him burning slowly to ash, his books and papers arranged in such precise order that at dinner time they had to sit on the floor in the living room and eat off the coffee table. There he is at her bed at night, pulling the covers beneath her chin, tucking them in on either side. "Snug like a bug?" he asks her. She nods her head against the pillow, the only part of her free to move, and gazes at his lovely face only inches above hers, until she can no longer keep her eyes open.

Marina did not forget her father in his absence, nor did she learn to accept the situation over time. She longed for him. Her mother often said that Marina was smart in just the way her father was smart, and that explained why he was so proud that she excelled in the very things that interested her the most: earth sciences and math when she was a little girl, calculus, statistics, inorganic chemistry when she was older. Her skin was all cream and light in comparison to her father's and very dark when she held her wrist against her mother's. She had her father's round, black eyes and heavy lashes, his black hair and angular frame. Seeing her father gave her the ability to see herself, the comfort of physical recognition after a life spent among her mother's people, all those translucent cousins who looked at her like she was a llama who had wandered into their holiday dinner. The checkers in the grocery store, the children at school, the doctors and the bus drivers all asked her where she was from. There was no point in saying, *Right here, Minneapolis,* though it was in fact the case. Instead she told them India, and even that they didn't always understand (*Lakota?* asked the gas station attendant, and Marina would have to work very hard not to roll her eyes because her mother had explained that eye-rolling was the height of rudeness and was never an appropriate response, even to very stupid questions). Being the child of a white mother and foreign graduate-student father who took his doctoral degree but not his family back to his country of origin after he was finished had become the stuff of presidential history, but when Marina was growing up there was no example that could easily explain her situation. In time, she came to tell herself that she practically *was* from India because after all her father was from there and lived there and she had visited him there every two or three years when enough money had been saved. These dramatic trips were discussed and planned as great events, and as Marina marked off the months then weeks then days on her calendar what she was longing for was not only her father but an entire country, that place where no one would turn around and look at her unless it was to admire her good posture. But then, a little less than a week before she left, the dreams would begin.

In the dreams she is holding her father's hand. They are walking up Indira Gandhi Sarani towards Dalhousie Square or following Bidhan Sarani in the direction of the college where her father is a professor. The farther they go along the more people start to come out of buildings and alleyways. Maybe the power has gone out again and the trams have stopped and all the fans in all the kitchens have stopped so that people who were in their apartments have come out to the street because the crowd is pushing in closer and closer as more people are joining in along the edges. There is the heat of the day to contend with and then the heat of so many bodies, their sweat and perfume, the sharp scent of spice carried in the smoke of vendors' fires and the bitter smell of marigolds strung into garlands, and all together it begins to overwhelm her. Marina can't see where she's going anymore, only the people pressing into her, hips wrapped in crimson saris and dhoti-punjabis knocking her from side to side. She reaches out her hand and pats a cow. She can hear the persistent music of jewelry weaving through the shouted conversations, bangle bracelets stacked halfway to the elbow and anklets covered in tiny bells, earrings that function as wind chimes. Sometimes when the masses shift her feet are lifted from the ground and for a moment she is held a few inches aloft, a small weight distributed over various points on other people's bodies as she drags behind her father like a low kite. She feels her shoe knocked loose from her foot and she calls for her father to stop, but he doesn't hear her over the roar of voices. She can still see the little shoe flashing yellow on the hard packed ground not two steps behind them in the crowd. It is perfectly still, untrampled, and though she knows she isn't supposed to, she lets go of her father's hand. She dives for her shoe but the crowd has already swallowed it, and as quickly as she turns back the crowd has swallowed her father as well. She calls for him, *Papi! Papi!* but the ringing of bells, the calling and crying of beggars, has taken the sound from her mouth. She doesn't know if he even realizes she's gone. Some other child could have attached himself to her father's hand when she fell off, in India the children are very fast. And then Marina is alone somewhere in the sea of Calcutta, folded inside the human current of chattering Hindi which she does not understand, her body swept along while she cries, at which point she would wake up sweating, nauseated, her black hair soaked to the skull. She would run down the hall to her mother's room, throw herself into her mother's bed, crying, "Don't make me go!"

Her mother took her up in her arms, put a cool hand on her forehead. She asked her what the dream was about but Marina always said she couldn't remember, something awful. She did remember, but wouldn't speak it for fear the words would somehow cement the images into reality. From then on she had the dream every night: she had it on the plane going over to Calcutta and woke up screaming. She had it in the flat her father rented for her and her mother not far from his office at the college so that they would not disturb his second wife, his second children. They were separated getting onto a bus, her father let her go while they were swimming in the sea at a crowded beach. After so many dreams that were so much alike she became terrified of sleep. She was terrified the whole time they were in India, so much so that at the end of every trip both of her parents agreed that it might all be too much for her. Marina's father said he would try to come to Minnesota more often, but that was never practical. Once they were back at home, after a week or two, the crowds that haunted her sleep would begin to dissipate, thin into smaller groups, and then break apart altogether. Slowly, Marina would forget them, and then her mother would forget, and within a year it would once again be decided that she was a much bigger girl now and maybe they should start thinking about a trip to India sometime in the future.

Was it possible that no one had troubled themselves to read the voluminous side effects of the Lariam? Marina liked to think she would have figured out the puzzle herself if her father hadn't died when she was in college. At that point she hadn't been back to Calcutta in three years. Had he lived and she had gone again, she would have been old enough to look into the medication herself, although it was true that a patient was less likely to question a set of symptoms she had always accepted. She had grown up believing that India gave her nightmares, seeing her father gave her nightmares, when all along it was the anti-malarial. The drug, not the circumstances of her life, destroyed her chance to be with her father.

"Of course I knew it was the Lariam," her mother said over the phone. "Your father and I were always worrying about it. You had such a terrible reaction."

"Then why didn't you tell me what it was?" Marina said.

"You don't tell a five-year-old they're going to have bad dreams. That's like giving them an invitation to have more."

"A five-year-old," she said, "I'll grant you that. But you could have explained it to me when I was ten, at least when I was fifteen."

"I couldn't tell you anything when you were fifteen. If I'd told you it was the pills that gave you nightmares you wouldn't have taken them."

"Would that have been the end of the world?"

"If you had gotten malaria in India then, yes, I suppose it would have been. The end of the world had it killed you. I'm surprised this is still a problem. I would have thought they would have come up with a better drug to take by now."

"They have and they haven't. The new ones don't make you so crazy but they also don't protect from all the different strains of malaria."

"So why in the world are you taking Lariam again?" her mother asked. It was the most important question and yet it only now seemed to have occurred to her. "Are you going back to India?"

What was so interesting about the nightmares now was the extent to which nothing much in them had changed. At forty-two she was still holding her father's hand, the people around them rose up like a tide and she was then forced to let him go. It had never actually happened, this physical wrenching apart, and still her subconscious clung to the fear. Things that had happened to Marina, the memories she saw as the logical candidates for nightmares, never entered her sleeping life, and she supposed that for this she should be grateful. In her own home she got up and turned the lights on in the bathroom. Her hands were shaking and she ran a wet washcloth over her face and neck, careful not to look at herself in the mirror. It was surprising to discover that understanding the origin of her dreams offered her exactly no comfort at two in the morning. In fact, all she could think of now was her doctor's careless admonition that she might want to jump off a roof. Her deepest fear, her father's hand slipping from her hand, had held steady even when it was kept undisturbed in a pharmacy without her for twenty-five years.

"What about the funeral?" Marina asked Karen Eckman. They hadn't seen each other all week, not since Marina had come with Mr. Fox on the day of the heavy snow. Now that she was leaving in the morning, both of the women thought it was important to say goodbye, though for different reasons. Marina wanted to see if Karen had given up on the idea that Anders might still be alive now that she'd had some days to sit with his death. Karen wanted to make sure Marina wasn't thinking of backing out.

It was after dinner when Marina came by and the lengthening day had just gone dark. The boys had brushed their teeth and were watching television in the den. They were now allowed a show before bedtime every night, a childhood luxury previously restricted to weekends. Marina said hello to them when she first came in and they barely turned their heads towards her, the youngest two muttering hello in low unison when their mother insisted, the eldest saying nothing at all. Mr. Fox had made a mistake in telling Marina that she had been the first choice to go find Dr. Swenson instead of Anders. She now saw the entire world in terms of alternate scenarios.

"A memorial service. You call it a memorial service when you don't have a body," Karen said.

"I'm sorry," Marina said. "Memorial service."

Karen leaned around the open archway to the den. The boys in their sweatshirts and flannel pajama pants slumped into the endlessly long corduroy couch. The smallest, palest boy lay over Pickles like a rug. They were bound to the television screen as if by wires. "It's amazing what they hear," she said in a low voice. "They don't even have to be listening but their ears just pick it up, then I put them to bed at night and one of them says, 'When are we having the funeral for Daddy?' " Karen poured herself a glass of wine and when she wagged the bottle in Marina's direction Marina nodded.

"Funeral," the middle boy called out without looking at them. He giggled for a second and then stopped.

Marina thought of that muddy ground where Anders was buried and reached for her glass. "I'm sorry," she said to Karen.

"Benjy, stop that," Karen said in a sharp voice. "No, no, it's just something I try to be aware of. Did Anders ever tell you I majored in Russian literature in college? I've been thinking I should find some Russian friends. Then we could talk anywhere. Or maybe it's just that we could talk about Chekhov anywhere." She took her wine to the other side of the kitchen and opened the louvered door to the big walk-in pantry. Marina followed her inside. Even the pantry was neat, bright boxes of cereal standing together in a line of diminishing height. Karen returned to her point, her voice lowered. "Sometimes I think they can hear the conversations people have about us down the street. If you listened to them talk you'd think they knew everything that was going on. I mean, they don't understand it all but somewhere or other they've heard it and they remember. Do you ever wonder when you stopped being able to hear everything?" Karen asked.

"I hadn't thought about it." Marina had no idea how much her hearing had deteriorated over the course of her life.

Karen looked blank for a minute as if part of her had walked out of the room and then, just as quickly, returned. "I got a letter today."

There was no question and still she said Anders' name, her heart thrumming like a hummingbird's heart.

Karen nodded and pulled one of those same blue envelopes out of the pocket of her sweater. She set it face up on the palm of her open hand and together they stared at it like a thing that could at any minute unfold a pair of wings. There was Anders' clear parochial penmanship across the front. *Karen Eckman . . . Eden Prairie.* Marina liked to tell him he was the only doctor she ever knew who wrote like a Catholic school girl. "It's the second one I've had this week," Karen said. "The other one came on Tuesday but he wrote it later, the first of March. He was sicker then."

Marina opened her mouth. There was something she was supposed to say but she couldn't imagine what it would be. He was dead, he was sick, he was not so sick. The story rewound until the only conclusion to draw would be that Anders gets better. He leaves the jungle and returns to Manaus. He flies from Manaus and starts again from home, only this time they know enough to refuse to let him go. Marina wondered how many letters were still out there and when they would drift in, their postal route having mistakenly sent them on a detour through Bhutan. A person didn't have to stretch very far to find a logical explanation for how this had happened, so why did Marina feel it necessary to tilt back her glass and take down all of the wine in a swallow?

"That experience, going out to your mailbox and finding a stack of catalogues and bills and a letter from your dead husband, there's not been anything in my life so far to get me ready for that." Karen unfolded the envelope and looked at the words but just as quickly looked away from them. She looked to Marina instead. "It makes you understand why e-mail is better," she said. "You get an e-mail from your dead husband and you know that he's alive out there somewhere. You get a letter from your dead husband and you don't know anything at all."

"Can you tell me what he said?" Marina was whispering. Maybe the letters were the one thing the boys didn't know about yet. She wanted to ask if there was anything about Dr. Swenson and where they were working. She wanted to know where in the jungle she should look.

"It isn't really about anything," Karen said, as if that was something she should apologize for. She handed Marina the letter.

February 15th

Would it alarm you too much to tell you I am often alarmed in this place? What you deserve is not honesty but the sort of husband who is capable of putting up a Brave Front. But if I put up a Brave Front now after telling you so much about how miserable I am, if I paid Nkomo or one of the Saturns to put a Brave Front together for me on a separate sheet of paper which I could then copy over in my own coward's handwriting, you would see through the ploy immediately. Then you would have to get on a plane and hire a boat and a guide and come down here to find me because you would know (having never seen a single Brave Front out of me in your life) how unimaginable things must be. So I won't alarm you by trying to muster up courage. You've always been the one with all the courage anyway. It's why you're staying home with three boys and I'm vacationing. It's why you were able to pull that nail out of Benjy's heel last summer with pliers. I am not brave. I have a fever that comes on at seven in the morning and stays for two hours. By four in the afternoon it's back and I am nothing but a ranting pile of ash. Most days now I have a headache and I worry that some tiny Amazonian animal is eating a hole through my cerebral cortex, and the only thing I want in the world, the only thing that would give meaning or sense to this existence, would be the chance to lay my head in your lap. You would put your hand in my hair, I know you would do that for me. Such is your bravery, such is my good fortune. Damn these ridiculous sheets of paper. There's never any space. I pray like a babbling fundamentalist now that I am in Brazil and tonight I will pray that the letter carrier sends this to you so that you can feel the full weight of my love. Kiss the boys for me. Kiss the inside of your wrist.

—A-

Marina refolded it and gave it back to Karen, who returned it to her pocket. She put her hand on a shelf near several boxes of microwave popcorn to steady herself. It was incalculably worse than the letter from Dr. Swenson. This was Anders announcing the onset of his own death, his voice so clear and plain he might as well have crowded into the pantry with them and read it aloud. "Who are Nkomo and the Saturns?"

Karen shook her head. "He mentions names sometimes but I don't know them. I can't even imagine how many of the letters got lost. The letter from Dr. Swenson could have gotten lost, the one saying he was dead." Karen ran a finger in an absent circle around the top of a can of peas. "I think I'd rather wait on the service until you come back. I'd like it if you could be here."

Marina looked down at her, blinked, nodded.

"I never say it to them," she said, looking towards the slightly open pantry door in the direction of her boys and their television, "that I'm not sure he's dead. I know they need to have one answer, even if it's the worst answer you could think of. Hope is a horrible thing, you know. I don't know who decided to package hope as a virtue because it's not. It's a plague. Hope is like walking around with a fishhook in your mouth and somebody just keeps pulling it and pulling it. Everybody thinks I'm a train wreck because Anders is dead but it's really so much worse than that. I'm still hoping that this Dr. Swenson, for some reason I couldn't possibly put together, has lied about everything, that she's keeping him, or she's lost him somewhere." Then Karen stopped and a sudden light of clarity came over her face and the panic fell away from her voice. "And I say that and I know it isn't true. No one would do that. But then that would mean he's dead." She put the question to Marina directly. "Is he dead?" she asked. "I just don't feel it. I would feel it, wouldn't I?" Her eyes filled up and she brushed the tears back with two fingers.

Nothing would be lovelier than a lie now, a single dose of possibility. But if Marina gave her that then she would be nothing but another fishhook in Karen Eckman's mouth. She said that Anders was dead.

Karen put her hands in her pockets, looked to the very clean wood plank floor. She nodded. "Was he writing to you?"

Marina understood the question but she left it alone. "He sent me a postcard from Manaus and two letters from the jungle very early on. They were mostly about birds. I showed them to Mr. Fox. I'll give them to you if you want them."

"For the boys," she said. "It would be good I think to keep everything together. For the future."

Marina was not claustrophobic by nature, and the pantry was as big as a hotel elevator, but she was ready to open the door and step outside. The canned green beans and bottled cranberry juice and packets of instant oatmeal in sweet, assorted flavors were beginning to press towards her, taking up more and more of the space. "I don't know how long I'll be gone."

"Well, whatever you do, don't stay." Karen tried to say this lightly. "That's the big mistake."

After they said their goodbyes, Marina left the Eckman house and walked out alone into the subdivision beneath the endless expanse of velvet night. She gave herself a moment in the enormous darkness to shake off the small, bright closet she had been in. She wondered if there would be some time in her life, ten years from now, or twenty, when she would not be thinking about that letter. *Such is your bravery, such is my good fortune.* Probably not. In his death, her officemate had become her responsibility. While she understood Karen's position on hope she wouldn't have minded a little bit of it for herself. How gladly she would go to Brazil to find Anders! But her job was to confirm his death and finish his work. All those years in the smallest lab at Vogel working on the same reports, they had grown accustomed to completing the other's data.

Marina filled her lungs with frozen air and smelled both winter and spring, dirt and leftover snow with the smallest undercurrent of something green. That was another thing she and Anders had in common: they were both profoundly suited for Minnesota. She wanted to develop a fear of flying that would keep her from ever going farther than the Dakotas in her car. Like her mother and all her mother's people before her, those inexhaustible blondes who staked their claims in verdant prairies, Marina was cut from Minnesota, the soil and the starry night. Instead of growing up inquisitive and restless, she had developed a profound desire to stay, as if her center of gravity was so low it connected her directly to this particular patch of earth. The frigid winds raced across the plains with nothing in their path to stop them but Marina, who stood there freezing for one more minute before finally getting into her car.

Back at home she found Mr. Fox waiting in her driveway, engine running and heater on. When he saw her he rolled down his window. "I've been trying to call you," he said.

"I went to tell Karen goodbye."

She could have told him about the letter but there was so little time left, and anyway, what could she say? This week hadn't gone the way either of them would have liked. They had seen each other mostly at the office in the presence of Vogel's board. Given the circumstances, the board had wanted Marina to have a complete and detailed account of their expectations for her trip. Did she understand exactly what was expected of her? Fly to Manaus, go to Dr. Swenson's apartment there, they had an address, Anders had found some people who knew where *la, la, la.* Marina was scrambled by the lack of sleep and agitated by the Lariam. She found herself sitting through those meetings and listening to nothing, moving her Vogel Pharmaceutical ballpoint in designs that resembled cursive writing. Even when she gave moderately articulate replies to their nervous questions she wasn't listening. She was thinking instead of her father and how she had missed his death because she hadn't wanted to leave school in the middle of the semester. As with so many other critical matters in her early life, she had been protected from the seriousness of the situation. She had been told only that he was ill and he hoped that she could visit soon. Given that information she had thought there was plenty of time, when in fact there had been none at all. She was thinking of her mother who had been asked not to attend his funeral and so waited in the hotel room in deference to the second wife. She was thinking of Anders and his birding guides and wondering if Dr. Swenson would have kept them. Anders would be so happy if she made the effort to look for some birds while she was there. She would use his binoculars to find them. Surely when Dr. Swenson said in her letter that she was keeping his few possessions this would include his binoculars. And his camera! She would use his camera to take pictures of birds for the boys.

"May I come in?" Mr. Fox asked.

Marina in the dark, in the cold of early April, nodded her head and he followed her to the door of her house and stood very close behind. He shifted to the left and then slightly to the right and then stopped and pressed himself against her back while she dug for her keys in her purse. He was trying to shield her from the wind. It was that tenderness that brought the tightness to Marina's throat and before there was a chance to stop herself she was crying. Was she crying for Karen and her letter? For Anders while he wrote it, or for those pajama-clad boys? Was she crying because of the Lariam, which made her cry at newspaper stories and radio songs, or because she really would have given almost anything to let this cup of Brazil pass from her? She turned and put her arms around Mr. Fox's neck and he kissed her there under her porch light where anyone driving by could have seen them. She kissed him and held on to him as if a great crowd of people were trying to pull them apart. The cold and the wind did not matter. Nothing mattered. They had played this thing all wrong. They had made terrible decisions about waiting to see where their relationship would go, about not being together openly. They agreed there was no point in becoming the topic of other people's conversations, especially if things didn't work out. Mr. Fox was always quick to tell her that he didn't think things would work out. The problem, he said, was his age. He was too old for her. Even when they were lying in bed, his arm beneath her shoulders, her head on his chest, he would talk about how he would die so many years before her and leave her alone. It would be better if she found someone her own age now and not throw away these good years on him.

"Now?" she would say. "Do I have to find someone else right this minute?"

Then he would press her closer and kiss the top of her head. "No," he would say, running his open hand down the side of her arm. "Probably not this exact minute. You could put it off for a little while."

"I could die first, you know. There's a perfectly good chance." She had said it because in truth Marina wanted very much for this relationship to work, and because there was a medical fact worth pointing out as well: the younger ones go first all the time. But coming into her house on this night she thought about those conversations in a different light, and so they kissed each other while thinking of her death rather than his. Logically speaking, Anders' death portended nothing for Marina, but Anders was dead and he hadn't thought it was a possible outcome for his trip. Karen hadn't thought it was possible or she never would have let him out the front door. Mr. Fox was sorry, genuinely sorry, that he had ever asked Marina to go and he told her so. Marina said she was sorry she had agreed. But Marina had been a very good student and a very good doctor and a very good employee and lover and friend and when someone asked her to do something she operated on the principle they had asked because it was important. She had succeeded in life because she had so rarely declined any request that was made of her, how would the Amazon be different? They banged their legs against the coffee table as they tried to move through the house without turning on lights. They pressed against a wall in the dark hallway. They fell into her room, into her bed, and stayed there until they had exhausted themselves with every act of love and anger and apology and forgiveness they could think of that might stand in for what they did not have the words to say. It was after all of that, when they were finished and had fallen asleep, that Marina started screaming.

It was a while before she could explain herself. As much as a minute passed before she could be fully awakened and so kept on in the world of her dream in which screaming was the only possible option. When she opened her eyes Mr. Fox was there and he was holding her upper arms and looking like he was about to start screaming himself. She almost asked him what was wrong, then she remembered.

"I'm taking Lariam," Marina said. There was no saliva in her mouth and without the lubrication the words were sticking on her teeth. "It's the side effect. Nightmares." She was on the floor with the bedspread around her bare shoulders. She covered her face with her hands and thought she could hear the sweat running down her neck. Her flight from the St. Paul–Minneapolis airport left at six forty-five in the morning and she still had a little last minute packing to do. She wanted to be sure to water the plants and take all the perishables out of the refrigerator. She was awake now, wide awake. She would just stay up.

Mr. Fox, who was crouched down in front of her, put his hands gently on her knees. "What in the world did you dream?" he said.

And even though she wanted to tell him the truth because she loved him, she could not imagine putting the dream into words. She told him the same thing she used to tell her mother: it was something generically awful, she didn't remember.

When Mr. Fox drove her to the airport it was twenty degrees. Marina clicked off the radio before they had the chance to announce the windchill. The dark of morning seemed deeper than anything night had been able to come up with. They were addled by their decisions, their lack of sleep. They didn't take into account how early it was and that the drivers in that fierce commuter traffic for which they had allotted so much extra time weren't even awake yet. When he pulled into the lane for departing flights it was five fifteen in the morning.

"I'll come in with you," he said.

She shook her head. "I'm going to go on to the gate. Anyway, you need to get home, get ready for work." She didn't know why she said it. She wanted to stay with him forever.

"I have a little going-away present," he said. "I was coming over to give you this last night but I got sidetracked." He leaned across her to open the glove compartment, from which he took a small black zippered pouch. He pulled the zipper back and took out a complicated-looking phone. "I know what you're going to say, you already have a phone. But trust me, it isn't like this. They say you can make a call from anyplace in the world on this thing. You can check your messages, send e-mail, and there's a GPS. It can tell you what river you're on." He looked so pleased with it all. "It's all charged up and ready to go. I programmed in my phone numbers. I put all the instructions in the bag. I thought that maybe you could read them on the plane."

Marina looked at the bright silver face. It could no doubt shoot and edit a short documentary film about a pharmacologist who goes to the Amazon. "I'm sure I'll need to."

"The man at the store told me you could make a phone call from Antarctica."

Marina turned and looked at him blankly.

"I want to stay in touch with you, that's all I'm saying. I want to know what's happening."

She nodded and put the phone and the phone's tiny manuals in her purse. For a moment they both sat quietly. Marina thought they were working up to goodbye.

"About the dreams," he said.

"They'll stop."

"But you'll keep taking the Lariam?"

They were bathed in the fall of light pouring out through the high sheets of glass in front of the airport. Why did airports always have such ridiculously high ceilings? Was it meant to ease you into the notion of flight? Mr. Fox looked at her very seriously and so she said, "Of course."

He sighed and took her hand. "Good," he said, and gave the hand a squeeze. "Good. There must be a huge temptation to throw them in the trash if they give you dreams like that. I don't want you going down there—" He stopped himself.

"And getting a fever," she said.

Mr. Fox seemed suddenly distracted by Marina's hand, as if he were making a study of its shape and size. It was her left hand, of course, he was on the left side of the car, and he took his own left hand and slid the tips of his fingers down her third finger, as if he were putting a ring there, except there wasn't any ring. "You'll go down there, find out what you can, and take the next flight home." He lifted his eyes to hers. "Do you promise?"

She said yes. He was still holding on to her finger. She wanted to ask him what it meant, if it meant what she thought it meant, but if she was wrong she couldn't bear the answer at this particular moment. They got out of the car together. Marina, with the finely honed sense of a native, would say that the windchill had fallen into negative numbers, although the woman on the radio had said tomorrow the temperatures would climb back up near forty. Such were the inconsistencies of spring. He took her bag out of the trunk of his car and he held her and kissed her and exacted one more set of promises of how careful she would be and how quickly she would return, and when all of that was done Mr. Fox got back into his car and drove away. Marina stood there in the cold watching the taillights until she could no longer be certain which set were his, then she wheeled her bag into the airport's main terminal and pulled it up to an embankment of chairs. First she opened the zippered phone case he had given her and after removing the phone and the paperwork searched with some real sense of expectation for a ring. It was the only place he could have hidden it, and if he had, well, that would be something, because then she supposed she would use the phone to call him and say yes, she would marry him. But when she had untangled the cord to the charger and found nothing but her own foolishness she put it all back. She put the manuals in her carry-on just in case she was able to make herself read them on the plane and then she pushed the phone inside her suitcase. She ran her hands carefully around in her folded shirts and underpants and extra shoes until she found the small bag which bore a striking resemblance to the bag the phone came in, the one she used for pills: aspirin, Pepto-Bismol tablets, Ambien, broad-spectrum antibiotics. She took out the bottle of Lariam and without so much as a thoughtful glance dropped it in the trash can beside her. She felt that there was something deeply flawed in her imagination that she hadn't even considered the fact that the pills could just be thrown away.

Unfortunately, throwing away the pills did not throw away the dreams, not until whatever was left of the Lariam had cycled through her blood stream, and so with little more than three hours of sleep to back her up she tried to stay awake on the plane. Vogel had bought her a first-class ticket to Miami and then on to Manaus, and the big seat took her in its arms, tilted her back, and told her repeatedly to rest. At seven thirty in the morning the man beside her in a charcoal gray suit asked the flight attendant for a Bloody Mary. She wondered if they had given Anders a first-class ticket, or, for that matter, a cell phone with GPS. She doubted it. The recirculated air carried the lightest scent of vodka and tomato juice. Marina's head dipped to the side and there was Mr. Fox again, holding her ring finger, telling her to come home. Her head shot up.

Mr. Fox's wife was named Mary. Mary had died of a non-Hodgkin's lymphoma at the age of fifty-five. It was the same year Marina came to Vogel. If Marina was given to armchair analysis, and she was not, she supposed a case could be made that despite Mr. Fox's protests to the contrary, the very thing that drew him to Marina was the fact that she was younger and therefore less likely to re-create the situation he had already endured, although that hardly explained why he was sending her to Brazil. In the pictures of Mary that Mr. Fox kept out, one of her alone that was in the kitchen, and another in the den with their two daughters on a rafting trip, she looked like someone Marina would like. She had a good face, her eyes opened wide, her thick wheat-colored hair pulled back in a ponytail. Mary had taught math at a prep school in Eden Prairie that both of their girls had attended. "They gave us a great break on tuition," Mr. Fox said, holding the picture. "Ellie," he said, pointing to the smaller of the two girls, "looks just like her mother. She's doing her internship in radiology at the Cleveland Clinic, married an English teacher of all things. And this one, Alice, she isn't married." He moved his finger over to the darker of the two girls. "She's an international bond trader in Rome. She went to Italy her junior year at Vassar and that was it for her. She believed she was supposed to be Italian."

Marina stared at their faces. The girls were little, maybe six and eight. It was difficult to imagine them as doctor and banker. Mary in the picture was younger than Marina was now, her health shimmering like the pinpoints of light spreading out across the water behind her. They are standing on the bank of a river in front of an overturned canoe, pine boughs feathering the edges of the frame. They are holding up their paddles and smiling, smiling at Mr. Fox, who is himself not yet forty when he pushes down the button on the camera.

"I had thought that they would all stay here," he said, standing the picture back in the bookshelf. "Maybe the girls would go away to school, but then they'd come back and live near us, get married, have children. I hadn't given much thought to our dying back then but if you had asked me I would have said that Mary would outlast me by a good ten years at least. She was at the top of the actuarial tables. She ate her vegetables and went hiking and never smoked and had so many friends. I would have bet every dime I had on her." He tapped his fingers against the top of the frame. "It seems ridiculous now, doesn't it, that kind of naïveté?"

If anything, it seemed to Marina that naïveté was key. It was the thing that had allowed Karen to marry Anders and have those three children, their shared belief that he would always be there to take care of them. She and Anders both were too naïve to think that either one of them might die in these early years when they were both so essential to one another and to their sons. Had they thought for a minute that things might turn out the way they did they never would have had the courage to begin. Marina's own birth had been engendered by naïveté: her mother's, thinking that love would win out over the pull of an entire country; her father's, thinking he could leave a country behind for one Minnesotan. Had they not been so hopeful and guileless her birth would have been impossible. Marina reimagined her parents as a couple of practical cynics and suddenly the entire film of her life spooled backwards until at last the small heroine disappeared completely. Naïveté may be the bedrock of reproduction, the lynchpin for the survival of the species. Even Marina, who understood all of this, was still able to think that Mr. Fox was possibly, obliquely, suggesting they might marry.

Marina had been married once herself, though she didn't think it counted for much of anything now. They had married in the beginning of their third year of residency and divorced at the end of the fifth, and in the two and a half years that intervened they were virtually never awake at the same time. Marina often thought that if it hadn't been for the wedding, which was modest, it would have simply been a failed relationship with a nice man she really never thought of anymore. She had been naïve herself, thinking that they could make a marriage work at that particularly difficult point in their training, despite the fact that everyone they knew had told them otherwise. She was certain that love would prevail, and when it didn't, she had lost not only her marriage but her ingenuous self. Marina and her husband bought their own divorce kit at an office supply store and amicably filled out the paperwork at the kitchen table. He took the bedroom furniture, she took the living room furniture. In a gesture of kindness, she offered up the kitchen table and the chairs that they sat in, and because he knew she meant it kindly he accepted. Her mother flew to Baltimore to help her find a smaller apartment and pack up half of the wedding gifts that she hadn't wanted in the first place. What Marina had wanted very much was the chance to lie on the sofa in the living room and maybe drink a glass of scotch while crying in the afternoon but there wasn't time. She had turned thirty the week before. She had six hours left before she had to be back at the hospital. The thing that Marina was feeling the end of so acutely, the thing that made her want to take to the sofa in the middle of the day, was not the end of her marriage but the end of her residency in obstetrics and gynecology. Four years into her five-year program she had switched to clinical pharmacology, enrolled in a Ph.D. program, and doomed herself to another three years of school. Even though her mother had come to Baltimore to help her through her divorce, Marina didn't tell her what it was she was actually breaking up with. She didn't tell her that the life she had ruined was not her own nor Josh Su's but someone else's, someone she didn't even know. She did not tell her mother about the accident, nor about the Spanish Inquisition that had followed. She did not tell her about the switch to pharmacology until she was a year into the program and then she mentioned it so casually that it seemed like the most natural thing in the world. She did not tell her mother about Dr. Swenson.

Marina pulled her coat around her shoulders. Beneath the plane was a soft white bank of clouds that shielded passengers from the landscape below. There was no telling where they were now. She let her head tip back and thought that no harm could come from the smallest sip of sleep. She knew how to close her eyes for two minutes. It was a magic trick she had picked up in her residency, falling asleep in the corner of an elevator and then waking up on the right floor. She would give her head a quick shake and then walk straight to the patient's room, not exactly refreshed but, for the moment, reinforced. She pressed the button on the armrest and let her seat recline. She set her internal alarm for five minutes and gave in to the sleep that had been pulling at her since the nightmares had thrown her out of bed this morning. But this time when the elevator doors opened she was not in Calcutta. She was at Vogel, looking down the hallway at the tile floor and humming lights, and suddenly she changed her mind about everything. She should have told Anders about Dr. Swenson. It was hard to see what bearing her story would have on his trip to the Amazon but still she had chosen not to tell him as a means of protecting herself, not because he shouldn't have had the information. Anders would have been grateful for any insight, she could see that now, and it seemed possible that this one additional fact could have changed his outcome. He might at least have been wary. The more she thought of it the faster she went down the hall. All of the windows set into the doors of the labs and offices were dark. Everyone had already gone home.

Except Anders.

He was at his desk, his back towards her. She always got to work before him in the morning. He had to drop the boys off at school. She almost never came in and saw him sitting there and the joy that broke over her at the sight of his tall, straight back, his faded hair, made her cry out. "I was afraid I'd missed you!" she said. Her heart was beating so fast, 150, she thought, 160.

The look on his face was half surprised. "You did miss me. I was all the way out to the parking lot and I realized I'd left my watch." He slipped the band over his left hand, fastened down the catch. Anders always took his watch off in the morning, they all did, too much hand washing, too many times in and out of latex gloves. "What's wrong with you? You look like you've been running." He reached over and put his hand on her shoulder and then he started to shake her, gently at first and then forcefully. "Miss," he said, as if they had never met before. "Miss?"

Marina opened her eyes. The man in the suit was shaking her shoulder and the flight attendant was peering into Marina's face, entirely too close. When Marina opened her eyes she was looking directly into the woman's mouth, her lipstick a thick brownish pink, obscene. "Miss?"

"I'm sorry," Marina said.

"I think you were having a dream." The flight attendant pulled back, giving Marina a bigger picture. How early must she have gotten up this morning in order to put on that much mascara? "Would you like a glass of water?"

Marina nodded. The trick of Lariam was to figure out which part was the dream and which part was her waking life: Vogel she knew, Anders and the lab. It was the plane that smacked of nightmares.

"I don't like to fly myself," the suited man told her and held up his Bloody Mary. "I medicate."

"I don't mind flying," Marina said. There was something she had meant to tell Anders.

"It certainly seemed like you mind it," the man said. Maybe he was concerned, or bored, or inappropriately friendly, or midwestern friendly. Nothing was clear. She took the glass of water that was handed to her and drank it down.

"I have bad dreams," Marina said, and then she added, "on planes. I won't fall asleep again."

The man looked at her skeptically. After all, they were in this together now, seatmates. "Well, if you do, should I wake you up or just let you go?"

Marina thought about it. Either way it was a loss. She didn't want to scream in front of him and she didn't want him shaking her arm either. The intimacy of sleeping next to strangers, much less twitching and making noises, was unbearable. "Let me go," she said, and turned her shoulders away from him.

She had been going to tell Anders about Dr. Swenson. It was a funny business, the subconscious mind, thinking that it could rewrite history. It would never have occurred to her to tell him what had happened when he was alive, and now that he was dead she was certain she should have. The great, lumbering guilt that slept inside of her at every moment of her life had shifted, stretched. Wasn't it logical that guilt should awaken guilt? Marina Singh had had an accident a long time ago, and after that she had removed herself from the obstetrics and gynecology program. She had never told her mother, who thought that her daughter had had an illogical change of heart late in her training, or Mr. Fox, who never knew her to be anything other than a pharmacologist. The people who did know the details of what had happened, Josh Su, the friends she had at the time, one by one she found a way not to know them anymore. She no longer knew Dr. Swenson. With a great deal of concentrated effort she had found the means to stop repeating the story to herself. She no longer traced the events through the map of her memory, studying the various places where she had been free to make different choices.

Marina Singh had been the chief resident and Dr. Swenson was the attending. On this particular night, or as the review board had called it, the night in question, she was working at the County Receiving Hospital in Baltimore. It was a busy night but not the worst. Sometime after midnight a woman came in who said she'd been in labor for three hours. She had already had two children and she said she hadn't been in any hurry to come to the hospital.

"How are you feeling now?" the flight attendant asked.

"I'm fine," Marina said. Her eyes were dry and she concentrated on keeping them open.

"Well, don't feel embarrassed. This nice man here woke you up in time."

The nice man smiled again at Marina. Something in that smile implied that he was sheltering a small flame of hope that there would be a reward for his good deed.

"Some people's seatmates aren't so thoughtful," the flight attendant said. She was lingering. There wasn't much to do in first class, not enough people to take care of. "They let them snore and scream and carry on until you can hear them in the rear lavatory."

"I'm fine now," Marina said again, and she turned her face to the window, wondering if there was an empty seat at the back of the plane.

She tried to separate what had happened that night from her deposition. She tried to place herself back at the actual event instead of the endless and exhaustive retelling of that event. The patient was twenty-eight, African-American. Her hair was straightened and pulled back. She was tall, broad shouldered, enormously pregnant. Marina was surprised to remember how much she liked the woman. If the patient had been afraid she never showed it. She talked about her other children in between her contractions and sometimes through them: two girls, and now they were having their boy. Marina paged Dr. Swenson and told her the patient's contractions were four minutes apart and she hadn't begun dilating. The infant's heart rate was unstable. Marina told Dr. Swenson that unless the situation improved they would need to do a cesarean.

And Dr. Swenson said, she was very clear on this, that Marina was to wait. She was not to do the section without her.

"Can you see anything down there?" asked the man in the suit.

"No," Marina said.

"I don't know how you can stand it. Me, I can't do the window seat. If it's all they've got I pull the blind. I tell myself we're in a bus. I used to not be able to fly at all and I went to a class where they taught us to hypnotize ourselves into thinking we were on a bus. It works as long as I have a drink. Do you want a drink?"

Marina shook her head.

"Part of the paper?"

Marina looked at him. He was pale with high red cheeks, a fellow traveler who wanted her to ask him why he was flying to Miami and if that was his final destination. He wanted her to tell him she was going on to South America so that he could be impressed and ask her what she planned on doing there, and she would do none of that. She would do nothing for him.

She had done C-sections before but on that night she was told to wait and monitor and call back in one hour if there was no improvement. The fetal heart rate dropped and climbed, dropped and climbed, and still the patient wasn't dilated. Marina paged Dr. Swenson the second time, and she waited and waited but there was no call back. When she looked at the clock she realized that only forty-five minutes had passed, not an hour. The rules were intractable. She had not followed the rules. It was exactly the thing Marina had always admired about Dr. Swenson until she was the one trying to get her on the phone. The patient was a talker, and they had time to talk. She said she was exhausted but that it wasn't so much the labor. She said her two-year-old had kept her up all night the night before with an earache. Her husband had dropped her off in front of the hospital. He was driving their girls out to his mother's and that was two hours away. Two hours out and two hours back but at the rate she was going he'd be there for the birth so she said she didn't mind waiting. She wanted him there. He had missed the first two, circumstances, she said, not his fault. Her voice was strong, louder than it needed to be in the small room. "You always forget what childbirth is like," she said, "but I don't remember it being this hard." Then she laughed a little and said, "That's the whole point, right? You don't remember, because if you did remember no one would ever have kids again and then what would happen? That would be the end of everything." It was one thirty. It was two. It was three. No calls were returned. Marina delivered two other babies while the woman waited and both of the births were so easy they hadn't needed a doctor at all. Women for the most part knew how to push out an infant. Even when they didn't know there was no stopping them. Marina went back to check on the woman again. The doctor was terrified, the patient was patient. Back in the days when Marina played this film in her head every hour, waking and sleeping, this was the part she watched most carefully. She slowed down the tape to a crawl. She looked at every frame separately. She was not terrified that the patient would die or that she would lose the baby, she was terrified that she was doing something wrong in the eyes of Dr. Swenson. She was thinking that if she had followed instructions and waited another fifteen minutes to call the first time then none of this would be happening. Surely she had learned her lesson now. Surely Dr. Swenson was almost there. The nurses understood all of this. Even as they were prepping the patient for surgery and calling the anesthesiologist to wake him up they were saying, We're just getting things ready for Dr. Swenson so she can walk right in. Marina should have called another doctor but she never even thought of it. She had stretched the time out too far trying to cover herself. If she hadn't waited so long, if she hadn't waited until everything was crashing and there was no other choice but to go ahead, she would have taken more time.

The plane dropped sharply and then righted itself. It was an air pocket, a blip, but for a split second every person on the plane heard the same voice in their head, *This is it.* The man in the suit grabbed her wrist, but by the time his hand was on her arm it was over, forgotten, everything was fine. "Did you feel that?" he said.

She hadn't started in the right place. The deeper truth of the story was someplace years before this, at the beginning of her residency, or in medical school that first day of class when she saw Dr. Swenson down in the pit of the lecture hall. There were no words for how much she admired her, her intelligence, her abilities as a doctor. All of the students did. In every moment Dr. Swenson's students were eager and anxious. She didn't bother to learn their names and yet they lived their lives to the letter of her law. She was harder on the women in the group. She would tell them stories of her own days in medical school and how when she came along the men knit their arms together to keep her out. They made a human barricade against her, they kicked at her when she climbed over them, and now all the women were just walking through, no understanding or appreciation for the work that had been done for them. It wasn't that Marina had ever wanted to be like her, it wasn't in her. She had just wanted to see if she was capable of spending five years of her life living up to Dr. Swenson's standards, and she wasn't. All of a sudden she felt drunk. Somewhere very far away she could feel the presence of a man beside her. He had let her go. She could never have told this story to Anders, even if it would have put him on his guard, even if that might have been the thing to save his life. He had three sons of his own, after all. The skin of the patient's belly was stretched to the point of startling thinness, like a balloon that had been blown up too far. Marina remembered there was a sheen to it. She cut the skin, dug through the fat for the fascia. She had thought there was no time left. Her hands were working at triple speed, and there was the uterus. She thought that she was saving the baby's life because she was so fast, but the instant she realized he was occiput posterior, looking straight up, the blade had caught his head right of center at the hairline, cutting until she stopped in the middle of his cheek. It used to be that she could feel it in her own face, the straight incision, the scalpel slicing through the eye. The child's father could feel it when he came back to the hospital that night to find his wife sedated and his son scarred and blinded in one eye. Marina met him in the hallway and told him what she had done. She saw him flinch in exactly the way she had flinched. He was not allowed to see the baby then. The specialists were already working but some things cannot be set to right.

They did not terminate her residency. Marina remembered this with no small amount of wonder. When all of it was over and the lawsuit was settled, she was allowed to go back. The patient had liked her, that was the hell of it. They had spent the whole night together. She wanted the settlement money but she didn't want Marina's head on a pike. She said that other than that one mistake she'd done a good job. That one mistake. So Marina was left to mete out a punishment for herself. She could not touch a patient or face her classmates. She could not go back to Dr. Swenson, who had said in the deposition that the chief resident had been instructed not to proceed alone. Over the three hour period the fetal heart rate kept getting lower but every time it reversed. It kept coming up. Maybe in another hour or two she would have dilated. Maybe in another ten minutes the baby would have died. No one knew the answer to that. Marina was a sinking ship and from the safety of dry land Dr. Swenson turned her back and walked away. Marina suspected in the end Dr. Swenson had no idea who she was.

Anders was never going to stay home. Not when there was a chance to leave in the winter and see the Amazon, to photograph the crested caracaras. And anyway, he had already left, he was already dead, she was flying to Brazil in hopes of finding out what had become of his body. She had been up all night with the patient, she had been up all night blinding the child, and now her eyes dropped, opened, dropped. This was the cost of going to find Dr. Swenson: remembering. She went to the lab at Vogel even though she had promised the man beside her on the plane that she would not.

She went down the dark hall to their dark lab and there she picked up the picture of the Eckman boys that sat on Anders' desk, all three of them caught in a fit of hilarity that would hereafter be thought of as belonging to another lifetime. The picture, whose small subjects were so incandescent they seemed to throw off a little light of their own in the dark room, was in her hands when the door opened again. Anders had forgotten what this time? Wallet? Keys? It didn't matter. She only wanted him back.

"Come now, Mari," her father said. "It's time to go."

It was so perfect that Marina nearly laughed aloud. Of course he was there now, of course. There was a part of the dream that did not follow her into waking—this part—where her father comes into the room and says her name. The part when they are together for a while, the two of them, before things go wrong. The way things ended always obliterated the genuine happiness that had come before and that shouldn't be the case. The truth was so much more complicated than that. It was made up of grief and great rewards and she needed to remember all of it. "I was looking at this picture," she said, and held it out to him. "Aren't these handsome boys?"

Her father nodded. He looked good in his yellow kurta and pressed trousers. He looked fit and rested, a braided belt circling his trim waist. Marina hadn't thought of it before but they were very nearly the same age now. She understood it was the business of time to move forward but she would have been glad to stay exactly in this moment.

"So you're ready?"

"I'm ready," she said.

"Good, alright then, hold on to me." And he opened the door and they stepped out together into the empty hallway of Vogel. For a moment there was a wondrous quiet and Marina tried to appreciate it while understanding that it couldn't last. One by one the doors opened and her colleagues came out to meet her father and shake his hand and behind them came Indians, more and more of them, until it felt like all of Calcutta was pouring in beside them, raising their voices over the din of other people's conversations.

"I know where the staircase is," Marina said into his ear. "We can get there."

Her father couldn't hear her, it was simply too loud. They pressed ahead, holding on to each other for as long as was possible.

Three

The minute she stepped into the musty wind of the tropical air-conditioning, Marina smelled her own wooliness. She pulled off her light spring coat and then the zippered cardigan beneath it, stuffing them into her carry-on where they did not begin to fit, while every insect in the Amazon lifted its head from the leaf it was masticating and turned a slender antenna in her direction. She was a snack plate, a buffet line, a woman dressed for springtime in the North. Marina handed over her passport to the man at the desk whose shirt bore all the appropriate badges and tags of his office. He looked hard at her picture, her face. When asked, she said she was visiting Brazil on business. While her planned response to the question "How long will you stay?" was *two weeks,* she changed her mind just as she opened her mouth.

"Three weeks," she said, and the man stamped an empty page in a booklet filled with empty pages.

Marina squeezed into place at the crowded baggage carousel and watched the river of bundled possessions flow past. Such enormous suitcases piled on top of one another like sandbags ready to stem a rising tide. Marina waited and watched for her own unassuming luggage, looking away only long enough to help a stranger drag a foot locker to the floor. She thought of Calcutta, the madness of the baggage claim that gave only the slightest preview to the madness of the streets outside. She and her mother and father were alone together among the thronging masses, her father shepherding them from the path of young men with roller carts. Sari-wrapped grandmothers guarded the family luggage by sitting on top of it, zippered soft-sides that strained to open against a series of exterior belts. Marina shook the image from her head, turning her full attention to the scene at hand. She tried to stay hopeful through the dwindling: the suitcases, the crowd, one by one they all left. A pair of child's swim goggles remained on the belt and she watched them pass again and again. She made a mental list of the items a smarter person would have kept in a carry-on: the dictionary, the zippered bag with the phone, the Lariam, which was in a trash can in the Minneapolis–St. Paul airport.

The unhappy people who crowded the office of lost luggage pressed against the stacks of unclaimed suitcases and together they raised the temperature in the little room some fifteen degrees beyond the heat in the vast cavern of baggage claim. A small black metal fan sat on the desk and stirred hopelessly at the air in a two foot radius. One by one they approached the girl at the desk, making fast conversation in Portuguese. When Marina's turn came she handed over her ticket and the address of her hotel without a word, and the girl, who had had more than a little experience with these situations, pushed forward a laminated sheet of pictures of various bags. Marina touched the suitcase that most resembled hers. The printer churned out a piece of paper that the girl then handed back to Marina, circling a phone number and a claim number.

Marina went past security and customs and stepped out into the lobby full of people who were looking behind her. Young girls stood on their toes and waved. Taxi drivers hustled for fares, cruise directors and Amazon adventure guides herded their charges into groups. An assortment of cheap shops and money changing stations vied for attention with bright colors and brighter lights, and right in the middle of everything stood a man in a dark suit holding a neatly lettered sign with two words:

Marina Singh.

So certain was Marina Singh that she was alone in this world that the sight of her own name written in a heavy black marker and properly spelled (how rarely anyone found the energy to include that final "h") made her stop. The man holding the sign appeared to see everything, and though there were easily five hundred people to choose from, he very quickly turned to her. "Dr. Singh?" he said. He was quite far away. She did not hear her name as much as see it shaped by his lips and she nodded. He walked towards her and the sea of life parted easily around him. He held out his hand. "I am Milton."

"Milton," she said. She had to remind herself that an embrace was not in order.

"You are quite late. I was concerned." And he looked concerned. His eyes peered into hers for any sign that things had not gone well.

"My luggage was lost. I had to go to the claims office. To tell you the truth, I didn't know that anyone would be here to meet me."

"You have no luggage?" Milton said.

"I have an overcoat." She patted at the coat and saw that one sleeve was almost to the floor. She pushed it back in the bag.

On his face she saw a look of sorrow and responsibility. "You'll come with me?" He took the small bag from her and put his hand very lightly on her upper arm, moving her a few steps backwards into the crowd.

"I filled out all the forms," she said.

He shook his head. "We must go back."

"But we can't go back through security." To move backwards through a security door, a door clearly marked to indicate that all traffic flowed in one direction, was as likely as going back in time, but there was Milton, his hand now resting on the shoulder of the security guard. He leaned his body slightly forward and whispered something to the man with the gun and the man with the gun held up his hand to stop the people who were pouring ahead to let Milton and Marina through. They walked the wrong way through customs where a man in uniform had two hands deep inside a woman's purse. He then held out one of those hands to Milton and Milton shook it as they passed.

"I'll need your paper," Milton said to Marina, and she handed it to him. Already they were moving past the carousels. They stepped into the claims office which was now crowded with different people who had lost their luggage on later flights. They pushed against one another, angry and sad, thinking they had been the only ones.

The girl working behind the desk saw them, or sensed them, as soon as they stepped inside the door and she raised her head. "Milton," she said, smiling, and then she was off on a tear of Portuguese. Marina put together the girl's opening and then lost the thread—"Isso é um sonho." The girl waved them up to the front where she and Milton began a conversation in passionate animation. When a man who had waited more than an hour for a word of recognition began to protest, the girl made a clucking sound with her tongue and silenced him. Milton gave her the computer printout and she read the report she had typed up herself as if it were a document of compelling mystery, then let out a long sigh. From his wallet Milton took a business card and quickly folded a bill around it, talking, talking. The girl took it from him and he kissed the tips of her fingers. She laughed and said something to Marina that may or may not have been lurid in nature. Marina looked back at her, dumb as a sock.

The outside air was heavy enough to be bitten and chewed.

Never had Marina's lungs taken in so much oxygen, so much moisture. With every inhalation she felt she was introducing unseen particles of plant life into her body, tiny spores that bedded down in between her cilia and set about taking root. An insect flew against her ear, emitting a sound so piercing that her head snapped back as if struck. Another insect bit her cheek just as she raised her hand to drive the first one away. They were not in the jungle, they were in a parking lot. For an instant the heat lightning brightened up an ominous cloud bank miles to the south and just as quickly left them in darkness.

"Do you have what you need in the small bag?" Milton asked hopefully.

Marina shook her head. "Books," she said, "a coat." The manual for the phone that was lost. A neck pillow for sleeping on the plane. A copy of *The Wings of the Dove,* which she brought because she thought it was long enough to see her through the entire trip. A copy of the *New England Journal of Medicine,* which contained a chapter of Dr. Swenson's report—"Reproductive Endocrinology in the Lakashi People."

"Then we must get you some things tonight," he said. His brother-in-law ran a store in town. Milton took out his cell phone, assuring her the brother-in-law would be amenable to meeting them with the keys despite the late hour, not a problem, and Marina, who very much wanted a toothbrush, accepted.

Milton was careful to maneuver around those potholes which could be maneuvered around. He drove cautiously through the ones that could not. People clumped together on corners of busy streets waiting for a light to cross, but when the lights changed they continued to stand there. Girls dressed for dancing pushed strollers past walls pasted over in handbills. An old woman with a broom swept debris through the middle of an intersection. Marina watched all of it thinking of Anders, wondering if he had seen these same people on the night he arrived. She couldn't imagine things in Manaus changed very much from one night to the next. "Did you drive Dr. Eckman?" Marina asked.

"Eckman," Milton said, as if it were an object whose English name was unfamiliar to him.

"Anders Eckman. He came here just after Christmas. We work for the same company."

Milton shook his head. "Do many of your doctors come to Brazil?"

Exactly three, Marina thought, and then she said, "Not many." Of course no one would have thought to get Anders a car and driver. Anders would have found his luggage and taken it to the taxi line, opened his Portuguese phrase book and rehearsed the sentence, "What is the fare to the hotel?" It occurred to Marina now how close she was to him here. She thought of him standing in that same airport, his feet planted on the same asphalt outside. They had been divided by only a scant handful of months, one of them slipping out the back door while the other was coming in the front. It was then that an entirely different idea came to Marina. "Did you ever drive a woman named Dr. Swenson?"

"Dr. Swenson, of course. She is a very good customer. Do you work with Dr. Swenson as well?"

Marina sat up straighter then and as soon as she did she felt her seat belt lock into place. If Vogel hadn't bothered to hire a driver for Anders they certainly would have found one for Dr. Swenson, or Dr. Swenson would have found one for herself. It would be a car as clean as this one, a driver as strikingly competent. "Do you know where she lives?"

"In Manaus, yes. It isn't far from your hotel. But Dr. Swenson is rarely in Manaus. Her work is in the jungle." Milton stopped then, and Marina saw him glance at her in the rearview mirror. "You know her, yes?" He should not be talking about the people he drives. He should not be talking about Dr. Swenson.

"She was my teacher in medical school," Marina said, offering up this bit of her past so easily it felt like a lie. "Many years ago. We work for the same company now. I've come here to find her. Our company has sent me to talk to her about the project she's working on."

"And so you know," Milton said, his voice relieved.

"I have her address in town but no one is able to reach her where she's working. Dr. Swenson won't use cell phones."

"She calls me from the pay phone at the dock when she comes to the city."

"And it doesn't matter if you're driving someone else . . ." She was speaking from her own, distant experience.

Milton nodded then, keeping his eyes straight ahead. "There's never any warning when she's coming, when she leaves. Sometimes months go by and she doesn't come in from the jungle. I grew up in Manaus. I wouldn't spend so much time out there."

"Nothing bothers Dr. Swenson," Marina said.

"No," Milton said, but after more consideration he added, "except not being picked up at the dock."

In a few more turns Milton brought her to another part of the city where people walked through the streets arguing or holding hands, oblivious to the fact it was night and there was nothing going on around them in any direction. Up ahead a man sat on a low cement step and Milton pulled the car over. Immediately the man stood up and opened Marina's door. He was tall and thin, wearing a pink cotton shirt that would have covered two of him. He greeted them in clipped Portuguese. He clearly was not as pleased to be coming out late as Milton had suggested.

"Negócio é negócio," Milton said, turning off the ignition. He introduced his brother-in-law, Rodrigo, to Marina, as Rodrigo took her hand to help her out of the car.

Rodrigo said something to Milton when he unlocked the door to the building. Milton then flipped on the lights. Inside it smelled of sawdust. He checked to make sure the door was locked behind them.

Rodrigo turned off the lights and Milton turned them on again. Rodrigo covered his eyes with his hands as if trying to ensure darkness, all the while making quick use of a language Marina did not speak. She blinked, her eyes dilated and blind and then flooded with electric light. The store was nothing but a large square with wood plank floors and every conceivable item crammed inside: canned food and clothes and pills, sunglasses, postcards, bags of seed, laundry soap. The colors of the boxes and bottles climbing up and up to the high ceiling made her dizzy. The general tenor of the argument between the two men was clear to her even if she didn't understand the words. They were taking turns flipping the switch from off to on to off and she was to make fast work in the light while she had it. She picked up a red toothbrush, deodorant, toothpaste, shampoo, insect repellent, sunblock, two cotton shirts, T-shirts, a straw hat. She held a pair of pants up to her waist and then dropped them on the counter. The suitcase might arrive in the morning or she might never see it again. She picked up a package of underwear and then a cluster of elastic hair bands. "So when was the last time you saw Dr. Swenson?" Marina asked.

"Doctora Singh conhece a Doctora Swenson," Milton said to his brother-in-law. Marina heard both of their names. In a gesture that struck her as being particularly Indian, Rodrigo pressed his palms together in front of his lips and made a slight bow of his head.

"She is an excellent customer," Milton said. "She buys all the provisions for the camp here. It is something to see the way she comes into the store. She stands right in the middle, right where you are, and points to what she wants and Rodrigo brings it down for her. She does it all without a list. It's impressive."

"Muito decisivo," Rodrigo said. "Muito rápido."

"It used to be one of the other doctors might come in for supplies. Dr. Swenson would be working very hard on her medicine and so she would send someone else into town, then two days later there she would be at the dock. She'd say they hadn't bought enough things, or the right things. In the end she told me sending someone else was only time wasted. Sometimes she sends in Easter with a note if there is something special she needs, but that isn't often. He couldn't do all the shopping himself."

Rodrigo disagreed. Milton ignored him. "Rodrigo knows her very well now. There are certain items he orders just for her."

"Other doctors?" Marina said. Outside she could hear voices and then the rattling of the door handle, and then the slapping of hands against glass. The crowd wanted in.

"It hasn't been a month since she was here." Milton looked at Rodrigo and asked in Portuguese, "Um mês?" Rodrigo nodded. "That could be inconvenient for you," Milton said. "I've known her to be gone for three."

Marina pictured three months in this city she had yet to see in daylight, wearing these clothes, memorizing the manual for the missing cell phone. She would buy a boat and head down the river herself if it came to that. She asked if there was anyone who would know how to find her.

Milton tilted his head from side to side as if weighing out his thoughts. "If anyone did it would be the Bovenders, but I don't really think that they know."

"Dr. Swenson não lhes diria nada," Rodrigo said. He could follow the conversation well enough in English but did not speak it. He brought out a hooded rain poncho folded into a clear plastic sack and a small umbrella. He handed them to Marina and nodded at her with a gravity that insisted she add them to her purchases.

"You have another idea?" Milton asked his brother-in-law in English.

"The Bovenders," Marina said.

"They are the young couple who stay in her apartment. No doubt you'll meet them. They are very hard to miss. They are travelers." Milton closed his eyes. "What is the word?"

"Boêmio," Rodrigo said disapprovingly.

Milton opened his eyes. "They are young bohemians."

Rodrigo was making a list of everything Marina was taking, writing down the prices with a pencil. She held a single yellow flip-flop against the sole of her shoe, then she put it back to try another. She picked up a prepaid phone card. Anders would have found the Bovenders easily enough if they were living in Dr. Swenson's apartment. He had the address where her mail was delivered, he would have gone there first. In the store there was an irregular clicking sound, a tapping that wasn't coming from the people who were taking turns trying to force open the door. It sounded like someone was hitting the edge of a watch against a counter. She looked up to the ceiling to see some hard-shelled insects dashing themselves against the fluorescent tubing. From where she stood they didn't appear to have wings.

"Estoque!" Milton called out to the people clustered on the other side of the glass. He continued to shout at them in Portuguese. Rodrigo shut off the light again. In the dark he put her purchases into tissue thin plastic bags.

"What do they want?" Marina asked.

Milton turned and looked at her. "They don't want anything," he said, pointing out the way in which their situation was different. "They're just looking to pass the night."

When Rodrigo finally did open the door to let Milton and Marina out it became clear that the crowd wasn't as large as it had appeared when viewed through a pane of glass, maybe twenty people, and some of them were children. They looked dissipated standing there in the open street, as if there had never really been the energy needed to push their way inside. Still, they waited around to voice their disappointment, which they did in a half-hearted manner.

When Rodrigo opened the car door for Marina she suddenly realized she hadn't paid for anything. The featherweight sacks containing everything she had taken were looped over her fingers and she held them up to the two men. "I haven't paid," she said to Milton. The members of the dwindling crowd who hadn't wandered home leaned in towards her, hoping to make out the contents of her bags.

He shook his head. "It all goes on account, yes?"

"Whose account?"

"Vogel," Rodrigo said. He reached into one of the bags and showed her the carbon of the bill, a neatly printed record of everything she was leaving with.

Marina started to say something and then let it go. If it seemed odd to her that a general store in Manaus had direct billing with an American pharmaceutical company, it did not seem odd to the two men. She thanked them both and said good night to Rodrigo, who, under Milton's translation, wished her luggage a safe return. Because he opened the back door of the car for her that was where she sat for the very short ride to her hotel. When they reached their destination, Milton gathered up the few things she had and walked her inside.

She had a room at The Hotel Indira. She could not imagine that whoever booked it had known enough to mean it as a joke. From the grand exterior she entered a lobby of palm plants and tired brown sofas that slumped together as if they had come as far as they could and then given up. Milton checked her in and then came back to give her the key. After a pleasant wish for a good night he left her there, having circled his cell phone number on his business card. She realized that without Milton she might have slept in a chair in the airport and then checked in for the morning flight back to Miami. Even when she was in her room and had hung her coat on a metal bar that was attached rather nakedly to the wall, she thought about that flight. She sat down on the edge of the bed and fished a pair of reading glasses out from the bottom of her purse in order to see the endless series of microscopic numbers from the phone card she had bought in Rodrigo's store. Somehow it was only one hour earlier in Eden Prairie. After so much travel she was a scant hour from home. Mr. Fox answered on the second ring.

"I'm here," she said.

"Good," he said. "Good." He cleared his throat and she heard some rustling around. She wondered if she had woken him up. "I thought I'd hear from you earlier. Did you get some dinner?"

Marina thought about it. She must have eaten something on the plane but she couldn't remember. "My suitcase was lost. I'm sure they'll bring it tomorrow but I wanted you to know I don't have the phone."

"You put the phone in your suitcase?" he said.

"I put it in the suitcase."

Mr. Fox was quiet for the briefest moment. "They always find them these days. Usually they bring it to the hotel in the middle of the night. Call the desk as soon as you wake up in the morning. I'll bet it's there."

"The driver took me to get some things. At least I have a toothbrush now. Thank you for that, by the way."

"For the toothbrush?"

"For Milton, the driver." She put her hand over the receiver and yawned.

"I'm glad he's helpful. I'm sorry I'm not more helpful myself."

She nodded, for all the good it did their conversation. Maybe she should have waited until tomorrow to call. The draperies were open and she looked out onto the city, that infinite sea of tiny lights. In the dark, in the distance, she could have been anywhere. She closed her eyes.

"Marina?" he said.

"I'm sorry," she said. "I think I fell asleep."

"Go to bed. We can talk tomorrow."

"Unless the phone doesn't come," she said, and then she remembered. "Or you can call me at the hotel."

"I'll do that," he said. "Get some sleep."

"I'll write you a letter," she said. She did not remember hanging up the phone.

Manaus wasn't difficult to figure out. It catered to tourists and travelers and shippers, who, in this accommodating city, were free from all import duties. Everyone was either getting off of boats or getting on them, and so the streets had been laid out in such a way that one always had the feeling of walking away from the water or towards it. By the third day Marina could navigate easily. Once she got a fix on the river's position everything else fell into place. She went to the market hall at six in the morning when the world was out to accomplish as much as was humanly possible before the truly devastating heat began. The smell of so many dead fish and chickens and sides of beef tilting precariously towards rot in the still air made her hold a crumpled T-shirt over the lower half of her face but she took the time to stop and look at the herbs and barks at the medicine table, the snake heads floating in what she sincerely hoped was alcohol. A black vulture the size of a turkey walked down the aisles like all the other shoppers, looking for whatever fish heads and entrails were to be had underneath the tables. The bloody scraps were hard to find. Marina bought two apple-flavored bananas and a pastry from a woman who kept hers under a crumpled sheet of waxed paper. After that she went down to the river to watch the boats. She spent a great deal of time looking at the water, which was the color of milky tea and completely opaque even when she walked down a dock, squatted on her heels, and stared directly into it. She did this often. She couldn't see a quarter of an inch below the surface. She was waiting for Dr. Swenson.

Waiting for Dr. Swenson to appear would have been a clear waste of time had there been some other means of putting time to better use. Waiting for her suitcase was simply not a full time job, even though Tomo, the young man at the front desk of her hotel, was kind enough to call the airport twice a day and inquire as to its status. There were also the Bovenders to wait for. Marina had the address of Dr. Swenson's apartment and so every day she had written to them, putting both the names Bovender and Swenson on the envelope and neatly printing her request for contact along with her hotel information. From what Marina could tell from the building's architecture and neighborhood, and from the well-appointed lobby where she left off her letters at the desk every morning, it was one of the city's better residences. She wondered what it was costing Vogel to keep a pied-à-terre in Brazil that was mainly inhabited by bohemians who didn't seem to be home much themselves. Of course, it was possible that the bohemians had gone on. They had been described as travelers after all, and this was clearly a city where people who had somewhere else to go would not be inclined to stay. She nodded again to the concierge who as always took her envelope with an enormous grin and great, energetic nodding.

"Bovenders," she said pointedly.

"Bonvenders!" he replied.

She decided that her project for the afternoon would be to cobble together a note in Portuguese to hand him tomorrow. It would be better if she could explain to the concierge, as well as to the mythical Bovenders, what she was after.

All of Marina's activities—waiting at the river, waiting outside the apartment building, wandering through the city in hopes that she might be struck by some piece of inspiration that could lead her in the direction of Dr. Swenson—were punctuated by rain, blinding, torrential downpours that seemed to rise out of clear skies and turn the streets into wild rivers that ran ankle deep. People moved calmly from the open spaces and pressed their backs against buildings, sharing whatever room there was beneath various overhangs while they waited for the storms to pass. Several times a day she had the opportunity to be grateful to Rodrigo for pushing the rubberized poncho on her.

Of course there were times when neither the poncho nor the awnings were enough and the rain drove Marina to run in her flip-flops back to the hotel, every drop pricking her skin like a hornet. The chemicals in her sunscreen mixed with the DEET in her insect repellent and when she tried to wipe the water from her face it burned her eyes until she was half blind. Back at the hotel she showered and napped and did her best with the James novel, and when she'd had enough of that she read about the reproductive endocrinology in the Lakashi people.

As Anders had tried to explain to her when she had been so disinclined to listen, the Lakashi were an isolated tribe in the Amazon whose women appeared to continue to give birth to healthy infants well into their seventies. Securing accurate ages on the women was of course an inaccurate science. Still, it did not undermine the point: old women were having babies. The Lakashi were reproducing for up to thirty years beyond the women in the neighboring tribes. Families containing five generations were commonplace, and aside from what could perhaps be called a heightened exhaustion, they all appeared to enjoy a state of health commensurate to that of their indigenous peers. Birth defects, mental retardation, problems with bones, teeth, vision, height, weight, everything came out as average in both mothers and children as compared to members in neighboring tribes over a thirty-five-year period of study.

Marina rolled over onto her back and held the journal above her. *A thirty-five-year period of study?* That would mean that while Dr. Swenson was, to the best of her knowledge, teaching a full load at Hopkins she was also studying the Lakashi in Brazil? Of course, who knew what she did on the weekends, spring breaks, Thanksgiving vacations. It was possible she had been flying to Manaus all those years and hiring a boat to take her down the splitting tributaries of the

Rio Negro. Had it been anyone else she would have been certain the whole report was an ambitious fraud, but Dr. Swenson had always exhibited a relentless energy that defied all human understanding. If someone had told Marina that while she was stumbling through her rounds half asleep in Baltimore, Dr. Swenson was taking the red-eye to Brazil to collect data, she would have been impressed but not amazed. In fact, the very paper she was reading included research from a dissertation for which she had been awarded a doctorate in ethnobotany from Harvard. It seemed there was a great deal about Dr. Swenson she didn't know.

When the rains came hard and caught her out too far to run back to the hotel, Marina would go to the Internet café and pay five dollars to look up information about Dr. Swenson or her tribe, but as she sat there trying not to let her hair drip on the keyboard she found there was remarkably little information to be had. Google Annick Swenson and there were course descriptions, appearances at medical conferences, papers—mostly related to gynecological surgery—some tedious postings from medical students who complained that Dr. Swenson's classes, and probably all of their classes, were unfairly difficult. Most of the mentions of Lakashi linked back to the *New England Journal of Medicine* article, although the name also came up in relation to the famous Harvard ethnobotanist Martin Rapp, who had first interacted with the tribe while taking plant samples in 1960. His interest in them as a people appeared nominal, as his writing about their habits was limited to which species of fungi they did and did not consume. There was a single picture of him, an extremely thin sunburnt man with light hair and a straight English nose who stood a head above the natives on either side of him. They were all holding up mushrooms. Marina read everything she could find about Dr. Rapp and the Lakashi in hopes that there might be some clues as to their location, but the most specific directive she found was "central Amazon basin."

Leave it to Dr. Swenson to somehow manage to keep the Internet out of her business.

"Tell me they've found the suitcase," Mr. Fox said as soon as he answered the phone. Mr. Fox had somehow become more focused on whether or not she had made successful contact with her luggage than with either Dr. Swenson or the mythical Bovenders.

"Apparently the airport code for Manaus is MAO. Madrid is MAD. The theory is that an O starts to look like a D after a certain number of suitcases and so they start sending bags to Spain."

"I'm going to mail you another phone," he said. "I'll get it programmed and shipped down there tomorrow. You're going to need more Lariam soon anyway. Make a list of what you want."

"Nothing," she said, looking at the rings of insect bites that braceleted her wrists and ankles, hard red bumps that she longed to dig out with her fingernails. "I don't need anything. The second you send another phone my suitcase will show up and then I'll have two."

"So then you'll have two. You can give one to Dr. Swenson. There may be someone she wants to call."

In fact, Marina enjoyed not having a telephone. She had started out as an intern with a pager and then added to that a cell phone that later turned into a BlackBerry. In Manaus, there was an almost indescribable sense of freedom that came from wandering around in a strange city knowing that she was unreachable. "Speaking of Dr. Swenson, I've been reading about the Lakashi."

"It's always good to read up on people before you meet them," Mr. Fox replied.

"It's an interesting article but she doesn't exactly give anything away."

"Dr. Swenson doesn't mean to give things away."

"So what's the secret ingredient? Does she even know? Certainly the Lakashi don't know. I don't care how primitive these women are, if they understood what they were doing that was causing them to remain fertile unto death they'd stop doing it."

Mr. Fox fell silent on his end and Marina waited.

"You know and you don't want to tell me?" Marina said, laughing. Surely his secretary, the very serious Mrs. Dunaway, had walked into his office at that moment and forced him to wait on his reply.

"It isn't a matter of want," Mr. Fox said finally.

Marina had relaxed into the conversation and spread herself out across the bed but a bolt of incredulity forced her to sit upright again. "What?"

"There is an agreement of confidentiality—"

"I'm in *Brazil,*" she said. "I found a lizard in the bathtub this morning the size of a kitten. I don't know where Dr. Swenson is or how to find her and now you're saying you aren't going to tell me how the Lakashi women maintain fertility? Is there something I still need to do to merit your trust?"

"Marina, Marina, it has nothing to do with you. It's contractual. I'm not allowed to talk about it."

"It has nothing to do with me? Then why am I here? If this has nothing to do with me then I would very much like to come home now."

In truth, she did not care. She did not care that the Lakashi were having 3.7 times the number of children as compared to other indigenous Brazilians over the course of their lifetimes. She didn't care where they lived or if they were happy or if they wanted the children they had. What she did care about, cared about very much in fact, was that her employer, who had virtually proposed marriage and then sent her off to the equator after one of Vogel's employees had died there, now refused to share with her the basic information of the research in question. "When I find Dr. Swenson and all those pregnant Lakashi people, am I supposed to avert my eyes so I won't figure out how they're managing this? Do they make it a practice of killing anyone who finds out their secret?" And then she saw Anders standing ankle deep in the muddy river, holding a single blue envelope in his hand. "My God," she said. "My God, I didn't mean that."

"They chew some sort of bark while it's still on the tree," Mr. Fox said.

Marina did not care at all about the bark or the trees. "I didn't mean that."

"I know," he said, but all the light had gone out of his voice, and in another couple of sentences they had wrapped it all up and gotten off the phone. Marina put her shoes on and went back out into the street. The rain had stopped and the sun was beating the pavement and buildings and people and dogs into a flat sameness. She didn't want to walk to the river or the market hall and so she walked for a while around the square in the choking humidity thinking of how Anders must have walked around the square as well. Maybe he hadn't felt hopeless when he came here. Maybe he was glad to go on day-long birding excursions into the jungle and drink pisco sours alone at the bar at night. Marina bent over to look at the carved trinkets that a group of natives were selling off a blanket. She picked up a bracelet that could have been smooth painted beads or red seeds with holes drilled through the centers. She let the woman on the blanket tie it to her wrist with a complex and permanent set of knots and then bite off the ends, her lips somehow never touching skin. One of the children, a narrow-chested boy of nine or ten, looked through the menagerie of tiny carved animals that were spread out in front of him and picked out a white heron that was two inches high, a tiny fish caught in the needle of its beak, and he handed it to her. Marina had meant to refuse it, but once she held it up she thought it was in fact very fine, better than anything else she had seen, and so she agreed to buy the heron and the bracelet for a handful of bills she thought worked out to be about three dollars U.S. She put the little bird in her pocket and walked down a series of side streets, careful to keep all her turns in mind. She wasn't in the mood to get lost. The farther she walked the more she noticed that no one was looking at her. The small boys with stacks of T-shirts and dazzling butterflies pinned to boards inside cheap wooden frames didn't follow her. The ice cream vendors didn't call to her, nor did the man with the mustache and a small monkey on each shoulder who was barking at tourists in Portuguese. With her black hair caught back in a barrette beneath the hat she'd bought and her cheap clothing and her flip-flops, she was able to pass in Manaus the way she was never able to pass in Minnesota. Here they looked at her and seeing someone who looked something like a woman they knew, looked away. When she was spoken to it was only a simple greeting, that much she understood, and she nodded her head in recognition and kept walking. Anders would have been mobbed everywhere. He was so blue-eyed and overly tall, his skin was very nearly luminous, as unfamiliar to these people as snow itself. Any passerby could see deeper into Anders than he could the Rio Negro. Marina thought of all the times he'd come to work on Monday after a weekend spent paddling the boys around some lake in the summer, and how his skin would be scorched, his lips and nose already starting to peel. "Haven't you heard of sunblock?" Marina said. "Hats?"

"They keep all that information from men." He didn't wear a tie to work on those days and his shirt collar stayed open. The sore, red visage of his neck was something Marina made a point not to look at. Who thought it would be a good idea to send Anders to the equator? Her own skin was darker now. The sun had extended its reach past the hats and creams. It was inevitable.

When Marina turned again, a turn that was as aimless as all the others she had made, she found herself back at Rodrigo's store. There were no crowds out front this time, no one peering in the window. In the daylight it didn't appear to be such a compelling attraction.

The street outside was empty of people, empty of cars. In fact when she went inside, thinking she would say hello, buy a bottle of water, there was only one young couple in the store, a man and woman in their twenties pointing up to something that was over their heads. The woman was long-limbed and tan in a red sundress and she stretched to try and reach for whatever it was she wanted. Her long yellow hair, which was held away from her face by a large pair of sunglasses pushed back on her head, was the brightest aspect of the room, as it seemed that Rodrigo was no more inclined towards electricity during the day than he had been at night. The young man, who may have been a little taller than the woman, stood back in his T-shirt and baggy shorts and watched her stretch. His hair was pale brown and shaggy and his face, which was nearly too pretty, was half covered up in what was either a beard or several days spent not shaving. They hadn't noticed her come in, and so Marina watched them, in part because they made an unusual sight for Manaus, and in part because she was sure that they were the Bovenders.

She had pictured the Bovenders as being closer to her own age, without any of the drama inherent to so much bony attractiveness, but the minute she walked in the store she revised the imaginings of her idle mind. There was a tattoo banding the young man's ankle, a decorative vine, and around the woman's ankle a small gold chain. Marina had exactly one word of description to work from, bohemians, and these were the only two bohemians she had seen in three days.

Rodrigo came into the store from a room behind the counter. He told the couple something in Portuguese and the young woman disagreed and once again reached above her head helplessly while the young man folded his arms across his chest. Was it the soap pads she wanted? When Rodrigo turned for the ladder he saw Marina standing just inside the open door and in the course of a single second he placed her, remembered who it was she wanted to find, and was pleased at the luck of being the one to make the introductions. "Ola!

Dr. Singh!" he said, and when the young couple turned to see who it was Rodrigo knew, he opened his hands towards his other guests. "Bovenders."

The young Bovenders, in possession of a highly evolved social instinct, were beaming as they walked towards her. If they had been working to avoid her they were masters at hiding it. In fact, it seemed as if meeting her in this store on this afternoon was the very thing they were most looking forward to in all the world and they would not hold it against her that she had come a little late. "Barbara Bovender," the young woman said, extending her hand. She smiled to show the slight disorder among her large white teeth.

"Jackie," the young man said, and Marina shook his hand as well. The accent she thought was Australian but she wasn't positive. They seemed too tan to be English.

Rodrigo said something to Barbara and she squinted at him slightly when he spoke, as if she were translating each word separately and then reassembling them into a sentence in her head.

"Nos?"

"Dr. Swenson," he said.

"Yes, of course," Barbara said, looking almost relieved. "You're looking for Dr. Swenson."

"People don't look for us," Jackie said.

"That's because nobody knows where we are," Barbara said, and then she laughed. "That makes it sound like we're hiding."

Marina tried to put this couple together in her mind with Dr. Swenson. She tried to picture the three of them standing together in the same room. She could not. "I've left letters for you."

"For us?" Jackie asked. "At the apartment?"

"At Dr. Swenson's apartment building. I left them at the desk."

At this point Rodrigo got the ladder and climbed up towards the ceiling to get a box of dryer sheets. The hierarchy in which different items were desired, needed, and sold, could clearly be charted based on what was closest to the ceiling and what was closest to the floor. Dryer sheets appeared to be hovering on the edge of obscurity for everyone in Manaus save Barbara Bovender.

"All the mail goes straight into a box," Jackie said. "Annick picks it up when she comes into town."

"Or she doesn't," Barbara said. "She isn't very good about the mail. I've told her I'd open it for her, sort it all out, but she says not to bother. I think at the heart of it she just doesn't care."

Jackie turned then to face his wife. Was she his wife? The Bovenders could have been siblings or cousins. The general resemblance they bore to one another was striking. "She has a lot on her mind."

Barbara nodded, half closing her eyes, as if she were considering all the many weights Dr. Swenson had to bear. "It's true."

"We have a postbox," Jackie said. "That way when we get to the next town they'll forward it on."

"Are you leaving?" Marina asked.

"Oh, we will, sooner or later," Barbara said. She looked over at Rodrigo who now had the box of dryer sheets in his hand. "We're always leaving. We've stayed here longer than anywhere."

Somehow Marina was hoping she didn't mean Manaus. She couldn't imagine how she would last out the week. "In Brazil?"

"No, here," Jackie said, and held up his open hand as if he meant to say that they had spent an endless stretch of time in Rodrigo's store.

Barbara then got a serious look on her face and tilted the slender rack of her shoulders towards Marina. "Do you know Annick?"

Marina hesitated so briefly that neither of the young people saw it. "I do," she said.

"Well, then you know. Her work is so important—"

Jackie interrupted her. "And she's been really good to us, my God."

"It's not like I think we're helping her," Barbara said. "We're not scientists. But if *she* thinks we're helping her, if there's anything we can do to contribute, then it's not a problem for us to stay for a while. It's not a problem for me anyway. I can do my work anywhere. It's really harder for Jackie."

"What do you do?" Marina said, using the pronoun in the plural.

"I'm a writer," Barbara said.

Jackie raised his hand and ran his open fingers through his hair. "I surf," he said.

Harder, yes. Marina thought about the bath-warm water of the Rio Negro inching along towards the Rio Solimões so that they could flow together into the Amazon. She was planning to ask him something about this, how surfing constituted work or how he planned to solve the current problems of his employment, when the only other person she knew in Manuas came through the open door. When Milton saw the three of them together he was extremely pleased. He had left his suit in the closet at home and was dressed for the weather. All his light cotton clothes were neatly pressed. "Perfect!" he said. "You found each other without me."

Marina extended her hand to the driver. Because she knew him to be a problem solver she was especially glad to see him again. "I was just out taking a walk."

"A bad time of day for walking but this is very good," Milton said. "I am relieved. I have been telling them to go to your hotel."

Jackie had wandered off to pick up the store's lone can of tennis balls. It seemed that there was nothing Rodrigo hadn't thought of. Barbara in turn shot her eyes to Milton who seemed startled by the severity of her glance. "I'm sorry," he said, before he knew what he might be apologizing for.

Barbara sighed and tried to brush a medium-sized insect off the front of her sundress. It was hard-shelled and black and the tiny spikes on its legs held stubbornly to the fabric but she seemed not to notice any of this. She put her thumb beneath her index finger and gave the bug a single, dislodging flick. "You'll forgive me," she said to Marina, who imagined she would. "Part of what we try to do is keep Annick hidden—from the press that comes down, from other doctors and drug companies trying to steal her work. You never know who someone really is no matter what they tell you."

"I am terribly sorry," Milton said.

"The press comes here?" Marina said.

Barbara looked at her. "Well, they will once they hear about her research. They did before we got here. What really matters is that people shouldn't distract her. Even people with very good intentions." She was trying to be firm but she lacked experience.

"Dr. Singh works for Vogel," Milton said in an attempt to make up for his indiscretion. "She and Dr. Swenson are employed by the same company. They sent her here to—" He looked at Marina but he had to stop there. She hadn't told him why they'd sent her.

"Vogel"—she looked at Marina—"I'm sorry but that is my point exactly. Vogel is the worst. All they want to know is what her *progress* is. How can she be expected to do her work if she's constantly being monitored? This is science. This may change the course of everything. She can't just stop and meet people. Do you know that you're the second doctor that Vogel's sent to see her since Christmas?"

"I do," Marina said. If she were in any way inclined to have compassion for the girl she would have stopped her then, but at the moment she did not. Jackie had come back now and he kept the can of tennis balls in his hand. Maybe he wanted them. Maybe he knew a court nearby where they could play.

"You know Dr. Eckman?"

"We worked together."

Barbara shrugged her pretty shoulders which were gold along the tops and gold down her arms. "Well, if he's a friend of yours, I'm sorry. He's a perfectly nice guy but he was a huge distraction. He hung around here forever, always asking questions, always wanting to go along. He was a distraction to *my* work. I can't even imagine what he must have been like for Annick."

"He took me birding," Jackie said.

"I tried to explain to him that Annick didn't have the time, but he wasn't going to go until he saw her. She finally came and picked him up. For all I know he's still out there."

"He isn't," Marina said. "Or he is. He's dead." It wasn't the girl's fault of course, not any of it, but Marina found her sadness transposed itself easily into anger.

Jackie put down the tennis balls then and took Barbara's hand in a gesture of sympathy or solidarity. She watched the color drain from the girl, from her face, her neck, all the blood was rushing to her heart. Even the gold receded from her shoulders.

"Dr. Swenson buried him at the research station where she works. She told us that in a letter. She sent us very little information about his death, but, as you say, she's busy. Dr. Eckman's wife wanted me to come down to see if I could find out what happened. She wants to know what she should tell their children."

Three women came into the store then, one of them holding a baby, and in another minute a couple came in behind them. It seemed that they all knew one another, the way they were talking. The woman with the baby passed her baby over to another one of the women so that she could look at cooking oil.

"I need to sit down," Barbara said. She did not say this dramatically. The two Bovenders left the store together to sit on the cement steps out front. Almost immediately Jackie came back in to get her a bottle of water.

"Ah, your poor friend," Milton said to Marina. "I am very sorry."

Marina nodded, unable to focus her eyes on Milton or the Bovenders or anything in the store.

When the Bovenders did get up from the steps, after Barbara had finished her bottle of water, they did not come back into the store. Rodrigo wrote out the same well-ordered receipt to charge to the Vogel account and then gathered up the things they'd wanted and put them into bags: dryer sheets, tennis balls, a new sun hat, mangoes and bananas. Marina in her rush to be unpleasant had likely broken the one thread she could have followed into the jungle. Maybe they found Anders annoying, but in his affable way he had managed to wear them down. Still, she liked to think if she had been the one who died and he was coming in as the replacement, his patience would have been limited as well.

Four

Jackie sat up front with Milton on the way to Ponta Negra while Marina sat with Barbara in the back. They kept the windows down. In the wind tunnel that roared through the backseat, strands of Barbara's hair would intermittently fly out and strike Marina in the face even though Barbara did her best to gather her hair in her hands and hold it down. Jackie was prone towards car sickness, and the road to the beach was neither smooth nor straight.

"It wouldn't be better if you were cool?" Milton asked Jackie. Jackie said nothing.

"He needs the fresh air," Barbara shouted from the back.

Marina might have noted that the air was not particularly fresh but she refrained. The Bovenders had invited her to the beach and she was determined to be grateful that they had extended themselves. When he was invited to come along on the outing and bring his car, Milton had said they needed to leave no later than six a.m. The beach, like the market, was strictly a morning affair. But the Bovenders would not hear of six. They claimed they were useless until nine at the very earliest, and while Milton and Marina were waiting for them in front of the apartment at that designated hour, the Bovenders did not make an appearance until nearly ten. It was, Marina thought, a bad start. "Wouldn't you get motion sickness from surfing?" she asked, raising her voice to be heard over the din of circulating air. They were going fast; Jackie had said he wanted to go fast in order to get out of the car as soon as possible.

"Not a problem," he said.

"He can surf a killer wave but on boats," Barbara said. "My God, he can't even look at a boat. He can't walk down a dock."

"Baby, please," Jackie said, his voice weak.

"Sorry," Barbara said, and turned her head towards the window.

"I don't have any problems when I drive," Jackie said.

As they rounded another hairpin curve a silky white goat trotted into the road and Milton slammed the brakes. Marina, who was not given to car sickness in the least, felt her stomach lurch up. The people in the car understood that the goat had escaped his fate by no more than four inches, but the goat understood nothing. It looked up, mildly puzzled, sniffed the blacktop, and then went on. Jackie opened the door and vomited lightly.

"I can't let you drive," Milton said.

"I know," Jackie said, and he covered his eyes with his hand.

The night before at dinner the Bovenders had made a list of everything Marina should see while she was in Manaus. "There isn't much to do around here," Jackie had said, "so you really ought to make the effort." They offered to take her to the beach and the Natural Science Museum but both required a car. Barbara took out her cell phone at the dinner table and called Milton. His number was programmed in.

The Bovenders had come to her. They had waited nearly a week after their unfortunate first meeting but then they called. They wanted to hear about Anders. They assumed, incorrectly, that Marina knew a good deal more about his death than she had told them.

"But what did Annick say?" Barbara leaned in close enough that Marina could smell her perfume, a mix of lavender and lime.

"She said that he died of a fever. That's all I know. And I know that she buried him there." The restaurant was dark with a cement floor and dried out palm fronds hanging over the bar. There were two pinball machines in the corner and they chirped and clanged even when there was no one there with the change it took to play them.

Barbara ran a tiny red cocktail straw in circles, nervously stirring up the contents of her glass. "I'm sure it would have been almost impossible for her to get the body back."

"But people do," Marina said. "I realize Dr. Swenson isn't sentimental but I imagine she would have felt differently had it been her husband. Anders' wife would have liked to see him buried at home." She would have liked it had he never gone in the first place.

"Annick has a husband?" Barbara said.

"Not that I know of."

"Did you speak to Annick about what should be done with Dr. Eckman?" Barbara was more inclined to do the talking. Jackie was busying himself with the hard salted strips of plantains that were served in the place of chips.

"From what I understand she doesn't have a phone. She wrote a letter and by the time it got to Vogel he'd been dead two weeks." Marina took a sip of some fruited rum punch Jackie had ordered for all of them. "She wrote the letter to Mr. Fox."

Barbara and Jackie looked at one another. "Mr. Fox," they said together ominously.

Marina put down her drink.

"Do you know him?" Barbara asked.

"He's the president of Vogel," Marina said, her voice even. "I work for him."

"Is he awful?"

Marina looked at the girl and smiled. In truth she was irritated with Mr. Fox. He had gone ahead and sent her another phone and several different antibiotics and enough Lariam to see her through another six months in South America. If he had intended it as a message, it wasn't a message that pleased her. "No," she said neutrally, "not awful at all."

Barbara waved her hand. "I shouldn't have said that. But you have to understand—"

"We're very protective of Annick," Jackie said, nibbling the side off a plantain strip.

Barbara nodded vigorously, giving her long, jeweled earrings a good swing. Barbara had overdressed for dinner, wearing a sleeveless silk top in emerald green. She was such a pretty girl. It must be hard for her, Marina imagined, to have no place to go. "Of course you'd be upset about your friend. We're upset about Dr. Eckman ourselves, but whatever happened it wasn't Annick's fault. It's just that she's very focused. She has to be."

Now that Marina was in the Amazon it seemed that there was probably no end of things that could kill a person without any assignment of blame, unless perhaps the blame was assigned to Mr. Fox. "I never thought it was her fault."

This news came to Barbara as a great relief. "I'm so glad!" she said. "Once you understand Annick you know there's nobody like her. I was thinking that maybe you hadn't been around her in a while, or you'd forgotten," she said, seeming to know things she could not possibly know. "She's such a force of nature. Her work is thrilling, but really, it's almost beside the point. She's what's so amazing, the person herself, don't you think? I try to imagine what it would have been like to have a mother like that, a grandmother, a woman who was completely fearless, someone who saw the world without limitations."

Marina could remember that exact feeling. It was a thought so briefly held and deeply buried that she could barely dredge it up again:

What if Dr. Swenson were my mother? She made a mental note to call her mother before she went to bed tonight, even if it was very late. "But what does that have to do with Mr. Fox?"

"He bothers her," Jackie said, as if he had suddenly woken up and found himself in a restaurant, in a conversation. His blue eyes peered out brightly through the fringe of his overly long bangs. "He writes her letters asking her what she's doing. He used to call her."

"That's when she got rid of the phone," Barbara said. "It happened years before we got here."

Marina took the slice of pineapple off the edge of her glass, dipped it into her drink and ate it. "Is that really so intrusive? She does work for him after all. He is paying for everything, her research, her apartment, this dinner. Isn't he entitled to know how things are going?"

Barbara corrected her. "*He* doesn't pay for it. The company pays for it."

"Yes, but the company is his job. He runs it. He hired her. He's responsible."

"Is the person who commissions van Gogh responsible for the painting?"

Marina wondered if she would have come up with a similar quip of logic when she was twenty-three or however old Mrs. Bovender actually was. She was quite sure she would have felt the same way. It was exactly Dr. Swenson's brio she had been drawn to, the utter assuredness with which she moved through the world, getting things done and being indefatigably right. Marina had not met her like again, and she was glad of that, and she was sorry. "I suppose that van Gogh would be responsible for making good on his sale, and that if he didn't show up with the painting after a vastly extended period of time it would be within the rights—"

Barbara put her cool hand on Marina's wrist. "I'm sorry," she said. "Mr. Fox is your boss, Dr. Eckman was your friend. I shouldn't be running on about this."

"I understand your point," Marina said, making a conscious effort to get along.

"We'll try to find a way to get word to Annick, and if we can't we'll just entertain you ourselves until she comes back."

Marina took a long pull off her drink, even though there was a distinct voice in her head telling her not to. "You don't have to do that."

"Of course we do," Barbara said, and sat back peacefully in her chair as if everything had been decided. "It's what Annick would want."

By ten o'clock the world was a furnace cracked open in a closed room, but just outside of Manaus people crowded the river's bank on a Wednesday to lie across towels spread out in the sand. Children played in the shallows while adults swam wide circles around them. Their voices, the screaming and laughing while they splashed one another, sounded less like words and more like the call and answer of birds. Milton in his infinite wisdom had brought a large striped umbrella in the trunk of his car and stabbed it repeatedly into the sand until it was able to stand upright and provide a circle of shade. It was in that limited field that he and Marina sat on towels, their arms around their knees. Marina had gone to buy a swimsuit from Rodrigo that morning and the only possible option, which is to say the only one-piece, was cheap and bright and had a small skirt that made her look like an aging figure skater. She wore it under her clothes now, unable to imagine what had ever made her think she would go into the water. The Bovenders, who had no interest in the umbrella or its protection, were, without their clothes, unnerving. Jackie wore a pair of cutoff shorts that rode dangerously below the sharp protrusions of his hipbones, while Barbara's bikini was carelessly tied together with a series of loose strings. It seemed that the desired effect of their swimwear was to make their fellow beach-goers feel a strong breeze could strip them bare. At one point Jackie yawned, tilted forward into the sand,

and raised himself into a handstand. The muscles in his arms and back separated into distinct groups that any first year medical student would have been grateful to study: pectoralis major, pectoralis minor, deltoid, trapezius, intercostal. The people on neighboring towels pointed, calling for their children to watch. They whistled and clapped.

"Not sick anymore," Milton said.

Jackie brought his feet to the ground and sat again. The vine that encircled his ankle was hung with tiny clusters of grapes. "I'm fine."

"That's why I married him," Barbara said, half of her face shielded behind enormous black glasses. "I saw him do that at the beach in Sydney. He was wearing his boardies. I said to my girlfriend, 'That one's mine.' "

"Marriages have been built on less," Marina said, although in truth she didn't think this was the case.

"Do you swim?" Milton asked her. He was wearing his trousers and his white short-sleeved shirt. He showed no signs of removing them.

"I know how," she said, "if that's what you're asking."

Barbara stretched along her towel, her oiled body reflecting light from every surface except for the few discreet areas covered by fabric. There was a small, circular diamond hanging in the gold chain of her anklet and it glinted along with her skin. "It's so hot," she cried quietly.

"Hot is what we do best," Milton said. He had a little straw hat sitting on the top of his head and somehow it made him look cooler than the rest of them.

"Let's go for a swim," Jackie said, and leaned over to smack his wife's stomach lightly with the flat of his open hand. Her whole body jumped an inch off her towel.

"The water is only going to be hotter," she said.

"Up, up, up," he said, and stood himself, leaning down to pull her to her feet. She paused a moment to shake the sand out of her pale hair. It was for the other beach-goers as great a spectacle as her husband standing on his hands. They were halfway to the water, their arms draped against each other's naked waists, when they turned back to their compatriots. "You're coming, aren't you?" Jackie asked.

Marina shook her head. "Go, go," Milton said. "We'll come and watch." He got up stiffly and helped Marina to her feet. "They want us to see how pretty they are in the river."

"They were pretty enough just lying there," Marina said.

"We are the parents," Milton said. "We have to watch."

Marina went along with a sullen sense of duty, but out from under the umbrella the world was a different place. It had not been cool beneath the candy colored stripes, but away from them the sun meted out a pummeling that was stunning. She stopped for a moment to spot the Bovenders as they walked into the brown water holding hands. On a few occasions since arriving in Brazil she had been as hot but she had always been able to step into the shade, to go into a café for a can of soda, return to her hotel room and stand in a cold shower. She had come to know in advance when the heat was about to overwhelm her as clearly as if there had been a thermometer built into her wrist and so she had been able to save herself accordingly, but looking out at the water and the sand she was uncertain of where she could go. She was melting into the people around her, into Milton. There was a little ice chest beneath the umbrella that Milton had brought with them—cool bottles of water and beers for Jackie. She could rub a piece of ice against her neck. Far ahead of them the Bovenders sank into the water and blurred into all of the other children around them as they swam away. With everything in her she cursed them for being unwilling, unable, to wake before nine. After all, she had been tired herself. She had taken a Lariam fresh from the new bottle Mr. Fox had sent the night before and at three in the morning she had woken herself, and no doubt everyone else in the Hotel Indira, with her interminable screaming. *Someone is stabbing a woman to death,* was the thought she had swimming up through sleep before she realized where the sound was coming from. After that she was finished for the night, no more sleep, just waiting.

"You do a good job of this," Milton said, keeping his eyes towards the river. "I admire your patience."

"Believe me, I have no patience."

"Then you create the illusion of patience. In the end the effect is the same."

"All I want to do is find Dr. Swenson and go home," she said slowly. The words coming out of her mouth felt hot.

"And to get to Dr. Swenson and to get home you must first get past the Bovenders. The Bovenders are the guards of the gate. It is their job to keep you away from her, that's what they're paid for. I have no idea if they know where she is, but I am certain that no one else knows. They like you. Perhaps they'll figure something out." An arm went up in the water and waved and Milton raised his hand and waved back.

Where in the world was the rain? Those blinding cataracts that she had endured day after day? She needed one now. It didn't necessarily cool things down but at least for a while it blocked out the sun. "They couldn't like me."

"They think you're very natural. Mrs. Bovender told me that. They see you as a person who is honestly grieving her friend and trying to get information about his death."

"Well, that's true," she said, although that description only covered her obligations to Karen.

"They're starting to think that Dr. Swenson would like you," Milton said.

Marina felt the top of her head turning soft as the sun worked into her brain, unloosening its coils. "Dr. Swenson knew me once already. I'm quite certain she had no feelings for me one way or the other." She mopped at her face with a large red handkerchief Rodrigo had pressed on her that morning. When she declined it once he had made her a gift of it, though probably it went on Vogel's account all the same. Under her clothes she felt the swimsuit with every inhalation. It wrapped around her body like an endless bandage, growing larger and looser as it soaked her up. She kept pushing the cloth against her face. Her vision was clouded by the sweat in her eyes. She could only make out the most basic elements of the landscape: sand, water, sky.

"What the Bovenders require is diplomacy," Milton said. "They just need some more of your time. They want to study you and make sure you are what you seem."

Marina squinted out towards the waving line of the horizon. "I don't see them anymore." What she meant to say was that she thought she might faint. At that point she might have said Milton's name. She didn't fall, but she was thinking of falling, and with that thought he took her arm and walked her over the remaining expanse of sandy beach to the river. He walked her into the water up to their knees and then up to their waists. It was like a bath, silky and warm. The current was so slight it barely disturbed her clothes. She wanted to lie down in it. Milton dipped his own handkerchief into the water and spread it wet over the top of her head. "It's better, isn't it," he said, though it wasn't a question.

She nodded. Jackie had been right to make Barbara go in. It was lifesaving. When Marina looked down she saw nothing, just a line where her torso vanished into the water. All around them children kicked their rafts and jumped off one another's shoulders. "How do you know what's under there?" she asked him.

"You don't," Milton said. "You don't want to."

When Marina got back to the hotel room and checked her cell phone she had two messages from Mr. Fox, one from her mother, and one from Karen Eckman, whose number showed up in Anders' name. She might as well have been home. She was feeling slightly sympathetic towards Dr. Swenson's refusal to have a phone at all. She took a cold shower, drank a bottle of water, and went to bed, where she had a dream about losing her father in a train station. When

Barbara Bovender called on the hotel line at nine that night she woke her up. "We wanted to check on you," she said. "I'm afraid we nearly killed you this afternoon with our idea of fun."

"No, no," Marina said, disoriented by sleep and heat and dreams. "I'm fine. I just haven't gotten used to all of it yet. I suppose it takes some time."

"It does!" Barbara said, sounding gleeful for no reason. "I'm so much better at it now than I used to be. The secret is not to let the heat keep you in. Jackie swears the air conditioning weakens your immune system after a while. The more you get out the more you get used to it. You should come over to the apartment and have a drink."

"Now?" Marina said, as if she might have something else to do.

"A little walk at night would do you good."

Maybe the Bovenders were the guards at the gate but it was also true that they were lonely. There was nothing keeping Marina at the Hotel Indira. Tomo had moved her to a bigger room two days before, a reward that acknowledged the length of her stay, but it was still as musty and dismal as the one before it. There was a better view but the same metal bar attached to the wall for clothes. Marina looked at her wool coat, even from a distance she could see the lacework of holes the moths had eaten near the collar. She said she'd come over.

Walking through the city streets past all the closed up shops, Marina could understand how exciting it would be to see one of them open now. If there had been a light on in Rodrigo's store tonight she would doubtlessly have gone and stood with the crowd on the street, craning her neck to try and see what was going on inside. She had not come up with a time line for how long she would wait in Manaus if the waiting continued to be nothing but an exercise in frustration, but she could feel herself coming to the end. Marina was used to being good at her work but she was no good at this. The same concierge who had been sitting at the desk in the lobby of Dr. Swenson's apartment building at eight in the morning was sitting there still at nine-thirty at night.

It appeared he was very glad to see her. After all, she hadn't been by in several days. "Bovenders," she said to him, and then touched her index finger to her chest. "Marina Singh."

When Barbara Bovender opened the door and invited her in, Marina had the sense that she was crossing a portal from the wasteland of Manaus to another world entirely. Granted, she had spent more than a week in a badly furnished hotel room wearing the same three outfits she rinsed out in the bathtub at night. She was very far from beauty, and yet she had to think that this place would have struck her as beautiful no matter where she came across it. She praised it lavishly, sincerely.

"You're so sweet," Barbara said, walking her down a hallway past a series of small framed works on paper that could not have been Klee and yet looked like Klee. The hallway brought them into a large open living room with a high ceiling. Two sets of tall French doors were open onto a balcony and a breeze that Marina hadn't felt anywhere in the city stirred the edges of the sheer silk curtains that had been drawn aside. The breeze smelled like jasmine and marijuana. From the height of the sixth floor the river appeared to be rimmed in small, blinking lights. If Marina didn't focus her gaze she could have been in any number of splendid cities. "It's a wonderful place," Barbara said, looking at her home with impartial judgment. "I'm sure the bones have always been good but it really was a wreck when we got here."

"Barbara's done amazing things," Jackie said, taking a small hit off a joint and holding it up to her. Marina shook her head and so he brought her a glass of white wine instead, kissing her on the cheek when he gave it to her as if they were old friends. She was surprised how much the kiss startled her, more even than the joint. Jackie raised his hands, motioning to the walls around him. "The woman who lived here before us, Annick's last assistant, had her sisters strung up in hammocks all over the place."

Barbara took the joint from her husband, allowing herself a modest inhalation before stubbing it out in a small silver ashtray. She gave herself a moment and then exhaled. "Annick just wanted something nice. That was the only thing she said to me about it. Of course you would, wouldn't you? Coming in from all that time in the jungle, that's not so much to ask. Good sheets, good bath towels—"

"A decent glass of wine," Jackie said and raised his glass as an indicator that they should all drink up.

There was something perfectly spare about it all, a bouquet of some sort of white flowers she had never seen before on the dining room table, a long, low leather bench in front of an equally long white sofa, walls that were painted a shade of blue so pale it might not have been blue at all, it might have been the evening light. And then there were the Bovenders themselves, whose many physical attributes were highlighted by the elegance of their surroundings. Barbara's stacking bracelets seemed to have been carved from the same wood as the floor boards so that one might notice how the color of the floor complimented the warm color of her skin. Still, it was difficult to imagine Dr. Swenson perched on that sofa. Marina doubted Dr. Swenson's feet would touch the floor. "Where do you go when she comes in?"

Barbara shrugged. "Sometimes we just move to the guest room. It depends on whether or not she needs us for anything. If we have some time we go to Suriname or French Guiana so Jackie can surf."

"I need to get to Lima," he said, glad to have the topic turn in his direction if only for a sentence. "The waves are exploding there, but getting flights from Manaus to Lima is an unbelievable bitch. It would take me about as much time to walk there."

Marina wandered over to the balcony. She couldn't take her eyes off the river; that thick brown soup was a mirror in the darkness. "I wouldn't have expected there would be something like this in Manaus," she said. She wouldn't have expected the Meursault either, and she took another sip. She couldn't help but wonder what all of this was costing. It couldn't really matter to Vogel. The expense of one apartment in the Amazon for a researcher who didn't use it was nothing when put against the potential profits of fertility.

"There was a lot of money here once, you have to remember that," Barbara said. "It used to be more expensive to live in Manaus than in Paris."

"They came, they built, they left," Jackie said, dropping himself down on the sofa and stretching his bare feet out on the bench in front of him. "When there wasn't any money to be made in boiling the rubber out of the jungle anymore that was it, instant history. The people around here were very glad to see those people go."

"I think there's a lot about this city that's still very elegant. This building is as good as anything you'd find in a real city," Barbara said. "And Nixon takes care of everything at the front desk like a professional. I tell him all the time he could get a job in Sydney."

"Nixon?" Marina said.

"Seriously," Jackie said, his eyes lightly pinked.

"Well, he isn't much for delivering the mail," Marina said, and then she thought again. "Unless you did get the notes I sent you."

Barbara stood a little straighter. In her heels she was taller than Marina. "We didn't. I told you that."

Marina shrugged. "So much for Nixon."

"All the mail goes into a box for Annick." She walked away and came back from another room holding a neat looking steel crate with handles on either side, the kind of thing an idle girl would order from a design catalogue to be delivered to Brazil when putting mail into a cardboard box seemed too messy. "Look," she said. "I don't even check it. Annick says straight in the box and so there it goes. I keep it in her office." She put the crate down on the bench near her husband. There was a pale V marked across the tops of his brown feet where his flip-flops had interfered with his tan. "I used to answer the letters, to tell people they couldn't come to see her, but in the end Annick decided that any interaction was a form of encouragement so she told me to stop."

"These people take no as encouragement," Jackie said.

Marina came and sat beside the box, putting her glass of wine down on the floor. She did not ask. She slipped her fingers into the back and moved the letters forward. She didn't have to go very far before she found her own handwriting on the hotel's white envelopes. "Bovender," she said, dropping the first one on the bench and then going back to find the other two. "Bovender, Bovender."

Jackie leaned forward and plucked the paper from the envelope. "Dear Mr. and Mrs. Bovender," he began.

"Please!" Barbara said, and covered her ears with her hands to make her point. "It makes me feel like a total idiot. From now on I'll look at the mail, I promise."

Marina looked up at her. "Don't you pay the bills?"

Jackie shook his head. "They all go straight to Minnesota. I bet that was something to set up."

Of course, so no one would be bothered. Marina went back to the box. The magazines stood up neatly at the side, *Harper's, The New Yorker, Scientific American,* the *New England Journal.* There seemed to be a host of letters from Vogel, letters from other countries, envelopes from hospitals, universities, drug research companies that were not her own. Her fingers kept flipping, flipping.

Barbara peered over the edge and watched her employer's correspondence sift through the hands of someone she in fact did not know at all. "I'm not so sure we should be doing this," she said in a tentative voice. It seemed it was just now occurring to her that bringing out the entire box of mail might not have been her best decision. "Unless you wrote us more letters. She doesn't like for us—"

But there it was. Marina didn't have to go so deep into the crate. It wasn't such a very long time ago that he had been here. "Anders Eckman." She dropped the blue airmail envelope on top of the stationery from her hotel. Jackie pulled up his feet quickly, as if she had set down something hot.

Barbara leaned forward, looked without touching. "My God. Who do you think it's from?"

Anders Eckman, in care of Dr. Annick Swenson, a particularly inaccurate phrasing. "His wife," Marina said. Once she had identified Karen's handwriting she could find the letters quickly. Everything she pulled from the box now would have been written after he had gone into the jungle. Writing in care of Dr. Swenson in Manaus was the only chance Karen had of reaching him once he had left the city, there were no other addresses. Before he was in the jungle she would have called him or e-mailed or, if she was feeling sentimental, sent him a letter at the hotel. Karen would have told him about the boys and the snow, told him to come home now because he was sounding worse, and anyway, they obviously had not thought this through well enough at the outset. Marina knew the contents of every letter that passed through her hands and one by one she dropped them onto the bench where Jackie's feet had been. She could see Karen sitting at the island in her kitchen, perched on top of a high stool, writing page after page in the morning after she had taken the boys to school and then again at night when she had put them to bed, her head bent forward, her blond hair pushed behind her ears. Marina could read them as if she were standing over Karen's shoulder. *Come home.* The letters came singly and in pairs. They came in groups of three. Karen would have written every day, maybe twice a day, because there was nothing else she could do to help him. But she didn't help him. Marina did not doubt that Anders knew Karen was writing him and knew that her letters had hit a wall in Manaus. He would have known his wife's loyalty as a correspondent. But by not receiving those letters he never knew that she was hearing from him. Anders would have died wondering if any of his letters had made it out of the jungle. Who wouldn't imagine that the boy in the dugout log would have simply taken the coins he was given and let the envelopes float in the water as soon as he had rounded the bend in the river, and that those letters were divided between the fish and the fresh-water dolphins? In the meantime, Karen Eckman turned her love into industry, writing her husband with a diligence that was now spread across a low leather bench in Dr. Swenson's apartment.

At some point Barbara had gone to sit next to her husband. They held their wine glasses and watched the growing stack of mail with a flush of guilt on their cheeks. "What will you do with them all?" Barbara asked once Marina had combed the box for the final time.

Marina leaned over to pick up the few strays that had fallen onto the floor. "I don't know," she said. "I'll take them. I don't know what I'll do with them."

"This one's different," Jackie said, and picked up a smaller envelope from the pile.

Marina took the envelope, giving it the most cursory inspection. "It's from me."

"You were writing to him too?" Barbara asked.

Marina nodded. There would have been notes from the boys in there as well. Karen would have addressed the envelopes for them.

"Were you in love with him?"

Marina looked up, her hands full of thin blue envelopes. Barbara Bovender was more interested now. She leaned in closer, a glossy chunk of hair swinging forward. "No," Marina said. She started to say something sharp and just as quick had another idea entirely: yes. The very thought of it brought the blood to her cheeks. Yes. She hadn't loved him when he was alive, and not when that letter was written, but now? She thought of Anders when she went to sleep at night and when she woke up in the morning. Every street she walked down she imagined him standing there. She imagined being with him when he died, his head in her lap, just so she wouldn't have to think of him alone, and for a minute at least she had fallen in love with her dead friend. "We worked together," she said. "We did the same research. We ate lunch together." Marina picked up the letter she had written. It was no doubt full of statistics on plaque reduction she had thought he might enjoy.

She was glad he'd never received it. "You get used to people. You get attached to them. It was seven years. But no." As far as Marina was concerned the evening was over. She rested the stack of letters in her lap. She was tired and sad, and she couldn't imagine that she and her hosts had anything left to say to one another.

But the Bovenders wanted her to stay. Barbara said she could make a light supper and Jackie suggested that they watch a movie. "We got a copy of *Fitzcarraldo,*" he said. "How crazy is that?"

"You could even sleep over if you wanted," Barbara said, her pale eyes brightening at the thought. "It would be so much fun. We'll just agree now that we'll stay up too late and have too much to drink."

The twenty years between Marina and the Bovenders formed an impenetrable gulf. For whatever she thought of her hotel room, she knew a slumber party might well kill her. "I appreciate it, I really do, but all that sun this afternoon wore me out."

"Well, at least let Jackie walk you back to your hotel," Barbara said, and Jackie, in an unexpected flourish of chivalry, was on his feet at once and looking for his sandals.

"I'm fine," Marina said. She put the bundle of letters in her bag. She wanted to go quickly now, before there was another offer to decline.

Barbara began to wilt as soon as it was clear her company was leaving. Her inability to come up with something more enticing to offer had defeated her. "We manage to make a worse impression every time we see you," she said. Marina assured her it wasn't true. Barbara leaned a shoulder against the wall. It couldn't be said that she was blocking the exit, she didn't have the girth for that, but clearly she was stalling. "It would be better for me if you didn't tell Annick about the letters," she said finally, twisting her bracelets. "I don't think she'd like it if she thought I was letting people go through the mail, even though you were completely right to get the letters from Dr. Eckman's wife."

Marina thought of all the times another resident had asked her not to tell Dr. Swenson something, the lab results that had not confirmed a diagnosis, the details of a badly handled exam. She remembered Dr. Swenson's canny knack for knowing all of it anyway. "I'm hardly in a position to tell her anything."

Barbara took Marina's hand in her two cool hands. "But you will be, when you see her again."

"These letters belong to Anders and to Karen. They aren't anyone else's business."

Barbara gave her the slightest smile of genuine gratitude. "Thank you," she said. She squeezed Marina's hand.

Once Marina was back at the hotel she put the letters on the night table and looked at the neat stack they made. She didn't like having them there. They were certainly too personal to leave in Dr. Swenson's box but they were too personal to be with her as well. She moved them to the night table's shallow drawer beside a Portuguese Bible before calling Karen. She had a need to hear her voice, thinking it would tamp down the guilt for that sudden bout of love she'd felt for Karen's husband.

"It's so late," Marina said. She hadn't thought about the time until she dialed.

"I never sleep," Karen said. "And the worst part is nobody calls after eight. They're afraid of waking up the boys."

"I didn't think of that."

"I'm glad. Nothing wakes them up anyway. I called you this morning. Mr. Fox gave me your cell phone number."

"You've heard from him?"

"He checks on us." Karen yawned. "He's a better person than I thought he was. Or he's lonely. I can't tell. He says you haven't found her yet."

"I found the Bovenders."

"The Bovenders!" Karen said. "My God, how are they?"

"Anders talked about them?"

"And very little else for a while. They drove him out of his mind. He did not love the Bovenders."

"I could see that."

"He felt like they were stringing him along, like they were always about to produce Dr. Swenson but they never quite got around to it. He was never really sure whether or not they knew where she was, but he spent a lot of time being nice to them."

"Well then, I guess I'm right on schedule. How much time was he in Manaus before he found Dr. Swenson?"

Karen thought about it. "A month? I'm not positive. I know it was at least a month."

Marina closed her eyes. "I don't think I can spend a month with the Bovenders."

"What did they say about Anders?"

"They didn't know he was dead," Marina said.

There was a long silence on the line after that. Back in Eden Prairie, Marina heard Karen put down the phone and then there was nothing to do but wait. Marina laid back across the bed and stared at the pale water stain on the ceiling that she had contemplated every night since she changed rooms. She wished she could put her hand on Karen's head, stroke her hair. *Such is your bravery. Such is my good fortune.* When Karen did come back her breathing had changed.

"I'm sorry," Marina said.

"It comes on so fast," Karen said, trying to catch her breath. "They didn't know he was dead because she didn't tell them. Why wouldn't she tell them?"

"She didn't tell them for the exact reason you just said—they have no means of communication. She only comes to town once every few months. She doesn't even check her mail." Marina didn't know what she was going to do with the letters but she wasn't going to tell Karen that she had them. That much she could at least be certain of. From thousands of miles away Marina listened to her crying. The boys were asleep in their beds. Pickles was asleep. "Should I call Mr. Fox?" she said. It didn't seem like a good idea but it was the only one she had.

Karen put down the phone again and blew her nose. She was trying to get a hold of herself, Marina could hear it. She made the sounds of a person who was trying to wrestle an enormous sorrow to the ground. "No," she said. "Don't call him. This happens to me now. It's part of it."

"I want to tell you something different," Marina said.

"I know you do."

"It's terrible here, Karen. I hate it."

"I know," she said.

That night, which was her first night of fever, she dreamed that she and her father were paddling a small boat down a river in the jungle and that the boat turned over. Her father drowned and she was left alone in the water. The boat had gotten away. Marina had forgotten that her father didn't know how to swim.

"Now I have something you're going to like," Barbara said on the phone.

Marina hadn't heard from the Bovenders since her visit to their apartment several days before and since that time she had not left the hotel and had very seldom left her bed. She wasn't entirely sure if the preventative medicine that worked against insect borne diseases was making her sick or if she had in fact contracted an insect borne disease in spite of the medication. It also seemed entirely possible that all of her symptoms, which included body aches and a peculiar rash around her trunk, were psychosomatic—she was willing herself into illness in order to bring this all to an end. But then she wondered if Anders hadn't reached the same conclusion. *I have a fever that comes on at seven in the morning and stays for two hours. By four in the afternoon it's back and I am nothing but a ranting pile of ash. Most days now I have a headache and I worry that some tiny Amazonian animal is eating a hole through my cerebral cortex.* Marina had only read that letter once and still she knew it by heart. "What will I like?" she asked Barbara Bovender, because in truth she could not think of one single thing in Manaus that sounded appealing.

"We're going to the opera! Annick keeps a box and the season opens tomorrow. We have her tickets!"

"She keeps a box at the opera?" Marina didn't have the energy for indignation but really, was there no end to this?

"Apparently there was a season several years ago when the rains got so bad she had to come into the city for a long time. She said the opera saved her."

"Well, I don't think it's going to save me. I'm sick. I need to stay where I am."

"Did you eat something?" Barbara asked. It was the logical question. The market stalls were filled with things that would kill anyone who didn't have several generations of the proper bacteria in their gut.

"It's just a fever," Marina said.

"High or low?"

"I don't have a thermometer." She was bored. She wanted to get off the phone.

"Alright," Barbara said. "I'll be over in about an hour. And I'm bringing some dresses for you to look at."

"I don't want company and I don't want dresses. I appreciate the gesture but trust me, I'm a doctor. I know what I'm doing."

"You have no idea," Barbara said lightly.

Tomo, the concierge, in an act of dogged perseverance and faith that far outreached anything Marina herself was capable of, had continued to call the airport every day regarding her luggage. It had been located momentarily in Spain and then lost again. He was also the hotel employee who was sent up to her room whenever someone called about the screaming, and now he was looking after her because she was sick. He brought her bottles of syrupy cane juice and carbonated soft drinks and hard, dry crackers that stood in for meals. The truth was that Marina, stranded and in decline, elicited the sympathy of the entire hotel staff, but they all recognized that Tomo was in charge of her.

So when there was knocking on her door, how much later she couldn't say (sleep was like an anesthetic she broke out of and then slipped into again), Marina assumed it was Tomo. She put on the extra bed sheet that was her robe and answered the door.

Barbara gave her a hard stare up and down before speaking. "Oh, you are rough," she said with her long, flat vowels. "Why didn't you call me?"

Marina, disappointed that now she wouldn't be able to go right back to sleep, retreated into her room, which was dark and stale. The Australian followed her.

"I've brought you things." Barbara held up a small, dirty paper sack and a tapestry overnight bag as if they were enticing offers. The housekeepers hadn't been in for a couple of days because Marina could not stop sleeping. Bits of crackers were scattered over the floor like sand. Mrs. Bovender turned on the light switch by the door and then opened the blinds. "You shouldn't be living like this," was all she had to say.

"My standards have changed." Marina burrowed down into the bed. One would think it would be difficult to fall asleep in front of someone you barely knew but in fact it was the simplest thing in the world.

Barbara took a paper cup out of the bag and pried off the lid. "Here," she said, and held it out to her. "Sit up. You're supposed to drink it while it's hot."

Marina leaned forward and sniffed the contents of the cup. It was the river, boiled down to its foulest essence. It was even the color of the river. The steam that rolled off the surface was like the heavy morning mist. "Where did you get that?"

"From the shaman stand in the market, and don't say anything dismissive about the shaman until you've given him a try. I've been bitten by half the insects in this country. I've had some awful fevers, some sores I wouldn't even talk about. Jackie had food poisoning once. He ate some sort of grilled turtle from a vendor, which was idiotic in the first place. I was positive he was going to die. The shaman's saved us every time. I could practically open an account with him."

The shaman would no doubt have direct billing with Vogel. "But I haven't been to see the shaman," Marina said, applying logic where no logic could be applied. "What is he basing his diagnosis on? You haven't seen me either."

"I explained the situation. Actually, Milton explained the situation for me after I explained it to Milton. The shaman and I don't exactly speak the same Portuguese, and I think it's important to get it all right. Milton hopes you're feeling better, by the way." She pressed the cup against Marina's breastbone and held it there until she took it in her hands.

"This is idiocy," Marina said, looking down at the cloudy liquid. The cup was warm. The smell came up to her in layers: water, fish, mud, death.

"Drink it!" Barbara said sharply. "I'm tired of trying to help you. Drink it all down, one swallow, come on. This is what we do down here in hell."

Marina, so surprised by the force of the order and by the look of mad frustration on Barbara Bovender's face, did what she was told and took down the whole foul cup in one long swallow. It was not entirely liquid, it was thicker near the bottom, viscous, and there were tiny bits of something hard and twiglike that caught in her throat.

The canoe they were in was a log and it rolled over to the side and she was thrown down with her father into the water. The water filled up her eyes and nose and mouth. She sank before she could swim and all she could taste was the river. She had forgotten until now how the river tasted.

"Put your head back and pant," Barbara said. "Don't throw it up." She got down on her knees in front of Marina, putting her hands on Marina's knees. Mr. Fox had said the difference between Marina and Anders was that Anders hadn't had the sense to come home when he had first fallen sick, but oh, it wasn't a matter of whether she was willing. It was all a matter of able. A chill passed through her, a great shuddering wave that washed over her wet skin and made her spine convulse.

"Okay," Barbara said quietly, patting at her knee as if it were the head of a very small dog, "here's the other thing. You're going to be really sick now, but just for a little while, an hour or so, maybe two. It all depends on what needs to break down inside you. Then you're going to be absolutely fine. You're going to be better than fine. I'd be happy to stay with you. I'm free all afternoon."

Marina looked at her guest but all she could really make out was the light of her hair which appeared to be receding down a tunnel. She said she did not want her to stay.

Barbara sat back on her heels looking disappointed. She took Marina's cold fingers in her hand and bounced them. "Okay, I'll come back then at five and we can talk about what dress you're going to wear tomorrow. I brought a few that I think will be pretty on you. It's good that you have a friend who's as tall as you are." She waited. "Are you going to be sick now? Try to wait as long as you can. The longer you can hold it down the better it works. Panting really helps."

Lines of sweat began to run down Marina's forehead, down from the crown of her head, down the back of her neck. A clear, thin mucus came from her nose at a rate that exceeded both the perspiration and the tears that were pouring from her eyes. She did not lift her hand to her face. She let the slick wall pour unabated. It was early still but she realized very clearly there was nothing she could do to stop this from happening. The trembling shook her hard enough to knock her teeth and she tried to keep her mouth open. Even if there were an antidote she would never get to it in time. This was the end of the end. She knew what it felt like now. If she lived to see it come again she would call it by name. In one of her last clear thoughts, Marina wondered if she had been murdered, or if by taking the cup herself, she had committed suicide.

Far outside the city the tree frogs were calling her, and the deep, rhythmic pulse of their voices set the blood flow to her heart.

Marina woke up on the cool tile of the bathroom floor, her head resting on a pile of towels. She opened her eyes and watched a bright red spider of medium size slip beneath the sink cabinet. The details of the time that had elapsed, she didn't know how much time it was, were not clear, and for that she was grateful. She breathed in and breathed out, moved her fingers and toes, stretched open her mouth and closed it again. The shaman-induced illness had left her and in the violence of its departure had scraped out whatever illness she had had in the first place. She was alive, possibly well. Her hip was sore from the angle she had been lying at but that hardly seemed important. Carefully, slowly, she pulled herself upright and then moved the short distance over the ledge of the bathtub where she sat in the bottom just to be safe and let the hot shower beat against her head until the water slipped to lukewarm. After that she brushed her teeth and drank a bottle of water. She was sore and raw but she experienced that distinct mental clarity that marked a fever's end. She rolled her head from side to side. She walked naked into the bedroom, a towel around her head, to find the room was clean and Barbara Bovender was sitting in a chair by the window reading the *New England Journal of Medicine.*

"Look who's up!" Barbara said.

"You were leaving," Marina said, but very little sound came out. She coughed, trying to reset her vocal cords which had been stripped from vomiting. "You were leaving." She found the bathrobe sheet folded on the foot of the bed and pulled it around her.

"I was going to, but you got sick so fast. It really went right to work on you. I thought I should stay just to make sure you didn't fall and hit your head on the toilet, anything like that. But you're better, right? I can tell just by looking at you."

"I am," Marina said. She couldn't bring herself to thank the person who had so recently poisoned her, nor could she deny that the poison had improved her circumstances.

"I've never read this article," Barbara said, holding up the journal. "It's fascinating, even the science parts which I really don't follow. I kept thinking about how lucky it was that things worked out so that I was sitting in your hotel room for a couple of hours. I have to tell you, I really didn't understand Annick's work at all before this. To think of being able to wait and have your children whenever you want them, forty, fifty—sixty even, that would be amazing." Barbara stopped and looked at her hostess. "You know, I've never asked you, do you have children?"

"I do not," Marina said. The air conditioning had been turned up to high and she was starting to shiver in the cold. "I'd like to get dressed now." For the first time in days she was hungry.

"Oh sure, of course." Barbara got up from her chair. "Do you mind if I borrow this? I know Jackie would want to read it."

"Fine," Marina said.

"Try the dresses on and let me know which one you like." Barbara stopped at the door. "I really am so glad it all worked out and that you're better. I'll tell the shaman, he'll be so pleased. We'll pick you up tomorrow at seven, alright?"

But she didn't mean it as a question. Before Marina had a chance to answer, Barbara Bovender and the *New England Journal of Medicine* were gone.

Five

The point of an evening at Teatro Amazonas was not so much to see an opera as it was to see an opera house. They had tickets for Gluck's *Orfeo ed Euridice,* but only because there had to be tickets for something. The building itself was the performance, the two long marble staircases curving up in front, the high blue walls piped with crisp white embellishments, the great tiled dome that must have been torn from a Russian palace by a monstrous storm and blown all the way to South America, or so a tourist had told Marina one morning when she stopped to take a picture of it with her phone. There was no real explanation for how such a building was conceived for such a place. Marina thought of it as the line of civilization that held the jungle back. Surely without the opera house the vines would have crept up over the city and swallowed it whole.

"The natives swear that nobody built it," Barbara said, taking the tickets out from her tiny black lacquered evening bag. "They say it just happened."

Jackie nodded. It was the version of which he most approved. "They say it was brought down in a space ship for some prince because this was the only place he could have sex."

Barbara Bovender was wearing a short ivory-colored dress that showed the full length of her leg, a shameless expanse of tanned calf and thigh that was exaggerated by a very high pair of evening sandals. It was a dress she had first offered to Marina and Marina had declined. Every dress Barbara had brought over in her tapestry bag was missing some essential piece of fabric: the front or the back or the skirt, leaving Marina to decide which part of herself she could best afford to leave uncovered. The ivory dress had a modest neckline and long sleeves but was short enough to embarrass a third-grader. In the end she settled on a long straight dress of dark gray silk that left bare her arms and back because Barbara consented to lend her a wrap, even though she said it ruined the lines. Once Marina's fever had broken and the vomiting had stopped, she was in fact grateful, not only for her shaman cure (though she wished she had taken a vaccine for hepatitis A before leaving on her trip) but for the loan of an inappropriate dress and the chance to go to the opera. She appreciated having a reason to scrub beneath her fingernails, to leave her room in the evening, to listen to music. What's more, Mrs. Bovender came back to her hotel before the performance to pin up Marina's hair and apply her eyeliner as if she were a bride. Marina had had many friends in her life who could recite the periodic table from memory but not since high school had she had a friend with a particular talent for hair. When Barbara was through with her considerable work she led Marina to the mirror so that she could be overwhelmed by the results, and Marina, who didn't remember looking as beautiful on her wedding day, obliged. "You have to make a point of looking nice every now and then," Barbara said, clamping a significant gold cuff around Marina's wrist. "Believe me, if you don't do it down here then everything is lost."

When the three of them moved through the lobby, the crowds of opera goers turned to watch them pass. Jackie, slightly stoned, with his lightly tinted glasses and glossy hair, looked like a man who was likely to arrive with two women. He wore a white linen shirt with white embroidery down the front, a surfer's version of formal wear. Marina was only sorry to think that this beauty she was doubtlessly incapable of replicating was being spent on the Bovenders. After all, Mr. Fox enjoyed the opera. It wasn't so unreasonable to think he could have visited her here. She imagined the weight of her hand resting inside his arm.

The usher unlocked the door to their box with a heavy brass skeleton key that he wore around his neck on a velvet cord. He made a slight bow to each of them while distributing the programs. The three of them had eight red velvet chairs to choose from. Marina leaned over the brass railing on their balcony to watch the prosperous citizens of Manaus find their way to their seats. The inside of the house was a wedding cake, every intricately decorated layer balanced delicately on the shoulders of the one beneath it, rising up and up to a ceiling where frescoed angels parted the wandering clouds with their hands. When the chandeliers began to dim, Jackie put his hand on his wife's thigh and she crossed her other leg over to pin him there. Marina turned her attention down to the orchestra. With a face of pure serenity, Barbara leaned towards Marina and whispered, "I love this part." Marina didn't know what part she meant, and didn't ask, but when the house was dark and the overture rose up to their third-tier balcony she understood completely. Suddenly every insect in Manaus was forgotten. The chicken heads that cluttered the tables in the market place and the starving dogs that waited in the hopes that one might fall were forgotten. The children with fans that waved the flies away from the baskets of fish were forgotten even as she knew she was not supposed to forget the children. She longed to forget them. She managed to forget the smells, the traffic, the sticky pools of blood. The doors sealed them in with the music and sealed the world out and suddenly it was clear that building an opera house was a basic act of human survival. It kept them all from rotting in the unendurable heat. It saved their souls in ways those murdering Christian missionaries could never have envisioned. In these past few days of fever Marina had forgotten herself. The city was breaking her down along with the Lariam, her sense of failure, her nearly mad desire to be home in time to see the lilacs. But then the orchestra struck a note that brought her back to herself. Every pass of the cellists' bows across the cellos' strings scraped away a bit of her confusion, and the woodwinds returned her to strength. While she sat in the dark, Marina started to think that this opera house, and indeed this opera, were meant to save her. She knew the story of Orpheus, but it wasn't until the singing began that she realized it was the story of her life. She was Orfeo, and there was no question that Anders was Euridice, dead from a snake bite. Marina had been sent to hell to bring him back. Had Karen been able to leave the boys, she would have been Orfeo. It was the role she had been born to play. But Karen was in Minnesota, and Marina's mind was filled with Anders now, their seven years of friendship, the fifty hours a week they spent charting lipids, listening to the rise and fall of each other's breath.

Barbara opened up her tiny purse and handed Marina a Kleenex. "Blot in a straight line beneath your eyes," she whispered.

A woman sang the role of Orfeo in a baggy toga, her hair slicked back and caught beneath a crown of gilded leaves. She stood there center stage, a lyre in her arms to cover her breasts, and sang her sorrow to the chorus.

Jackie leaned across his wife. "Why is it a woman?" he whispered to Marina. Marina dabbed her nose and bent in to tell him that the alternative was to find a castrato for whom the part was originally written, but a hand reached between them and thumped Jackie on the shoulder with two hard taps.

"Quiet," the woman's voice said.

Marina and the two Bovenders straightened their spines as if the same small voltage had run up the carved chair legs and through the velvet seats. They began to turn, the three of them together, but the hand came back between Barbara and Marina and pointed to the stage. That was how they watched the rest of the opera, their eyes forward and their entire consciousness turned behind them to focus on Dr. Swenson.

Dr. Swenson! Back from the jungle and here at the opera with no announcement at all. And now they were made to wait, not to get out of their seats like reasonable people, step into the stairwell or go down to the lobby to begin the conversation that should have been started weeks ago. At first Marina had thought about how she would feel once she saw Dr. Swenson, but the longer she had stayed in Brazil the more she came to consider her chances of finding her to be hopeless. The scenarios she had run in her mind involved going home to tell Karen and Mr. Fox that she had failed. Euridice was behind Orfeo as they trudged the long road up from the underworld, Euridice constantly harping, complaining, her lovely soprano voice turned into a droning saw—*Why won't you look at me? Why don't you love me?* Dear God, even in her enormous beauty she was unbearable. Marina fixed her eyes forward and willed herself with everything in her not to turn around. She noticed that Jackie's hand was no longer sandwiched between his wife's thighs and that they were both staring at the stage with great concentration, no doubt wondering if they had properly aired the apartment, made the bed, returned all the lacy scraps of underwear to their proper drawers. Marina, who had folded the shawl in her lap once the lights went down because it was less than perfectly cool in this third-tier box, considered the visage of her naked shoulders and back that were presently obstructing Dr. Swenson's view of the stage, the complicated twist of her hair held in place with two black sticks ornamented with tiny gold fans as if she were a Chinese princess. She imagined herself in a hospital room, sitting at a patient's bedside in her dark gray silk, and suddenly Dr. Swenson came into the room behind her. *I was paged,* Marina said to her, trying to explain the lack of fabric in her dress. *I've been at the opera.*

Her own fear surprised her most, the dull thumping deep in her bowels that was associated with the instruction that she might now open her test booklet and begin. Or even later, being called on in Grand Rounds, *Dr. Singh, if you would then explain to us why the numbness persists.* Marina would have expected anger, confrontation. It wouldn't matter that someone was singing, that everyone around them would hear her. *I want you to tell me what happened to Anders!* was what she had planned to say. What a thought. She had nothing to say to Dr. Swenson. She was waiting to hear what Dr. Swenson had to say to her. *Dr. Singh, of course I remember, you blinded that child in Baltimore.* The sweat under her arms came down her rib cage in an unimpeded line, and because of the way the dress was cut, fastened behind her neck and low across her back, it did not pool into a stain until it was nearly at her waist. Orfeo could not take it another minute, the badgering, the chilling doubt. *Isn't it proof enough that I've come to hell for you?* he could have said. *Couldn't you trust my love and wait another twenty minutes while I navigate this narrow path?* But no, it didn't work that way. He had to see her. He had to reassure her of his love. He had to shut her up. He turned to his beloved and in doing so he killed her all over again, sending her down to that pit of endless sleep where the story had first begun.

With everything in her, Marina willed the singers to stop singing, the musicians to put down their instruments in recognition of the unbearable anxiety emanating from the third tier. Such is the stuff of dreams. It wasn't enough that in this opera the dead were alive and then dead again due to the botched efforts of the protagonist, there were still more reversals of fortune and a very long dance segment to endure, but the ending did at last arrive. Marina and the two Bovenders applauded violently, all the repressed energy of waiting finally able to release itself into their slapping hands. "Brava!" Jackie called when the mezzo came forward on the stage.

"It was hardly as good as all that," Dr. Swenson said behind them.

As if that sentence were their permission, they stood and turned, the three of them, Dr. Swenson's chorus. "Probably not," Barbara said, as if this were a conversation. "But it's just so lovely to go to the opera."

"Great seats," Jackie said.

Marina, who was considerably taller in Mrs. Bovender's shoes, neglected to take Dr. Swenson's height into account and so looked directly over Dr. Swenson's head when she turned. She saw another person in the box, a man in a suit who stayed beneath the eaves. Milton mouthed to her a silent hello.

Barbara put her arm around Marina's shoulder and pulled her close. The gesture could have been seen as possessive or loving and yet Marina suspected it was really an attempt by the younger woman to remain standing. She could feel Barbara Bovender's heartbeat as she pushed in hip to hip, rib to rib. A low current of trembling rumbled between them and she could not be sure which of them was the source. "Annick, you know my friend Dr. Singh," Barbara said.

"Dr. Singh," Dr. Swenson said, and offered her hand, neither confirming nor denying what she knew. The last thirteen years had not touched Dr. Swenson, except that her skin, which had seen very little sun in those Baltimore winters, was now quite tan, and her hair was more white than gray. It still floated around her broad, open face in the same disorganized cloud Marina remembered. She was blue-eyed, bright, her small hand round and soft in Marina's own. Her clothing was wrinkled, sensible, making no concessions for a night at the opera. It seemed possible that she had come directly from the dock. This woman who had fixed the course of Marina's life looked for all the world like somebody's Swedish grandmother on a chartered tour of the Amazon.

"I'm very glad—" Marina began.

"Sit, sit," Dr. Swenson said, and sat herself to set the example. "She's going to sing the Villa-Lobos."

"The what?" Barbara said.

Dr. Swenson answered her with a tremendous glare and took the fourth chair in the first row next to Marina while the soprano, the tedious and beautiful Euridice, put a modest hand to her breast and bent her head forward to receive the maelstrom of applause. The Villa-Lobos, Brazil's singular contribution to the classical repertoire, was considerably more beautiful than the Gluck, or the soprano was inclined to sing the vocalise with more tenderness than she had been able to bring to her previous role, and for the briefest moment Marina was able to forget what was behind her (Anders' death) and all that there was still to come (the now inevitable trip into the jungle with her professor) and she listened. It took eight cellos and a human voice to quiet her mind.

"Now that was worth coming in for," Dr. Swenson said, when finally, after fifteen minutes of thunderous applause, the soprano reluctantly tore herself from the proscenium. As they picked up their programs and opened the door to the box, Dr. Swenson addressed Marina directly. "What did you think of the Gluck, Dr. Singh?"

Tell us about the patient, Dr. Singh. Marina stopped herself. "I'm afraid I'm not a good judge this evening. I was distracted."

Dr. Swenson nodded as if this was the correct answer. "I feel certain it's better that way. The Gluck in one's memory is always more satisfying than the Gluck itself." She turned and led the way down the hall to the staircase and the four others followed behind. Milton took Marina's arm for the stairs and she was grateful for the kindness. She spent very little time in high heels and she could feel a sway in her ankles.

"No one was expecting her?" Marina said. She made her voice quiet but the crowds were pouring into the hallways now and filling up the space around them, everyone chattering to one another, to their cell phones. The air clicked with the hard, bright syllables of Portuguese spoken by Brazilians well pleased with their evening out.

"There is no expecting Dr. Swenson," Milton said, tightening his grip on Marina's arm as two young girls cut through the crowd at a gallop pace, their party dresses flipping up behind them to show white underskirts as they took the stairs three at a time. "But there is suspecting. She doesn't like to miss the opening of the season. I didn't take any bookings for tonight though there were plenty of people who wanted to come in a car. That is not because I expected her, but because I suspected."

Marina had lost sight of Dr. Swenson but not the Bovenders, who were a dozen steps ahead. Mrs. Bovender especially was a virtual lighthouse. "I would have appreciated you passing your suspicions along."

"I might have made you worry for nothing then. She doesn't always come. She doesn't always do anything."

"I understand that, but had I known there was any possibility of her being here tonight I would have worn my own clothes."

Milton stopped on the stairs, forcing the people behind him to stop. "There is something wrong with your dress? How could there be something wrong with this dress?"

Up ahead Marina saw the Bovenders ride the river of humanity out the front doors of the opera house, their bright heads bent down. She could assume they were talking to Dr. Swenson or at least that they were listening to her. She ignored Milton's question and tugged him forward.

The night air was heavy and warm but there was a slight fish-smelling breeze coming from the river. Marina and Milton found the other three on the great tiled landing in front of the opera house, their faces turned in the direction of that breeze. Countless thousands of insects poured towards the electric lights that bathed the sides of the magnificent building and flooded over into the terraces and the streets below them. Even in the noise of the crowd Marina could hear the thrumming of wings, the various pitches of buzzing sounds they made. Their enthrallment of the light reminded her of the audience at the end of the final aria. They were driven mad by it. They could never have enough.

"The Bovenders tell me that nothing has changed since I've been gone," Dr. Swenson said as Milton and Marina approached them. "Is that true? An entire city and nothing changes?"

"I can't think of any changes in the last ten years," Milton said.

"There must be something," Dr. Swenson said. Her face was tilted up and the spotlight above her head seemed to shine on her alone. It was as if she had been cut out of light and pasted onto a dark background, powerfully removed from the crowds around her the way she was in memory. Even though this was exactly the person Marina had been looking for, she could not overcome the feeling that two very distant points in her life were now colliding in a way that should be relegated only to bad dreams. The last time she had actually seen Dr. Swenson was the day before the accident. Throughout the inquisition they had no contact and after the inquisition she left the program. She hadn't thought of that before.

"Well, Marina's here now," Jackie offered.

"I would prefer something I didn't already know."

Milton thought for a moment. "Rodrigo is stocking flea collars in his store. He says you can put them under your pillow, it keeps things out of the bed."

Dr. Swenson nodded her head approvingly, as if this were exactly the piece of information she had hoped to uncover. "I'll get some in the morning."

That was when a slightly built boy, a Brazilian Indian, wandered towards them, slipping easily between adults without touching their clothes. He was noticeable even in the crowd because he represented two groups that were largely absent from the evening: children and Indians. He wore a pair of nylon shorts and a green T-shirt that said "World Cup Soccer." He looked like the boys who sat on blankets in the square selling bracelets and small animals carved out of nuts. He had the same dark silky hair and eyes that appeared overly large, when in fact it was his face that was too small. Logic would dictate that this child would be selling something as well, children were industrious in Manaus: hawking fans and postcards and butterflies in wooden boxes, but his hands were empty.

"Easter!" Barbara Bovender cried, and dropped down to sit on the back of her heels, a perilous maneuver in so short a dress. She held out her arms to the boy who ran into them, burying his face in her neck.

"It's the hair," Dr. Swenson said. "He never can get over it."

Jackie leaned over to pick the child up and his wife came up as well. The boy had filled both of his hands with her hair and was studying it intently, a luminous rope thrown down from the gods. He was too old to be picked up and clearly it delighted him. "I think you're bigger," Jackie said, jostling him up and down as if trying to guess his weight.

"He isn't bigger," Dr. Swenson said. She tapped the boy on the chest and when he looked at her she spoke. "Dr. Singh." She raised her right index finger and touched that hand to her left wrist, then drew a line up her throat with one finger and pulled that same finger into the air from her mouth. Then she pointed at Marina. He let go of Barbara's hair and gave Marina his hand.

"Look at that!" Jackie said, as if this were a particularly clever trick for a boy. "He can shake." As a reward he tossed the child up in the air a few inches, up and down and up and down, until he laughed a strange, seal-like laugh and had to let go of her hand.

"It's nice to meet you," Marina said. The child's enormous eyes fixed themselves to her and did not look away. "You could have brought him to the opera," she said to Dr. Swenson. Had he come with her? "There were plenty of seats."

"Easter's deaf," Dr. Swenson said. "The opera would have been more tedious for him than it was for us."

"It wasn't such a bad opera," Barbara said to the boy.

"He likes to wander when he has the chance," Dr. Swenson said for him. "He likes to take a look around town." Easter, perched in Jackie's arms, his attention rightfully returned to Barbara's hair, did not turn his head. Even with good hearing he would have seemed too small to be walking the streets of Manaus alone in the dark.

"I would have gone with you if I'd known you were out here," Jackie said to the boy. "We could have cut out together."

"He could have come. I think he would have liked seeing all the people," Barbara said. "There's a lot to look at in the opera house even if you can't hear the music."

Dr. Swenson looked at her watch. "I think this is enough of a reunion for now. Dr. Singh and I should have a talk. I assume you don't mind the late hour, Dr. Singh. Milton tells me you've been waiting."

Marina said that she would be glad to talk.

"Good. So the rest of you go on. I'll see you in the morning. Milton, tell Rodrigo I'll be at the store by seven."

"May I drive you somewhere?" Milton asked.

Dr. Swenson shook her head. "It's a perfectly good night. I'm sure we can manage a walk. Can you manage, Dr. Singh?"

Marina, in her column of gray silk and her high heels, was not entirely sure she could manage, but she said that a walk would be good after sitting so long.

"We'll take Easter back to the apartment," Barbara said. The child had begun to braid the section of her hair that he was holding on to.

Dr. Swenson shook her head. "He hasn't eaten. He'll come with us. Put him down, Jackie, he isn't a monkey."

Jackie set Easter on the ground and the boy looked from one party to the other. In spite of not having heard he seemed to be in tacit agreement with the plans. "We'll see you later then," Jackie said, finding the part in the boy's hair with his fingers and smoothing it down. Then, remembering what in fact was new, he held out his hand and Easter shook it goodbye. "Brilliant," Jackie said.

The streets around the opera house were made of flat stones fitted together into an uneven jigsaw and Marina found herself wishing that Milton had come with them, if not to drive then at least to keep his hand under her arm. Marina was a very tall doctor who worked in a lab in Minnesota and those three things: the height, the work, and the state, precluded the wearing of heels, giving her little experience to draw from now that she needed it. She shifted her weight forward onto her toes and hoped not to wedge the heel of Barbara's shoes into a crevice. Even as Marina slowed, Dr. Swenson kept to her own unwavering pace, a trudge of metronomic regularity that Marina remembered. In her khaki pants and rubber-soled shoes, she was quickly a block ahead without seeming to notice that she was alone. Easter stayed behind them both, perhaps to alert Dr. Swenson in the event that Marina went down. The crowd from the opera had dispersed and all that remained were the city's regulars who stood on the street corners in the dark trying to decide whether or not to cross. They watched Marina as she pulled her borrowed shawl up over her shoulders.

"Are you coming, Dr. Singh?" Dr. Swenson called out. She had gone around a corner or stepped into a building. Her voice was part of the night. It came from nowhere.

Are you coming, Dr. Singh? She would dip so quickly into a patient's room that suddenly the residents would lose their bearings. Had she gone to the right or the left? Marina squinted down the street, the darkness broken apart by streetlights and headlights and bits of broken glass that showered the curb and reflected the light up. "I'm coming," she said. Her eyes shifted constantly from one side of the street to the other in a slow nystagmus. In order to steady herself, she made an organized list in her mind of all the things that were making her nervous: it was night, and she wasn't exactly sure where she was, though she could have easily turned around and found her way back to the opera house and from there, her hotel; she was unsteady in her shoes, which, along with the ridiculous dress, made her the human equivalent of a bird with a broken wing to any predator who might be out trawling the streets late at night; if there was a predator, she now had a deaf child to protect and she wasn't exactly sure how she would manage that; as she felt the blisters coming up beneath the sandals' straps she could not help but think of the countless explorers throughout history who had been taken down by the lowly blister, then she reassured herself that there was very little chance that this was how she would meet her end given the three different types of antibiotics Mr. Fox had sent along with her Lariam and the phone; and since this was a list of anxieties, she could not neglect the most pressing fear of all: assuming she made it to her destination tonight, she was then to sit down with Dr. Swenson and have a discussion about what exactly? Vogel's rights and interests in Brazil? The location of Anders' body?

Then, without so much as a footfall to announce him, Easter came up from behind her and put himself in the lead. At first she thought he must be bored by how slow she was and figured he meant to leave her, but instead he aligned himself to her pace. He would have been in easy reach had she just put out her hand. He had made himself her seeing-eye boy. As she watched his back, his shoulders barely wide enough to hang a shirt on, half the anxieties on her list fell away. With one hand she held Mrs. Bovender's wrap firmly to her chest while her other hand was full of the silk of her skirt which she held up in order not to trip on it or let it drag in the pools of muddied rain left over from the late afternoon deluge. The night air pressed against her, moving roughly in and out of her lungs. It was very recently that she had been ill. Despite the pins and the spray and the black lacquered sticks with the gold Chinese fans, she could feel random sections of her hair breaking free and sliding damply down the back of her neck. When they reached the corner, Easter turned right, and without question or thought, she followed him.

Two blocks later, at about the point she was certain she would not be able to take another step, Easter dipped into a restaurant Marina had never seen before, on a street she couldn't remember. He could not have seen Dr. Swenson go in but there she was, sitting at a table in the corner, a bottle of soda water in front of her that was already half consumed. If possible, the room was slightly darker than the night she had come in from and a small, single candle on every table stood in place of the stars. Half a dozen tables were occupied, a dozen more were empty. It was late. The boy, having completed his job, cut the shortest path between the other customers and sat in a wooden chair beside Dr. Swenson. Had she brought him in with her from the jungle or did Easter, along with Milton and the Bovenders, have his place on Vogel's payroll? Dr. Swenson tilted the bread basket towards him and he took a piece and laid it nicely on his plate. Marina tried not to limp as she made her way towards them. For a moment she stood at the table saying nothing, her resplendence melted in the heat, and waited for the other woman to acknowledge her arrival. She could have waited for the rest of her life. "I lost you," Marina said finally.

"Clearly you didn't," Dr. Swenson said. "Easter knew where we were going."

"I didn't know that Easter had been informed."

Dr. Swenson was looking at the menu through a pair of half glasses. "I'm sure you realized soon enough. This place is a bit farther but that's why the opera crowd avoids it. I can always get a table."

Marina pulled out a chair beside Easter, across from Dr. Swenson, and felt a significant throbbing in her feet as the blood shifted back up her legs. She decided to be grateful for the chair and for the audience.

After taking in all the information the menu had to offer, Dr. Swenson laid it down. Now that she knew what she would have for dinner she was ready to begin. "Allow me to be direct, Dr. Singh," she said, folding her glasses back into their padded case. "It will save us both some time. You shouldn't have come. There must be a way of convincing Mr. Fox that continual monitoring does not speed productivity. Maybe that can be a project for you when you return home. You can tell him I am fine, and that it would better suit his own purposes to leave me alone."

A waiter approached the table and Dr. Swenson proceeded to order for herself and the child in broken Portuguese. When the waiter turned to Marina she asked for a glass of wine. Dr. Swenson added to the order and sent the waiter away.

"I'm glad you're fine," Marina said. "And you're right, I've come to find out about the progress of the drug's development, that's part of the reason I'm here. But I was a close friend of Dr. Eckman's. I am a friend of his wife's. It's important for her to understand the circumstances of his death."

"He died of a fever."

Marina nodded. "So you wrote, but she would like to know more than that. It would help her to be able to explain to their children what happened."

Easter sat at the table without fidgeting, both of his feet on the floor or nearly on the floor. He tore neat pieces off his bread and ate them slowly. He did not seem to be the least bit bothered by waiting, which caused Marina to wonder if he had had a great deal of practice.

"Are you asking me if I know what caused the fever, if it had a name? I do not. The list of possibilities is too long. I suppose at this point checking his recent vaccination records would be a place to start. I can also give you a list of antibiotics he failed to respond to."

"I'm not asking you what kind of fever it was," Marina said. "I'm asking you what happened."

Dr. Swenson sighed. "Is this my deposition, Dr. Singh?"

"I'm not accusing—"

Dr. Swenson waved her hand, brushing the words out of the air. "I will tell you: I liked Dr. Eckman. Every aspect of his visit was a great inconvenience to me but there was something ingenuous about him.

He had a sincere interest in the Lakashi, in the work. You were a friend of his and so you know this about him, he had a singular ability for demonstrating interest, if it was in birds or in the estrogen levels in the collected blood samples; he asked a great many questions and took in every word of the answers he was given. He was polite and affable even when I was trying to convince him to leave, which, you should note to his wife, I did constantly." She interrupted herself to finish her glass of water and before the empty glass had come to rest on the table it had been refilled by the hovering waiter. "Mr. Fox was an idiot to send him down here. I've hardly ever seen a man so ill suited for the jungle, and that's saying a great deal. Most people are ill suited for the jungle. The heat, the insects, even the trees made him anxious. Now, one would think when a person comes to a place where he doesn't want to be and he is not wanted, he would have the sense to go. Dr. Eckman lacked that sense. He told me that the company needed me to speed up the progress of my work, that they needed to see my records, bring in other researchers, move as much of the project back to Vogel as soon as was possible. I believe our entire exchange could have taken place in an hour, fifteen minutes if both parties were succinct, but there was something about Dr. Eckman. It was as if he needed to see everything for himself. He had come a long way and by God he wasn't going to take my word for the fact that there was a drug in development. He felt the need to retrace the entire course of my work. He was going to rediscover the Lakashi tribe himself. He was going to find the roots of their fertility himself. He refused to let his misery inform his actions."

A small man in a dirty white apron came out of the kitchen with two plates of yellow rice covered over with chicken. The meat was the same color as the rice and was glossy and loose on the bone. He gave one to Dr. Swenson and one to the child, whose face became incandescent with joy when he saw what was for dinner.

"We haven't had much luck keeping chickens," Dr. Swenson said. "We have both been looking forward to dinner." She tapped Easter's hand and at that permission he picked up his fork and began to pull the meat apart by holding the chicken in place with two fingers. She tapped his hand again and handed him a knife. "We have Dr. Eckman to thank for Easter's table manners. All this is new. It frankly wasn't anything I'd stressed before, the Lakashi table manners are not our own, but I've kept up with it. Dr. Eckman took such an interest in the child. I can only think he was missing his own—" She stopped and looked at Marina, leaving the question unspoken.

"Boys," Marina said. "He had three boys."

Dr. Swenson nodded. "Well, you could see it. I don't suppose I'd thought of this before but surely a great part of my sympathy for Dr. Eckman came from his kindness to Easter."

The original waiter returned and put a piece of tres leches in front of Marina, who shook her head at the sight of it. She was thinking of those three boys on the sofa, the ones whose hearing was so acute that adult conversations were forced into the kitchen pantry and conducted in whispers.

"I ordered it for you," Dr. Swenson said, and sent the waiter away. "It's good cake. It goes with the wine."

Marina saw the boy eyeing her dessert, caught between the joy of his own meal and the longing for hers. "How long was Anders with you before he got sick?"

"It would be hard to say since I don't actually know when he was infected. In retrospect, I think he may have picked up something here in Manaus and brought it out with him. I didn't know Dr. Eckman before this. It's possible that I never saw him when he was completely himself."

"You did," Marina said. "You met him at Vogel before you left. He was on the review committee for your financing." She pictured Anders leaning against her desk. He had been so certain Dr. Swenson had liked him.

Dr. Swenson nodded, her attention given over fully to her chicken for the moment. "Yes, of course, he told me that. But I didn't remember him. I wouldn't have any reason to remember him."

"Of course," Marina said, and for the first time it came to her with certainty: *She does not know me.*

The older doctor took a bite of rice. "It's difficult to trust yourself in the jungle," she said. "Some people gain their bearings over time but for others that adjustment never comes. It's simply too foreign. We can't find a common application for what we already know. I'm not just thinking of moral issues or rules of law, though both of those apply, but the simple concrete facts of existence aren't what we're used to. Take the insects, for example. Hundreds of thousand of new species are discovered around the world every year, and who knows how many other species vanish. The means by which we separate out the deadly from the merely irritating are extremely limited considering that the insect that just bit you might not have even been classified yet, and at what point does constant irritation itself become deadly? You're bitten by so many things, there's no way of keeping track. You simply have to accept the fact that whatever it was probably isn't going to kill you." She motioned to Marina with her fork. "Did you know your arm is bleeding, Dr. Singh?"

Marina had let the shawl slip behind her in the chair and she could see now that there was a thin line of dried blood about six inches long that came from a puncture of her right biceps. Dr. Swenson took the unused napkin from the fourth place at the table and dipped it into her water glass. "Here," she said. "Clean yourself up."

Marina took the napkin and wiped her arm, taking a minute to apply some pressure to the wound as washing it had started up the bleeding again.

"I'm sure it's nothing," Dr. Swenson said, working industriously to get the last of the chicken off the bone, "but it goes to my point. It's easy to become hypochondriacal out here but the more dangerous state is hypochondria's opposite: the insistent voice that says you must be overreacting to things, and so in turn you begin to ignore real symptoms. Doctors, I'm sure you know, are notorious for this sort of behavior, and I think it may have been the case with Dr. Eckman. His substantial fears actually led him too far in the other direction. Every time I asked him if he was sick he would exhaust himself denying it. When it became ridiculous for him to deny it, I told him I was sending him back. No, no, no, he said to me, like some sort of child who doesn't want to miss his part in the school pageant, he would be better in a day or two. I couldn't make his decisions for him, Dr. Singh, though believe me, I tried. He had waited for me a long time in Manaus and he wasn't about to turn back around without completing whatever mission he imagined it was his responsibility to complete. The next thing I knew we were setting up an infirmary. He required nearly constant attention." Dr. Swenson looked over at Easter, who had picked a chicken bone up from his plate and was gnawing on it. She raised a hand to tap him and then lowered it instead. She let it go. "Do you see the problem here?" she said to Marina, her voice maintaining every inflection of composure. "The man who had been sent to prod me along in my work was keeping me from it. He had crossed over a line from feeling that he would recover quickly to feeling he was too ill to travel. He told me he wanted to wait until he was in a better condition. He didn't want to be out on the river. He was afraid of the river. What he wanted was to be home, but getting home from the Amazon requires a great deal of effort and after a certain point he no longer had that in him. I liked Dr. Eckman well enough, but I don't believe that makes any difference to the story. He was an impediment to me when he was well and he was an impediment when he was sick. I will not have him be an impediment now that he is dead. I will not attempt to retrace every moment of his illness when I cannot alter its outcome. I am sorry that his wife will have to bear that, but there was nothing I could do about it then and there is nothing I can do about it now. He made his own choices. He received the best care we could have given him considering our resources, but Dr. Eckman died. Does that shed any more light on the subject? I wasn't with him at the end. If there were some final words, a message, I missed it."

Marina sat at the table and thought of her friend dying of a nameless fever in some room or some hut at the end of the world. Karen Eckman made her promise she would ask if Anders was dead. Instead she asked Dr. Swenson if he had died alone. It was a sentimental question but she wanted some other picture in her mind than the one she had.

"When he died? No," she said. Her eyes cut over to the boy for an instant and then back to Marina. "Easter was with him."

Easter, who was possibly the age of the oldest Eckman boy, or the middle one, had seen him out. His plate was scraped clean and wiped down with bread, a neat pike of chicken bones stacked in the center. She gave him her cake and in return he gave her such a smile that she wanted the waiter to come back so she could order another piece and give him that one as well.

"It isn't a story to bring home," Dr. Swenson said.

"No," Marina said.

"The story isn't meant for her anyway." Dr. Swenson tapped the corners of her mouth with her napkin. "It's a story for you. Without getting into the details over dinner, you will trust me when I tell you that Dr. Eckman suffered. I mean it to be a cautionary tale."

Marina nodded, trying to find some untapped vein of stoicism within herself as she wanted very much to cover her face with her hands at the thought of Anders' end. "I understand that."

"I don't imagine that anyone has been too worried about this back at the pharmaceutical plant, but Dr. Eckman's death was difficult for me as well. I was cautious to begin with and now I am doubly so. I'm not looking to take on a new responsibility. If you want to know how my work is going I will tell you: I am behind schedule. This is a delicate piece of science. I give it every waking moment of my life but at this point it still requires more time. I understand that it is not an unlimited number of years I have in which to finish this, both from Vogel's perspective and from my own." Dr. Swenson signaled the waiter to bring the check and drank the last of her water. "Someday I would like to leave the Amazon myself, Dr. Singh. I am used to this place but I am not in love with it. I have every possible incentive to complete this project as quickly as possible. Mr. Fox seems to think that I'm enjoying myself so much that I would need a series of Vogel emissaries to remind me that the goal is to finish. You may report back that I have not lost sight of the goal."

Marina nodded. She understood that she was being given her ticket home.

Dr. Swenson put both of her hands on the table and gave it a gentle tap to signify that their interview was now concluded. "Easter and I will walk you back to your hotel. We'll go right past it on the way to the apartment. There we will say good night and goodbye. This won't be a long visit for me. You understand I need to get back."

Marina cautiously moved her toes side to side. Her feet had swollen while she had been sitting and the straps of her sandals were now cutting deep into the skin. She reached under the table and, with some effort and a sharp strike of pain, pulled the shoes off. Easter, having finished the cake, ducked to look.

"I'm afraid I won't be able to walk back," Marina said. What harm would there be in telling the truth now? She was finished.

Dr. Swenson called out to the waiter and Marina clearly understood her to say Milton's name. The waiter nodded. "He'll come and pick us up," she said. She motioned for Easter to hand her one of the shoes and she looked at it as if it were a rare archeological find. "It's difficult for me to understand why a woman would choose to do that to herself." She returned the silver sandal to its mate.

"It is a mystery to me as well," Marina said. She would not try to defend the shoes. They were indefensible. She would walk barefoot for the rest of her life before she'd put them on again.

"Barbara tells me you were a student of mine," Dr. Swenson said. Perhaps it was the shoes that made her think of it, she was wondering how a student of hers had learned so little about the workings of the human anatomy.

"Yes," Marina said. All of her fears were floating away from her now. What difference did it make? One by one she met them and then let them go.

"That would have been Johns Hopkins?"

Marina nodded. "I'm forty-two."

Dr. Swenson signed her name to the bill and left it on the table. It would no doubt be mailed to Vogel. "Well, I must not have done a convincing job if you went into pharmacology. But then here I am developing a drug. I suppose we both wound up in the same field after all." She reached down to the floor and handed Marina's sandals to Easter to carry. He seemed very pleased to have the job. "None of us knows how life will work out, Dr. Singh."

Dr. Singh was in the process of agreeing with that exact impossibility as Milton, who must have been idling the car outside, walked in the door to take her home.

That night Marina spent a long time in the bath paying attention to her various wounds: the turned back flaps of skin that dotted her toes and heels, the pillowy blisters that had yet to drain, the different bites that were itching or bleeding or bruised, she scrubbed them all with soap and washcloth until the skin around the red lesions was red as well, then she dried off and slathered up with salve. All of this had to be done before calling Mr. Fox. It didn't matter how late it was. She was planning on waking him up. She was hoping even that waking him up would give her something of an advantage in their conversation. She pictured the phone ringing on the night table beside the bed she had on occasion fallen asleep in but in which she had never slept an entire night, the very bed she hoped to go home to. Mr. Fox answered on the fourth ring, his voice alert and composed. He would have given himself two rings after waking to collect himself.

"Tell me you're fine," he said.

"Some blisters," she said, gently pushing at one of them on her toe, "but absolutely fine. I found Dr. Swenson." She said it straight out. She did not wait for him to ask her because he had asked her every time they spoke, as if finding Dr. Swenson was something that might have happened and then slipped her mind. She told him about the opera house, about Easter and the dinner. She told him what had been said about Anders and, in trying to recreate the conversation, she realized how little of a conversation it had actually been. She could report that the project was behind but moving forward. Even if she lacked the details she was sure about the essential fact: Dr. Swenson wanted to see this done more than anyone, and she would get it done, on that point she had been very convincing, though she had neglected to say when she projected the drug might be submitted to the FDA.

"No time line?" Mr. Fox said.

"Nothing absolute," Marina said, but in truth she hadn't asked. Why hadn't she asked? All these years later, she still listened to Dr. Swenson as a student listens to a teacher, as a Greek listens to an oracle. She didn't question her, she simply committed the answers to memory.

"Don't worry about that," Mr. Fox said. "It was a preliminary meeting. You're smart not to push her yet. Do you think you'll leave tomorrow?"

"Tomorrow or the next day. It depends on tickets. I'll be on the first plane that has a seat."

"You'll take a plane?" Mr. Fox asked.

"To come home."

The line was quiet, and into that silence Marina did not extend herself. Even as she realized the error of her assumption she wanted to stay with it for as long as possible. Her hopeful imagination had let her drift all the way home. She had no luggage. They had never found her luggage. Everything she had acquired in Manaus would be left behind, save the little white heron and the red beaded bracelet that was knotted to her wrist. Through the window of the Minneapolis–St. Paul airport she saw white blossoms. She drank the honeyed breeze as she stepped outside.

"Don't quit this now," Mr. Fox said. "Not after all the time it's taken to find her."

He would still be saying this after six months, after a year, *Don't quit this now.* Maybe he wanted her to stay until she could promise she was bringing back the chemical compound for fertility in her pocket. "I delivered the message," Marina said. In retrospect she was not entirely sure that she had said anything but she was certain that any message she delivered to Dr. Swenson would never be listened to anyway. Dr. Swenson didn't listen to Marina, or Anders, or Mr. Fox. Listening was not Dr. Swenson's habit. Marina was not going to change the course of the river. "Anders delivered the message. She told me that. She understands exactly what it is you want and I believe she will get it to you as soon as is humanly possible."

"It isn't the sort of thing you can take someone's word on. The drug could be finished or she could never have started it. This is a project of enormous importance and expense. You need to find out where we are in development," Mr. Fox said, and then he added the word "exactly."

She looked at her feet, bright and raw in the overhead light, slick with Neosporin. "You'll have to find somebody else."

"Marina," he said. "Marina, Marina." He said it with tenderness in his voice, with love.

She could smell her own capitulation coming on from a mile away. It was her nature, her duty. She told him good night and hung up the phone. She couldn't blame him much. Inside the envelope of his own warm, dry sheets, he really couldn't understand what he was asking her to do. When she was still at home, she hadn't been able to imagine this place either.

It was a Lariam day. She had been putting it off since this morning, but what difference did it make? She always wound up taking it in the end. The pills she had so cavalierly tossed in the airport trash had managed to find her again. Tomo never complained about having to come up from the front desk to settle her screaming by banging on her door. And if she dealt with intermittent nausea, paranoia, my God, she could hardly pin that on the Lariam. Even if she went home tomorrow she would have to take it for another four weeks. It was the drug's way of reminding the patient that the trip isn't over. The trip would be in the bloodstream, in the tissues. All the potential disasters of the place would continue to linger inside. Marina set the pill on her tongue and swallowed it with half a bottle of water which was sitting on her dresser, then she turned out the light. She was becoming accustomed to the dip in the middle of the mattress, to the foam-rubber pillow that smelled like cardboard boxes, to the sound of the water piping into the ice machine down the hall and then, hours later, the dumping release of its little frozen charges into the bin. She wondered how long these things would stay with her once she was home again. She wondered how long Anders would stay with her, and what it would be like to settle back into their lab alone and who would eventually come to replace him. She wondered how long it would be that she would think of him every day, and what it would feel like to realize that days had passed and she had forgotten to think of him at all. She thought about the stack of letters that Karen had written sitting in the drawer of the table beside the bed. She thought of Anders buried in the jungle floor three thousand miles from Eden Prairie. As tired as she was, it kept her awake. When the mind could no longer bear the news—Anders is dead—it busied itself with the details: Where is his camera? Where are his binoculars?

When Marina woke up she was standing in front of the window in her hotel room with no memory of having gotten out of bed. It was freezing. She and her father had been at the campus of the University of Minnesota where he had done his doctoral work in microbiology. The snow was coming down hard. All she could really remember were the Indians coming out of all the buildings, and how the women in their red and purple saris completely changed the landscape, the men in pink shirts broke the whiteness apart. They shivered in the arctic wind until the colors began to vibrate, making a sea of trembling, snow-covered poppies. She had gone to sleep with the air conditioner left on high and now the inside of the hotel window was so wet that she wondered from the stupor of interrupted sleep if it was finally raining inside. Beads of water streaked down the glass, reducing the view of the world outside to a deep purple darkness punctuated by balls of glittering light. The cold air blew gale force at the cheap cotton nightgown she had bought from Rodrigo. She squatted down in front of the unit beneath the window, her hair blown back by the wind, and blindly pushed the little buttons until the system gave one final frozen exhalation and died. She was shaking, and unsure how much of that was the temperature and how much was a dream. All she could be certain of was that she had been trying to go home and that she couldn't because of the snow. She wasn't going home. Maybe Mr. Fox had whispered in her ear all night, but while she slept the world shifted away from the airport and towards the docks. The clear resolve she had had in the restaurant seemed to have broken like a fever sometime during the night and as she was waking up she could feel Minnesota recede with the rest of her dream. She would not get back into bed now. She was finished with that bed. Like a somnambulist half awake she gathered up everything that belonged to Barbara Bovender, the gray silk dress that was muddied around the hem, the savage shoes, the wrap, the hair pins, and put them all together in a plastic bag. Then she opened every drawer and removed the meager contents. She folded what she owned and put it into small piles on the dresser. As she went to every corner of the room, she told herself that what mattered now was movement, that the point was not so much to get home as it was to leave Manaus. She was certain of nothing except the fact that she wouldn't spend another night in the Hotel Indira. She put the packet of Karen's letters on top of her three folded shirts. She didn't have a bag for what she owned but that, she imagined, would be the least of it.

By six o'clock she had dressed and left. The early morning city had the tick of action, children were on their blankets, the painted bowls and crude flutes and beaded bracelets they had to sell were all in even lines, the women were moving towards the market hall, not briskly but faster than they would move at any other point for the rest of the day. Dogs trailed along far to the sides of the streets, heads low and watchful, the shadow and light making valleys between every rib.

It seemed in all of Manaus only Nixon was still asleep. In the lobby of the Swenson-Bovender apartment building, his face was pressed sideways against the desk, his hands stretched out in front of him and open wide. Marina gave herself a moment to watch such a deep and dreamless sleep, feeling a fondness for him she couldn't account for unless it was just the fact that there were so few people in this city she knew by name. She imagined he was a good man even though her only evidence was his fidelity to this post.

She sat down in the lobby to write the Bovenders a note, but after going to the trouble of locating paper and pen found she had no idea what to say. She couldn't thank them. They were the grand jury after all, keeping her there in the holding cell of the Hotel Indira for two weeks while they decided if her case was fit for Dr. Swenson to hear. Or maybe she should thank them for managing to make their decision in two weeks. They had kept Anders for over a month, an entire wasted month of life while his boys rode their bicycles alone through the slush of spring. Marina was distracted by the sound of Nixon's labored respiration. Then, on his desk, he stopped breathing. Twenty seconds, thirty seconds, she was just about to get up when at forty-five seconds he gasped, his back heaving, and then began to breathe again. Still asleep, he sighed and turned his face in the other direction. Apnea. There was nothing she could do about that.

She settled back into the winged chair in the lobby's small conversational grouping of furniture where she sat by herself. If Marina couldn't thank the Bovenders, she found she couldn't blame them either. At twenty-three she would have gladly done their job. She might have stayed in the position until she was forty-three if certain events had played out differently. Without the Bovenders there to remind her, she might have forgotten what it was like to be enthralled, to fall hard in love for principles and a singularly remarkable mind. They were little more than pretty children, feather-light, proven capable of no end of lies, and yet there was something in their shiny nature that made them indestructible. She would have given anything to take them to the jungle with her. So in the end she put down the truth as she knew it at that exact minute. *I will miss you.* She wrote their name on the bag and added twenty dollars U.S. for the cost of cleaning the dress, knotted it all together and left it on the desk beside one of Nixon's sleeping hands. Dr. Swenson tended to be early. If rounds began at seven she was on to the first case at six-thirty. It didn't take long to figure out the clock. Marina didn't want to meet her in the lobby for fear it might look like an ambush. She walked quickly to Rodrigo's store. It was busy then, all the stores were busy. She fixed herself a cup of coffee from the pot on his counter and found a nylon duffel bag while he waited on customers. She picked up more sunscreen, more bug spray. It was important not to think too deeply about what she would need or she might wind up taking all of it. Everything went on the Vogel account, down to the coffee. She picked up another box of Band-Aids, a second pair of flip-flops. She was looking at a length of netting that was meant to hang over a bed when Dr. Swenson came in with Milton.

Rodrigo saw them first. There wasn't room enough for Dr. Swenson and all the women who had come in for flour and thread, things they could easily wait until later to buy. He began to rush his other customers by shouting at them and no one objected to his harassment. A few of them put down whatever was in their hands and left the store immediately, while others grabbed a few more things off the shelves nearby and rushed to the counter to pay. Maybe they knew Dr. Swenson. Maybe they were as anxious to leave as the clerk was to see them go. Rodrigo, always so careful to write up bills of sale, gave a quick visual assessment of the pile of goods and barked out a price that each woman paid without question. Dr. Swenson noticed none of this. Her chin was pointed up. She was mainly interested in the high-shelf items, the goods ignored by the daily foot traffic of Brazilians. She was muttering her thoughts to the ceiling and Milton was writing them down. She would not have noticed Marina had Marina been dipped in yellow paint, and Milton, who never looked up from his pencil and pad, had missed her as well. One by one the customers fled the store. Marina followed the last of them to the counter to have her purchases added to her account. Rodrigo, who seemed to understand exactly the decision that had been made, added in an extra hat, three more cotton handkerchiefs, several rolls of LifeSavers.

"You're up very early, Dr. Singh," Dr. Swenson said to the ceiling.

Milton, startled, looked up. "There you are!" he said. "Then finding you this morning is one thing I can cross off my list."

"You said you'd be here early," Marina said. "And there were a few things I needed myself."

"There's no end to what one needs in the Amazon," Dr. Swenson said. "What isn't eaten by insects is quick to rot. That's why our friend Rodrigo does such a booming business. Nature provides a state of constant turnover. Still, I would think if you are leaving today you'd be better off making your purchases at home, unless you're looking for souvenirs."

There was nothing to do but say it. Marina told her she would be coming along. This did not seem to surprise Dr. Swenson. She took the news as if it were both unpleasant and expected. "You've been talking to Mr. Fox."

Marina looked up towards the high shelves as well, wondering what she might be seeing there. "At the very least I should get Anders' things."

"Raisins," Dr. Swenson said to Milton, who added it to the list. "Tapioca." She turned to Marina. "Does it matter at all that you are not invited?"

It would be easier had she been invited but to the best of her knowledge Dr. Swenson had never welcomed students to her classes or interns to the program or patients to the hospital. She couldn't see how this experience should be any different. "Not really."

"Dr. Rapp always said that people would attach themselves to an expedition." She moved very slowly, putting her hand first on a box of crackers, next on a bag of coffee. Milton continued to write and then Rodrigo was writing as well. An older woman with a baby tied across her chest in a bright red scarf opened the door and, seeing the people who were inside, turned and left without comment. "Certainly they did with him. I saw it myself. An endless succession of mongrels and malingerers, the laziest dropouts who fancied themselves explorers. He made his policy clear: he was not responsible for their food, their shelter, their safety, or their health. He didn't waste his time discouraging them because frankly there was no discouragement they could not withstand. All of the energy they could have put into their intelligence they had used to develop their tenacity. But what I quickly learned was that their tenacity was for going, not for staying. Once they were out on the trail they fell like flies. Some took a day, two days, others were gone in a matter of hours, and Dr. Rapp never stopped for them. He remained beautifully consistent: he was there to work and he would continue to work. He would not ferry back the weak and the lame. They had chosen to get themselves in and they would simply have to figure the means to get themselves out. People were quick to accept these terms until they themselves were weak. Then they changed their tune entirely, then they said Dr. Rapp was heartless. They couldn't slander him as a scientist but they said no end of scurrilous things about him as a man. He hadn't rescued them! He hadn't been their father and mother! I will tell you, none of that troubled his sleep. If he had made them his responsibility, either by dissuading them from their ambitions or by bailing them out of their folly, the greatest botanist of our time would have been reduced to a babysitter. It would have been an incalculable blow to science, all in the name of saving the stupid."

The air, ever heavy, now was paralyzed. Milton had slipped his pencil and pad in his pocket without thinking, and Rodrigo had put his pencil down as well. While Dr. Swenson continued to calculate how much food she would need to take back with her, the other three stood breathless and unblinking. Marina felt as if she were trying to remember the answer when there hadn't been a question posed. They were all waiting. "I don't think you'll find me to be nearly that much trouble," she said finally.

Dr. Swenson, who had been distracted by a small bin of socks, did not look up. "As much trouble as what?"

"The mongrels," Marina said. "The malingerers."

"Don't be so self-referential. I was telling you a story. I wasn't telling a story about you."

At that Milton inhaled as abruptly as Nixon at his desk. "There you go," he said, willing himself to accept the explanation. "How many cans of apricots?"

Dr. Swenson waited a moment, as if making a tally in her head. "A case more than usual," she said, looking at Marina. It was impossible to know how many apricots a person would eat once they had been removed from civilization.

It was agreed then that Milton would pick Marina up in front of the Hotel Indira at eleven, and despite the heat of that hour she was standing ready at the front of the hotel, tucked beneath the awning with her half-empty bag. She had said goodbye to Tomo, who was more than happy to store her coat and sweaters until she returned. She had not said goodbye to Mr. Fox. This city, so busy when she woke up that morning, was practically empty now. The dogs pressed themselves into doorways beneath thin strips of shade. The cars drove by slowly, as if every driver was trying to decide if he was the one who was supposed to take Marina to the docks. They looked at her carefully and tapped their horns.

When Milton did arrive, Easter was in the passenger seat. When he saw Marina through the open window, he reached both of his arms out to her as if he were hers alone in all the world. There was something brilliant about being recognized, the happiness on his face entirely disproportionate to his knowing her. Marina went to him and took both of his small hands in her hands and he gave her an enthusiastic shake. Milton put a thumb on the boy's shoulder and pointed to the backseat. Easter immediately flipped backwards, a trick he had been saving.

"Forgive me," Milton said in a tired voice when she got in the car. He was sitting on a folded towel, his shirt and pants and hair soaked through. Even the small straw hat on the back of his head was wilted and damp. There could have been a rainstorm blocks from here that Marina never saw. He could have fallen in the river.

"Forgive you for what?"

Milton shook his head. "It took us longer to load the boat." He took out a smaller towel and wiped down his face.

Easter was craning his entire upper body out the window to see as far as he could in every direction: boy as turtle, car as shell. The wind dried out last night's soccer shirt and ruffled the dark, wet curls against his neck. Looking at him, Marina realized he was a marker. The boat was loaded, Dr. Swenson was on the boat. If Milton hadn't taken Easter there would have been no reason for her to wait the minutes it took for him to drive to the hotel. "It's not as if I had anywhere else to go," she said.

"He likes the car," Milton said, tilting his head back.

"I'm sure he does."

The dock was farther up river than Marina had been before. The wooden planks on the walkway were warped by the endless succession of sun and hard rain. A collection of rusted tugs and houseboats that looked like they had been pieced together over the course of many generations bobbed between the low-riding water taxis. From the top of the bank she could see the freighters and cruise ships in the distance lining up against the great cement piers. Below her was a small figure pacing beneath the shade of a black umbrella.

"We are late, Milton," Dr. Swenson called. The engine of the boat was running and a pale lavender smoke spread out across the water.

"This would be the time to change your mind," Milton said quietly. "If you are inclined to change your mind."

Easter flew ahead of them now, running in flip-flops, forsaking the perilous steps for the more perilous slope of mud and rock and weed. The boat was a pontoon, the kind of boat her father had rented for a weekend every summer when Marina was young and her parents were married. Her father was not much for boating but the pontoon he said was like a pony rented out for children: stolid and low, not given to sudden movements.

"I'll be fine," Marina said. She was in motion now. She was as good as on the river.

"I don't remember telling you to take Easter along," Dr. Swenson said when they reached the old pontoon with a flat metal roof. The boy was standing behind her now, his hands on the wheel in an imitation of steering. There were boxes stacked neatly around the circumference and the boat sat low and even in the water.

"I don't believe you did," Milton said. He gave Marina his hand to board and in the moment she held his hand she thought about him the way she thought about the Bovenders. It would all be better if he would simply board the boat behind her.

Dr. Swenson tapped Easter on the shoulder and pointed to the lines, at which point the boy jumped off the boat and untied them. He curled his toes around the edge of the dock and pushed the boat away. He let it go so far that for one horrible instant Marina thought he wasn't coming either, but then he leapt, his child's bones filled with springs, and landed with both feet planted on the deck.

"Travel safely," Milton said, and raised his hand up to them. He was the only person on the dock and he stood there as if they were the *Lusitania*. He was waving them back instead of waving them on.

Easter was firm at the wheel now. The child steered the boat out into a low swirl of current, a seriousness in his eyes as he scanned the wide horizon. Dr. Swenson, safe beneath the boat's cover, closed her umbrella. Marina dropped her bag at her feet and held on to the railing. Milton receded but stayed in place, his arm raised as he grew smaller and smaller. Dear Milton. She waved to him. She hadn't made it clear how grateful she was. After all those empty hours to spend in any conversation in the world, they had left in a matter of minutes with no discussion of where they were going or how long it would take them to get there or when they might think of coming back. But somehow none of that mattered anymore. Marina hadn't understood the enormity of the river until she was on it. The sky was spread over in white clouds that banked and thinned depending on the direction she turned in. Some of the clouds had covered over the sun so for the moment it was cooler, and the breeze of their forward momentum kept the insects down. The birds shot out from the banks and cut over the water. Marina thought of Anders at the bow, his binoculars raised.

How glad he must have been to finally leave this city. Marina never would have believed it until she was on a boat herself but the water was an enormous relief. "Beautiful," she said to the one member of the party who could hear her.

"We always feel better heading home," Dr. Swenson said.

Six

There was traffic on the Negro, barges and tugs, water taxis with rotting thatched roofs where river swallows nested, dugout canoes containing entire families—sisters with babies and brothers and cousins and grandfathers and aunts holding open umbrellas, so many people crammed into one log that the lip of the boat sat nearly level with the surface of the brown water as one man in the back rowed carefully on. The smaller boats stayed near the shore, while a cruise ship, white as a sailor's dress uniform, churned up the center aisle. Easter remained fiercely alert, his damp hair pushed back by the breeze, his eyes sweeping slowly side to side. He pulled the throttle to cut his wake in deference to the boats that were smaller, and he waved to those larger boats that cut their wake for him. Every appearance was that of an orderly world. Then the boy would turn and look behind him, and when he did he would nod to Marina and Dr. Swenson and they would nod back.

"Does he drive all the way?" Marina asked, not having any idea how far they were going.

Dr. Swenson nodded. "He likes it." She was sitting on a box of canned hash while Marina stood. "What boy wouldn't want to drive the boat? It gives him standing in the tribe. I drive or Easter drives, no one else. A few of the men have outboard motors that they've traded for over the years, but they've never captained a boat like this. It forces them to show respect when they see how much I trust him. He's good with the engine, too. He's figured it out."

Marina was no judge of children but she would say that Easter looked too young to captain a boat or fix an engine or walk alone in a city at night, though not a mile back she had seen a child alone in a child-sized log who could not have been more than five, a spear lying over the bow, his paddle even as it went in and out of the water. "How old is Easter?"

Dr. Swenson looked up and gave a squint in Marina's direction. "Shall I ask him?"

If Dr. Swenson had not been changed by time or experience or geography or climate, was it possible that Marina had not been substantively changed either? Was she in fact the person she had been in medical school, in grade school? "You'll have to forgive me," Marina said, and then set about restating the question. "I don't know any more about the Lakashi than what you've written and you've written nothing about their ability to record time. Does anyone know how old anyone is? Do his parents know?"

"You make no end of suppositions, Dr. Singh. Is that a habit of yours? I have to say that was one thing I admired about Dr. Eckman: no preconceived conclusions whatsoever. A truly open mind is a scientist's greatest asset. He must have been very thoughtful in his research. Had the circumstances been different I could have imagined asking him to stay on."

Marina was not in the least bit unsettled by the praise for Anders. She knew the role of compliments in Dr. Swenson's pedagogy: they were used not to raise one person up but to tap another down into place. She was only sorry that she didn't have Anders to repeat it to, no doubt he would be shocked to hear such kindness after his death.

"You, however, suppose that Easter is Lakashi. He is not. I of course cannot be certain where he came from as he simply appeared in camp one morning and could neither hear nor speak. Were I to follow your example, I would suppose that he was Hummocca based on the shape of his head and the arrangement of his sinuses. The Hummocca have sinus cavities that are less pronounced than the Lakashi. Their faces are more curved, not quite so flat, but the difference is subtle. The Hummocca are somewhat smaller as well, and this goes to your original question about his age. I say all of this based on a single brief and unpleasant encounter with the tribe many years ago. Still, I find that fear can sometimes heighten our powers of observation to a point of great clarity. I remember the heads of the Hummocca so vividly it was almost as if I had dissected one."

A double-decker tourist boat glided by without slowing and for a moment they were caught in its churning wake. As they pitched forward and back, rolling like a barrel in the little waves, Marina grabbed on to a pole and Easter raised his fist at the bigger boat. A tourist on the upper level pointed a camera in their direction. Dr. Swenson dropped her head for a moment, as if willing the other boat to sink through powers of concentration.

After the worst of the rolling had abated, Dr. Swenson lifted her head, her blue eyes bright and ringed in sweat. "Always buy a pontoon," she said, panting lightly as if making an effort not to vomit. "You cannot imagine how hard that wake would have hit us had we not been in a pontoon. But I was making a point: Easter is a very small child, I would go so far as to say he is stunted. This could have been caused by a consistent lack of nutrition. It seems quite possible that no one was willing to give much of the tribe's resources to a deaf child, or it could be that whatever illness rendered him deaf also rendered him small but now I am straying into what can only be called guessing, which is never helpful. Given his skills, his ability to learn, I would think him to be a twelve-year-old of normal, perhaps above-normal, intelligence. I'll have a more precise judgment when he reaches puberty. The onset of puberty in the Lakashi male falls consistently between thirteen-point-two and thirteen-point-eight, a much narrower window than you find in American males. Whether or not this holds true of the Hummocca I am afraid I will never know. Do you have children, Dr. Singh?"

Marina was at least three questions behind. She wanted very much to know about the unpleasant encounter but, feeling she had been called on to give the easiest answer, merely shook her head. "None."

"That's good. Dr. Eckman had no business coming down here leaving three children behind. Are you married?"

"I am not."

"Good again." Dr. Swenson nodded her approval before turning her face towards the breeze. The sky spooled blue above the river in both endless directions. "This is a business for old maids, and I don't say that derogatorily, being one myself. I feel better about you being on the boat knowing your circumstances."

Speaking of suppositions, how much light could being unmarried and childless shed on her circumstances? Did it mean that no one would miss her terribly if she were to die, that there wouldn't be the same set of complications brought about by Dr. Eckman's death? Marina said nothing but sat down on the deck near Dr. Swenson's feet. The sun edged beneath the boat's awning and she wanted more of the shade.

Dr. Swenson leaned to the side and patted her case of canned hash with an open hand. "I prefer to sit on a box. A box doesn't protect one from the roaches but I like to think it sends a message: We are on another level. There is a case of grapefruit juice there. I would recommend that."

Obediently, Marina got up and pushed the box of juice forward, sat. They passed a handful of open houses built onto stilts. Several children, all of them too young to be standing alone in the water, were standing waist deep in the river, waving.

"As for Easter's parents—" Dr. Swenson stopped then and looked at the captain's small back. She tilted her head. "*Parents* seems a very sentimental word to use in his case. The man who inseminated the woman, the woman who pushed the child out of her body, other members of the tribe who may or may not have tried to raise that child when the original duo failed in their responsibilities: his parents have not been in evidence. The Hummocca left it up to the Lakashi, which, considering the nature of the tribe, strikes me as a startling act of humanity. I would have thought them more inclined to abandon a child in the jungle to starve to death or be eaten. All of which is to say he has been with me some eight years now, eight this past Easter. I suppose I am his parents."

"It sounds as if the Hummocca may have left Easter for you then and not the Lakashi, assuming they knew you were here." Marina realized she had made another assumption as soon as it was out of her mouth but this one Dr. Swenson let pass.

"Oh, they knew I was here," she said, nodding her head. "Everyone knows everything eventually. Upon first consideration a person believes herself to be very isolated in the jungle but it isn't the case. Word travels between the tribes, although I've never figured out how it happens as many of them refuse to communicate with one another. It would make a brilliant dissertation topic if you ever become interested in furthering your education." (Marina would have mentioned her Ph.D. as well as her M.D. but there was not a glimmer of a break.) "I say it's the monkeys," Dr. Swenson said. "But then I tend to blame the monkeys for everything. 'A white woman is living with the Lakashi.' News like that goes up and down the river in a matter of hours. Then one afternoon a boy is cutting at a tree with a machete and when his arm goes back he sinks the blade into his sister's head. Amazing that this sort of thing doesn't happen every fifteen minutes out here. So I found a needle and some gut in my bag and I sewed the girl up. It was mostly blood, she was a very dramatic bleeder, but one hardly has to go to medical school to sew up a head. It didn't take many events like this, a snake bite, a breech birth, and suddenly the whole of Brazil knows there is a doctor available off the Negro. Now, you must understand this, Dr. Singh, so few people do: I am not Médecins Sans Frontières. I have not come to the Amazon to be a family practioner. I am simply a person who made certain mistakes at the onset. They didn't know me as a doctor when I arrived. The Lakashi knew me as a member of Dr. Rapp's party. They thought I was like Dr. Rapp, that I was there for the flora and not for them. For the first few years I came alone they were forever bringing me mushrooms and various fungi to look at. They lugged so many fallen trunks of enormous, rotted trees back to camp it would have sent any mycological society into a frenzy. The fact that I took their temperature and drew blood samples and measured their children was completely lost on them, they continued to see me as the person they first met—as an extension of Dr. Rapp. And it had been my intention to be like him, to float on their misguided perceptions, but then I sewed up that girl's head. It was my fatal mistake. The next thing I knew sick people were being paddled up the river to receive my care, and a deaf child had been left off for me to deal with."

The deaf child had gotten her to town. He had ferried her guest to the restaurant after the opera and loaded the boxes on the boat and steered the boat through the river. The deaf child was not without his uses. "What would the alternative have been?" Marina asked. "Going back to that first girl."

"The bleeder. The question is whether or not you choose to disturb the world around you, or if you choose to let it go on as if you had never arrived. That is how one respects indigenous people. If you pay any attention at all you'll realize that you could never convert them to your way of life anyway. They are an intractable race. Any progress you advance to them will be undone before your back is turned. You might as well come down here to unbend the river. The point, then, is to observe the life they themselves have put in place and learn from it."

Marina felt remarkably unmoved by this. "So go back in time, do it again: there is a child standing in front of you with a machete in her head. What do you do?" The farther they went down the river, the fewer boats they saw. From time to time there was still a group of people, mostly very small children, in clusters on the shore but they were thinning out. It felt good to ask a question twice. It was something she could never have managed in the past.

"That's a dramatic flourish, Dr. Singh. Did I tell you the child had a machete in her head? I said she was cut. There was no doubt that she had a skull fracture. I picked out bone fragments with my tweezers but there was nothing else to be done about that. If she was draining cerebral spinal fluid she didn't do it in front of me. I sewed her up, I gave her some antibiotic ointment, hooray for me, now I can meet your expectations of decency, unless of course your expectations include my taking her back to Manaus for an X-ray. But the actions you admire are not thoughtful, they were automatic, the actions I had brought with me from my Western medical background. The question you should be asking is what would have happened to the girl if I hadn't been there? There was someone in the tribe who had managed these situations before me and I suppose that he, in this case it was a he, would have used the available means to help her. Would it have been a sterile needle? I think not. Would she have died? Very doubtful. And while you are moralizing, ask yourself this question as well: What happens to the girl whose brother cuts her after I've gone? Does the tribe still have faith in the man who sewed up heads before me? Has he kept up with his own skills or was he too busy watching mine? I don't intend to be here forever."

"The man who puts the girl's scalp back together, the one you are respecting, do you think his methods are as successful as yours?"

"Now you are being purposefully ridiculous. I have very little respect for what passes as science around here. There's nothing a Westerner loves more than the idea of being cured by tinctures made of boiled roots. They think this place is some sort of magical medicine chest, but for the most part the treatments here consist of poorly recorded gossip handed down throughout the ages from people who knew very little to people who know even less. There is much to be taken from the jungle, obviously—I am here to develop a drug—but in most cases the plants are as useless as the potted begonia that grows on your kitchen windowsill. The ones that do have potential can only be medicinal when they are properly employed. For these people there is no concept of a dosage, no set length for treatments. When something works it seems to me to be nothing short of a miracle."

Marina remembered that cup of sludge Barbara Bovender had brought her from the shaman's stand and wondered if she was no more than a Westerner given to the charms of boiled tinctures. It was a cure she would never admit to now.

Dr. Swenson brightened for a moment. "I'll tell you what the locals do have a real genius for, and that's poison. There are so many plants and insects and various reptiles capable of killing a person out here that it seems any idiot could scrape together a compound that would drop an elephant. As for the rest of it, people survive regardless of the care they get. The human animal is too resilient for it to be otherwise. It is not for me to meddle."

"I appreciate your point. It's only that I believe in the moment—the child, the blood—it would be hard not to act."

"Then perhaps it will actually open up some of my time to have you here. I'll send the daily medical emergencies to you."

Marina laughed at this. "Then I know they'd be better off with the local medical care. I haven't threaded a needle in nearly fifteen years." Suddenly Marina realized she couldn't remember sewing up that last woman she'd operated on. She remembered lifting out the infant, and at that instant realizing what she had done. She remembered one of the nurses taking him away, but what came after that? Where was the needle? She didn't leave the patient there, uterus and abdomen open to the world, but she could not find a picture in her memory of closing.

"It comes right back," Dr. Swenson said. "You were my student. Believe me, I pounded it all in there."

Marina was still looking for the conclusion to the surgery in her mind when she had another thought. "What about Dr. Rapp?"

"What about him?"

"Wouldn't he have sewn up the girl's head?"

Dr. Swenson snorted. "He most certainly would not have, and not because he wasn't a medical doctor. He had a perfect understanding of human physiology and the steadiest hands I have ever seen in my life. He could have grafted a vein by a campfire had he thought it was necessary. But Dr. Rapp had no self-aggrandizing notions about his role in the tribe. He never set himself out to be the great white hero. He never took a single specimen more than what was absolutely needed. He disrupted nothing."

"So he would have let her bleed to death."

"He would have respected the order that was in place."

Marina nodded, thinking perhaps she was luckier than she realized to have found herself with an expedition still capable of making errors of compassion. "Is Dr. Rapp still alive?"

She might as well have asked if President Kennedy had survived his assassination attempt. "Do you read, Dr. Singh? Do you live in this world?"

It was a beautiful question to be asked by a woman on a boat who was taking her down a river into the beating heart of nowhere. "I do," Marina said.

She sighed and shook her head. "Dr. Rapp died nine years ago. It will be ten years this August."

And Marina, sensing that sympathy was in order, said that she was sorry to hear it, and Dr. Swenson thanked her.

"Were you studying mycology at the time? Is that how you came to work with Dr. Rapp?" It seemed possible, after all; anything was possible. She may have been coming down here as an operative for the CIA.

"I was a student of Dr. Rapp's, and the location of his classroom was unpredictable. I followed him through Africa and Indonesia, but the Amazon was the source of his most important work. He studied botany, and I was free to study the workings of a true scientific mind. As an undergraduate at Radcliffe I wasn't allowed to take his class at Harvard, Harvard couldn't have stood for anything as radical as that, but Dr. Rapp let me travel on the expeditions. He was the first teacher I encountered who saw no limitations for women. As it turned out he was the only one."

They were quiet for a long time after that, both staring off at different aspects of the jungle as it rolled past them, the same bit of scenery recycled indefinitely. Two hours later, Easter left the protection of the right-hand bank and crossed the width of the Negro to the left. There he turned up a tributary that was in every way similar to the countless other tributaries they had passed, and while it was unmarked, it was the exit ramp from the interstate, the one that would eventually take them to the street where Dr. Swenson lived. No other boats followed them though the entrance was wide at the mouth. In a matter of minutes the nameless river narrowed and the green dropped behind them like a curtain and the Negro was lost. Marina had thought that the important line that was crossed was between the dock and the boat, the land and the water. She had thought the water was the line where civilization fell away. But as they glided between two thick walls of breathing vegetation she realized she was in another world entirely, and that she would see civilization drop away again and again before they reached their final destination. All Marina could see was green. The sky, the water, the bark of the trees: everything that wasn't green became green. *All in green my love went riding.*

Dr. Swenson announced that lunch was now in order. "The boy deserves a break. He stands up there so rigid that I think he would shatter if a nut hit him just right. There is no way of communicating that one should relax, do you realize that? You can shake out your arms and swivel your neck and it all looks like nonsense." Dr. Swenson put her hands on her thighs and pushed up but she did not stand. She was thicker around the middle than she had been in Baltimore and the weight and the long time sitting seemed to keep her tied to her case of hash. Dr. Swenson, so far as Marina could calculate, would be in the neighborhood of seventy. It was possible at this point that even Dr. Swenson was tired. Marina stood up and extended her hand. Dr. Swenson rubbed her knees for a minute, looking pointedly away, then she took the hand. "Thank you for the assistance," she said. She stood up and then let Marina go. "These are different days. For all I know about the body this is still not what I expected." She went over and tapped Easter on the shoulder, then made a turning motion with her wrist and pointed to the shore. He nodded, keeping his eyes ahead. "He won't go in right away," Dr. Swenson said, coming back to where Marina was standing. "There's a spot he likes where he can tie up to a tree. The anchor makes him nervous. It's not reliable. Once he dropped it off and we had a devil of a time getting it back in the boat. There's a lot for an anchor to get caught on in this river."

Marina looked over the side of the boat. She couldn't even imagine it. "How long have you been coming out here?"

"Dr. Rapp first found the Lakashi"—Dr. Swenson craned back her head, looked towards the tops of the trees—"it was fifty years ago, I suppose. I was on that trip, standing right on the stage of history. I remember coming down this very river for the first time. It was a glorious day. I had no idea that I would be coming back for the rest of my life."

"It doesn't seem that anything much has changed," Marina said, looking to the riverbank and the straight wall of plant life, not a single person on the shore now, not a hut, a boat, in any direction.

"Don't be fooled by the scenery," Dr. Swenson said. "Things were very different then. You didn't turn a corner and find a square mile of forest burned into a field. You didn't see the constant smoke the way you do now. And the Lakashi, even they're different. They lose their skills as fast as the basin loses forest. They used to make their own ropes, they wove cloth. Now even they manage to buy things. They cut down two or three trees and tie them together, float them to Manaus and sell them, that's enough money for kerosene and salt, a river taxi ride back home, maybe some rum if they can strike a good deal, but for the most part they are terrible at dealing. They pick up clothing in town, the very junk that Americans drop off at the Salvation Army box. One time when I was visiting, this was years ago, the tribal elder, a man they called Josie, met me at the dock wearing a Johns Hopkins T-shirt. I had left my class at Hopkins that morning and flown to Brazil and taken a boat down a half a dozen splitting rivers only to be greeted by a Johns Hopkins T-shirt." She shook her head at the memory of it. "Dear God, he was proud of that shirt. He wore it every day. In fact he was buried in it."

"So you would teach all week and see patients and then fly down here on the weekends?"

"Not every weekend, nothing like that, though if there had been enough time or enough money I might have. There was so much work to do down here. I would leave late Thursday night after my last class. I only had office hours on Friday, and I didn't keep office hours. I never believed in them. Questions are for the benefit of every student, not just the one raising his hand. If you don't have the starch to stand up in class and admit what you don't understand, then I don't have the time to explain it to you. If you don't have a policy against nonsense you can wind up with a dozen timid little rabbits lined up in the hall outside your office, all waiting to whisper the same imbecilic question in your ear."

Marina clearly remembered being one of those same Friday rabbits herself, waiting for hours in the chair beside the office door until another student coming down the hall had the decency to explain that she was waiting for nothing. "The department chair didn't mind that you didn't keep hours?"

Dr. Swenson lowered her chin. "Did you attend parochial school as a child, Dr. Singh?"

"Public," Marina said. "And so you came back on Sunday and taught Monday's class?"

"It was a red-eye coming back. I'd land Monday morning and have the taxi take me straight to campus." She stretched her arms overhead, the straying springs of her white hair reaching out in every direction. "I never looked my best on Mondays."

"I never noticed," Marina said.

"That's one thing I have to give to your Mr. Fox: he made it possible for me to stay down here and do my work. I can't say I am undisturbed, as he makes every effort to disturb me himself, but I am free of the madness that comes from trying to conduct meaningful research when your subjects are in another country. I've been down here full time for ten years now. The first three years I pieced together grants but the constant search for funding was more time consuming than flying back and forth to teach. There wasn't a major pharmaceutical company in the world that wouldn't have been willing to foot the bill for this but in the end Vogel won. I give credit where credit's due."

Easter slowed the boat and then put it in reverse, which, with their forward momentum, achieved a sort of churning stillness. He steered it into what appeared to be a slight indentation in the solid wall of trees and then took the rope that was already in his hand and flung it over a branch that hung out over the water at a better angle than all the other branches.

"Well, that worked out nicely," Marina said when the rope was safely caught. She would rather talk about branches and rope than *her Mr. Fox*.

"It always works out well. That's Easter's tree. That's the one he waits for. He knows exactly where to go."

Marina made a slow circle. Thousands of trees, hundreds of thousands of trees as far as she could see on both sides of the river without a single clearing. Branches ad infinitum, leaves in perpetuity. "He remembers one branch? I don't see how it would be possible to remember one branch." From time to time a flock of birds would explode shrieking from the tangled greenery but the jungle looked so impenetrable that Marina couldn't imagine how birds were able to fly into it. How could one bird ever make its way back to the nest? How could Easter remember the best place to tie the boat?

"It has been my observation that Easter remembers everything," Dr. Swenson said. "When I said I believed that his intelligence may be above average I didn't mean it sentimentally."

Every act the boy performed was done with a graceful efficiency of movement: he shut down the engine, tied a knot, turned around to nod at Dr. Swenson.

"Very good!" she said, holding two thumbs up.

Easter smiled. The minute they were properly moored he became a child again, the one that Marina had first seen outside the opera house, the one Jackie had held in his arms. The boat was now the responsibility of the tree and for these moments he could be on his own. He pointed to the water and looked again to Dr. Swenson. She nodded, and as quickly as she could move her head he pulled off his T-shirt, showing them the smooth brown skin of his chest, the matchstick of his torso. He scrambled on top of two boxes of canned apricots and flying up and over the ropes that stood in place for a proper railing he launched his body rocket-wise, up and over, up and out, out and into the brown water with a resounding splash, his knees pulled up to his chest, his chin tucked in, his arms lifted up to the light. And then he was gone.

Marina was at the edge of the boat in two steps while Dr. Swenson made herself busy looking for something in a brown paper bag. The water was velvety, undisturbed by the weight of so small a boy. It didn't even trouble itself to give up a reflection the way most water would. There was nothing on the surface and nothing beneath it. "Where is he!" Marina cried.

"Oh, that's part of the trick. He thinks he's scaring me to death. That's the big fun of it all." Dr. Swenson rooted through a bag of loose items. "Do you eat peanut butter? Americans are all determined to be allergic to peanuts these days."

"I can't see him!" The water was as impenetrable as the earth itself. The boy had been swallowed whole, a minnow, a thought.

Dr. Swenson raised her head and, looking in Marina's direction, she sighed. "There is a great temptation to tease you, Dr. Singh. Your earnestness makes you very vulnerable to that, I'm sure. The child has the lungs of a Japanese pearl diver. He'll resurface two-thirds of the way across in a direct line with the boat." She waited one count. "Now."

And up came the head of the boy who flipped his wet hair aside and raised his hand and waved. The light on the planes of his face made him golden. Even at this distance she could see his enormous inhalation before he dove again, this time kicking his legs up straight so that the light caught the pink soles of his feet before they disappeared. Marina sank down on the case of apricots, the place from which those feet had so recently catapulted, and she cried.

"Peanut butter and marmalade," Dr. Swenson said, dealing out six slices of bread along the top of a box as if it were a poker game. She twisted closed the plastic bag with a piece of wire and picked up a battered knife with a long narrow blade. She stuck the blade into a jar of marmalade. "Rodrigo got the Wilkins and Son. Now there is a man who knows how to keep his customer's business. One underestimates the pleasures of marmalade until one has been separated from it. Be sure to enjoy the bread. When this loaf goes that's it, no more. It just doesn't keep. I bring back yeast and they bake some but it has almost nothing in common with the store-bought bread. This, I must say, is delicious."

She had thought he was dead, and as stupid as that was she could not control her imagination. Of course the boy could dive, could swim. He would come back in the boat and take them where they needed to go. How had she become so dependent on a deaf child in less than twenty-four hours? What in the world was she crying for?

"Pull yourself together, Dr. Singh," Dr. Swenson said, keeping her attention fixed on the even distribution of peanut butter over bread. "He'll be back on the boat in a minute and it will upset him greatly to see you carrying on. He's a deaf child. He does everything to make you forget that, so it is your responsibility as the adult to remember. You can't explain to him why you're crying. I have not invented a sign with which to convey foolishness, so you cannot tell him you are just being foolish. You'll frighten him, so stop it." Easter was on the surface now doing an extravagant backstroke and the sound of his splashing was soothing to both of the women in the boat. Using the same knife, Dr. Swenson cut the sandwiches into triangles and left them there on the box. "Come and get your lunch now," she said to Marina. It was an imperative rather than an invitation.

Marina pressed her eyes against the sleeve of her shirt. "It just scared me. That's all," she said. Neither her voice nor her explanation sounded convincing.

"We aren't even there yet," Dr. Swenson said, and took a triangle of sandwich for herself. "You're going to have to toughen up or as God is my witness I will put you on the shore right here. There are more frightening things in the jungle than a boy going swimming in a still stretch of river."

After Easter was back on the boat, as sleek and damp as a seal, and the sandwiches had been eaten (he handled the peanut butter jar with such gentle affection afterwards that Dr. Swenson consented to make him another), it was announced that there would be a nap. "Sesta," Dr. Swenson said, and clapped her hands. The Portuguese made it sound essential. "It is said the sesta is one of the only gifts the Europeans brought to South America, but I imagine the Brazilians could have figured out how to sleep in the afternoon without having to endure centuries of murder and enslavement." She tapped Easter and pointed to a low trunk in front of the steering wheel, then she closed her eyes and rested her head against her folded hands in a child's pantomime of sleep. Having his directions, the boy pulled two hammocks from the box and then set to clipping them onto poles beneath the shade of the boat's tarp.

"Before I came to the jungle I didn't believe in napping," Dr. Swenson said, choosing the hammock nearest the steering wheel for herself. "I thought of it as a sign of weakness. But this country could make a napper out of anyone. It is important to pay attention to what the body is telling us." She settled herself into the long piece of fabric and when she leaned back and lifted up her feet the hammock swallowed her whole. Marina looked at her teacher, a low-hanging lump cocooned in striped cotton swaying from side to side, the energy of her lying down to rest creating motion. "Go to sleep now, Dr. Singh," the muffled voice said. "It will do your nerves a world of good."

It was as if Dr. Swenson had vanished from the boat, as surely as Easter had vanished from it when he went over the side. Marina watched the hammock until its motion had settled. It was a magic trick: wrap her in a blanket and she's gone. The quiet that was left without her was layered, subtle: at first Marina heard it only as silence, the absence of human voices, but once her ear had settled into it the other sounds began to rise, the deeply forested chirping, the caw that came from the tops of trees, the chattering of lower primates, the incessant sawing of insect life. It was not unlike the overture of the opera in which the well-trained listener could draw forth the piccolos, the soft French horn, a single meaningful viola. She leaned out from the shade's protection and looked into the sun. Her watch said two o'clock. Easter sat on the deck in front of one of the many boxes that made up their furniture, a ballpoint pen in his right hand. Marina touched the empty hammock and then pointed to him. She folded her hands together and rested her head on them.

Easter shook his head, pointed to her, the hammock. He closed his eyes and dropped his chin. When she only stood there watching him he pointed again, this time using the pen for emphasis. She was supposed to go in the hammock.

It wasn't a bad idea. She was tired. Still, she had the feeling that vigilance was in order. Didn't someone need to stay awake and watch the jungle? Didn't someone need to make sure the child did not fall overboard?

Easter got up and spread out the fabric with both hands, holding it open for her like an envelope and nodding instructively, as if perhaps the operation of a hammock was confusing to her. So he would watch the jungle. He would make sure she did not fall into the water. Obediently, she sat down, she lay down, and when she was settled in, Easter put his hand on her forehead and held it there as if she were a sick child. He smiled at her, and smiling back she closed her eyes. She was on a river in a boat in Brazil. She was in the Amazon taking a nap with Dr. Swenson.

She had had a good imagination as a child, though it had been systematically chipped apart by years of studying inorganic chemistry and charting lipids. These days Marina put her faith in data, the world she trusted was one that she could measure. But even with a truly magnificent imagination she could not have put herself in the jungle. She felt something slip across her rib cage—an insect? a bead of sweat? She kept still, looking out through the top of the hammock at the bright split of daylight in front of her. The midday heat tacked her into place. She thought about medical school, the fluorescent halls of that first hospital, the stacks of textbooks that made her back ache as she lugged them home from the library. Had she known that Dr. Swenson caught the last flight to Manaus after Thursday's lecture on endometrial tissue, would she have wished that she could come along? Could she have seen herself in the Amazon at the side of her teacher on an expedition that forged ahead in science's name? Dr. Swenson certainly had no trouble envisioning herself in the Amazon with Dr. Rapp when she was a student. Wasn't it possible that she could have managed the same? Marina attempted to shift the knot of her hair to one side so that she was not lying on it so directly and in doing so set herself back into a gentle rocking. The answer was no. Marina had been a very good student, but she only raised her hand when she was certain of the answer. She excelled not through bright bursts of inspiration but by the hard labor of a field horse pulling a plow. On the few occasions Dr. Swenson noticed her she had approved, but she had never been able to remember Marina's name.

When the rocking stopped Marina tilted her hips back and forth to start it up again. There were layers upon layers of scents inside the hammock—the smell of her own sweat which brought up trace amounts of soap and shampoo; the smell of the hammock itself which was both mildewed and sunbaked with a slight hint of rope; the smell of the boat, gasoline and oil; and the smell of the world outside the boat, the river water and the great factory of leaves pumping oxygen into the atmosphere, the tireless photosynthesis of plants turning sunlight into energy, not that photosynthesis had an odor. Marina inhaled deeply and the scent of the air relaxed her. Brought together, all those disparate elements turned into something wholly pleasant. She wouldn't have thought that would be the case.

Marina closed her eyes. She could feel the boat wagging gently in the current of the river as it pulled on its line. She could feel the light and layered motion of the water coming up through the boat and up the poles that held the hammock and from there into the hammock and into her bones, and that was the movement that sent her to sleep.

Her father was there, but he was in a terrible rush. She was going back to the university with him. He was late for the class he was teaching and the streets of Calcutta were packed in a human knot, more and more people pushing to find their place on the pavement, so many students rushing to get to class themselves. She held his hand as a way to keep from losing him in the crowd and she thought of how they must look, the two of them holding hands. When a woman walking quickly in the opposite direction with a sack of rice on her head wedged herself between them as if there was no other way she could possibly go, Marina latched onto the back of her father's belt before he had the chance to slip away. She was trying to outsmart the dream. She knew it well enough by now. Her father was so fast! She was looking at the little bit of gray in the back of his hair, which was still very thick and mostly black, when suddenly a man with a cart full of bicycle tires rushed at them. How could he get so much speed in this crush? The dream was intent on its own historical set of rules—it is written that the two of them must be divided—and so he rammed his cart between them as if he meant to go through her arm. The blow hit her with such velocity that she went flying up into the air. It was like a dream, and for the instant she was above the crowd she saw everything, all the people and the animals, the terrible shacks that lined the road to the grand houses, the beggars and their bowls, the gates of the university, her father's slim shoulders as he dashed ahead unencumbered by her weight. She saw everything, the impossibility of everything, before she crashed down on the pavement, the entire weight of her body coming onto her elbow.

"Is it a snake?" Dr. Swenson shouted at her. "Have you been bitten, Dr. Singh?"

Marina was on the deck of the boat. It was a very slight distance to fall. Suspended in her hammock she had been no more than three feet off the ground, but be that as it may the ground had come up hard and knocked the wind out of her. When she opened her eyes she saw feet in tennis shoes and beside them, small brown feet. She took another minute to breathe.

"Dr. Singh, answer me! Is there a snake?"

"No," Marina said, her left cheek pressed hard to the filthy wood.

"Then why were you screaming?" The boat was moving now and Dr. Swenson gave Easter a poke in the shoulder and pointed him back to the wheel. They had resumed their journey at some point and for a minute there had been no one driving.

Oh, she could think of so many reasons to be screaming, not the least of which was the fire in every bone on the left side of her body. Marina eased over onto her back. She moved her left fingers gently and then explored the range of movement in her left wrist. She moved her feet from side to side to complete the inventory. Nothing broken. The fabric she had been sleeping in was now hanging just above her face. "I was having a dream."

Dr. Swenson reached up and unclipped Marina's hammock from the pole and then walked around her to the other side to take the hammock down. It had the effect of someone throwing open the draperies. The sunlight flooded her vision. Without intending to, Marina was looking up the bottom of Dr. Swenson's shirt and saw the soft white ledge of her belly where it met the line of her drawstring pants. "I thought you had been bitten by a snake."

"Yes, I understand that." Marina was shivering slightly in the heat. She closed her right hand, tried to feel her father's belt.

"There are lanceheads in these parts and they aren't geniuses for hanging on to their branches. It is as stupid a snake as it is deadly. Everyone here knows someone who met their end stepping on a lancehead. They are perfectly camouflaged and they do nothing to get out of the way or make their presence known except for sinking their teeth into your ankle. Easter once kept me from putting my foot in the middle of one all coiled up in our camp. It must have been two meters long and it didn't look any different from a pile of leaves and dirt. Even when he showed it to me I didn't see it at first." She stopped and gave herself a quick shake.

"Was I about to step on one?"

"They do occasionally fall into boats," Dr. Swenson said tersely. "They like to get under things or into things. A hammock is a reasonable place for a snake to hide. It was startling, your screaming. I had to turn you out to see if there was a snake in there with you."

"You turned the hammock over?" Marina had assumed she had thrown herself out in the course of her dream.

"Of course I did. Did you expect me to find the snake without waking you?"

Marina shook her head. Had there been a two-meter snake in her hammock, flinging it onto the ground while flinging Marina on top of it would likely not have saved her from being bitten, but where snakes were concerned people often made hurried decisions. She closed her eyes and covered them with both hands. Dr. Swenson would have thought she was thinking of the snake but she was thinking of her father. No one said anything for a while and then she felt something very cold tapping against her shoulder.

"Sit up," Dr. Swenson said. "Drink a bottle of water. Sit up now. There's ice on the boat. Do you want any ice?"

Marina shook her head.

"Ice is a luxury confined to this moment. If you want any ice, this is your chance. Sit up now, Dr. Singh. I can't stand to see a person lying on this deck. It's vile. You had a dream. Now sit up and drink your water."

Marina sat up and then, remembering the cockroaches, she pulled herself back onto the box of grapefruit juice. Her head hurt. Then she noticed that the box she was sitting on was covered in letters, letters she was sure hadn't been there earlier. It was a printed uppercase alphabet of an irregular size, or most of the alphabet. The letter K was gone, and when she moved her thigh she saw the Q was missing as well. Some letters, like the A, were perfectly rendered, while others, R and Z, were backwards. At the end of the string of letters were two words, EASTER and ANDERS, followed by a rudimentary drawing of a snail. Marina touched her fingers to Anders' name. "What's this about?"

"That is one of the many legacies left by your friend Dr. Eckman. I'm sure there are more I have yet to come across. In the brief amount of time he was with us he managed to teach Easter the fundamentals of table manners as well as the alphabet, or most of the alphabet. I see the K is missing."

"And he can write their names."

"I thought it was interesting that those were the two words he chose to teach the boy. Easter, well, that makes sense, but Anders? Still, he was very sick at the end. Maybe he felt it was a way to be remembered."

Marina could see him sitting on a log, a pad of paper out across his knees, Easter pressed in close beside him. Of course he could teach a boy how to make his letters. He'd done it three times before. It wouldn't make any difference to him that Easter couldn't hear. *This is who you are,* Anders tells him, pointing to Easter's name. Then he points to his own, *This is who I am.*

"Dr. Eckman wrote everything out for him, a sort of study chart. Easter practices constantly. I let him keep Dr. Eckman's pens when he died. For a while he was making letters all over his arms and legs but I put a stop to that. I don't know how much of the ink is absorbed through the skin but it can't be good for a child. It's a bad habit when there's plenty of perfectly usable paper. I don't know what he thinks the letters are exactly, but he remembers them, most of them. He gets them in the right order."

"Maybe he thinks of them as something that belonged to Anders."

Dr. Swenson nodded. She watched the boy watch the river. "Easter cries out in his sleep. It's the only time I've heard his voice, but he has one. Months go by and I don't hear him, but since Dr. Eckman died he's had nightmares every night. It's a terrible sound he makes." Dr. Swenson turned then and let her eyes stay on Marina's. "It's a shame you can't talk to him about it. It's something that the two of you have in common. I will assume that the issue for you is mefloquine and that Mr. Fox did not send me a doctor with a debilitating mental illness."

"I'm taking Lariam." She wished she could bring back the box of grapefruit juice for Karen. It was, all things considered, a remarkable achievement.

"I've seen my share of screamers down here but when it happens I never think of Lariam. In the moment I always think it's a snake."

"Better to be safe."

Dr. Swenson nodded. "Lariam is for tourists, Dr. Singh. I sincerely hope you are a tourist, out of here in the next canoe. But short of that I suggest you throw those pills in the river. Do you think I take Lariam? A person can't live here having screaming nightmares and paranoia and suicidal fantasies. The jungle is hard enough without that."

"I haven't been suicidal."

"Well, good for you. It can still come. I knew a young man who walked into the river one night and didn't walk out. The natives saw him, thought he was going for a swim."

"I don't take it because I enjoy it, believe me."

"Ever more the reason not to take it. It affects certain people quite seriously. I would say given this display that you're one of them."

Marina drew a slow breath in, held it, let it out. She could feel herself coming back even as the fire was raised in her arm. "All the same though, I'd rather not get malaria."

"Well, I wouldn't say it's rampant. I haven't gotten it, or I got it once but it wasn't here. And there is after all a cure."

"Was Anders taking Lariam?"

Dr. Swenson put her hands in her hair and gave her scalp an aggressive scratch. "He didn't scream in his sleep so we never had the opportunity to discuss it. Are you asking me if Dr. Eckman died of malaria?"

It hadn't been what she was asking, though it was a perfectly reasonable question. "It seems possible."

"Malaria is something of a specialty of mine," Dr. Swenson said. "So I can tell you no. Not unless it was *P. falciparum* that turned cerebral. That would be a true rarity, of course, there isn't a great deal of *P. falciparum* in these parts."

P. falciparum, P. vivax, P. malariae, and there was one more. When was the last time Marina needed to know the strains of malaria?

"*P. ovale,*" Dr. Swenson said.

"You think he might have had *P. ovale*?"

"No, that's the one you can't remember. Mention a strain of malaria to any doctor and they try to remember the other three, but no one remembers *P. ovale*. You see very little of it outside West Africa. Do you have the same dream every time?"

Marina had been too recently asleep to understand everything, too recently on this boat, too recently discussing snakes, too recently in Calcutta, too recently with Anders. *P. ovale*? "More or less."

"I find mefloquine interesting in that way, how it taps into a single pocket of the subconscious. You could just as easily use it as a treatment as you could a preventative medicine. There's no sense suffering in advance. It wouldn't do you much good with cerebral malaria but as I said, that would be an extremely rare presentation in Brazil. What are your dreams about, Dr. Singh?"

What are your dreams about? her mother asked her when she was a child screaming in her bed. *What did you dream?* Mr. Fox asked, his hands holding the tops of her arms. "My father," Marina said. "I'm with my father and then we're separated somehow. I can't find him."

Dr. Swenson stood up with some difficulty. The interview had reached its conclusion. "Well, that doesn't sound too bad."

Marina would concede the point. When presented as a single sentence without embellishment it didn't sound bad at all.

Seven

At dusk the insects came down in a storm, the hard-shelled and soft-sided, the biting and stinging, the chirping and buzzing and droning, every last one unfolded its paper wings and flew with unimaginable velocity into the eyes and mouths and noses of the only three humans they could find. Easter slipped back inside his shirt while Dr. Swenson and Marina wrapped their heads like Bedouins in a storm. When it was fully dark only the misguided insects pelted themselves into the people on board while the rest chose to end their lives against the two bright, hot lights on either side of the boat. The night was filled with the relentless ping of their bodies hitting the glass.

"Dr. Rapp used to say how easy it was for the entomologists," Dr. Swenson said, turning her back to the onslaught. "They only had to switch on a light and all their specimens came running."

Marina was less comfortable in the jungle now that she couldn't see it. She felt the plant life pressing against the edges of the water, straining towards them, every root and tendril reaching. "Not only do the specimens come to you, they then have the decency to kill themselves."

"This is worse than a hailstorm," Dr. Swenson said, spitting a small winged beetle onto the deck. "We can do without the lights." And then she turned off the lights.

In an instant the veil of insects lifted and Marina saw nothing as she had never seen nothing before. It was as if God Himself had turned out the lights, every last one, and left them in the gaping darkness of His abandonment. "Shouldn't Easter be able to see where he's going?" she asked. She could barely hear the sound of her own voice over the engine. A boy who could find a single branch in a thousand miles of uninterrupted trees could surely find his way home in the dark. She was the one who wanted the lights back on.

"Open your eyes, Dr. Singh," Dr. Swenson said. "Look at the stars."

Marina put her hands out in front of her and batted at the air until she found the rope at the edge of the boat. She held tightly to it when she leaned to the side. Beyond the spectrum of darkness she saw the bright stars scattered across the table of the night sky and felt as if she had never seen such things as stars before. She did not know enough numbers to count them, and even if she did, the stars could not be separated one from the other, the whole was so much greater than the sum of its parts. She saw the textbook of constellations, the heroes of mythology posing on fields of ink. She could see the milkiness in everything now, the way the sky was spread over with light. And when, finally, she could tear herself away from the theater above them to look forward again she saw yet another light blinking like a mirage on the horizon. It was small and orange and as they came towards it, the light appeared to stretch into a single line, and when she thought she had the line fixed in her vision it broke apart. It scattered and spread, bits of it popping on and off. "There's something up there," she said to Dr. Swenson, and in another minute she said, "It's fire." What she meant to say was *Turn the boat around.*

"Indeed," Dr. Swenson said.

It was a dozen fires, and then the fires tripled, and then Marina could no longer count them. What had been a line had spread into layers, and in those layers the circles of light lifted and fell. Was the fire in the tops of trees? Was it somehow burning in the water? Easter turned the lights of the boat back on and instantly the fire began to leap. A ululation of voices exploded the night, the ringing sound of countless tongues hitting the roofs of countless mouths. It filled the entire jungle and poured up the river in a wave.

There were people on the banks of the river.

They were going to meet the tribe. That had always been the point of the expedition, so why hadn't Marina thought of it before now? What had made the jungle so uncomfortable all this time was its absence of people. All the jungle had offered thus far were plants and insects, clinging vines and unseen animals, and that was bad enough, but now Marina realized that people were truly the worst-case scenario. It was like being alone on a dark city street and suddenly turning a corner to find a group of young men staring menacingly from a doorway. "Lakashi?" Marina asked, hoping they were at the very least facing a known factor.

"Yes," Dr. Swenson said.

Marina waited for a moment, hoping for more than a one word affirmation. She was on an unnamed river in the middle of nowhere in the middle of the night feeling very much the same way she always felt with Dr. Swenson, like Oliver Twist holding up his empty bowl. Would it have been too much to ask for the simple acknowledgment that these were no doubt unfamiliar circumstances? Dr. Swenson could have even extended herself enough to tell the story of the first time she had encountered the Lakashi, *Lucky for me it was daylight then,* or, *I certainly was grateful that Dr. Rapp knew what to do,* but that of course would require Dr. Swenson to be someone else entirely. The boat crept its way towards the waving, spinning flames until they were close enough that Marina could just make out the shape of heads behind each of the fires, every man and woman waving a burning stick, children holding slim burning branches, jumping and calling. She could see the trails of sparks as they splintered off and flew in every direction, extinguishing themselves before they touched the ground. In their magnitude those sparks were reminiscent of stars. The sound was also more nuanced the closer they came to it: too forceful for any flock of birds, too rhythmic for any animal. Marina remembered a funeral her father had taken her to as a child, thousands of lights in paper cups floating down the Ganges, the people crowded onto the banks, walking into the water, cutting through the night air filled with incense and smoke. She could smell the rot of the water beneath the blanket of flowers. At the time the spectacle had frightened her so badly she buried her face in her father's shirt and kept it there for the rest of the night, but now she was grateful for the little she had seen. It didn't explain what was spread out before her but it reminded her of all the things she didn't understand. "What do you think has happened?" Marina asked. Some of the people on the shore were dropping their fire now. They were walking into the water and swimming towards the boat. It was quite clear to Marina how people could get on the boat but she wasn't able to see how she could get off.

"What do you mean?" Dr. Swenson said. *What do you mean, Dr. Singh, when you say stage-two cervical cancer?*

Marina, beyond words, extended her open arms to the shore ahead.

Dr. Swenson looked down at the men who swam towards them. They kept their long throats stretched up like turtles so that they could avoid getting water in their open mouths as they called and cried. Then she looked back at her guest as if she could not believe she was yet again being bothered by the timid rabbits and their foolish questions. "We've come back," she said.

Marina turned away from the ebullient welcome, the burning and hopping and splashing, the never-ending sound of *la-la-la-la-la*, and turned back to Dr. Swenson, who was nodding her head towards the masses with a sort of weary acceptance. "You were only gone for a night."

"They never believe it. It doesn't matter how many times I tell them. Their sense of time lacks—" But she didn't finish her sentence. The boat had sharply listed to the right as the men began to hang on to the pontoon on one side and then push themselves up. The case of grapefruit juice slid abruptly, hitting Marina in the ankles and very nearly throwing her into the ones who were just now pulling themselves out of the water. She caught a pole and righted herself. This was the reason Marina's father always insisted on renting a pontoon boat in those early summers: not only was it easier to navigate and impossible to sink, it would have been very easy to reboard if one of them had fallen over. But no one ever did fall over. The theory was not put to the test. Dripping, the men hoisted themselves on to the deck and stood. They were considerably smaller than Marina, though taller than Dr. Swenson, wearing nylon running shorts and sopping T-shirts that advertised American products—Nike and Mr. Bubble. One of them wore a Peterbilt hat. They slapped their open hands against Easter, his arms and shoulders and back, as if he were a fire that they were putting out. Easter, clearly pleased, slapped them away. There were seven men on the boat, and then there were nine, all of them crying out with piercing intent. The black water was churning with swimmers and from time to time Easter would swing down the light and shine it into the water which served to consolidate the men like tarpon. They looked up and waved. No one could fault Easter for driving over them, they were swarming, but when the slow moving pontoon pressed against a shoulder or head the man simply sank beneath it and then popped up again later, assuming it was the same man popping up there. How many boats throughout history had been met by such enthusiastic locals? On the deck a man was looking up at Marina now and he touched her cheek with a wet hand without making eye contact. Two men behind her petted her hair. A fourth man ran his fingers down her forearm in a way that was almost too gentle to be endured. It was as if she were being greeted in a school for the blind. When a fifth reached up and cupped her breast, Dr. Swenson clapped her hands together sharply.

"Enough of that," she said, and the men with their hands on Marina jumped back onto the toes of ones standing behind them who were waiting their turn, which caused all of them to still their tongues in their mouths and look at Dr. Swenson with expectation. In that moment Marina knew two things for certain: the Lakashi did not speak English, did not know the word *enough,* and that despite this minor hindrance they would do whatever Dr. Swenson told them. The snap in Dr. Swenson's voice had driven Marina's pulse higher than the men with their wet fingers. They, after all, seemed more curious than menacing. In this hierarchy, Dr. Swenson was the uncontested kingpin and Marina felt herself to be closer to the natives than to their ruler. "Go on," Dr. Swenson said, and pointed to the side of the boat, where one by one they walked obediently off the edge, often landing on some unfortunate in the water. "They are an extremely tactile people," Dr. Swenson said when the last one had disappeared with a splash. "They don't mean anything by it. If they can't touch it, it doesn't exist."

"They don't touch you," Marina said, running her sleeve over her face.

Dr. Swenson nodded. "At this point they know I exist. I've been able to do away with the rest of it."

There was a narrow dock sticking out of the bank, a single, beckoning finger, and Easter brought up the boat snug alongside it, at which point the men handed their burning sticks to the women and boarded the boat in an orderly fashion, picking up boxes and baggage and carrying them off into the night. Most of them gave Marina a tap on the shoulder or stopped to touch the side of her head, but there was work to be done and no one lingered. Now it was the women who were singing out, and as Marina left the boat with Easter and Dr. Swenson they raised their torches overhead to cast a wider band of light. They wore homemade shift dresses in dull colors and kept their hair in long braids down their backs. There were children tied across their chests in slings, children holding on to their ankles, children balanced on hips, their dark round eyes reflecting the fire all around them. Dr. Swenson trudged up the dirt path into the jungle, nodding from time to time at the women who trilled their vowels in rapture. The children on the ground reached out and touched Marina's pants, women ran their fingers around her ears and tapped at her collarbone. Occasionally a child, a very small one, would extend a hand to Dr. Swenson and the mother would snatch it back.

"They didn't know you were coming tonight," Marina said, hurrying a bit to be closer to Dr. Swenson. She even went so far as to put a hand on her arm. "Sometimes you stay longer in Manaus, two nights, three nights."

"Sometimes I stay a week," Dr. Swenson said, looking forward. "I don't enjoy it but it happens."

A pregnant woman reached into the path in front of them and pulled back a low-hanging branch from a tree.

"But if they have no sense of time, and you have no means of contacting them, how do they know when you're coming back?"

"They don't."

"Then how did they know to stage all of this tonight?"

Dr. Swenson stopped and turned to Marina. The terrible darkness was broken apart by so many separate fires that the shadows, like the voices, came at them from every direction. From time to time a chunk of burning stick would fall into a pile of leaves. It was hard to understand how the entire forest had not been reduced to a pile of smoldering ash. "I suppose they do it every night when I'm gone. I don't actually know. You can ask Dr. Nkomo in the morning. I'm going to say good night, Dr. Singh. Easter will get you settled from here. I'm tired now." As she spoke the words, Dr. Swenson began to weave a bit from side to side and Marina took a firmer hold on her arm. Dr. Swenson closed her eyes. "I'm alright," she said, and then she looked at Marina. She seemed to struggle for her breath. "Sometimes this is more difficult than I had imagined." Dr. Swenson held out her hand and a woman standing beside the path, a woman with one sleeping child tied across her chest and two more children, twins perhaps, holding either calf, took that hand and led her forward into the night. As Dr. Swenson walked away, all the light and sound went with her, the crowd formed itself around the fire she was holding. It should have been Marina who asked for a torch because before very long she was standing alone in the dark.

She would have worried about Dr. Swenson then, how the Amazon appeared to be defeating her, but instead thought of the lanceheads. She wondered if they slept on the ground or in the trees and, if it was in the trees, did their coils ever loosen in the night? Her best bet was to follow the crowd, to stay within the light, but after taking a few steps she felt uncertain as to where she should put her feet. There was so much crackling and breaking all around her. Small thorns tugged at her clothes and she was certain something was crawling on her neck. Just as she was about to call out she saw a light coming up from the direction of the dock, a light that formed itself in a long, steady beam. A flashlight! She felt as if she had never seen anything so modern in her life. Clearly it was Easter who was coming for her. Easter didn't use a flashlight like a boy. He kept the light focused on the path. He didn't shine it in Marina's eyes or illuminate the tops of trees. When he got to her he took her hand and together they walked further into the jungle. There was a sort of narrow path, although it could have been nothing more than a random break in the growth of underbrush. Marina stayed one step behind Easter, putting down her feet in the places from which his feet had been lifted while Easter cleared everything in their way, low-hanging vines and spiderwebs of such size and strength they could have easily ensnared a small pig. Marina's attention was so wholly focused on her feet that she didn't see where they were going until they stopped. The place that Easter brought her to was a tin box built onto stilts. He leaned over and lifted up a rock, took out a key, and unlocked the door. Marina had not expected a door in the jungle, much less a lock. Inside the room Easter swept the flashlight over a table and some chairs, stacks of boxes, some of which she thought she recognized: the juice, the hash. They were in the storage room. Easter, who kept hold of her hand even now, led her to the back of the room where they went through a second door and out onto a wide porch, or maybe it was a room as well. It was hard to tell. There was no breeze other than what was stirred up by a hundred thousand wings of flying insects. Easter pointed the light to a long column of mosquito netting that was suspended from the ceiling and fanned out over a cot. He pointed to her, to the cot. All of this would be different in the daylight. Nothing would feel so daunting once she could properly see.

When she sat down on the edge of her bed, Marina realized that in her concern about fire and snakes and the wandering hands of the natives she had walked off and left her suitcase on the boat, and while she would have liked to change out of her clothes and brush her teeth she wasn't even sure where she could find a basin of water. She could imagine no pantomime for Easter that would express her desire to be accompanied back to the boat and she wasn't about to make the trip on her own, and so she decided to forget about the whole business. What she would have liked was the telephone. She should have called Mr. Fox before they left Manaus. She knew by now he would have left a dozen messages and that when she listened to them in the morning she would be able to chart the panic mounting in his voice. It had been nothing but petulance on her part, his punishment to spend the day not knowing where she was, and now that it was too dark to try and find the phone there was no way to comfort him. Or maybe he would think she was halfway to Miami now, coming home on the next flight the way she had told him she would, although Marina didn't think he had ever really believed her.

She took off her shoes and pointed to Easter. *You sleep?* He turned the flashlight to a wall six feet from the foot of her bed and showed her a hammock, an empty casing waiting for a boy. Then, handing her the flashlight, he pulled off his shirt and climbed inside while she stood there shining the light in his direction, dumbstruck by the little hanging cocoon he made. By her good fortune, she was sleeping in Easter's room. She tried to imagine it was a stroke of extraordinary kindness on Dr. Swenson's part when in fact it was probably the only bit of available space covered by a roof. It didn't matter; she realized now she could never have slept there without him. In her cot, beneath her net, Marina could easily calculate the ways in which her circumstances could have been worse. She stretched out and clicked off the light, listening to the steady breathing of the jungle. This was better than the Hotel Indira. The cot was no less comfortable than that bed. Clearly the Lakashi were prepared for guests no matter how insistently Dr. Swenson claimed to dislike them. People had come and stayed here before and probably they had all lain beneath this mosquito net thanking God that Easter's hammock was six feet away. Marina opened her eyes. In the dim light of the moon she looked into the white cloud of her net. Anders would have slept here. Easter was with him when he died, that's what Dr. Swenson had said. She sat up. Anders. It came over her, this dark, this porch, this cot. In his fever he looked through this net. Marina got up, put her feet back in her shoes. There had to be a pen somewhere. She got the flashlight, checked the small figure of Easter supine in his cloth. She had nothing, not a handbag, a rucksack. She went back into the storage room. Now that she held the light she could see that it functioned as nothing more than an outsized closet—boxes and boxes, plastic bins, plastic tubs, boxes of food, bottles of water, smaller boxes of test tubes and slides. She found a broom, a pile of cloths, a giant spool of twine. There was not a drawer or a shelf. There was not a logical place to put a pen, there was no logic to any of it. And then she remembered that Anders' pens had gone to Easter when he died. That was the boy's legacy, a handful of Bics. She went back to the sleeping porch, shined the light on some buckets, traced the beam of light around the line where the wall met the floor, and there, just beneath the hammock, she saw a metal box, bigger than the kind used for documents and smaller than the kind used for tackle or tools. She went down on her knees and reached beneath the boy, slid the metal over the rough hewn planks of flooring. There was no lock, just a fold-over hasp that kept the box shut. On the top was a small metal tray full of feathers and she held them up in groups of two and three and four, more than two dozen feathers in colors Marina had never realized feathers came in, lavender and iridescent yellow, each one perfectly clean, the barbs zipped up tight. In the tray there was a rock that in its size and marking looked startlingly like a human eyeball. There was a perfect fossil of a prehistoric fish pressed into shale and a rolled-up red silk ribbon. Beneath the tray was a blue Aerogram envelope with the word EASTER written on the front and when unfolded read: *Please do all that is within your power to help this boy reach the United States and you will be rewarded. Take him to Karen Eckman.* There was his address, his phone number. *All expenses will be reimbursed. REWARD. Thank you, Anders Eckman.* Beneath that, the note was written out again in Anders' college Spanish. He did not speak Portuguese and so the Spanish was his best chance. Marina sat back on her heels. There was a pocket-sized spiral notebook that contained the alphabet, a letter on each page, each of them printed in uppercase, and at the end the word *Easter* and then the word *Anders* and then the word *Minnesota.* Anders' driver's license was in the bottom of the box along with his passport. Maybe Easter had wanted his picture or Anders wanted him to have it. There were three twenty dollar bills. There were five rubber bands, a half dozen pens, a handful of coins, American and Brazilian. Marina was dizzy. She had meant to wake the boy up, to write the word *Anders,* one of the three words he knew. She would point to the word and then point to her bed. *Did Anders sleep here?* but she didn't have to ask the question now. She put everything back the way she had found it. She arranged the feathers, closed the lid, and slid the box to the wall. She turned off the flashlight and followed the moon back to Anders' bed and crawled inside. He had shown her his passport the day it came in the mail. The cardboard cover was stiff. His picture captured nothing of him. Even the color was off. The picture on his driver's license was better. "You didn't have a passport?" she asked him.

"I did," he said, sitting on her desk and looking over her shoulder so he could see it again. "My junior year of college."

Marina looked up at him then. "Where did you go?" Marina regretted that she had never spent a year abroad. She could never bear the thought of being so far from home.

"Barcelona," he said, lisping shamelessly. "My parents wanted me to go to Norway. But who leaves Minnesota for a semester abroad in Norway? When I was there I never thought I'd go home. I used to write the letter in my head to my parents, explaining that I was meant for sun and sangria and siestas. I was the happiest American in Spain."

"So what are you doing here?"

Anders shrugged. "My time was up. Somehow I wound up going home. I went to medical school. I never went back." He took the passport from her and looked at it again. "Don't you think the picture is good? I look so serious. I could be a spy."

Marina didn't dream that night. Whatever price the Lariam exacted on her subconscious had been paid that afternoon on the boat, but at some point when she was asleep and dreaming of nothing she was awakened by a breathless cry, the high, hopeless call of an animal in a trap. Marina sat up. "Easter?" she said. She turned on the flashlight and saw such a struggle in his hammock that her immediate thought was a snake. She leapt to her feet, meaning to grab the edges of the fabric and flip it over, to save the boy from what was devouring him, but by the time she had made it out of her net she understood what was happening and she took just a second longer to listen to the sound of his voice, then she reached inside and put her hands on his shoulders. She knew how to wake a person from a dream, how no one ever did it and how it should be done. She shook him gently, letting him flail beneath her hands. He was sweating, shaking, his eyes rolled back. She made all the appropriate sounds he couldn't hear. She whispered, *Okay, it's alright now.* She could not have stopped herself. She took him in her arms and let him cry against her neck while she made him promises, her hand tracing circles in the narrow space between his shoulder blades, and when he could breathe easily again and was falling back into sleep she straightened his hair with her fingers and turned to go back to her bed and he followed her there and climbed beneath the net. Marina had never slept with a child before, not since she was a child herself and had slumber parties with other girls, but it wasn't a science. She made a space for him beneath her arm and pulled his back against her chest and before there was another thought they were both asleep, safe in the white tunnel of net.

At some point during the night the fire juggling, fiercely screaming Lakashi had been replaced by a working-class tribe, a sober group of people who went about the business of their day without fanfare or flame. Marina found them by following a path to a clearing on the banks of the river, although when she had walked through this spot the night before she would have sworn it was solid jungle. There were women washing clothes in the river and washing children, women gathering sticks into baskets and braiding the hair of girls, every movement they made exposed to the merciless sunshine. There was a large assortment of naked toddlers slapping the water with their hands and stamping in puddles, so many toddlers and crawling babies that Marina wondered if she had wandered into the tribal day care. There were fewer men in evidence but still there were a handful of them carving down the inside of a very large log. They were shirtless, shoeless, and when Marina walked by them they gave her a brief, disinterested glance as if she were a tourist and they had seen her kind before. Boats, of course, were key to river life, and other logs carved into boats were jumbled together on the shore, and in the water a man was paddling away. Two small girls came by wearing shorts and no shirts, each of them with a tiny monkey around her neck that held on to its own prehensile tail with its hands to form a clasp. The monkeys both swiveled their heads towards Marina and showed her their pointy yellow teeth in extravagant smiles. The monkeys alone looked her in the eye. Then one of the monkeys caught sight of some infinitesimal life form in the hair of his little girl and reached up and snatched it off her scalp and swallowed it.

Marina had not as yet been able to locate the two people she knew on this river. Easter was not in her bed when she woke up this morning, not in his hammock, and she marveled at the thought that anyone could be quiet enough not to wake her, especially a child who was himself unacquainted with sound. She hadn't found Dr. Swenson yet either but that she imagined would be more of a challenge. Dr. Swenson was either standing right in front of you or she could not be located, and in this case there was no waiting outside her office door hoping she would turn up.

The pontoon boat swayed lightly on its rope at the edge of the dock exactly where it had been left the night before and Marina took this as a sign that for the moment all was well. When she went on board the men who had been scraping at the log stopped what they were doing and stood up straight to stare at her, their curved knives tapping against their thighs. It was a matter of seconds before she established her bag was not on board. The deck was empty and there was no place a piece of luggage could be hidden away. Marina ran her tongue over her teeth and thought again of her toothbrush. The morning was already hot and the air was thick with the smell of leaves rotting and leaves unfolding. Down by the water the mosquitoes helped themselves to her ankles and dug a well into the nape of her neck. One flew down the back of her shirt to bite beneath her shoulder blade in a place she would never be able to scratch. She wanted this suitcase much more than she had wanted the one that never arrived in Manaus. She wondered if somewhere in the storage shed where she was sleeping there might be a case of insect repellent, and for the first time she considered the word *insecticide* in relation to the word *homicide.* Suddenly she felt a shift among the Lakashi, a collective straightening of spines that was followed by an animated chatter she could not parse into any words she knew. Then she saw a very tall black man as thin as a drinking straw emerge from the jungle, his small wire glasses glinting sunlight. He dipped his head in every direction in a gesture that was less than a bow but considerably more than a nod, and from every corner the people stood and dipped their heads in return. A few of them called out a phrase of greeting and he repeated it back to them, capturing perfectly the same rhythmic swing at the end of the sentence that threw the crowd into raptures. The women held up their babies and wagged them towards him, the men laid down their knives. They proceeded then to engage in a sort of call-and-response, a person in the tribe throwing out a phrase and the tall man repeating it. No matter how complicated a sentence they served he managed to volley it back. The Lakashi were rocking side to side in complete satisfaction, at which point the man gave a much lower bow that seemed to indicate it had all been great fun but now was the time to return to work.

"Dr. Singh, I presume," he said, walking around a fire to offer his hand to Marina. He wore khaki pants and a blue cotton shirt that looked as if they had been banged out repeatedly on rocks. "Thomas Nkomo. It is a pleasure." His English was so musical and so clearly not his first language that Marina wondered if he had learned to speak it through singing.

"A pleasure," she said, taking his long, thin hand.

"Dr. Swenson told us you would be returning with her. I had wanted to meet you last night, to say welcome, but with everyone turning out to greet you I could not even get close."

"I don't think it was me they were coming to greet." Dr. Swenson told him she would be returning with her?

"The Lakashi like to make things happen. They're always looking for reasons to celebrate."

Marina nodded to the crowd behind them who had sat down to watch their conversation as if it were a theater piece. "You speak their language beautifully."

Thomas Nkomo laughed. "I'm a parrot. What they give me I can return to them. It is the way I learn. They know some Portuguese, the traders come through or they go to Manaus, but I make an attempt to speak Lakashi. One must not be shy where language is concerned."

"I wouldn't know how to start with this one."

"You must first open your mouth."

"Do you understand Lakashi?"

He shrugged. "I know more than I think I do. I have been here two years now. That's time enough to pick up something."

Two years? Just behind the thick scrim of leaves Marina could make out the shape of some huts, a vague outline of civilization. Was there a sort of suburb in the trees that she couldn't see, a place where people could bear to live for years at a time? "So you're working with Dr. Swenson?" Surely Vogel knew and failed to mention to her that they were paying other doctors to work on-site.

"I am working with Dr. Swenson," he said, but he sounded like he was parroting again, that he either didn't believe what he was saying or he hadn't understood the question, then he added, "Our fields of research overlap. And you, Dr. Singh? Dr. Swenson tells us you are employed by Vogel. What is your field?"

"Cholesterol," Marina said, thinking that in all probability no one in the rain forest had ever considered their cholesterol nor did they need to. There were so many lanceheads to step on. "I work as part of a group that does long-range tests with statins."

With that Thomas Nkomo put his long, elegant hands together and pressed the tips of his fingers to his lips, his head moving sadly, slowly from side to side. She saw his gold wedding band bright as a beacon against his skin. The Lakashi, who never stopped watching him, were leaning forward now, concerned to see the distressed look on his face. It was a very long time before he said anything at all. "You are here about our friend then."

Marina blinked. Of all the other doctors who had come here before her the chances were good that only one of them was interested in cholesterol. "Yes."

He sighed, his chin down. "I had not put this together but of course, of course. Poor Anders. We have missed him very much. How is his wife? How are Karen and the boys?"

Car-*ron* was how he said her name. It had never been feasible for Karen to make this trip and yet Marina wanted her there to see the suffering on Thomas Nkomo's face, to be the recipient of such gracious sympathy. "She wants me to find out what happened to him. There has been very little information."

Thomas Nkomo's shoulders slumped forward. "I don't know what to say. How can we explain this to her? We thought he would recover. People in the jungle get extremely sick, fevers are common things. I am from Dakar. In West Africa I can tell you that the very young will die suddenly and the very old will die slowly but the people in the middle, healthy men like Anders Eckman, they pass through these illnesses in time. We are doctors here." He covered his heart with his hand. "I am a doctor. I was not expecting this."

As if in response to this show of emotion the Lakashi stood abruptly and gathered their children and their knives. They made quick work of putting twigs and clothing into baskets and in less than a minute every last one of them had retreated into the jungle.

Thomas Nkomo glanced nervously at the sky. "We should go now, Dr. Singh. The storm will be heavy. The Lakashi have the most uncanny meteorological abilities. Come with me, then, yes? I will show you the lab. You will be impressed by what we have made in our primitive circumstances."

To the west she could see the storm heading up the river and feel the sudden shift in the texture of the air. Dr. Nkomo put his hand against her back. "Now, please," he said, and they began to walk quickly in a direction Marina had not been in before. Birds came reeling past the water and dived straight into the canopy overhead while other things, things that Marina couldn't make out exactly, darted up trees. Then there was a single, nuclear flash of lightning that was followed some milliseconds later by a clap of thunder that could have cracked the world in half, and then, because these things come in threes, there was rain. Marina, half blinded by the light and deafened by the boom, suddenly thought she would drown standing up.

There had been many occasions in Manaus when Marina had outrun a storm, or outrun the worst of it, she had pounded up the street in her flip-flops, finding shelter beneath an awning before the sky broke apart, but to run in a jungle one must have been born in a jungle, otherwise the roots and vines are snares, leg breakers, with mud that slicks the landscape into oil. The Lakashi had long since vanished with the birds and those other skittering unknowns, all of them back to home and nest and hole, leaving the place empty for Marina and Dr. Nkomo who made slow progress on the uneven path. Every drop of rain hit the ground with such force it bounced back up again, giving the earth the appearance of something boiling. Marina moved her hands from tree to tree, steadying herself on branches, trying to regulate her breath in the flow of water.

Dr. Nkomo tapped one of his long fingers against her fingers. "Excuse me, but it is not the best idea," he said loudly. "You never know when there is something hiding in the bark you shouldn't touch."

Marina pulled her fingers back quickly and nodded, then she turned her palms up and washed her hands in the rain.

Dr. Nkomo went on, more or less shouting to pitch his voice above the roar of the storm. "I leaned against a tree once and a bullet ant bit through my shirt, bit into my shoulder. You may know it by the genus, *Paraponera*?" He removed his glasses, which the rain had rendered useless, and put them in his shirt pocket. "It was only one ant, as long as my thumbnail, and I was in bed for a week. No one likes to complain of such things but the pain was memorable. No bullet ants where you are from, is that correct?"

Marina thought of the crickets and the meadowlarks, the rabbits and the deer, the Disney book of wildlife that slept in the wide green meadows of her home state. "No bullet ants," she said. Her scalp was soaked, her underwear, the ground beneath her feet loosened as streams of water sluiced between the trees. They heard a high whistle piercing through the thunder and wondered if it was their imagination. Imagination played a major role in the jungle, especially during a storm. They stopped and waited until the whistle came again and then a silence. Marina turned her head and saw that what she had taken for a tree to her left was actually a pole. There were four poles, and five feet above her head there was a platform, and above that a palm roof. Four Lakashi leaned over the edge, watching. Dr. Nkomo looked up, waved, and the four waved back.

"It is an invitation," he said to Marina. "We should go up, yes?"

Marina, who could barely hear for the water building up inside her ears, climbed the ladder first.

The single wide, open room that was the house was miraculously dry given the absence of side walls but the roof was several feet wider than the floor in every direction and dipped down low on the sides. Marina and Dr. Nkomo both looked up instinctively to admire this barrier between the rain and their heads while one of the women sat on the floor intricately knotting three very long palm fronds together into shingles as if to demonstrate how such things were possible. She was so taken with her work that she seemed not to notice the arrival of the guests, and yet Marina was certain she had been leaning over the edge of the floor and staring at them thirty seconds before. The sound of water pummeling palm fronds was infinitely more gentle than the sound of water beating against her skull and she was grateful to this woman for the work she did. Two men, who may have been thirty or fifty, came over to slap their hands against Dr. Nkomo's chest and back, though the slaps were more respectful and restrained than the ones that had been meted out to Easter the night before. Then, chatting endlessly with one another, they picked up pieces of Marina's sopping hair, examined her ears briefly, and let the hair drop. A much heavier woman in her sixties or seventies was chopping up a pile of whitish roots using the floor as her cutting board and the same knife that had recently been in the employ of the boat builders. Because there were two men in the room there was a second similar knife on the ground behind her. There was a teenage daughter, replete with pimpled skin and bitten nails, who cast her gaze aimlessly around the room as if she were hoping to catch sight of a telephone, a sprinting toddler of two or three who wore a very small version of the crude shift dress that all Lakashi women seemed to wear, and a naked boy baby crawling at a good clip across the splintered planks. Marina quickly calculated the speed at which the baby was traveling and the remaining length of the floorboards and immediately leapt across the room, catching the boy by his small brown foot just as his left hand had reached into the empty air in front of him.

"Aaaahhh!" the crowd said, and laughed. Marina, breathless, looked over the edge where the water from the roof churned into a pit of mud and vines like it was pouring off Niagara Falls. She dipped an arm beneath the child's midsection and carried him back to the center of the room again. The baby was laughing too. What was the joke, exactly? That she really thought he was going to go over the same way she had thought that Easter would not break the surface of the water again? That this was how they ensured an intelligent race, by letting the careless babies fall like ripe fruit from the trees? She held the child beneath his arms to face her. He was no doubt thinner than the average American model but very healthy, kicking and gurgling with pleasure. The toddler stopped her running for a minute to pick up the unemployed knife and began to knock it against the floor behind the older woman. The baby then urinated on Marina, a long exuberant stream against the front of her already soaking shirt. The men laughed harder now and the women laughed more sedately, shaking their heads at all the silly foreigners in the world who don't know enough to hold a baby in the right direction. The toddler's knife got stuck in the floorboards and after a momentary wail she pulled it out and plunged it back again, missing the old woman's back by six inches. "Could you pick up that knife?" Marina said to Dr. Nkomo.

Dr. Swenson would no doubt have argued for respecting the natural order in which babies sailed off the edge of a flat earth and toddlers played with the knives they would one day need to understand in order to feed themselves. These children had escaped without major injury before Marina arrived and chances were no doubt good that they would continue to exist after the company departed, but still, Dr. Nkomo was willing to pry the knife from the unwilling hands of the little girl, and when he had handed it to one of the men she put her face down on the floor and wept. The woman weaving shingles stood up and said something to Dr. Nkomo, pointing at Marina, pointing at him. The teenage girl came and took the baby away.

"Have I done something already?" Marina asked.

"It is something about your clothes," he said. "Clothes is the only word I recognized, and maybe I am not sure of that."

The older woman now got up stiffly from the floor and began to unbutton Marina's shirt. Marina caught the woman's fingers and shook her head but the woman simply waited until Marina let her hands go and then she started again. Her touch was both patient and persistent. It made no difference to Marina that there was urine on her filthy, soaking clothes but there was no way to explain that. When Marina stepped away the woman followed her. She was considerably shorter than Marina, they all were, and so Marina was left to look at the part in her gray hair, the long braid that went down her back. Her dress pulled against her belly and her belly pressed against Marina's groin. The woman's belly was high and hard and suddenly Marina saw the woman's arms were thin, her face and legs were thin. Only her stomach protruded. Marina considered this as she stepped away from her again and again until it seemed possible that they might both go over the edge. Marina stopped, considering the ways to extricate herself while the woman resumed the work with the buttons, her stomach pressed against her, and then she felt the baby kick.

"My God," Marina said.

"I think she wants to wash your shirt," Dr. Nkomo said, seeming deeply embarrassed. "Once they are on to an idea it is very difficult to dissuade them."

"She's pregnant. I felt the baby kick," Marina said. "It kicked me."

The baby kicked again as if grateful for the recognition and the woman lifted her face and shook her head at Marina as if to say, *Kids, what can you do?* Her forehead was deeply creased and her neck was wattled. There was a dark, flat mole of an irregular shape on the side of her nose near the eye that could have been a melanoma. Buttons undone, she helped Marina out of her shirt and Marina let her take it. What was it that Anders had said? *Lost Horizon* for ovaries? How many children had this woman undressed and how many of the people in this tree house were her children? The toddler weeping for her knife? The woman weaving the roof? The men waiting to get back to carving their boat? The other woman came with a rag that was small and not particularly clean and rubbed down Marina's arms and back, rubbed her stomach and neck. She touched Marina's bra and said something to the older woman who leaned her nose between Marina's breasts to inspect the lace edge of the white cups more closely. Dr. Nkomo busied himself with the toddler, his back decisively pointed in her direction, but the other two men folded their arms across their chests, watching the show with interest, and Marina was not bothered by any of this. She had been kicked by a fetus whose mother was at the very least sixty and could easily have been more than seventy. The teenage girl stood in front of Marina and held up her arms until Marina understood that this was an instruction and not a game. She held up her arms as well. It was the girl's clear intention to drop a shift dress over Marina's head but the height discrepancy between them did not allow for it and so Marina pulled it on herself. No sooner was it covering her head and somewhat twisted than one of them pulled down her pants and began to rub her legs with the cloth as well. She stepped up obediently, one foot and then the other, and the pants were taken away. Marina stood there like the others now in her loose trapeze dress full enough to take her through an entire pregnancy because among the female Lakashi all clothes were maternity clothes. Without zippers or buttons, Marina saw the way in which they looked like candidates for a rustic insane asylum. The outfit was considerably shorter on her and the women poked at her knees and laughed as if there was something vaguely scandalous about knees. The women sat down on the floor and Marina sat with them and put her hands back on the woman's stomach, waiting for the baby to move again while the one who made shingles pulled back Marina's hair with a carved comb and braided it more tightly than her own mother had ever managed to braid it when she was a child. The teenage girl bit off a single piece of the palm frond with her teeth and tied off the end of her braid while the baby swam beneath Marina's hands. She would say six months along. Marina realized then she had not touched a single pregnant woman since it stopped being her business to touch them. How could that be possible? After all the countless bellies she had run her hands over in her training, how had she let them all go?

"You knew, didn't you, about the Lakashi, about why Dr. Swenson is here? Anders told you?" Dr. Nkomo asked, the little girl in his lap, playing with his glasses. She was gentle as she folded the arms in and out.

"I'd been told, but I can't say I necessarily believed it. It's something altogether different to see things for myself."

"It's true," Dr. Nkomo said nodding. "I had read Dr. Swenson's papers but I was still very surprised. I have thought too much about the fertility and reproduction of mosquitoes and not enough about the fertility and reproduction of women. That's what my wife would say. She says if we wait much longer for a baby she will have to come and live among the Lakashi in order to get pregnant."

Marina reached back and moved the base of her braid back and forth, trying to loosen it up before it gave her a headache. "I thought your research was in fertility with Dr. Swenson."

"Ah," Dr. Nkomo said, taking his glasses back from the little girl and in doing so breaking her heart all over again. "We work together. We are colleagues, but we do not share the same field of study. Our fields overlap."

Their hosts followed the conversation intently, their faces turning from speaker to speaker as if they were watching a tennis match. "What is your field of study, Dr. Nkomo?"

"Please," he said, "call me Thomas. I suppose you would say I focus on the drug's off-target toxicity, except in this case it isn't toxic. The drug has exhibited benefits unrelated to fertility."

There were questions to ask, namely what the benefits were and who was paying for his research, but at that moment Easter appeared over the top of the ladder, every bit as wet as he had been coming up out of the river and over the side of the boat. Marina understood the look of panic on his face. He was sure she was dead as she had been sure he was dead. His eyes went quickly around the room, passing over her and stopping only briefly on Thomas Nkomo. He started to go down the ladder again but she stood up quickly and when he realized it was her in that dress with her hair braided he bounded up the last few rungs of the ladder, his T-shirt stretched out by the rain, the mud making a solid cake up to his knees. He began slapping his open hands against her arms, her hips, her back. He could not stop himself. She was his responsibility and he had lost her.

The Lakashi nodded and clucked their tongues and pointed at him but Easter would not look in their direction and so they gave up. There was no teasing the deaf if they refused to look at you.

"The rain is letting up," Thomas said, craning his head to look beyond the edges of the roof. "Or maybe it's stopped now and the trees are just dripping. It's very difficult for me to tell the difference between the current rain and the continued falling of the rain we've already had."

"I don't mind getting wet again." Marina put her arm around Easter's shoulders. She was thinking about his box, the pens and feathers, Anders' open letter to the world on his behalf.

"Then we should go." Thomas began a series of deep nods around the room.

"How do you say thank you?"

"To the best of my knowledge the word doesn't exist in Lakashi. I've asked other people that question and no one comes up with anything."

Marina looked at her hosts, who stared expectantly as if they were hoping she would figure it out. "What about in Portuguese?"

"Obrigado."

"Obrigado," Marina said to the pregnant woman but there was no change in expression. She put her hand on the woman's belly again but the baby was quiet.

Easter tugged at the cloth of Marina's dress, then he held out his shirt, pointed at his shirt, and then pointed at her. Marina looked around the room. There were a few hammocks strung between poles, some piles of blankets and clothes on the floor, some baskets with roots and some baskets with twigs, but she did not see her shirt and pants. In truth, if he hadn't mentioned her clothes she probably would have gone right down the ladder without them, she was so distracted by what she had seen. She shook her head. Easter then went to the pregnant woman and held out his shirt to her between two fingers and pointed to Marina. The woman seemed to have no idea what he was getting at. Marina did a pantomime of unbuttoning her shirt, taking her fingers down the front of her dress where the buttons would have been, but again the woman shrugged.

Thomas then said a word, *basa* or *basi*, which was probably the word he believed meant clothes, but it was met with the same blank expression as the Portuguese word for thanks. He held out his own shirt and pointed to Marina. The younger woman took her place on the floor and resumed the twisting and knotting of palm fronds as if there had never been visitors at all and then, in what was the most damning gesture of false innocence, the teenage girl sat down to help her. The baby was settled on the floor and given a palm frond to play with and he put the tip of it in his mouth and sucked contentedly.

"I believe you've been scammed," Thomas said.

"Out of my clothes?" Marina couldn't quite imagine such a thing was possible even as she stood there in a smock. Easter crossed the room and started digging through a pile on the floor and one of the men came over and smacked him on the side of the head with the flat of his hand.

"This isn't good," Marina said. "I don't know where my luggage is."

"The bag you came with from Manaus?" Thomas said. "Wasn't it on the boat with you?"

She turned to him. Suddenly the dress felt very small. "Of course it was on the boat with me but, my God, coming into all that fire and screaming, all these men climbing on board from the water, and then the next thing I knew Dr. Swenson was going up the dock. I wasn't going to stay there and find my luggage."

"Of course," Thomas said. He did not offer her a single word of encouragement. He did not tell her as anyone would that this was a very small village and surely there was no place for her bag to go. The teenage girl was up now, slapping at Easter's hands, and then the littlest girl, the toddler, came over and she hit him as well. "We should go now, Dr. Singh," Thomas said.

"Please," she said, surprisingly heartbroken over such a small loss. "Call me Marina."

Eight

Marina had been in the jungle for a week before Dr. Alan Saturn, whom she thought of as the first Dr. Saturn, said he would borrow Easter and the boat and make a trip to the trading post two hours away to mail some letters. (The trading post was not a trading post at all but a larger village down river where the more advanced Jinta Indians had their camp. They were, for a small price, willing to hold letters and money until a trader passed through from Manaus, which they did with some frequency. For a larger price, the traders would then take the letters back with them to mail—no small request as the mail was going to Java and Dakar and Michigan and they themselves were not men born with a natural inclination to stand in long post office lines.) Once the trip was established, everyone save Dr. Swenson broke from work to sit down for some time after lunch to commit themselves to paper. Dr. Budi gave Marina three blue tissue Aerograms from her considerable stack and Alan Saturn said he would stand her for the stamps. Marina, whose luggage had yet to be recovered, had spent the past seven days in her Lakashi dress, though she had been given an identical spare out of either guilt or compassion by an anonymous tribe member. Nancy Saturn, the second Dr. Saturn, had given her two extra pairs of underwear and Thomas Nkomo had a toothbrush still in the plastic wrap. He put it in her hand very discreetly. It seemed to Marina that these were among the kindest gifts of her existence.

"This is why I don't loan out the boat," Dr. Swenson said, looking around the lab as the doctors scattered with paper and pens, those charming dinosaurs of communication. "Once you say it's leaving no one seems to think there's any work to do."

But work was all there was to do. Marina had been set up in the corner of the lab and been given the job of running tests on the compound for stability, to see whether it was degrading with heat and exposure. Like Anders, she was a small molecule person. Their work had been in pills and while it wasn't an exact match for the task at hand it was comfortably within her realm of experience. There was enough data piled up to keep her busy for years and she wondered if that wasn't Dr. Swenson's objective—to keep her busy. It was possible that they were feeding her problems they had already solved as a means of placating her or testing her competence. They had mice after all, they were clearly already onto testing the concentration of the compound in blood levels. Still, she knew that if she stayed in her corner looking over what they had given her she would be much more able to make a realistic assessment of how far they were from a first efficacious dose. She could sidle over to Dr. Budi from time to time—Budi was in charge of clinical research organization—and ask her questions about the Lakashi blood work. She could see now how ridiculous it had been to simply ask Dr. Swenson over dinner what her progress was. Working here she had the chance to make her own assessment, and that was what Mr. Fox had wanted all along.

And besides, if she wasn't working, what was she going to do with her days? The jungle, with its screeching cries of death and slithering piles of leaves, was hardly a place to go walking alone in the afternoons. Two of the young men from the tribe had dreams of learning English and German and becoming tour guides at one of the eco-lodges hundreds of miles away. They had seen the great white hope of the cruise ships while riding bundles of trees to Manaus. They had met the naturalists when visiting the Jinta. Because they were always looking to practice, they were willing to take a restless doctor into that deeper place off the available paths where the afternoon light was filtered out by leaves. With a great deal of hand gesturing, a few common words in four different languages, and a couple of glossy field guides with the name Anders Eckman printed inside the front cover, they would endeavor to give jungle tours, pointing out the neon colored frogs the size of dimes that contained enough poison in their clammy skins to take down twenty men. The scientists all agreed that they had never been deep into the jungle for more than eight minutes without thinking they would give everything they owned to be led safely out.

Sometimes in the late afternoons when the generator stumbled from the burdens of overuse and the scant electricity in the lab clicked off altogether (save the backup, backup generators that kept the blood samples in the freezers flash-frozen to arctic levels), the heat drove the doctors, save Dr. Swenson, into the river to swim, though the river was even worse than the jungle because in that murky soup there was no telling what was coming at you. As they treaded the water slowly, hoping not to kick up an attractive splash, the conversation turned not to the spectacular moth with wings the size of handkerchiefs that for a moment hovered over their heads, but to the microscopic candiru fish that were capable of swimming up the urethra with catastrophic results. Marina, who had no alternative, swam in her dress and hoped that in the slow agitation of her strokes she was washing it. They kept an eye out for water snakes whose heads rode the surface of the river like tiny periscopes, and reminisced about the vampire bats that had tangled their claws in the mosquito nets over their beds. No one stayed long in the water, not even Dr. Budi, who apparently had been something of a swimming star in Indonesia when she was a girl.

For entertainment not reliant on nature, there were outdated scientific journals and old *New Yorkers* but invariably something had eaten through the most interesting paragraphs. Dr. Swenson had a complete set of hardbacked Dickens and she kept the books wrapped separately in heavy pieces of plastic tarp and tied with twine. She would loan them out and then do spot checks to make sure they were being read with clean hands. A cinnamon stick was lodged in the plastic wrap of each volume, as ants, Dr. Rapp had once told her, would always avoid the scent of cinnamon. Dr. Swenson believed that ants would be the standard bearers for the end of civilization.

Other than the brief and unsatisfying diversions of walking and swimming and reading, all that was left for Dr. Swenson and Dr. Singh, Dr. Nkomo and Dr. Budi and the two Drs. Saturn, was the lab, and the lab was not unlike a Las Vegas casino. They existed there without calendar or clock. They worked until they were hungry and then they stopped and ate—opening a can of apricots and another can of tuna. They worked until they were tired and then they went back to their cots in the small ring of huts that sat behind the lab like the bungalows at the Spear-O-Wigwam Summer Camp for Girls at Mille Lacs. They read some Dickens before they went to sleep. At the end of her first week, Marina was halfway through *Little Dorrit.* Of all her possessions lost and gone she was particularly sorry to be without her James novel.

As for the Lakashi, they were patient subjects, submitting themselves to constant weighing and measurement, allowing their menstrual cycles to be charted and their children to be pricked for blood samples. Dr. Swenson deserved the credit for that and she accepted it readily, telling stories about the tireless cajoling and gift giving that had once been required for even the most basic examinations. "I tamed them," she said, taking not the least discomfort in the word. "It was our life's work, Dr. Rapp's and mine, earning their trust."

But if she taught them to tolerate her research she had not made them good company. They rarely offered to share their dried fish and regurgitated manioc root, not that anyone wanted it, but it was the most basic lesson in any Introduction to Anthropology class: the sharing of food was the primary symbol of harmonious communal living. Then again, Dr. Swenson strictly forbade the sharing of the scientists' food among members of the tribe as she believed that a jar of peanut butter was more corrupting to indigenous ways than a television set, so it was possible that the Lakashi's unwillingness to offer up their bread was only a matter of passive retaliation. It was Easter alone who ate from both tables, or, more accurately, both pots. The Lakashi didn't knock on the door of the lab to extend an invitation on the nights they decided for no discernible reason to dance until three in the morning, and they left no note when they cleared out, all of them together, which they did from time to time, leaving behind the most unnerving silence. When they came back twelve hours later they were red-eyed and quiet, walking on their toes in their collective indigenous hangover. Even the children smelled of a peculiar smoke and sat like stumps on the bank of the river, an entire line of them staring straight ahead without scratching their insect bites.

"We used to call it a vision quest in honor of the indigenous Americans," Dr. Swenson had said when Marina ran to the lab in a sweat-soaked panic asking what had happened to everyone. She had been in camp three days when, in the manner of a horrible scene from a science fiction movie, they all disappeared. "That was the perfect name for what they were doing until it also became the name of a video game and the rallying cry for every pack of middle-aged New Agers who were looking to legitimize their interest in psychedelics. I don't have a name for it anymore. I wake up and see they're gone and I think, Oh, it's time for that again."

"Have you ever gone with them?" Marina asked.

Dr. Swenson was working through a complicated looking equation in a spiral notebook but she didn't seem to mind carrying on the conversation while she wrote down strings of numbers. There were computers in the lab but between the undependable electricity and the overpowering humidity that from time to time seized the generators like a fever, everyone was more inclined to do their important calculations by hand, proving legions of math teachers correct. "No one goes with them now. In retrospect, I think it was only Dr. Rapp they were inviting and the rest of us held his coattails. Once he stopped coming on expeditions, the Lakashi simply went out in the middle of the night while we were sleeping. Never have I known a people who could one hour be as loud as a blitzkrieg and the next hour maintain perfect silence while walking through dried leaves. They can move their entire operation out of here without breaking a twig."

Marina waited for an answer to the question she had asked but Dr. Swenson's attention had fallen back to the math before her. It occurred to Marina that these sorts of conversations were exactly the reason the Bovenders worked so hard to keep Dr. Swenson separated from society. Society was nothing but a long, dull dinner party conversation in which one was forced to speak to one's partner on both the left and the right. "But you did go?"

Dr. Swenson glanced up for a moment as if surprised to see Marina was still there. "Of course, when I was younger. It seemed fascinating at the time, as if we had discovered something central to the identity of the people. It was very important to Dr. Rapp, it was important to the entire field of mycology. I picture all those students now, boys from Park Avenue and Hyde Park and Back Bay who had spent their previous summers in the Hamptons scooping ice cream, all marching off into the jungle ready to ingest anything that was given to them. The way they opened their mouths and closed their eyes you would have thought the Lakashi were distributing communion. Actually, the ceremony would have made a striking program for interdisciplinary studies—biology, anthropology, world religion. I certainly found it compelling as a medical student to see how long a person could sustain such a low heart rate. In the whole lot of them there wasn't a pulse over twenty-four. I once brought a cuff with me and monitored the Lakashi and the students every twenty minutes for five hours after they had reached a state of unconsciousness. Their diastolic pressure ticked in slightly above dead. I was only testing for my own interest but if I could have put together a committed control group it could have been an important study over time."

"Did you—" Marina wasn't exactly sure how to phrase the question.

"I did, of course, but mycology was never my field. I was more interested in recording the subjects. Let the botanist take notes on his own trip, I say. I was of great assistance to Dr. Rapp in this way. He never had a graduate student who was willing to abstain for purposes of observation. I didn't mind that, of course, I was glad to help the science. The real problem was the Lakashi themselves. Once the women realized I wasn't going on the trip anymore they started piling all the babies around me, all the children. I put a quick stop to that."

"The children were participating?"

"I suppose that conflicts with your ideas of good parenting. In retrospect, I can see how you would have preferred me to stop them, but I didn't know you at the time."

"That's fine. I'm not interested in the children," Marina said, and in fact she was telling the truth. From what she could tell, the Lakashi children were constructed out of titanium. They ate random berries and were bitten by spiders and fell out of trees and swam with piranha and they were fine. She could hardly see how a regular dosing of hallucinogens could make a difference. "But when you did go on the trip, as you say, did you enjoy it?" Marina had given her youth to studying, believing all the propaganda of the dangers of drugs while her worshiped professor was spending her weekends in the Amazon eating mushrooms. She felt she deserved to know at least secondhand if it had been any fun.

Dr. Swenson took off her reading glasses and pressed her fingertips hard against the bridge of her nose. "I keep hoping that you are more than you show yourself to be, Dr. Singh. I am just on the verge of liking you but you dwell on the most mundane points. Yes, of course it was interesting to take part in the ritual, that was what we had come here to do. It was slightly terrifying the first time, all of the screaming and the smoke, in that way it was a little like your experience coming up the river at night, except that you are all very close together in one giant, enclosed hut. Seeing God was worthwhile, of course. I doubt seriously that anything in our Western tradition would have shown Him to me so personally. I remember Dr. Rapp would feel quite humbled for several days after the experience and would continue to see a great deal of purple. We all would. But in the final assessment I am a person who loathes vomiting, and there is a great deal of vomiting involved in the Lakashi ritual. It is an unavoidable part of the program. The body isn't capable of processing that amount of poison without—" Dr. Swenson, who was sitting on a low stool in front of a table she used for her desk, closed her eyes as if she were remembering the experience. She kept her eyes closed for entirely too long.

"Dr. Swenson?"

She held up her hand and shook her head almost imperceptibly, warding off further questions. Then she stood up, looking watery and pale, and, going quickly out the door, vomited next to the front steps.

Dear Jim,

It is true that no one here has a telephone. I believe it has something to do with the humidity, which is the enemy of all machines. While I am told there is an Internet connection in a village several hours west of Manaus (which is nowhere near us anyway) it only works when there have been two entire weeks without rain, which means de facto no connection. The second phone you gave me, along with my second suitcase, disappeared after my arrival in the Lakashi Village. I have been a poor steward of my belongings. It has been so long since I've been able to tell you where I am that I worry by now you must think I'm dead. I am hoping the mail service comes through for me and you get this letter quickly. I've been here a week and this is my first hope of getting a letter out of the village, though Dr. Nkomo told me that when Anders was here he would stand on the banks of the river with a letter in his hand and watch for any passing dugout canoe. What I most want to say is that you shouldn't worry about me. Life among the Lakashi has been better than expected. I have a small job in the lab and over time I feel I will be able to discern how much real progress has been made on the drug. While everyone is friendly no one is particularly forthcoming as to what aspects of the research they are responsible for. I will tell you that the pregnancies are astonishing. Ages are difficult to document in the older members of the tribe (Dr. Swenson began to document the children when she first arrived fifty years ago) but there are pregnant women here who seem clearly to be in their seventies. The more I see the more I understand your commitment to this drug, no matter how much time it takes to reach the first human dose.

Marina was at the end of her fold-over sheet and she hesitated at her closing. *Love* was not a word that had made its way into their parlance and yet she was certain it was implicitly true. She couldn't see how, given all that had happened, that there would be anything shocking about its introduction here. And so she wrote it in ink, *Love, Marina.*

She followed this letter with very brief notes to her mother and Karen in which she used most of her paper explaining why the note was so short. After all, the boat was leaving soon and she didn't want to keep anyone waiting. She promised to start longer letters immediately and save them for the next departure.

It was true that Anders had been impatient with the mail system, several people had commented on that. He would take Easter to the river and they would stand for hours waiting for anyone to paddle past, then when finally someone did, he would have the boy swim out with the letter and the money. Dr. Budi said he tried to get a letter in every boat that went by just to increase his chances that one or two might actually find their way home to his wife. But after a while he was too sick to go down to the water himself, too sick to spend so many hours in the sun, and so he sent Easter alone. It did not require a great deal of inquiry on Marina's part to put this together, nor much conjecture to fill in the missing pieces: Anders, sick, wrote letters to his wife. Easter, worried, did not want to leave Anders for the amount of time it would have taken to find a boat going past. The traffic on their little tributary was thin at best and on some days not a single person floated by. While Easter would have understood the ritual of giving the blue envelope to someone in a boat, he could not have understood what a letter was or what it represented, only that Anders wrote and wrote. He would have only just come back to the sleeping porch and his friend would want to send him out again with another envelope.

The first time Marina found one of those blue paper rectangles in her bed, perfectly sealed and addressed to Karen Eckman in Eden Prairie, she froze as solidly as a blood sample in the very bottom of the freezer. She leaned over the railing and shined the flashlight into the night jungle looking for a flash of Anders running away, her heart in full arrhythmia, but it didn't take her long to figure out who had delivered it. For Easter, these envelopes were his most precious possessions and therefore his best gifts, and because he knew he had come to them through a direct act of disobedience, they carried the added enticement of guilt. The letters were so secret he would not keep them in his lock box with the feathers. Wherever they came from he doled them out slowly, one every other day, every third day, beneath the sheet, beneath the pillow, folded in her extra dress.

Let me tell you the virtue of fever: it brings YOU here. I would have preferred it take me home and once or twice that's happened but for the most part YOU arrive at 4:00 and take me out of this bed and we walk through the jungle, and Karen, you know EVERYTHING about the jungle. You know the names of all the spiders. You are afraid of nothing. I am afraid of nothing when you are here. Let me live in this fever. It is so much worse now, the hours I am well

Then nothing. Maybe these were the letters Anders didn't finish, the ones he started and forgot, and Easter picked them up off the floor while Anders slept and tucked them away. Of the three she had received so far two were only paragraphs and the third was a scant two sentences:

What was the name of the couple who lived next door to us in the apartment building on Petit Court? I see them here constantly and I cannot think of their names.

Now everyone had finished his or her letter except for Dr. Budi who seemed to approach the question of what to say as a spatial problem. She would stare for a long time at her paper and then turn her eyes up to the ceiling as if trying to calculate exactly how many words she needed to express her feelings and how many inches there were left on the paper for those words.

Alan Saturn stood in front of Dr. Budi and tapped the table with his fingers. "Give it up," he said.

"You could have told me last night that you meant to go today." She was a fine-boned woman of indeterminate age who wore her black hair in a single braid in the manner of the Lakashi. She folded her letter into thirds and ran her tongue along the glue strip.

"Nothing happens here," Alan said. "No one needs that much time to write a letter."

Dr. Budi reached into the pocket of the cotton smock she wore and pulled out several small bills which she handed over to Dr. Saturn along with the envelope. Then, without further conversation, she returned her attention to her work. In her devotion to her task, Dr. Budi was an archetype of a particular sort in the medical community, as much as the ill-tempered surgeon or the addicted anesthesiologist. Any time a group of doctors came together, there was always the one whose car would be in the parking lot when the others arrived at dawn and whose car would still be there when the others pulled away after midnight, the one who was standing at the nurses' station at four a.m. reviewing a chart when it wasn't her weekend on call, the one the other doctors privately ridiculed for having no life and yet with whom they felt a gnawing and irrational sense of competition. What was remarkable was how ably Dr. Budi filled this role even when there was no hospital, no parking lot, and no patients. When all they did was work, Dr. Budi worked more. She claimed that she had already read all the Dickens.

"Have you ever been to Java?" Alan Saturn asked Marina. "Anywhere in Indonesia?" She had followed him down to the dock with the Lakashi, not even asking herself why she was doing it. A departure, an arrival, she was beginning to see their appeal as a diversion. She was certain one of the men was wearing a pair of her pants rolled up at the cuffs. Pieces of her clothing walked by her from time to time and there was nothing to do but watch them pass. She shook her head.

"It's my theory that Budi is more suited to the tropics than the rest of us. This air, these smells, they must be second nature to her. She looks up so seldom I imagine she thinks she's home." Dr. Saturn was working to loosen a knot in a rope that held the pontoon boat to the shore and in his struggles he made the knot more intractable. Easter came down the dock and thumped him on the shoulder. His point was clear. "Now, take Nancy and me coming from Michigan," he said, "well, that's going to be harder. It doesn't matter how long we're here or how often we come, we never fully acclimate. The foreignness of the place is always going to be a distraction for us."

"Dr. Swenson was born in Maine and she doesn't seem distracted."

"Dr. Swenson may never be cited in conversations about how normal people respond to their environment." Some freakish brand of great white bird with a wing span of a pterodactyl flapped down the river towards them. It had a bare black head, a long black bill, and a red ring around its skinny neck. They all stood paralyzed by the sight of it, watching until it took a hard left into the foliage and vanished. Dr. Saturn formed his hand into a visor against the afternoon sun. "Anders would have known what that was."

After a flurry of turning pages, Benoit held up the picture of the bird in Anders' book, thrilled to have found it so fast. He showed it to Dr. Saturn, who nodded approvingly at the correct match. "Jabiru stork," Dr. Saturn said.

Benoit, one of those young men who hoped for a career in tourism, had as a child been collected for a missionary school that had popped up briefly several tributaries away. Thanks to a group of Baptists from Alabama he could read and write in Portuguese and had memorized Bible verses which he could recite at will, skills that had made him one of the least contented members of his tribe. Marina came over to look at the picture.

"I've brought hats!" Nancy Saturn said, coming down to the water. "I have two. Now you can come with us." She handed Marina a wide brimmed hat and when Marina hesitated, Dr. Saturn took it from his wife and put it on Marina's head. The age span between the Drs.

Saturn was greater than the span between Mr. Fox and Marina. One could imagine, though it had not been said, that he had once been her teacher. Marina recognized the way the wife leaned towards the husband when he spoke as it was not unlike the way she had often leaned towards Dr. Swenson. In one late-night conversation over a bottle of pisco brandy in which the first Dr. Saturn was holding forth on matters of tropical medicine, the second Dr. Saturn actually took a notebook out of her pocket to write down something he had said. She was discreet, and the paper might have gone unnoticed had Dr. Swenson not asked her rather loudly if she wasn't capable of simply relying on her memory. Dr. Swenson leaned decisively away from the female Dr. Saturn, whom she clearly regarded as a gate-crasher, a hanger-on, though the younger woman, a botanist with a degree in public health, was probably best qualified to be of assistance. Certainly her credentials were closest to Dr. Rapp's. "I never rely on my memory when I'm drinking," was what Nancy Saturn had said.

Easter turned the key and the motor of the pontoon boat began to spit and cough. All of the Lakashi pressed forward now and Marina felt herself jostled from side to side by the shirtless men in running shorts and the women with their pregnant bellies. She found herself looking at their ears and the strings of seeds and animal teeth around their necks and suddenly she realized she had not dreamed of India all week. Her father, who had been missing from her life for so many years, was gone again, and for an instant she had a vivid recreation of that hollow, hopeless feeling of having lost him in the crowd. As she wondered if the Lariam was out of her system now, a mosquito bit the back of her knee.

"Jump!" Alan said, jumping onto the boat himself with the rope in his hand. Immediately the current caught the boat and pulled it away from the shore. He turned around and reached his hand to Marina. "The entire tribe is going to be on board in five seconds," he called. "Hesitation is the same thing as a straight-up invitation around here."

It was true, the Lakashi were poised to begin boarding, all of them.

Benoit pushed ahead of the pack and jumped without solicitation. He clearly meant to go somewhere, and Nancy followed him. Two more Lakashi leapt onto the boat but before they had gotten their balance Benoit tipped them back into the water, and then Marina jumped without ever meaning to go. Easter laughed at her flat-footed landing and she went and stood behind him, both of her hands on his shoulders. Every night they went to sleep separately, he in his hammock and she in her cot beneath the netting, and every night his dreams woke them both. His dreams, not hers, and she would go and scoop him up, bring him back in with her where they would sleep out the rest of the night in her little bed. They had gotten good at it. In only a week they had learned how to stretch and turn in unison.

The Lakashi were wading into the river and with the cross of breaststroke and dog paddle they favored, they swam. Marina looked at their dark heads in the water and wondered if she would have swum out too, just to have something to do. Nancy Saturn removed her hat and waved it at them, showing the short auburn hair she cropped herself. She called out an enthusiastic series of farewells—goodbye in English and *tchau* in Portuguese and then some sort of humming sound followed by a high pitched cry that essentially meant *I am gone from you* in Lakashi. After her fourth or fifth repetition they finally turned around and swam back to shore. It wasn't as if they ever would have caught the boat. Easter was gunning the engine now that Dr. Swenson wasn't on board.

"They only want a little recognition," Nancy said, watching and waving as they fell farther and farther behind. "If you don't acknowledge what they're doing they just keep doing it. Frankly, I don't think they're such good swimmers. You can't have half the tribe drowning on the way to the trading post."

"Nancy would have made a great social behaviorist," Alan Saturn said, dropping a very tan arm over his wife's shoulders. "Dr. Rapp would have loved her. There were so many things we missed back then that Nancy picked up on the very first time she came out here."

"You knew Dr. Rapp?" Marina asked.

Nancy raised her eyebrows briefly and then sighed with the recognition of what was to come. "How in the world did you miss that lecture?" she said, stepping out from under her husband's arm and rifling through her bag for sunblock and bug gel. She handed one tube to Marina and began to use the other on herself.

Alan Saturn lifted his sunglasses to better show the delight in his eyes. "I was his student at Harvard! I was actually enrolled in that famous mycology class the year he broke his ankle in New Guinea and wound up coming back to teach for the entire semester. Those were the lectures that were published by Oxford University Press, and there have been no end of papers written on them. I'm sure you must have read some of them. There were a great many legends built up around that class. It was listed in the catalogue every year but Dr. Rapp virtually never made his way back to the classroom for more than a day or two. In reality it was taught by some graduate student who had been in the field himself and was qualified to do no more than read the notes and mark the tests. So while Studies in Mycology was considered to be one of the seminal classes at the university, no one but rubes actually signed up for it. Signing up for the class was as good as admitting you had no idea what was going on, so who better than me to enroll? When people realized what had happened, that the great man himself was coming back to teach, you had a situation where seniors and graduate students and in some cases faculty members were making cash offers to freshmen to give up their seats. I for one stood firm and was rewarded fortunes beyond that fifty bucks I turned down. I got to know Dr. Rapp that semester, I made sure of it, and so I was asked to travel with him in the Amazon for the next three summers in a row."

"Is that how you met Dr. Swenson?" Marina thought of her teacher taking the trouble to catch the red-eye back from Manaus. To the best of her memory Dr. Swenson hadn't missed a single class.

Nancy Saturn smeared a great handful of white paste across her face and began to rub it in. "To know Martin Rapp was to know Annick Swenson."

"Don't ruin the story," Alan said to her. He turned his attention back to Marina, that untapped source of listening pleasure. "Annick is several years older than I am, of course." This news was delivered for his own vanity, as Alan Saturn, with his thinning white hair, enormous white eyebrows, and perilously slender ankles, could easily have been taken as older than Dr. Swenson. The only thing that made Dr. Saturn seem younger was his younger wife. "She was coming down here years before me. They were, shall we say, quite inseparable in the field."

"She picked the boys who went on the trips," Nancy said. "Only boys. She held interviews in his office at Harvard. She was the one who picked Alan. Dr. Rapp didn't have the time to fill the rosters himself."

Marina could see him then, a tall and lanky undergraduate, a canvas rucksack on his back. "You knew him too?" she asked Nancy.

Nancy gave a small, snorting laugh and applied a layer of sunblock to her breastbone, reaching into the collar of her shirt to do the job right. "I came after Dr. Rapp."

Alan Saturn was ignoring her now. He was launched. A giant tree had fallen into the river and the roots and branches reached up through the water as if begging to be saved. A bright yellow bird with a long, slender neck sat on one of those branches and watched the boat as it passed. Benoit, having spotted the bird, began his frantic turning of pages. "Martin Rapp was more than my teacher. He was the man I wanted to be. He was fully engaged with his life every minute that he lived it. He didn't trudge along doing what someone else told him to do. He was never a cog in the wheel. He held his head up and looked at the world around him. Now, my father was a very decent man, worked as a tailor in Detroit back when there were men in Detroit who had their suits made. He worked until his hands were so twisted with arthritis he couldn't hold a needle. If a man came into the store and told my father what he wanted, the only word my father had for him was yes. It didn't matter if it was a ridiculous order, didn't matter if this guy showed up on Saturday morning and wanted his suit for Saturday night and there was already work piled to the rafters, my father said yes. And once my father said yes it was as good as done because that word was all he had in the world. He spent his life in the backroom of a store and the only thing he knew about his environment was that needle going in and out of the cloth. He did all this so my brothers and I could go to college and not be tailors and have the luxury of telling somebody no someday. So off I went to Harvard, the tailor's boy, from Michigan. The next thing I knew I was sitting in a lecture hall and in walked the great Martin Rapp, his ankle sunk in a plaster boot, his crutches swinging forward. He came up to the lectern and he said, 'Gentlemen, close your books and listen. We have nothing less than the world to consider.' We were awestruck, every last one of us. We would have sat there for the full four years of college. I remember everything about that day, that room, the giant blackboards, the light coming in those leaded glass windows. What I saw in front of me was the character of a man. It was the most remarkable thing, and I've never had that experience before or since. It was some sort of aura he had. From ten rows away I knew exactly who he was and I knew I would follow him anywhere."

"Here," Nancy said to Marina, "take the sunblock and give me the bug gel."

Marina took the sunblock but there was only so much sunblock could do. As careful as she had tried to be she was as dark as the natives now. Her own mother wouldn't recognize her.

"Listen to her," Alan said, declining to take the paste himself. "We didn't have sunblock back then. It was a melanoma that killed Dr. Rapp in the end. By the time they found it, it had spread everywhere there was for a melanoma to go. I cannot imagine all the years he spent in an open boat with no more than a straw hat and a white shirt for protection. It's amazing he lasted as long as he did. I came back to Cambridge to see him in the end and he was every bit himself. He was interested in his own death, fascinated by it. He was taking notes. He was in his eighties then, he couldn't go out to the sites anymore. When I asked him if he still did his meditation he said to me, 'Why would this time be any different?' That was the thing most people never knew about him: if he was in his house in Cambridge or he was in a tent in the driving rain outside Iquitos, he always meditated, and that's back in the days when only a handful of Indians and maybe a few Tibetans had even heard the word. He used to say we all had a compass inside of us and what we needed to do was to find it and to follow it. But we were undergraduates and for the most part we couldn't find our asses with our hands and so we followed his compass instead. Until we knew how to be men by our own standards we tried to be men like Dr. Rapp. We never would be, of course, but it was still a noble goal. I look out over this river now and I can see him, paddling the canoe along with the rest of us. In fact we would have stopped paddling, crying like children about our blisters and our splinters, and he would just keep on. He wouldn't say a word and then all of a sudden he would turn the boat so hard we would nearly capsize. He would take it to shore and the next thing we knew he was in the water and then into the jungle, gone. Gone! And there we were, alone. Ten minutes later he'd walk back out with a mushroom in a bag, a specimen that had never been recorded before. He'd be writing up the coordinates and taking pictures of the site, and then he was cleaning off the knife he'd used to cut the mushrooms from the tree on his handkerchief, the surest sign that the discovery was now complete. Everything he did was orchestrated, every movement was beautiful. We boys would scramble into the jungle trying to figure out what he'd seen and how he'd known those mushrooms were there, and when we'd ask him he would say, 'I keep my eyes open.'" Alan Saturn was moved by the memory. "'I keep my eyes open.' That was the lesson. I have to tell you those were the happiest summers of my life."

Looking along the edges of the river in the blinding daylight, the mesh of the jungle as tight as twenty chain-link fences stacked together, Marina could imagine that reaching in to pluck a single mushroom from the forest floor must have been an act akin to pulling a full grown sheep from a top hat, at once dazzling and pointless. Easter turned back from the steering wheel of the boat and waved to her. Benoit looked for birds in the trees.

"So why didn't you go back with him after that?"

"Malaria," Alan said, and gave a sigh for the memory of what he had lost. "I got it in Peru the summer after my junior year. Dr. Rapp had had malaria who knows how many times. He said I'd pull through it fine, but I didn't do so well. After I got home I ended up having to sit out the first semester of my senior year. By the time the summer came around again and Dr. Rapp was putting his crew together I was probably back to ninety-five percent but my father wouldn't let me go. I shouldn't blame him, I suppose. He thought he was protecting me, and I couldn't make him understand. My father had never seen the world so he didn't think it was much of a crime to keep me from it."

Nancy Saturn looked at her husband, great streaks of unabsorbed white paste still standing on her chin and around her ears. She waited for another minute to see if there was anything else forthcoming and then she asked him, "Finished?"

"Those are some highlights," he said.

"As many times as I've heard this story there are two things that never sit well with me," she said.

"Tell me," Alan said.

"Well, first, your poor father. Why must he always be made the drudge in opposition to the free spirit of Martin Rapp? He didn't want his son who still had occasional relapses of malaria to return to the jungle where he'd gotten it in the first place? That doesn't seem so criminal to me."

Alan Saturn considered his wife thoughtfully for some time, chewing over her criticism. He brushed some sort of leggy cricket out of his hair. "You have a valid point," he said finally. "But this is the story of my life, the story of how I related to my father and then later to my mentor, who, it is obvious enough, was a father figure to me. I'm not misrepresenting my father. I say he's a hard worker, a provider. But if I lean towards Dr. Rapp as a role model then that's my choice to make."

Nancy waited a long time before shrugging her shoulders. The shrug appeared to cost her something. "I can see that."

"I hear you, though," he said. "And I appreciate what you're saying."

Marina wondered if they had been through a great deal of marriage counseling or if it was possible that this was the way they had spoken to each other all along. It was such a long time ago that she had been married. She couldn't imagine she and Josh Su had, in their twenties, ever had such an exchange.

"You said there were two things," Alan said.

"Annick Swenson."

"She isn't in the story."

"She is implicit in every story about Dr. Rapp. Your story tells as much by what you leave out as what you put in."

"I leave out what was private in his life. Those matters didn't concern me and they didn't concern science."

"Listen to him," the second Dr. Saturn said, turning to Marina. "What is this, *Meet the Press*?" She pivoted back to her husband. "It absolutely did concern you. When one's role model brings his mistress along trip after trip with a dozen boys and you are one of those boys then it concerns you. It concerns you when you later go to his house and have dinner with your mentor and his wife."

"Dr. Swenson was his mistress?" Marina said. Just saying it brought a sour taste to her mouth. It was, she thought, a terrible word, and in no way representative. A mistress was a woman who waited in a hotel room.

"This is what I meant by private," Alan said pointedly to his wife.

"Mrs. Rapp lives in Cambridge and has three daughters. She is ninety-two. We send her grapefruit at Christmas. I'm not saying people don't have affairs, even very decent people, let us be so lucky as to fall into that category. But we cannot unbraid the story of another person's life and take out all the parts that don't suit our purposes and put forth only the ones that do. He was a great scientist, I will grant you that, and by all accounts a true charismatic, but he was also deeply unfaithful to two women and frankly that bothers me. It bothers me that the man you say you wanted to become was a lifelong philanderer."

"When did this start?" Marina asked.

"We *can* take the life apart. We do it all the time." The veins on Alan Saturn's temples were pressing forward with their new influx of blood. "Picasso put his cigarettes out on his girlfriends and we don't love the paintings any less for it. Wagner was a fascist and I can hum you every bar in the opening of *Die Walküre*."

"I don't know Picasso and I don't know Wagner!"

"And you didn't know Dr. Rapp!"

The shouting caused Benoit to raise his eyes from the field guide he was studying. He pointed to the top of a tree and said in English, "Look!" But neither of the Drs. Saturn looked, nor did Marina, and of course Easter missed it completely.

"I know his wife!" Nancy said, her voice high. "I know his mistress! If I didn't know those two women I feel certain you'd be right. It would be just another bit of gossip from the annals of history, but that isn't the case. You can't separate it out when it's someone you know. I can tell you he wasn't a good man."

"He was the greatest man I ever knew."

"He *left* you with a tribe of Indians in Peru when you had a fever of a hundred and five!"

"And they took me to Iquitos and eventually I got to Lima. It wasn't as if he stretched me out next to a log in the jungle and walked away. We all understood the terms of the agreement going in. Anyone who slowed down the group would be cut from the group. Dr. Rapp was there to work and we were there to learn."

"You were nineteen years old and he was picking mushrooms!" Nancy Saturn had a wild look in her eyes, as if she were telling the story of what had happened to her child and not her husband. "His mistress must have been through medical school by then. At the very least you would think *she* could have stayed with you."

Alan Saturn would have stormed away at this point, the desire to leave her was plainly twitching in his muscles, working through his jaw, but they were on a boat on a river in the jungle. "The incident you are referring to happened a very long time ago." His voice was steady and low. "I clearly made a mistake in confiding it to you."

"I'm your wife. It would have come out eventually." Nancy Saturn was not in the least bit ready to break away. She saw she had a game advantage and did not blink.

"You knew nothing about Annick and Dr. Rapp?" Alan said to Marina finally. There were still sparks of rage in his voice even when it was directed to her.

"Not a clue," Marina said. She would have liked to separate herself from the Saturns now, to find a place on the boat without roaches where she could sit down, because even though she could say that based on the information that had been presented Alan Saturn was wrong—Dr. Rapp had behaved badly, and Nancy Saturn was right, such matters were worthy of judgment—she found herself siding with Alan because there was much in his single-minded devotion to a mentor that sounded a familiar note. In this life we love who we love. There were some stories in which facts were very nearly irrelevant.

"Yes," he said, trying to slow his breathing, perhaps another learned technique. "Well, a private matter." Nancy opened her mouth but he put his hand gently on her forehead and used his thumb to rub in a clot of sunblock that was clinging to the roots of her hair. He cleared his throat. He was trying very hard to settle them both. "You see that river there?" He was speaking to Marina. He nodded towards a tributary. It would have been easily missed, the small opening folded into the jungle so discreetly. "You follow that river to the Hummocca tribe. It's two or three hours from here. They are the closest tribe to the Lakashi and yet in all the times I've been here I've never seen them." It was his one heroic attempt to change the subject. He took his hand from his wife's head and there passed between them a tacit agreement. They were on a boat. They were not alone. They would find a way to stop this.

"Dr. Swenson said that Easter was Hummocca," Marina said, understanding that her part in the play was to pretend that nothing had happened.

"No one really knows," Nancy said, weighing her words out carefully. "But it's the only logical explanation. The Jinta wouldn't have left him."

"Did anyone try and take him back? See if they were missing a boy?" Marina looked over at Easter but he did not turn his head in the direction of the smaller river. Benoit was showing him a picture. He was steering with one hand.

"Tribes are like countries," Alan Saturn said. "They each have their own national characters. Tribes like the Jinta are essentially Canadian. Other tribes, like the Hummocca, are more North Korean. Because we have no direct contact with them we have very little information about what they do, and the information we do have keeps us away."

"Dr. Swenson has seen them," Marina said. "She told me so when we were coming in."

"And that's all she's told you," Alan said. "The story doesn't go any farther than that one piece of information: she's seen them and they frightened her. Just the idea of Annick being frightened of something is enough to keep me away."

"They're cannibals," Nancy said.

"They *were* cannibals," Alan said, "which is only to say a small part of the meat was eaten in rituals, not that they subsisted on a regular diet of human flesh, and there haven't been any reports of it happening in the last fifty years."

They had passed the opening in the jungle now. Looking back over her shoulder Marina found it nowhere in evidence. Had they turned the boat around she wasn't sure that she could find it. "No reports in the last fifty years, but it doesn't sound like anyone is going up there taking regular surveys about their habits."

"They've shot poisoned arrows at traders," Nancy said. "Either they're not very good shots and the arrows have landed wide of the boats, or they are very good shots and they mean it to be a warning. If Easter were at some point in his life a Hummocca, no one has plans to send him back."

When they arrived at the trading post it seemed less like Canada and more like Florida. A dozen or so tourists had come with their guide in an open boat from their eco-lodge to watch the Jinta children in their grass skirts as they twitched their nonexistent hips in time to the thundering rhythm of drums. The drums were played by middle-aged men, shirtless and thick, who were most likely the fathers. The fathers had run stripes of what looked to be red lipstick down their noses and across their cheeks and thrashed their heads from side to side like members of a garage band. The drummers were good but their children were better, their wrists encircled in tufts of grass. There were twenty of them or more ranging from very tiny to a few who were slightly bigger than Easter, and they stamped out a complicated pattern of footwork and then hopped in a large circle on one foot while sounding out the hue and cry of warriors. The tourists, enchanted, took pictures with their cell phones. A girl of ten or twelve with a red hibiscus tucked behind her ear stepped forward to dance a solo with a boa constrictor around her neck and so nicely did it hang and sway from her arms that one could not help but be reminded that a feather boa was made to imitate a snake. The mothers of the dancers quickly spread cloths on the ground and set out an array of small blow guns, tiny carved white herons, and string bracelets woven with red seeds. Having been given an opportunity to shop, the white women began bartering, wanting a bracelet and a necklace for the price of the bracelet alone. One of the women handed her husband the camera and then came and stood beside Marina. "Take my picture with this one," she said. "She's twice the size of the rest of them."

Marina, in her Lakashi dress, put her arm around the woman's waist so that her own red seed bracelet would show in the picture.

Easter went and stood beside one of the men with a tall kettle drum and put his hands on either side of the base. After a minute he began to nod his head in time. A boy came out with a three-toed sloth and hung it around a tourist's neck and the animal, barely awake, tilted back its head and seemed to smile at her. The sloth, for posing in pictures, was an even bigger hit than Marina. A heavyset woman in a dirty T-shirt and cutoff jeans then arrived with a struggling fifty pound capybara in her arms. She held it on its back the way one would a baby, possibly thinking the large rodent would take a nice picture as well, but the animal squealed and writhed and then finally bit her so that she was forced to drop it and watch it sprint away into the undergrowth, shrieking in fear. That was when two very old men in enormous feathered headdresses came skipping slowly out of a thatched hut shaking rain sticks, and the dancing children fell into a line behind them. The elder of the two men, the one with no teeth, stopped and took Marina's hand, tugging at her gently.

"You're supposed to dance," Nancy said.

"I can't do this," Marina said.

"I don't think there's any choice."

Marina looked at the crowd and then at the Indians and the message on every face was exactly the same: no choice. And so she took the chief's hand which he then held high above his head, about the level of Marina's cheekbone, and together they did the slow skip forward while the men beat their drums and the tourists took their pictures and the children followed with their dances, their snake and their sloth. In this group Marina danced with the people who were not white while the white people watched them. It would never have been her preference to be part of a tourist attraction. One of the children handed her the sloth and she took it. She hung it around her neck and continued her dance, feeling the soft, warm hair against her skin. Had anyone given her a choice, she would have chosen instead to be back on the porch behind the storage shed beneath her mosquito netting reading *Little Dorrit*. Still, she knew it was somehow less humiliating, less disrespectful, to dance with the natives than it was to simply stand there watching them.

Dollars accumulated in a woven basket, offerings to the gods. The letters were given to the tourists' guide, who said he had two hours off in Manaus the next day and would mail them himself. Benoit had been talking to the man the entire time and receiving strong advice on the importance of English and German. He should speak Spanish as well. Portuguese was nothing more than a baseline accomplishment.

On their way back from the trading post, Marina and the Saturns gave Benoit all of their attention. They looked at every bird and monkey he pointed to and when he found the correlating picture in the book they told him how to pronounce the words in English, *spot-billed toucanet*. Alan had brought binoculars and showed Benoit how to use them. Perhaps the tourists had rubbed off on them because they behaved as tourists now. They kept their collective gaze focused on the water and the leaves and the sky and scarcely looked at one another at all. They caught a glimpse of pink dolphins and discussed birds. They took a few unnecessary turns up very small tributaries because Benoit pointed them out to Easter and Easter, being free of all agenda, was happy to oblige. Marina and the Saturns had burned through so much emotion earlier in the day that now they all felt remarkably placid, or perhaps only exhausted. They had not passed another living soul since they left the Jintas and the world seemed something silent and wide, belonging only to them. On the left there was what appeared to be a crisp field of floating green lettuce. Benoit tapped at Easter's arm and the boy turned the wheel and took them in.

Beneath the sounds of bird calls there was the most delicate sound of crunching, as if the boat were making its way through a lightly frozen pond in December and the ice, half the thickness of a window pane, was breaking apart to let them pass. Marina leaned over the front of the boat and watched the lettuce compact beneath the pontoons while behind them the plants knitted themselves back together, smoothing over the path they had made without so much as a damaged leaf. We are here, Marina thought, and we were never here. It was a green so much brighter, so much fresher than anything she'd seen in the jungle. Long toed birds strolled across the delicate meadow with such confidence it was tempting to think those tiny floating plants might hold the weight of a single pharmacologist. The question then was whether the water was a foot deep or twenty feet deep. Benoit smacked at Easter again and held up his hand and Easter stopped the boat. Benoit lay down on his belly then, his head and shoulders over the side. He had seen something. The Saturns came and leaned over him, Marina leaned over him. "Is it a fish?" Nancy said. "Peixe?"

Benoit shook his head.

"I don't see anything," her husband said.

Easter kept his eyes on Benoit, who, without looking at his captain again, pointed his hand to the left, to the right, and then a little back. Easter held the throttle low and scooted the big boat around in the smallest possible increments until Benoit, every ounce of his attention fixed into the sweet spring of lettuce, abruptly raised his hand and Easter killed the engine altogether. The silence was startling. The budding naturalist, still flat on his stomach, then dove that same hand down through the leaves and began to pull the colossus of all snakes into the boat.

Human instinct dictated first that the snake must be kept away from the face, and so Benoit straightened his arm to rigid as if wishing to cast it away from his body while holding on too tight for the snake's comfort. The reptile's long, recurved teeth snapped ferociously into the air, diving towards Benoit's wrist while Benoit whipped the head from side to side, buying time until he could close the distance between hand and head. He rolled onto his side and then his back, managing somehow to pull the first half of the reptile on board while it flailed like a downed electrical wire. At its neck the snake was as big around as Benoit's wrist, and from there its body, smooth scales of darkest green with black blotches on the back and then creamy light underneath, swelled into a size more in keeping with his thigh. The snake kept pulling up and pulling up, more and more of itself slithering up and onto the deck in thick, muscular rolls where it sought to make its way onto Benoit's body, extending out against him, kneading him, while Benoit struggled mightily to keep their two faces apart. Do not let the faces touch.

"Put it back!" Nancy screamed in English, the language that stood between Benoit and his dream of being a tour guide. "Drop it!"

"Fuck!" Alan Saturn said, and then repeated the word endlessly for good measure.

He had caught it sure enough but he hadn't caught it close enough to the head. There was too much available snake above Benoit's hand, and the snake's enormous gaping mouth sought purchase, its jaws opening wider than such a little head should reasonably dictate. In a flash there was evidence of many rows of smaller teeth lined up and waiting to clamp into skin. Only by swinging it wildly did he keep the snake from sinking into his wrist. Benoit seemed fixated only on the six inches of the snake between the top of his fist and the tip of its tongue while completely ignoring the enormous body that was working its way heavily onto his own body now, and Benoit, who was wet with sweat and the water the snake brought on board, was laughing. There on his back pinned like a wrestler in an unsporting match, he roared with a powerful joy while he tried to work the one hand upwards with the assistance of the other hand. Easter, ever helpful, grabbed onto the lower half of their guest and tried to pry it off of his friend. There was too much coiling and uncoiling for an accurate measurement but the snake appeared to be fifteen feet long, eighteen when it stretched. Benoit appeared to be five feet, five inches, and he was outweighed by as much as fifty pounds. The three doctors pressed away, screaming various invectives in an unhelpful language. Marina wanted to jump in the water and to run across the lettuce with the long toed birds, but who could say the snake didn't have a family down there? There was an odor none of them recognized, the smell of a furious reptile, an oily stench of putrid rage that sunk into the membranes of their nostrils as if it planned to stay there forever. The back half of the snake whipped up and made itself a knot around Easter's slender waist and wrapped and wrapped and at the moment its head swung past, Easter reached into the air, his hand a quarter second faster than the snake, and grabbed its throat just below the head, well above Benoit's fist. Easter had caught the snake that Benoit had caught.

Oh, the whooping! The triumph and revelry! They shook the jungle with their screams, Benoit and Easter, for sure enough Easter was screaming, and the sound was so piercing, so much like the agony of death, that all three doctors were sure the boy was bitten and they lunged forward with the instinct of human decency to save his life. But Easter was grinning madly as he gripped the snake while Benoit, who was considerably stronger, held fast below. They looked into the creature's mouth now like a carnival attraction while the tongue, a silvered spark of light, licked towards them.

"It's a fucking anaconda!" Alan said. "He caught an anaconda with his hands!" Alan Saturn seemed to be at the perfect intersection of the thrilling achievement of the Lakashi, the terror of Marina and his wife, and the rage of the snake, whose eyes had focused into two pinpoints of murderous desire.

Easter coughed.

Maybe Marina understood before he did but of course that would be impossible to say. In a moment everything was clear to her and she stepped through the wall of her own revulsion and fear and took the tail end of the snake that was pressed into Easter's hip. Its flesh was at once clammy and dry, cool despite the terrible heat of the day. She had once dissected a snake in a college biology class, a small black garter snake long dead and stinking of formaldehyde. She had cut it down the center and pinned it open on a wax-bottom pan. To the best of her memory that was the only snake she had ever touched. She touched the second one as she worked to pull it from the boy. When she had pried a little of it loose she moved her hands up the body, hand over hand like she was working her way up a rope, except the end of the rope then began to wrap around her wrist. It was a muscle like nothing she had ever encountered. It did not fight against her. It did not notice her. She pulled. Easter coughed again. Benoit could now see the problem as well: his friend was wrapped inside the snake and the snake had figured out a way to loosen the hand that held its neck. Benoit slid his hand up to cover Easter's hand just as Easter's hand fell away. Easter tried to work his own small hands between himself and the snake and when he exhaled to get just his fingertips in between them the snake felt the movement of his breath and squeezed. Easter's eyes shot first to Marina and there she saw the very soul of him in his fear and she pulled and Alan's hands were by her hands and they were pulling together, all of them, Benoit from the throat while Nancy Saturn cried for a knife, a knife, and then "*Jaca!*"

But Benoit could not hear her now. He was frozen to the snake that was in the business of killing his friend who may have been eleven or twelve but was very small for his age.

"Tell me there is a fucking knife on this boat!" Nancy said. Easter's lips were turning blue. From either the lack of oxygen or the weight of the snake he went down on his knees. It occurred to Marina that his spine could snap. They all went down to their knees. Marina knew there was a machete strapped to the steering column of the boat, the knife that Easter had used to trim away the branches when he tied the boat to a tree. In an instant she was up. The knife was nearly as long as her arm, as heavy as a tennis racket, and she put the blade just above Benoit's fist and with a single pass sliced off the head. It would have been the greatest moment of her life had cutting off the head killed the snake but the beheading changed nothing. On the deck the busy head continued to snap its murderous teeth, moving in a slow circle as the jaw opened and closed, while its body went about the business of strangling a boy.

"Jesus," she said. She could see the tendons standing out on Benoit's neck, she could see his crooked bottom teeth, his open jaw jutting forward in the exertion, the blood of the headless snake running down his arm. While Benoit continued to pull the top of the snake, the Saturns continued to pull the bottom, and in the middle Easter continued his death. Marina began to saw into the rolls of headless snake, her hand at Easter's head and the point of the machete at Easter's toes. Her objective was to cut through both coils simultaneously as she doubted there would be time to do this twice. At no point did Easter make a sound. He would not use another teaspoon of breath. He stayed stock still inside this jacket and kept his eyes on Marina. First there was a large vertebral column that required Marina to lean in as she sawed, as much as she would have leaned in to saw apart a human wrist with a long knife at a bad angle. She had worried about pressing too hard and cutting into Easter, but Easter was still very far away. She cracked the vertebra in the first coil and then worked the knife from side to side to break the second bend. She then cut through the ribs, the thick muscles that ran down to the belly scute, the cloaca. When she was very close to Easter she put the knife down and ripped the bit of the snake that was left with her hands. The heavy weight of the snake worked in her favor then, tearing itself as it fell to the deck.

Nancy Saturn picked the boy up, light as air this child, and stretched him out beside his murderer and blew into his mouth and blew, her lips reined in to cover so small a mouth. With one hand behind his neck she tilted back his head and with her other hand she blocked his nose and she blew until she saw his chest rise and none of them could tell whose breath it was. She stopped for a minute. It was his. Shallow and uneven at first but his own. She lifted up his shirt and lightly touched the red welts across his torso and Alan Saturn kneeled beside her and put his ear to Easter's chest. Benoit crouched away from them, his head against his knees, his back heaving with his breath, while on the other side of the boat Easter's eyes blinked. Marina sat down beside him then in the widening pool of blood and took his hand.

It was still daylight when they got back. Alan Saturn was driving the boat and even though a couple dozen Lakashi were waiting on the shore the branches they held in their hands had not been lit. When they saw the boat they stood up to watch but they did not jump or cry out. It could have been because the travelers had only been gone for half a day and it could have been because Dr. Swenson was not among them. Either way, everyone on the boat was relieved, though there was more to celebrate now than there had been in all their lives combined. But when Alan Saturn pulled up next to the little dock and the Lakashi came on board the boat, the calling and crying broke forth in earnest, not the theatrical display of the week before but a deep and abiding joy Marina had not seen. Three men picked up the three large chunks of the snake from the blood-slicked deck and a fourth man picked up the head, the very head Marina had meant to kick into the water though she had been unwilling to touch it again even with her foot. They carried off the pieces of the snake, each as heavy as a small tree, and hoisted them about their heads to show the ebullient crowd. There would be anaconda for dinner tonight. It would be a feast to tell the grandchildren about years from now. So many Lakashi slapped their hands against Benoit they were beating him. They held out their chunks of snake in a rare offer of inclusion towards the Saturns, who leaned into each other fiercely and declined. Easter stood to walk but when he started to sway almost immediately, Benoit lifted him into his arms and the Lakashi cheered for them while the boy cried out in pain. Marina led them back to the porch and had Benoit put Easter in her bed and when Benoit was gone she crawled beneath the net herself to lie beside him. They were alive and together and they reeked of snake.

It wasn't long before Dr. Swenson came and found the two of them there in the little bed, shoulder to shoulder holding hands, small Hansel, big Gretel. Easter had fallen asleep taking shallow breaths through his mouth, but Marina's eyes were open wide. Even after all this time it still wasn't completely dark. "The Saturns told me what happened." Dr. Swenson reached beneath the net and touched his hair.

"I don't know what happened," Marina said, her eyes straight up to the point where the net knotted together. "It doesn't make any sense. He saw a snake in the water and he pulled it onto the boat? Why would he do that?"

"Benoit wants to be a tour guide and the stock and trade of an Amazon tour guide is the ability to pick things up—tarantulas, Caiman lizards, all sorts of ridiculous things. Pulling an anaconda into a boat is an extraordinary accomplishment. I've never seen anyone manage it, and I've seen people try. Had it ended better he probably would have asked you to write a letter to the National Board of Tourism."

"It's a miracle the thing didn't bite one of them. I'll be seeing those fangs for the rest of my life."

Dr. Swenson shook her head. "Teeth," she said, "not fangs. I'm told the bite is extremely painful and it's a monstrous business getting the head disengaged, but it isn't a poisonous snake. What that snake was doing to Easter was a much more serious business than biting."

Marina turned her head to face her mentor. "What about his liver, his spleen? If we were home I could take him for a CT."

"If you were home he wouldn't have been squeezed by an anaconda.

He would have been hit by an SUV while riding his bike. His odds were better against the snake."

"What?"

"It's dangerous here, you don't need to tell me that, but it's more dangerous there. This is where he understands things, he knows how to get along. Maybe he's cracked some ribs, but you watch him, he'll be fine. Dr. Eckman had ideas about taking Easter home with him. He felt if the hearing loss were nerve-based he might benefit from a cochlear implant, but you can't change people like that. You can't make a hearing boy out of a deaf boy, and you can't turn everyone you meet into an American. Easter isn't a souvenir anyway, a little something you pocket on your way out to remind you of your time in South America. You kept your head, Dr. Singh, you saved his life. I commend you for this. But if you think the reward for saving the boy's life is keeping the boy, then I must tell you this is not the case. A simple thank you will have to suffice. He is not available."

It would have been the easiest thing in the world for Marina to tell Dr. Swenson that she had no idea what she was talking about, when what Dr. Swenson was saying was perfectly clear, she had simply put it into words before Marina had made it a complete thought, the same way she would answer the questions on Grand Rounds the split second before Marina had them formulated in her mind. Marina was in fact moments from coming to the conclusion that the thing to do would be to take Easter home with her, that it was what Anders had wanted, that it was what she wanted, that in some bizarre way this was the child of their union, the product of the seven years Anders and Marina spent together in a cramped lab. Easter was her compensation for what she had lost. Dr. Swenson had simply seen it before Marina, and in seeing it, she cut her off at the pass. "It was horrible," Marina said weakly, wanting at least some sympathy for what she was being asked to forfeit. She meant the snake.

"I'm sure it was." Dr. Swenson put her hand against the boy's forehead, checking for fever, and then dipped two fingers into his neck to count his pulse. "Did you ever want children of your own, Dr. Singh?"

And there she was again, anticipating the next emotion, following Marina's train of thought backwards: *I cannot keep this child. I should have had a child.* She wondered if she were particularly transparent or if Dr. Swenson just had a special knack for reading her. "There was a time," Marina said. She could not make peace with the stench of the snake. She was amazed that Dr. Swenson hadn't commented on that.

"And that time has passed?"

Marina shrugged. It was a peculiar kind of therapy, lying flat out with the child you had only now realized you wanted while being asked if you had wanted a child. "I'm forty-two. I seriously doubt my life will change so much in the next year or two that it would be possible." She was no longer sure about what she wanted from Mr. Fox, and hers was not an age for indecision.

"There will be nothing but time, don't you understand? That's what the Lakashi are offering. If I can have a child at seventy-three, then why shouldn't you have one at forty-three, forty-five? I'll tell you the truth, Dr. Singh, what I have discovered about these trees is not what I expected. It will not be what your pharmaceutical company expects. It is something much greater, much more ambitious than anything we had hoped for. That was Dr. Rapp's great lesson in the Amazon, in science: Never be so focused on what you're looking for that you overlook the thing you actually find."

Marina was sitting up now. She had disengaged her hand from Easter's though the two were fairly stuck together from where the snake's blood had dried and sealed them into one unit. She came outside her net. "You're telling me you're pregnant?"

Dr. Swenson blinked. For a moment she looked more surprised than Marina. "You thought I was fat?"

"You're seventy-three years old!"

Dr. Swenson folded her hands on top of her stomach in a universal gesture of pregnancy. It was something Marina was sure she had never seen her do. Her shirt rode up and showed the roundness of her belly. "I know you have seen women here who are my age or older and they are pregnant. I've heard you comment on them."

"But they're Lakashi." Marina wasn't sure if what she was saying was racist or scientific. This distortion of biology is for them, not for us. She could still hear them singing by the river, beating on drums, no doubt tenderizing the snake before they held it on sticks above the fire, or whatever one did to cook a snake in these parts.

"They are Lakashi indeed, so that is the question. We know that if they eat the bark consistently from the onset of first menses their ova appear not to deteriorate. But Americans wouldn't feed their daughters a monthly pill from the time they're thirteen on the off chance the child will want to wait until she's fifty to reproduce. What we have to find out is whether or not the bark can reinvigorate the reproductive capacity of the postmenopausal woman."

"And you're the test case? You couldn't find someone else to do this?"

"There are no postmenopausal Lakashi. That's the whole point."

"Then you get a Jinta. You don't take it yourself."

"How quickly we put our medical ethics aside. I developed this drug. If I believe in it, and clearly I do, then I should be willing to test it on myself."

"Who is the father?"

Dr. Swenson looked at her with the gravest disappointment, the disappointment she reserved for first year medical students. "Really, Dr. Singh, you are not serious."

Given the circumstances of the day, Marina would have sworn that there was nothing left to upset her, and still she felt her hands shaking. "I understand that you are conducting an extremely limited initial trial on yourself but the end result of this experiment will be a child and, with all good wishes for your longevity, you may not be around as long as you might like to look after it. If there is no father in the traditional sense, then what happens to the outcome?"

"There are plenty of children around here. Do you really think one more is going to break the tribe? I am very well regarded. Any outcome of mine, as you so warmly describe this child, would be welcomed and well cared for."

"You're going to leave it here? Annick Swenson's child will be raised by the Lakashi?"

"They are a decent, well-organized people."

"You went to Radcliffe."

"I didn't love it."

Easter slept through all of it. Marina looked down on him in the bed. His shirt and arms and face were smeared with blood. Somehow in all of this she hadn't noticed it before. She would get a cloth and wash him. She could wash him while he slept. "Imagine Dr. Rapp fathered a child down here," she said, remembering the example of Alan Saturn in his argument with his wife and working to calm her voice. "Should the son or the daughter of the greatest mind in botany just wander around in the jungle for the rest of his or her life, not having any access to their own potential?"

"Do you think his children aren't here? Do you honestly think such things never happened? You should ask Benoit to take you to the next vision quest or whatever you want to call it." Dr. Swenson shook her head and then walked over to sit in the one small chair in the room. She sat on top of Marina's second dress and her other two pair of underpants as the chair was where she kept her things. "I am very tired, Dr. Singh," she said and pushed back her hair with her hands. "I have sciatica in my left leg and the child is sitting on my bladder. It begins to thrash whenever I lie down. I am glad to have conducted this piece of research on myself because it makes me realize something I might not have otherwise taken into account: women past a certain age are simply not meant to carry children, and I can only imagine that we are not meant to bear them or to raise them either. The Lakashi are used to it. This is their particular fate. They can hand off their infants to their granddaughters. They don't have to raise them. That is the only reward for these late-life children: you know they won't be your responsibility. I had never felt old before this, that is a fact. I have avoided mirrors my entire life. I have no better sense of what I look like at seventy-three than I did at twenty. I've had some arthritis in my shoulder but nothing to speak of. I keep on. I have kept coming down here, kept up with my work, Dr. Rapp's work. I have not lived the life of an old woman because I was not an old woman. I was only myself. But this thing, this child, it has made me firmly seventy-three. It has made me older than that. By straying into the territory of the biologically young I have been punished. I would have to say rightfully so."

Marina looked at her teacher, looked at her feet filling out a battered pair of Birkenstocks, looked at the way gravity pinned her to the chair. She asked the most ridiculous question of all, only because she had been so recently asked herself. "Did you ever want to have children?"

"What is it you said to me just now? There was a time? Maybe there was a time. To tell you the truth I can't remember. From where I sit I would tell you that having a child is akin to plotting your own death, but I delivered thousands and thousands of babies in my day and it seemed at least in that moment many of the mothers were happy. I know it wasn't like this for the young." Dr. Swenson closed her eyes and though her head stayed balanced and upright she seemed to be asleep.

"Should I walk you back to your room?" Marina asked.

Dr. Swenson considered the offer. "What about Easter?"

Marina looked back at him, noted the regular rise and fall of his chest. "He's not going to wake up. He's had a long day."

"That's the one you want," Dr. Swenson said, bringing their conversation back to its beginning although this time she seemed to be offering him up. "One who's older, one who's smart, one who loves you. If someone ever told me I could have had a child like Easter I would have done it, only I would have done it a long time ago."

Marina nodded, and using both of her hands she pulled Dr. Swenson up from her chair. "We can agree on that."

"You were smart to stay with us, Dr. Singh. I kept waiting for you to go, but I'm starting to see that you are genuinely interested in our work."

"I am," Marina said, realizing for the first time that she hadn't been thinking about leaving at all. Then she took Dr. Swenson's arm and together they walked down the stairs and side by side on the narrow path back through the jungle to the lab.

At the lab, Marina borrowed some soap and a pot, and when she was in the river took off her dress and held herself under the warm clouded water for some time. There was a complicated, ineffectual shower rigged up behind the lab that required hauling bags of water up from the river and running them through a filtering system but it would have been no match for all she was hoping to remove. Bringing her head above the surface, opening her eyes to the light falling at a low slant across the water, she was surprised to find that she no longer felt afraid of the river. She would have thought it would be the other way around. She scrubbed her dress and then used the rough fabric of the dress to scrub herself, then sank a final time and swam back into her clothes. She emerged dripping from the water still stinking, though perhaps not as much. Then she convinced the Lakashi women to let her put a pot of water down at the edge of their fire and while she waited for it to heat up a woman came and sat behind her, combing out Marina's wet hair with her fingers and then braiding it. If there were men in the tribe who hoped to one day escape their circumstances by becoming naturalists, the women all seemed to share a common dream of hairdressing. There was no more denying their desire to groom than one could stop those little African birds from riding on the backs of crocodiles and pecking out insects, and while Marina had fought them at first, pulling their hands from her hair whenever they gathered it back, she had finally given over to it. She had learned to relax beneath their touch. While the woman braided and tugged, Marina watched the river, counting the fish that popped the surface. She counted eight in all.

When her hair was finished and the water was hot enough she carried it back to the porch. It was finally getting dark and the evening was lovely and young. While the bats spun out of dead trees to announce the dusk, Marina washed the snake off of Easter. He woke up just enough to squint at her vaguely while she worked her cloth down his arms and between his toes. She wiped his face and rubbed his hair and was very gentle as she wiped down his stomach and chest which were already blossoming into a spectrum of purple and green. When she was finished he turned himself over with great difficulty and let her do the other side. She spread a clean sheet beneath him the way she had seen nurses do, it was a skill she had forgotten she had: change a bed with someone in it. So he had been a cannibal once, if only in another lifetime. In light of all that had happened it was hardly worth mentioning.

Nine

It was on the fourth morning after the trip to the trading post that Marina saw Dr. Budi and the second Dr. Saturn walking through the jungle. It was very early, much earlier than she normally would be out, but something had crawled beneath the net above her bed and bitten her near the elbow and the bite, now swollen and hot, had prevented her from going back to sleep. She used what scant morning light was available to inspect the snake's long-lasting tattoo that had deepened the color of Easter's bruises to eggplant and spread from his armpits to his groin. When she had assured herself yet again that these bruises were merely horrible and not a sign of some underlying medical catastrophe, she dislodged herself from the sleeping child and went in search of the coffee that Dr. Budi, always working, was sure to have made. It was still fifteen minutes short of full daylight when she saw her colleagues on the other side of a giant termite mound, the ground between them trembling with industry. She waved and called good morning and they stopped abruptly, looking at her as if she were the last person they had ever expected to see in the Amazon. After a pause, Dr. Saturn leaned down to whisper something in Dr. Budi's ear and Dr. Budi, after what appeared to be consideration, nodded her approval. The two doctors then made their way towards her, cutting a wide berth around the termites.

"How's Easter?" Nancy Saturn said.

Marina gave Nancy the credit for saving Easter's life, for having the presence of mind to say the word *knife* when Marina was still attempting to win a wrestling match with a snake. It was Nancy Saturn who had set their salvation in motion. "He was sleeping when I left. Dr. Swenson gives him half an Ambien at night now, otherwise the pain wakes him up."

"Blessings from Allah on that," Dr. Budi said, nodding.

"We're going out to the trees," Nancy said casually, laying her hand on the bag of notebooks that hung across her chest. "Why don't you come along?"

Before Easter's accident, if pulling a snake into a boat can be called an accident, Marina had asked several times to see the trees, but her requests had been met by a vague evasiveness—they had already been or this wasn't the week to go. Since the anaconda, she had frankly forgotten about them. Her notions of what was important had shifted. The jungle was not short on trees and she had seen many of them. It was difficult to imagine that some would be so substantially different from the others. Still, now that the invitation had been extended she accepted with pleasure, feeling that her patience had been noticed and rewarded.

In fact, she had written just such a sentiment last night to Mr. Fox, sitting on the floor of the sleeping porch and using the chair as a desk because Easter had already gone to bed. (Since the snake, his hammock had hung empty until a marmoset took it up for afternoon naps. It was a filthy little creature.) *I find myself following your advice now that I have no direct way of reaching you. You would tell me to wait and observe. You would tell me there is more to this situation than I could immediately understand and you would be right, just as you were right to tell me to come here and right to tell me (I know this is what you would say) to stay. Look how agreeable I've become since I've been gone! I can hardly believe how close I came to getting on the next flight home. I would have suffered through Manaus only to miss the very thing I had come for.*

Far to the west, Budi and Nancy and Marina heard a rustling of branches as two young women laughing and talking in what Marina still considered to be an impenetrable language passed at a distance, nodding their heads with disinterest when they spotted the doctors. One of the older women was walking from the direction of the river holding the hand of a young girl. Three more suddenly appeared from behind a large, dead stump. "You would think they all had alarm clocks," Nancy said as more and more women stepped from the underbrush and headed in the same direction. They were on a path Marina didn't think she had been on before although she couldn't be sure. Paths opened up when she studied the undergrowth carefully and then disappeared as soon as she turned her head. She had a mortal fear of following one path into the jungle and then being unable to find it again when she was ready to go out. If Marina had it all to do over again she would have brought sacks of red yarn with her so she could tie one end of the ball to the foot of her bed every time she entered the labyrinth.

"It is the Lakashi biological clock," Dr. Budi said, and Nancy and Marina laughed. Dr. Budi smiled shyly, having made so few successful jokes in her life.

It wasn't often that Marina dwelled on the contents of either of her lost suitcases but there were moments, and this was such a moment, when she would have liked a real pair of shoes instead of the rubber flip-flops. She would have liked a long sleeved shirt that would have saved her arms at least from the smaller thorns, and a pair of pants to protect her from those random blades of grass which when brushed past at exactly the right angle could slice the shin like a razor. The small amount of blood that beaded and then seeped from her leg was an advertisement for all she had to offer. It felt as if they were going a very long way, but distances, like directions, were hard to measure. It could have been that this particular path (were they on a path?) had more fallen trees lying across it that required clambering over, more mysterious sinkholes of standing water heralded only by a sudden sponginess underfoot. It could be that they were only two or three straight city blocks away from their destination but that distance was meaningless given the obstacles they had still to overcome. Marina brushed her hand across the back of her neck and dislodged something with a hard shell. She had learned in time to brush instead of slap as slapping only served to pump the entire contents of the insect, which was doubtlessly already burrowed into the skin with some entomological protuberance, straight into the bloodstream.

The Lakashi women were singing now. No, they weren't singing. It was just that so many of them were talking at once and when their voices came together it sounded vaguely like a section of Torah as sung by a group of bar mitzvah boys whose voices had yet to change. "Do you know what they're saying?" Marina asked.

Nancy shook her head. "I catch a word every now and then, or I think I do. We had a linguist with us for a while. He had been a student of Noam Chomsky's. He said the language wasn't particularly difficult or even interesting, that all the languages in this region of the Amazon came from a single grammatical base with variations in vocabulary which meant at one point the tribes must have been connected and then split apart. It made me wish we had a language that was a little bit more obscure so we might have kept him. He made us some charts with phonetics so we can put together some basic phrases."

"Thomas is very good at it," Dr. Budi said. She held up her arm and the other two women stopped and waited while a very large, low slung lizard dragged itself across their path, its loose green skin hanging over the rib cage like chain mail. "I don't know that one," Dr. Budi said, watching it carefully.

Nancy leaned over to peer at the lizard as if it were someone she could almost place, then she shook her head. "Neither do I."

It was another twenty minutes past the lizard before they came to a clearing, or, if not a clearing, a place where fewer, thinner trees stood farther apart from one another, and all the trees were the same. There was no thick coat of undergrowth covering the ground, just a light wash of grass, there were no hairy ropes of vines strangling the trees, only the smooth, straight expanse of bark. Sunlight fell easily between the pale oval leaves and hit the ground in wide patches. "It's beautiful," Marina said, dropping her head back. Such sunlight, such pretty little leaves. "My God, why don't they live here?"

"Too far from the water," Dr. Budi said, looking at her watch and making a note of the time.

A dozen Lakashi women were already there. Marina knew most of them by sight even if she couldn't properly reproduce the series of tones that made up their names. Over the next few minutes two dozen more arrived and took their places against the trunks that were a buttery yellow color and ranged from ten to twenty inches around. Without ritual or fanfare, with no apparent consideration, the women went for bigger trees, the ones already bitten, and left the saplings alone. Pressing in like a partner for a slow dance, they opened their mouths and began immediately to scrape their teeth down the bark. The jungle on this morning was particularly quiet and so it was possible to hear them, a small sound amplified by so many women making it at the same time.

A few stragglers wandered in and stopped to greet the women at the trees around them who stopped their biting and chewing long enough to receive the greeting and return it. Two of the women who had a great deal to say to each other took opposite sides of the same tree and from a distance they appeared to be kissing. Women who had brought their children left them in a pile in the center of the trees and the older children herded the younger ones back when they tried to crawl away. One of the older women went into the group of children and led a girl of twelve or thirteen to a tree and the others stopped all at once, turning their heads from their trees to watch her. When the girl tilted her face to the side, looking uncertain of how she should approach it, the others hooted lightly and slapped their trees to make a kind of tree-plus-human applause. The thin branches trembled and shook the delicate leaves from side to side. The girl, whose hair was unbraided and disheveled by sleep, looked embarrassed to be the center of so much attention. She then began to nibble at the bark. After the others felt certain she was performing this primal act correctly they all went back to their work. From the nubile to the beldame they scraped and chewed without pleasure or distaste. They had turned the fairly exotic act of biting a tree into nothing more than factory work.

"This is important," Dr. Budi said to Marina. "The girl has just completed her first menstrual cycle. The Lakashi rituals are very brief, unsentimental. You are lucky to see such a thing on your first day."

Nancy Saturn turned some pages in her notebook. "I didn't realize Mara was menstruating."

Dr. Budi held up her book. "I have it."

There were more than enough trees for everyone, maybe two hundred of them spread over two acres of land. The tallest climbed to a height of sixty or seventy feet, but there were plenty of new trees coming up as well. In the places where a tree had been recently eaten, the absence of bark left a mark that was soft and white; growing back, it was the palest of yellows and then darkened over time so that most of the trees at the height of a Lakashi's head appeared to have been banded by decoupage.

It was easier to breathe in this place, and so easy to see! In every direction the vista was open. No more wondering what might be tearing through the jungle with its wet jaws hinged open. "I never thought there would be so many trees," Marina said. "I didn't picture it like this."

"It's actually just one tree," Nancy said. She was counting the women and marking them present by name in her notebook. "They're

Populas, like Aspens, a very rare phenomenon. It's a single root system. The tree is cloning itself."

"Very delicate," Dr. Budi said, nodding to herself.

"The root system changes the acidity level in the soil so that nothing much will grow here except for the trees and a little bit of grass. In a sense you could say the tree poisons the area it inhabits to make sure that nothing else will survive in its space and take the nutrients out of the soil or grow taller and block out the sunlight."

"Except the Rapps," Dr. Budi said. "The Rapps thrive right where they are." She pointed the tip of her pen towards the clusters of mushrooms that grew near the base of the trees, each cap a perfect golf ball on a tall, slender stem. The Rapps were a most unearthly shade of pale blue. They came so close to glowing in the light of day that she wanted to come back with a flashlight and see them in the dark. Marina couldn't imagine how she had missed them.

"*Psilocybe livoris rappinis,*" Nancy said. "They are considered to be the greatest single discovery in mycology. There has never been any evidence that this ecosystem is duplicated anywhere else in the rain forest, anywhere in the world. These trees you're looking at here, these mushrooms, this is it. As far as we know, these are the only Rapps in the world. Your passport to spiritual enlightenment."

"You've tried them?"

Nancy Saturn closed her eyes and nodded slightly, holding up one finger.

"Very sick," Dr. Budi said. "Interesting, everything you see, but too sick."

"So if the mushrooms are Rapps, are the trees called Swensons?" Marina asked. There was an inordinate number of lavender moths the size of quarters bobbing through the sunlight. Marina didn't remember seeing them before but then it would be difficult to notice such a small moth in the workaday tangle of vines that suffocated the rest of the jungle.

"The trees are called Martins," Dr. Budi said. "*Tabebuia martinii.*"

"It's actually the Rapps we're protecting," Nancy said. "All the secrecy about the work and the location, it's so no one can find the Rapps. Scientifically, it's the Martins that have presented such remarkable potential. The Martins really may prove to be one of the great botanical discoveries of our age. But people have been trying to get their hands on the Rapps ever since Dr. Rapp started writing about them. If the greater world knew where they were—"

Dr. Budi covered her eyes with her hand and shook her head.

"Exactly. This place would be overrun, drug dealers, the Brazilian government, other tribes, German tourists, there's no telling who would get here first and what sort of a war would ensue. The only thing I know for sure is that the Lakashi would be destroyed. Their entire existence is built around Rapps and while they have easily a hundred times more mushrooms than they need for their rituals they have no interest in drying and storing them. The Rapps present three hundred and sixty-five days a year and so the Lakashi just assume they're always going to be right here under the trees. I've been trying to grow Martins and, subsequently, Rapps, for three years now, and I'm not talking about growing them back in Michigan, I'm talking about growing them in the lab from root dissections, the same soil, the same water, and I can't do it."

"You will," Dr. Budi said.

Nancy Saturn shook her head. "It's too soon to say."

Dr. Saturn and Dr. Budi announced that they were talking too much and the window of time for work would not stay open indefinitely. They excused themselves and began going tree to tree asking the women questions that involved the use of four or five words of Lakashi. Nancy took a cuff out of her bag and was checking Mara's blood pressure. Marina took the opportunity to look at the trees: a small plastic placard, numbered and dated, had been staked in front of each one. She ran her hands over the scarred bark, sniffed at the wood. Had she seen them by a lake in Minnesota she wouldn't have given them a second look, or maybe one glance back, just because she had no memory of seeing such yellow bark. The Rapps she would have noticed, looking down at the small clump near her feet. They were like a cluster of exotic sea creatures that had washed up a thousand miles inland. How in the world had Dr. Rapp found this place? How had he known to look past the fire waving tribe on the shore and go a mile into the jungle? Marina cut a path between the trees. What a pleasure it was to walk! What a pleasure to take a large step and be able to see where her foot was landing. She raised her arms above her head and stretched. One by one the women stepped back from the trees and began scratching out whatever splinter of bark had lodged between their teeth with their fingernails. Budi picked a handful of women out of the crowd and wiped down their fingers with alcohol swabs and then pricked them to draw the small pipettes of blood. After making notes she carefully pressed the tubes into a small metal case. On the other side of the stand, Dr. Saturn went through a more challenging interaction as she handed three of the women long cotton swabs and waited while they reached beneath their dresses, made a quick flick with the wrist, and handed the swab back to her. Dr. Saturn then tapped the swab on a slide and on a piece of litmus paper.

"What in the world are you doing?" Marina asked.

"Checking the levels of estrogen in cervical mucus." Dr. Saturn's carrying case was a more complicated affair and she sat down on the ground to make her notations on the test tube where she deposited her swabs. "The slides are for ferning."

"No one does ferning anymore," Marina said. It was the slightly arcane process of watching estrogen grow into intricate fern patterns on slides. No ferns, no fertility.

Dr. Saturn shrugged. "It's very effective for the Lakashi. Their estrogen levels are quite sensitive to the intake of bark."

"How in the world did you convince them to—" She wasn't sure of the appropriate word. Self-swab?

"That," Dr. Saturn said, "is Dr. Swenson's genius. The training was in place a long time before I arrived. I cannot imagine how terrified of her they must have been to have gone along with it. These days it doesn't even seem to register as an invasion of privacy." The third Lakashi woman handed over her Q-tip without fanfare and Nancy bowed her head as she accepted it.

When the Lakashi had finished what had been asked of them, they walked off in groups of two and three and four, not looking back at the trees or acknowledging the scientists. They picked up the children who were too small to walk reliably and let the others trail behind as best they could. They were done.

"Do they come every day?" Marina watched as the entire lot of them receded into the thickening woods as if a school bell had been rung. They left without so much as a glance back to the doctors or the trees. Their work was done.

"They chew the bark every five days, though the entire female sector of the tribe doesn't come on the same day. Their visits are regular. How they figure the five days is beyond us as they have no apparent system for marking time. I can only assume that it has at this point become a biological craving. They don't come when they're pregnant. In fact the bark repulses them from what seems to be the moment of conception. Dr. Swenson confirms this. Because of this pregnancies seem especially long out here. We know about them for a full thirty-nine weeks. They also don't come when they're menstruating, though conveniently they're pretty much on the same cycle so we get a few days off every month."

"All of them?"

Nancy nodded. "It takes the new girls a while to get it straightened out and no one is perfectly regular after giving birth, but other than that."

Dr. Budi walked over to a tree near her and looked to find a place where the bark was darkest yellow and dry, then she leaned towards it and bit, her teeth making that same scraping sound. "You'll try it?" she said, looking back at Marina.

"I should take her vitals," Nancy said, pulling out the blood-pressure cuff again. "Budi, take her temperature."

"Why would I?" Marina said.

"We need people to test. People who aren't Lakashi. We do it."

"But I'm not going to get pregnant."

Nancy Velcroed a cuff around Marina's arm and began to pump it tighter and tighter. Dr. Budi held up a flat plastic thermometer and Marina, sure of nothing, opened her mouth.

"You would not be alone in that," Dr. Budi said.

"Believe me, there are plenty of things to test you for. You don't have to get pregnant."

"Thomas will tell you," Dr. Budi said, and then as if on cue, Dr. Nkomo broke through the thicket outside the stand of Martins and was walking towards them.

"I see I am sufficiently late," he said, bowing his head to the three women.

"Men and women don't come to the stand at the same time," Nancy told Marina. "The women chew the trees and the men gather the Rapps."

"Division of labor," Dr. Budi said. Nancy removed the blood-pressure cuff and pressed two fingers to the side of Marina's wrist to find her pulse.

"First time, yes?" Thomas said.

Marina nodded, keeping her mouth fixed to the thermometer.

"Ah, very good. Just remember to keep your tongue pushed down. Otherwise you can get splinters."

"Although we're geniuses at taking them out," Nancy said. "Pulse sixty-four. Well done, Dr. Singh."

Thomas brought his mouth to the tree beside him and, far above the band of scarring, began to scrape down the bark. Marina took the thermometer out of her mouth. "Wait a minute," she said.

"The Martins have many purposes," Nancy said. "For years Dr. Rapp thought that part of the hallucinogenic qualities in the mushrooms must come from the root system of the tree, that it must in some way be leached from the trees themselves, so he assumed that by chewing bark the women were, in essence, giving themselves a little bump. It was Annick who made the connection between the trees and extended fertility. Apparently he never noticed that they kept getting pregnant."

"She still is always giving Dr. Rapp the credit," Dr. Budi said, not as a correction, simply as a statement.

"If you look at their notes from that time it's quite clear." Thomas took a handkerchief out of his pocket and touched it to the corners of his mouth.

"It wasn't until 1990 that she made the connection between the Martins and malaria," Nancy said. "And that was definitely her discovery. Dr. Rapp was barely in the field by the nineties."

"She still gives him credit," Dr. Budi said. "Says he had mentioned it before."

Thomas Nkomo shook his head by way of acknowledging the sadness of a woman who was so quick to assign her achievements to a man. "This is the greatest discovery to be made in relation to the Lakashi tribe. Not the Rapps or the fertility but the malaria."

"I don't understand," Marina said, and she didn't, not any of it.

"Lakashi women do not contract malaria," Dr. Budi said. "They have been inoculated."

"There is no inoculation for malaria," Marina said, and the other three smiled at her, and Thomas bit the tree again.

Nancy Saturn pointed out the small purple moth resting on the white inner bark of the tree. It was the spot that Dr. Budi had recently chewed and there was still the slightest glimmer of saliva on the surrounding outer bark. "The Martin is a soft bark tree. Once the bark is broken the Lakashi have no trouble scraping through the inner bark and down into the cambium where the living cells are. This creates an opening, as you can see, a sort of wound in the tree, and into that wound comes this moth, the purple martinet."

"You can't be serious," Marina said, leaning in for a better look. "Is there anything he didn't name for himself?"

"The Lakashi tribe was not a Martin Rapp discovery. If it had been, this place would surely have been Rapptown." Nancy put a finger just beneath the moth which, like the Lakashi, seemed impervious to the invasions of its privacy. "*Agruis purpurea martinet.* It takes liquid from the pulp of the Martin, not the sap, which is deeper inside the tree. The insect subsists on the moisture in the wood itself. It ingests and excretes almost simultaneously, processing the proteins from the pulp. Once a year it lays its eggs."

"In the bark?" Marina asked. When the moth opened its wings it showed two bright yellow dots like eyes, one on either side, then it folded back up again. A butterfly rests with its wings open and a moth rests with its wings closed, she had read that somewhere years ago.

Nancy nodded. "Like the Martins and the Rapps, the purple martinets seem to exist right here. You'll see one in camp from time to time. They'll go as far as the river, but we have no record of it feeding outside this area. The key to fertility is found in the combination of the Martin tree and the purple martinet, although we haven't isolated the moths' excretions from the proteins in its larval casing. What we know is that it works."

Dr. Budi wiped an alcohol swab over her own finger and then pricked it herself.

"What about the blood samples?" Marina asked. "Can you actually read hormone levels on such a small amount of blood?"

"Nanotechnology," Budi said. "Brave new world."

Marina nodded.

"We've isolated the molecules as they are metabolized in the bark of the tree," Budi continued, "but we're still charting the impact of the Lakashi saliva, their gastric juices, plasma. What we don't know is what combination of factors is also giving the women protection against malaria."

Marina asked if the men in the tribe were susceptible to malaria and Thomas nodded. "After they have completed breast-feeding, the male babies are as likely as any member of comparable tribes to contract malaria, as are female children between the ages when they cease to be breast-fed and the onset of their own first menses, when they begin chewing the trees."

"So they aren't actually inoculated. The tree and the moth act as a preventative, like quinine."

Dr. Budi shook her head. "Preventative while breast-feeding, inoculated when eating the bark. The question is why the entire tribe hasn't evolved to eat the bark in their youth, but considering how many children die of malaria, there could be a terrible population explosion among the Lakashi were they all to live."

"But how do you know?" Marina asked. Her head was swimming with this. Had they convinced some men to eat the bark? How had they tested the children? "Could you get some of the women to stop eating the bark?" She looked up again at the trees. She could see now far away against the ceiling of sky the clusters of pink flowers that hung as heavy as grapes.

"There have been a few cases of women who were unable to conceive who after a while stopped participating in the group visits to the Martins," Nancy said. "But because they had already eaten the bark they were inoculated."

"Mostly we have experimented on ourselves," Thomas said.

"With what?"

Dr. Budi looked at her, blinked. "Mosquitoes."

"So what drug is being developed exactly?" Marina asked. A purple martinet dipped past her and then landed on the front of her dress, its purple wings opening and closing twice before flying off again.

"There is enormous overlap," Thomas told her. "In exploring one we learn about the other. They cannot be separated out."

Nancy Saturn was a botanist. She could be playing for either team. But Dr. Budi and Thomas and Alan Saturn all seemed to be on the side of malaria. "Is Dr. Swenson the only one working on the fertility drug?"

"That is certainly her primary project," Thomas said. "But we believe the answer to one is the answer to the other."

"It's a lot to take in," Nancy said. "We understand that. Just give the bark a try, see what you think. You probably won't be here long enough to be part of the tests but you should at least give it a go. The number of non-Lakashi who have had the chance to chew the Martins is very small."

"It is an honor," Dr. Budi said, leaning forward to take another bite herself.

What was it Anders had said to her? "Pretend for a moment that you are a clinical pharmacologist working for a major drug development firm. Imagine someone offering you the equivalent of *Lost Horizon* for American ovaries." Marina closed her eyes, pressed down her tongue, and opened her mouth. It was not as natural as it appeared. It was more like milking a cow, easy as long as someone else was doing it. The secret seemed to be in the angle of the head, not coming at the tree straight on. In truth the bark was nearly soft, yielding. It offered up the slightest amount of pulpy liquid that tasted of fennel and rosemary with a slightly peppered undertone that she could only imagine had to do with the excrement of the purple martinet. It wasn't bad, but then it couldn't be bad. Generations of Lakashi women and a handful of scientists would not persist in chewing a foul tasting tree. How had that first Lakashi woman thought to break the bark with her teeth, and how did that first moth, who must have been eating something somewhere before this, flutter in behind her? Marina pressed in somewhat harder and felt a sharp stab in her upper gum line but she was not deterred. She was not seventy-three. She was not so old at all, and there were plenty of women who had children at her age, women who certainly never went as far as this. As ambivalent as she was regarding her own ability to reproduce, she was not the least bit ambivalent about the science of the experiment. Now she wanted that global satellite phone. She would have called Mr. Fox from where she stood and told him what was possible.

Dr. Budi tapped her shoulder. "Enough now," she said. "Too much at first affects the bowels."

Nancy handed her a swab sealed inside a test tube. "For later," she said. "You could just drop it off on my desk."

Marina touched her fingers to her lips and nodded. "Did Anders come here? Did he try this?"

There was a look that passed between the other three, a very brief flash of discomfort. "He was interested in our work," Thomas said. "From the beginning. He was with us here for as long as he could be."

"I want to see where he's buried," Marina said, hoping it was here in the field of Martins. She hadn't asked before because she wasn't sure she would be able to bear the sight of it, looking down at all the ungodly growth and knowing that Anders was beneath that weight forever. But it would be easier to remember him in a beautiful place. She could describe all of this to Karen. She could explain the openness. Even if he wasn't here, this is what she would tell her.

"Ah," Nancy Saturn said, pressing the toe of her tennis shoe against the root of a Martin.

"We don't know," Thomas said.

"Who does know? Dr. Swenson knows."

After a period of silence it was Dr. Budi who spoke up. She was not one to leave a difficult job to someone else. "The Lakashi bury people during a ritual. They take the body away, they take the Rapps. It is a private matter for them."

"But he wasn't one of them," Marina said. She saw him laid out on a makeshift bier being carted off into the very trees he hated, Gulliver dead and dragged away by Lilliputians. "It makes a difference. It makes an enormous difference." She said it knowing full well it made no difference whatsoever. He was dead and that was all that mattered.

"They were very fond of Anders," Thomas said, patting her shoulder. "They would have given him every care."

"It was raining hard that week," Dr. Budi said. "It was very hot. The Lakashi would not bury him where we asked and we could not bury him ourselves."

"So you gave him up." She saw Karen so clearly in her mind, sliding down to her kitchen floor, taking the dog in her arms. Karen had felt it fully even then, never having seen this place. "It was the only thing Dr. Swenson said in her letter, that he had been buried in keeping with his Christian traditions. I don't even know if he had any Christian traditions but I doubt he planned to be buried in a jungle by a group of people eating mushrooms."

"She said it to comfort you," Dr. Budi said.

"Let's go back," Nancy said, and put an arm around Marina.

There was no one clear point of loss. It happened over and over again in a thousand small ways and the only truth there was to learn was that there was no getting used to it. Karen Eckman had wanted Marina to go to Brazil to find out what had happened to her husband, but now that she was here she understood what Dr. Swenson had told her in the restaurant that first night after the opera: it could have been anything, any fever, any bite. It never was remarkable that Anders had died; the remarkable thing was that the rest of them were managing to live in a place for which they were so fundamentally unsuited. Karen had wanted to believe that knowing what Anders had died of and where he was buried would make a difference, but it wouldn't and it didn't. At some point Marina would have to figure out a way to tell her that.

Marina went back to the porch with the taste of Martins still on her tongue and found that Easter was up and gone. She looked through the sheets to see if there was a letter from Anders but there was nothing. Easter was no doubt showing off his bruises to the other children. She had already seen him laying two sticks in the mud very far apart to show them how long the snake had been. She wondered at what point he had lost his hearing and if he understood enough about language to miss it when there was so great a story to tell. She would have loved to know how the snake had lodged itself in his memory, if he thought of it as the terror it was or as a great adventure, or maybe he didn't think of it at all except as the source of the dull ache in his chest. Marina had to admit she really didn't know what Easter thought about anything. His nightmares had abated since the snake, he no longer cried out in the night, though that could have been the Ambien or the comfort of sleeping the entire night in her bed. It could have been that once an anaconda had squeezed him half to death there really wasn't anything left to be afraid of.

Outside, Marina heard Dr. Swenson calling her name, and she went and leaned over the porch railing.

"You've been gone half the morning, Dr. Singh," Dr. Swenson said. She was with a Lakashi man wearing shorts and a gray T-shirt that he had sweated through. The men wore T-shirts as a means of dressing up, certainly anyone coming early in the morning to seek an audience with Dr. Swenson would find a shirt to put on. He was holding a small red canvas duffel bag with both hands. From this particular angle, looking down on the two of them from a height of eight or ten feet, she couldn't imagine that she had ever missed Dr. Swenson's pregnancy. She was nothing but belly.

"There was a lot to talk about," Marina said, and she had every intention of talking to Dr. Swenson about it as well: Anders' burial, and who was funding the research for the malaria vaccine. But the man standing next to Dr. Swenson was bobbing up and down on the balls of his feet and twisting his hands back and forth against the straps of the bag and it was difficult to concentrate on anything but him. He twitched like he was trying unsuccessfully to conceal the fact he was crawling with ants.

"Talk we will, Dr. Singh. It's not a short walk. There's plenty of time to catch up, but I need you to come with me now."

"What's the problem?" Obviously there was a problem. The man was moaning. She could hear him now above the din of the insects though he seemed to be making a concerted effort to be quiet in the same way he was trying his best, she could tell, despite all his movement, to stay still. It wasn't just that Dr. Swenson had convinced the Lakashi to submit to her tests, they were as afraid of her as any group of first-year interns. The clear accomplishment of the man in the gray T-shirt was that he wasn't screaming.

"You'll like this," Dr. Swenson said, and turned back to the path they had come down. "This will be right up your alley."

Marina was out the door and down the steps. Dr. Swenson did not wait for her and had continued to carry on their conversation alone. "I know how much you've been looking forward to practicing medicine while you're here. I think we've found you an opportunity."

Even with Dr. Swenson six or seven months pregnant Marina had to rush to keep up with them. The man was setting the pace and the pace was quick. She kept a close eye on the ground. Marina had a particular fear of breaking her ankle. "I didn't say that."

Dr. Swenson stopped and turned to Marina. The man now looked petrified. It was imperative they continue their forward motion. He raised up the bag in case she had forgotten it and began a quick monologue in Lakashi, but Dr. Swenson held up her hand. "You did. You remember, on the boat. We were discussing the girl with the machete in her head."

"I do remember," Marina said, marveling at how the panic rising up in her was obliterating all of her questions: Why did you give Anders over to them and why did you lie about it and there was something else after that but now she couldn't remember. "I thought it was right for you to attend to the cases that presented themselves."

"That presented themselves to me as a doctor, or you as a doctor. Either way, you waved the Hippocratic oath above our heads like a flag so now you'll have the chance to bask in its glory."

"I'm a pharmacologist."

To the man's great relief Dr. Swenson started walking again. The sun was high and bright and very hot. "Yes, well, I can't get on the floor and in this village things happen on the floor, and if you're planning to tell me that they should bring his wife to the lab, I've already suggested that. She can't go down the ladder. As much as I am opposed to hosting a medical clinic in my office, I am considerably more opposed to house calls."

"What's wrong with his wife?"

Dr. Swenson passed a dead log covered in bright red butterflies and the breeze that she made caused them to startle and disperse upwards into a bright red cloud. "It has something to do with the birth of a child. If you are ever betting on the nature of a local tragedy you'll never go broke putting your money on that one. For the most part they do it remarkably well but the sheer volume in which they reproduce brings forth a certain number of errors."

"Do you know what this error is?" Marina was walking faster and faster when everything in her was saying she should stop.

Dr. Swenson shook her head. "No idea."

"But you said you didn't want to interfere." Interference in the medical needs of an indigenous people suddenly struck Marina as the worst possible idea. She could see now the virtue in leaving them alone, of observing without imposition. "You distinctly said there was someone—"

"The county witch doctor, yes. His malaria has flared again. He's running such a fever we've been asked to go by and check on him later. There is also, you will be pleased to know, a midwife, who is presently in labor herself. She is being attended by the midwife-in-training, who is her daughter. The daughter would feel much more comfortable if we stopped in."

"Who told you this? It isn't possible."

"The messages are collected by Benoit, who brings them to Dr. Nancy Saturn. Benoit and Dr. Saturn can stumble along together in Portuguese. Frankly, the chain of communication is so weak that we might arrive and find out none of this is true. I do a better job communicating with Easter than I do most members of the tribe."

In the jungle they passed the stilted huts of several families who leaned against the railings and waved. An enormous fallen branch blocked the path for a moment but their scout dragged it away before they had the chance to wonder how they might crawl through. Marina began again. "Dr. Swenson, you have to listen to me. I am not the person for this job. There are other doctors here and any one of them, I promise you, is better qualified."

"Shall we ask the botanist?" Dr. Swenson said sharply. "Or one of the other three? I doubt they have ever been out of a lab in their lives. You forget I have worked with these *doctors* for several years now. They have a real talent for breeding mosquitoes and that is all the credit I will give them. You may be a pharmacologist, Dr. Singh, but before that you were a student of mine. You know how to do this, and if you don't I will be standing there reminding you. I cannot get down on the floor anymore. My leg won't allow it. I will not go to the trouble of telling you that you can turn back now and leave this woman to her fate because it would be a waste of my time and yours. You will do this regardless of how you feel about it. That much I know about you now."

Marina felt such a sudden weight in her feet that she looked down at them, sure she must have stepped in something.

"Cheer up, Dr. Singh. It's your chance to do good in the world."

Marina's scalp was wet with sweat and it ran down the sides of her face and the back of her neck. She was going over notes in her mind and finding that entire pages of them were missing. Of course there was a chance that everything was fine, that they would arrive to find nothing but a long labor and a nervous husband. If it were only a matter of delivering the child because everyone else was indisposed, well, she could do that. Anyone could do that. She was only hoping there would be no cutting involved. Where was the bladder exactly? When she walked away from her last C-section it had never occurred to her that this was a skill she might someday be called to use again. Why should she have stayed current, attended the conferences, read the journals? She wasn't even boarded in obstetrics. Any fireman or taxi driver could be called on for a vaginal delivery, but the unqualified were never asked to cut. Somehow this thought calmed her, and for a moment she allowed herself the pleasant picture of a baby slipping easily into her hands while her teacher watched. There was no reason to think this wasn't the way it would go.

"You're very quiet," Dr. Swenson said. "I thought you would have so much to talk about while we walked. Everyone back at the lab this morning was anxious to discuss your feelings."

"I'm trying to remember how to deliver a baby," Marina said.

"The brain is a storage shed. You put experience in there and it waits for you. Don't worry. You'll find it in time." With these nearly encouraging words they reached their destination. Had the Lakashi lived in a city, this particular hut would have been located in the outskirts of the farthest suburb. It was for the native who wanted privacy, who wanted a view of the river without a view of his neighbors. They knew it was the right house by the pitifully weak screaming that emanated from it. The man and the duffel bag bounded up the ladder ahead of them and was gone.

Dr. Swenson looked behind him, gauging the logistics. "When I think of finishing this project and going back to the States the thing I picture is a staircase. I suppose if I were more ambitious in my daydreams I would think of elevators and escalators, but I don't. All I want is a nice set of stairs with a banister. You are my witness, Dr. Singh. If I make it out of this country alive I will never climb another ladder again."

At seventy-three it was hardly a shocking oath to swear. Marina considered the length of Dr. Swenson's arms and legs against the width of her circumference. It did not seem possible. "Is there any way for me to help?"

"Not unless you strap me to your back. I believe I can go up but the coming down concerns me. I don't want to get stuck up there and wind up having to give birth in this hut myself."

"No," Marina said, though the thought of going up there alone was not without problems.

Dr. Swenson rubbed at her temples. "What do we know for certain, Dr. Singh? I am a seventy-three-year-old woman who is pregnant and short. But women who are older and shorter and more pregnant than I have made it up and down these ladders every day of their lives, including the day of their delivery."

The T-shirted man leaned over the floor and looked at them with expectation. "*Vir! Vir!*" he said.

"Oh good," Dr. Swenson said. "He has a little Portuguese. He says we should come." She looked up again. "I suppose we should."

"We also know for certain that none of those women was having her first child at seventy-three," Marina said. "They had a lifetime of experience in climbing the ladders, pregnant or not. They were used to it."

Dr. Swenson turned to her and nodded her approval. "Well said, and I admire your willingness to argue against your own best interests. Now stay one step behind me and prepare yourself to be an ox. You are very strong, aren't you?"

"Very," she said. And so they climbed, Marina stretching her long arms around her professor, her hands just beneath Dr. Swenson's hands, her strong thighs beneath Dr. Swenson's thighs, and up they went towards the wretched weeping and the husband's calls of "Agora." *Now!*

Benoit had been sent ahead with instructions that the family should have waiting a large quantity of water that had been twice boiled and twice strained, and the first thing they saw were the buckets, which were not clean themselves, sitting in a row. Benoit, who had avoided Marina since the incident with the snake, was nowhere in evidence. The woman lay on the floor in a pile of blankets and both the woman and the blankets were so wet they looked like they'd been dredged up from the river. Spreading across the floorboards beneath her was a dark, soaking stain. Their guide was kneeling beside his wife, holding her hand, rearranging her wet hair with his fingers while the other members of the household went about their business. An elderly man with no shirt stretched out in a hammock while two small children, a boy and a girl, pushed him back and forth, laughing ecstatically every time he swung away. Three women, one with a baby on her breast, were tying strings of red peppers together while a man in the corner sharpened a knife. When Dr. Swenson arrived at the top of the ladder she was panting and they all snapped up their heads in attention. She pointed to a wooden crate and one of the younger women ran to bring it to her. She sat down and was offered a gourd full of water which she accepted. Even the woman on the blankets quieted herself to acknowledge the honor she had been shown. To think that Dr. Swenson had come to her house!

Marina didn't know if she should first attend to the patient or the doctor, when in fact she wasn't sure she had the skills to help either one of them. "There's the bag," Dr. Swenson said, and gave a nod towards the floor. "You'll find what you need. I'll tell you, I'm impressed to have managed this." She covered her heart with her hand. "I haven't gone up a ladder since this whole ordeal began."

Marina unzipped the bag and ran her hand in circles inside, heartsick to see how little she had to work with. There was a bar of soap in a box, no scrub brush, some packaged, disinfected towels, packaged gloves, a prepackaged surgical kit, some various medications that rolled around the bottom of the case looking paltry. There were two silver shoehorns with their ends bent back. Marina held them up. "What are these?"

"Shoehorns!" Dr. Swenson reported happily. "Rodrigo got a whole box of them once years ago. They make brilliant retractors."

Marina put the shoehorns in her lap and bowed her head. "How can I sterilize them?"

"How can you sterilize anything? You can't, Dr. Singh. This is what it is. Go ahead and wash up in the first bucket," Dr. Swenson said. "I'm catching my breath."

The water in the first bucket was tepid and Marina ground the soap into her skin over and over again, wondering how it was possible that she was where she was, that what was about to happen was in fact happening. Surely she had participated fully in every step it took to get to this place, agreeing whenever she had meant to decline, but still, it wasn't such a long time ago that she was back at Vogel charting lipids and Anders was alive. She was trying to dig out the dirt from underneath her fingernails when the woman on the blanket let out such a cry she jumped. What Marina needed was to deputize a nurse, someone had to open the packages. She called to one of the three women, jerking her head until the woman reluctantly laid down her peppers and came over. Marina handed her the soap and did a pantomime of washing and opening the packages while the woman stared at her as if Marina had lost her mind. She wondered if she would have to act out every stage of the surgery, but now she was getting ahead of herself. No one had said there would be a surgery. Dr. Swenson had situated her crate next to the woman on the blankets. Marina came over with her nurse who continued to scowl at the bother of it all until Dr. Swenson made eye contact with her and the eye contact settled her at once.

Marina pulled on her gloves, got down on her knees. When the woman on the blankets looked at her, Marina pointed to herself, "Marina," she said. The woman gave her a weak nod in return and said a name no one could hear. Having made the introductions, Marina soaped the woman's genitals and thighs, bent up her knees and showed the nurse how to hold them. "It would be nice to have a clean blanket to put her on."

"If you had a clean blanket you would want a sterile one, and a sterile blanket makes you think you can't do anything without a table and a light, and from the table and the light it is a very short step to needing a fetal heart monitor. I know this. Check and see how dilated she is."

Again, Marina looked at the woman as she slid in her hand to check the cervix. There was enough room for a well placed baby of normal size to make an easy exit and Marina felt a great wave of relief come over her. "She's wide open." She moved her hand around, feeling for the baby. As it happened, the basic construction of the female body had not changed since she had done this last. Having the patient on the floor made no difference: there was the baby, though she was quite certain that was not the baby's head she was feeling. "It's breech," she said. It wouldn't have been her first choice but she could manage it. "I'm going to have to try and turn it."

Dr. Swenson shook her head. "That takes forever, causes a great deal of pain, and half the time it doesn't work anyway. We'll do a section."

Marina removed her hand from the woman. "What do you mean it takes forever? Where do we have to go?"

From her perch on the wooden box Dr. Swenson dismissed the suggestion out of hand. "There's no point in putting her through all of that if in the end you'll have to do the section anyway."

Marina sat back on her heels. "The point is we don't have anything approaching sterile conditions. The chance of her dying from a postoperative infection is enough to indicate that turning the baby is worth a try. I don't have a nurse to help me with a surgery, I don't have an anesthesiologist."

"Do you think we keep an anesthesiologist around here?"

"What do you have?" Marina pulled off a glove and poked through the bag.

"Ketamine. And don't go throwing gloves away. This isn't Johns Hopkins."

"Ketamine? Are we planning on sending her out to a disco later? Who in the world uses Ketamine?"

"Here's the news, Dr. Singh, you get what you get, and I was lucky to get that."

"I'm going to try and turn the baby," Marina said.

"You're not," Dr. Swenson said. "It is enough that I had to go up that godforsaken ladder. I would appreciate it if you did not make me get down on the floor as well. Even if it were possible to take my leg out of the equation, I have edema in my hands." Dr. Swenson held up her hands for exhibition. Her fingers were swollen out straight and the skin was pulled tight. Ten little sausages.

"Dear God, when did that happen?" Marina reached up for a hand and Dr. Swenson jerked it away.

"I would have a difficult time with the scalpel. I have a difficult time with a pencil. All that said, either you are going to do the cesarean or I am. Those are the choices."

"What is your blood pressure?" Marina asked.

"I am not your patient," Dr. Swenson said. "You would do well to keep your attention on what is in front of you."

The man in the gray T-shirt looked from Dr. Swenson to Dr. Singh, holding his wife's hand. Clearly, their disagreement concerned him. It did not concern his wife, who took the opportunity to close her eyes for the two minutes she had between contractions. Had someone asked Marina whose opinion was more valuable on the question of whether or not to proceed with a cesarean—the former head of obstetrics and gynecological surgery at Johns Hopkins who had not touched the patient, or the obstetrics and gynecological surgery dropout who was touching her first patient in thirteen years—Marina would cast her lot with the former. Still, being the latter, she was sure she was right, and equally sure she wasn't about to physically prevent her mentor from taking over the case. That left her one option. "Tell me how to use the Ketamine," she said.

The Ketamine was put in a syringe, which, once the needle had been inserted into the vein, was taped to the inner arm so that it could be slowly tapped in as needed, and with that tapping the patient ceased to whimper. Marina washed and dried the woman's belly, straightened out her legs, and, putting on clean gloves, showed her nurse how to hold the skin taut. She had her nurse's attention now. The woman was wide-eyed and still while Marina slid the scalpel into the skin. Once she felt the knife insert, it occurred to her that this was not her first surgery after so many years. It wasn't a week ago she had cut through the snake. The subcutaneous fat welled up through the line of the incision like clotted cream dotted with the first bright beads of blood.

That cut, which passed without a sound save a small gasp from the husband, drew the sudden attention of everyone in the hut. Even the old man pulled himself out of the hammock and brought the two children over to see. The other two women, and the man with the knife, all gathered round for the show, leaning forward and pushing a little to get the best view. Marina felt someone's knees against her back. "This isn't helping," she said.

Her nurse, hands steady on either side of the incision, barked out an order, and the circle immediately took one big step back.

"Now we're looking for the fascia," Dr. Swenson said. "I didn't bring my glasses. Do you see it there, under the fat?"

"I've got it," Marina said. She took the nurse's hands and put a shoehorn in each one. She dug the horns into the incision and showed the woman how to pull. There was the uterus. Despite the drowning flood of adrenaline she recognized it all—bowel and bladder, it was perfectly familiar. Why was that so surprising? She had given up her profession, not her knowledge. Marina, half blinded by her own sweat, turned her face to Dr. Swenson who picked a shirt up off the floor and wiped her down. Dr. Swenson then leaned forward and blotted off the face of the nurse, who was wrestling mightily to keep the cavity open wide with her shoehorns.

"Now take the bladder down," Dr. Swenson said. "Don't nick it. You see the bladder, don't you?"

"I do," Marina said. It was a miracle to see anything without direct light. She cut into the uterus carefully, avoiding everything that was not meant to be cut, and the blood boiled up into the cistern of the belly. Blood, combined with the great slosh of amniotic fluid, made a dark and raging ocean Marina could not get past. The hot liquid broke over the floor and pooled beneath the doctor and her patient. "How in the hell do you do this without suction?"

"There's a bulb in the bag," Dr. Swenson said.

"I need another set of hands."

"You don't have them. Make do."

Marina grabbed at the bulb which shot out of her bloody glove and skidded across the floor where it was caught, like all balls, by a five-year-old boy loitering nearby. "Christ!" Marina said. "At least get somebody to wash it off."

And Dr. Swenson, without a word, motioned for the bulb to be run through the bucket with soap and water and so it was returned to Marina who used it to pull up a half pint of liquid that she then shot onto the floor beside her. She did it again. There, beneath so many layers, she could see the baby face down, feet to the head, bottom lodged firmly in the pelvis. Marina tried to sit the baby up but it was stuck.

"Lift the breech," Dr. Swenson said.

"I'm trying," Marina said, irritated.

"Just tug it up."

Marina moved the shoehorns to the inside of the uterus and motioned for the nurse to pull, to really pull, which this woman who was herself doomed to a lifetime of constant reproduction did with all her might while Marina reached in and tried to pry the baby out. It was wedged into the mother like a child who had shoved himself into the tiniest cabinet during a childish game and could then not be coaxed out. The muscles in Marina's shoulders and neck strained, her back pulled. It was a physical test of strength, 142 pounds of Marina Singh against six pounds of baby, and then with a great sucking sound the baby dislodged. The man with the knife put his hand on Marina's back to keep her from falling over. Red and white and shining, one entire boy flipped over on the mother's chest.

"Look at that. Could that have been easier?" Dr. Swenson gave a single, decisive clap. "Give the baby to them now. They know all about this." No sooner were the words spoken than the slippery child was out of her hands, the thick liver of placenta going with him. The entire crowd bore him away, the old and the young made off with the astonishingly new. They had proof of something spectacular happening now. As many births as there had been no one was completely inured to the charms of infants. "Do you remember the rest of it? Massage the uterus now. This is the part I always liked, reconstruction, restoring order to the chaos." Dr. Swenson leaned forward for a better look. "The baby is gone, he's someone else's problem, and you can pay more attention to the details. There isn't the same sense of urgency."

From the other side of the room the baby was crying now and the husband, still fixed to his wife's hand, craned his head towards the sound. "Tap the Ketamine," Dr. Swenson said. "There's no point in her waking up now." Marina suctioned out the belly again and set to work on the heavy stitches, a procedure as delicate as closing a Thanksgiving turkey with kitchen twine. The nurse, so much braver than one would have imagined, moved her shoehorns back knowledgeably while Marina reassembled everything she had taken apart: the uterus sewn, the bladder placed back on top.

"This is a good man," Dr. Swenson said, nodding to the husband. "He stayed right with her. You don't see that. They like to go fishing. Sometimes when they hear it was a son they'll come in for a look, but that's about it."

"Maybe it's their first," Marina said.

Dr. Swenson shook her head. "I should know that. I can't remember."

Marina was making her last knot when the baby was returned. She slid the Ketamine out of the woman's arm and lay the baby there in its place, though the mother, who was just barely flicking her eyelids, did nothing to hold it. It was a good looking baby, two furry eyebrows and a rounded mouth, swaddled in striped yellow cloth. He gave half a cry and half a yawn and everyone seemed to find this charming.

Marina was stiff coming up off her knees. "See?" Dr. Swenson said, pointing. "It's hard enough for you."

Marina nodded, taking off her gloves, and looked at the blood on her arms, the blood on her dress, the tidal pool of blood in which she had been sitting. "Good Lord," she said. She looked in the bag for a blood-pressure cuff.

Dr. Swenson shook her head. "You don't realize how much blood there is when you have all those other people waiting there to sop it up for you. This is a perfectly reasonable amount. You wait and see, she'll be fine. They'll both be fine."

The nurse came over and covered the woman with another blanket. "It would be good if we could just move her to someplace that was dry," Marina said. "I can't leave her lying in all of that."

"There are certain things we cannot expect the Lakashi to do," Dr. Swenson said. "They cannot perform cesarean sections. That is a matter of training and equipment. They do know that a sick woman should not be left to lie on a sodden blanket, and they know perfectly well how to clean up. You will come back tonight and check on your patients, Dr. Singh, and come back again to check on them tomorrow. You'll see how well they manage without you."

The woman who had been nursing a baby when they arrived had handed that one off and was now nursing the new one while his mother slept on the floor. The father came to Marina, who was putting the contents of the used surgical kit back in her bag, and very lightly slapped her back and arms with his open hands. Then the others came over, all except the woman nursing and the woman sleeping, and did the same. The two children hit her legs and the old man reached to slap her ears. Marina in turn pounded the back of her nurse who had never flinched or turned her head during the surgery and in return the woman gently slapped Marina's face with the back of her hand.

"Come now," Dr. Swenson said. "Once you get started with this it can go on for hours. You'll come home with more bruises than Easter."

It took some navigation to get Dr. Swenson down the ladder but there were so many Lakashi waiting for her at the bottom with their arms stretched up that they would have simply caught her had she fallen and borne her aloft all the way back to the lab. She gave herself a few minutes to catch her breath and while they waited a crowd assembled. Clearly the news of their success had spread. The natives made a thick ring around Marina and Dr. Swenson, chattering and clapping their hands together once Dr. Swenson made it clear they were to keep their hands to themselves.

"Everyone is admiring you," Dr. Swenson told Marina in a raised voice.

Marina laughed. There was a woman behind her holding on to her braid, staking out the territory as her own. "You're just projecting. You have no idea what they're saying."

"I know their happiness. I may not know the details of every sentence but believe me, there are many ways to listen and I've been listening to these people for a long time." The crowd was moving forward and the two doctors moved with them. "They think you will replace me," Dr. Swenson said to her, "the way I replaced Dr. Rapp. Benoit told them you were the one who killed the snake to save Easter and that you brought the snake back for them. Now they've seen you cut out a child and keep the mother alive. That's a heady business around here."

"They didn't see that," Marina said.

"They most certainly did," Dr. Swenson said, and lifted up her hand towards the sky. "They were in the trees. The entire surgical theater was full."

Marina looked around at the faces of all the beaming Lakashi. What would have happened if the woman hadn't lived? If the child were dead? "I didn't look up," she said.

"Just as well, too much pressure. You did a fine job. I could tell you were a student of mine. You made a classic T-incision. You kept the opening in the uterus small. You have very steady hands, Dr. Singh. You are exactly the person I want when I deliver."

What a thought, delivering the child of the person who taught her to deliver children. "I won't be here when you deliver," Marina said, and took comfort in the knowledge. "How far along are you?"

"Just over twenty-six weeks."

"No, no," she said. "That's not even possible. Who were you planning on delivering the baby?"

"The midwife. I'll be honest, I had envisioned an experience as close to the Lakashi's as possible, but as time goes by I'm thinking more about the need for a section. I'm doubting that my pelvis will spread. Chewing the Martins does nothing to reverse the aging of one's bones. I'm going to need a section and there's no one else here I'd trust for that."

"Then you'll go to Manaus."

"A woman my age can't go to the hospital to have a baby. There would be too many questions."

"I would have to think a woman your age couldn't avoid going to the hospital." Marina looked at Dr. Swenson and seeing that she wasn't listening began again. "Even if I was going to be here, and trust me, I'm not, you don't know what kind of complications you might have. You're breaking ground here, you can't just expect to have the baby on your desk. You just saw me perform my first surgery in over thirteen years. That hardly qualifies me to deal with anything that could come up."

"But you could. I saw you work. At some point I realized I should have made better plans for this inevitability but now you're here. You're a surgeon, Dr. Singh, and all the pharmacology in the world isn't going to change that." She shook her head. "Pharmacology should be reserved for doctors who have no interpersonal skills or doctors with uncontrolled tremors who are prone to making mistakes. You never did tell me why you changed your course of study."

Some members of the crowd around them had begun to sing and some others to tap their tongues against their palates, making a noise of cheerful wailing. The children cleared the path ahead like a pack of hungry goats, snatching up every leaf and twig, ripping out vines, knocking down spider webs with a stick, until the trail was as neat as anything found in a national park. "You never told me why you changed yours," Marina said.

"I had no choice. I saw the work that needed to be done and I had to do it myself. You can't draw the world a map to this place and have everyone come running in, trampling the Rapps, killing off the martinets, displacing the tribe. By the time they understood what they were doing, it would all be dead. The conditions for this particular ecosystem have yet to be replicated. Eventually, yes, but for the time being if it is going to happen it's going to happen here. For years my study was strictly academic. I wanted to record the role of Martins in fertility. I had no desire to synthesize a compound. I've never believed the women of the world are entitled to leave every one of their options open for a lifetime. I believe it less now that I am pregnant. Give me your hand, Dr. Singh, this leg is killing me. Yes. We can walk a little slower than the rest of them." With that the Lakashi, who had at times an uncanny ability to understand English, cut their pace in half. "But when I discovered the link to malaria all of that changed. No scientist could be on the threshold of a vaccination for malaria and not make an attempt at it. I've been very careful about the people I've brought here. They are all extremely committed, respectful. I wouldn't have any of them take out my appendix, but as far as the drug's development is concerned they have made remarkable progress."

"How do you know it works?"

Dr. Swenson used her free hand to pat her stomach. "In the same way I know the fertility aspects work. I test them. I've been regularly exposing myself to malaria for more than thirty years now and I've never had it. Dr. Nkomo, Dr. Budi, both of the Saturns, we all have regular exposures. I've exposed the Lakashi. I can show you all the data. It's the combination of the Martin bark and the purple martinets. We know it now. It's just a matter of replicating it."

"And what about Vogel?" Marina asked.

"Vogel pays for it. I would have said I had been careful in choosing Vogel as well, but Mr. Fox has grown too restless for me. He isn't interested in what can be accomplished. He only wants to see where the money's gone. Not that I think some other company would have been better. They all claim to support science without any real understanding of what science entails. Dr. Rapp spent half of his life down here, he did the most important work in the history of his field and he only scratched the surface of the mycology that was available to him. These things take an extraordinary amount of time. They can take lifetimes. You would think they would be grateful that I've given them my life, but someone like Jim Fox would be incapable of understanding that. Sending Dr. Eckman here was a disaster for all of us. His death was very bad for morale. For a week or two I thought I might lose all of them. But then you came, Dr. Singh, and as much as I've fought the intrusion I can see you have a place here. You get along well with everyone, your health seems excellent, and I think you'll be able to soothe Mr. Fox, convince him that things are progressing nicely and we'll just need a little more time."

"But why would I do that? I work for Vogel. They're paying out enormous sums to develop the drug that you brought to them, that you proposed. You haven't even told them about the malaria vaccine and that seems to be all you're working on. Why would I want to cover for you?" Marina balanced the weight of Dr. Swenson on her arm. The farther they went the more Dr. Swenson leaned against her.

"It isn't a matter of covering anything. This isn't a lie told in school. The drugs are intertwined. We have not been able to separate them out. Look at me. I am clearly pursuing my work in fertility even if my interests lie in how it relates to malaria. What I'm interested in personally really doesn't matter when either way we end up in the same place. When we get one drug we'll have the other, and I don't see the harm in making an American pharmaceutical company pay for a vaccination that will have enormous benefits to world health and no financial benefits for company shareholders. The people who need a malarial vaccine will never have the means to pay for it. At the same time I will give them a drug that will, if anything, undermine the health of women and make them a truly obscene fortune. Isn't that a reasonable exchange? Eight hundred thousand children die every year of malaria. Imagine an extra eight hundred thousand children running around the planet once this vaccine is in place.

Perhaps instead of trying to reproduce themselves, these postmenopausal women who want to be mothers could adopt up some of the excess that will surely be available."

Marina, as usual, felt that she was five steps behind in the conversation. "It seems you should give Vogel a chance. You may find they're as interested in the vaccine as you are."

"Your trust would be charming if it weren't so simplistic," Dr. Swenson said without a trace of rancor in her voice. "Because if you're wrong, and I am fairly certain you are wrong about an American pharmaceutical company wishing to foot the bill for Third World do-gooding, then we lose everything. That is not a risk you are allowed to take when the outcome of an incorrect assumption amounts to such a significant annual loss of lives."

They were back in the village, having picked up a great many more Lakashi on the way. It looked to Marina like almost the entire tribe was assembled.

"Come to the lab," Dr. Swenson said, patting the arm that she held with her other hand. "Dr. Nkomo will show you our mosquitoes."

"Let me take a swim first," Marina said. "Get the blood off."

Dr. Swenson shook her head. "Use a basin. I'll have some men bring some buckets of water over for you. No sense getting into the river all covered in blood. You never know who might mistake you for dinner."

"I went into the river when I had half an anaconda on me," Marina said, looking down at her dress which had stiffened as it dried.

Dr. Swenson nodded her head. "We're being more careful with you now."

When Marina went back to the sleeping porch the sheets on the bed had been straightened and there was a letter lying on top of the pillow. She reached carefully into the netting and took it out. She didn't want to touch anything until she'd had a bath and still she slid a finger around the edges of the envelope, turning it back into a sheet of paper. All that was there was her name, *Karen Eckman, Karen Ellen Eckman, Mrs. Anders Eckman, Karen Smithson, Karen Eckman.* The letters were scrawled and uneven. A few times the pen had torn the paper. He had printed the words but his hand was shaking. Maybe he had folded this one up and kept it with him in the bed. Maybe this one he had never even thought to mail.

Ten

Every morning Marina extricated herself from the sleeping limbs of the lightly drugged child and took the path to the field of Martins. She didn't follow the native example and wait for five days to pass. She was thinking it was possible that five days from now she would be out of this place and so she wanted to stuff herself with the bark, to turn herself into medical evidence before she went home. Her goal was to make up for all the bark she hadn't eaten in the past and anticipate the bark she would never eat in the future. This was her moment, the perfect now. She didn't mind making the trip deep into the jungle by herself anymore, though there was never a morning when she didn't run into other women eventually, both Lakashi and the doctors. Dr. Budi said there was scientific precedent for going to chew the trees so often at the beginning. They said they'd had a loading dose as well. Maybe it was just the excitement of the discovery, or maybe it was something the body had been starved for all along. Dr. Budi told Marina that even at this early stage she would be inoculated against malaria and that her window for monthly fertility would be extended from three days to thirteen. Beyond that, Marina had begun to wonder if there wasn't something mildly addictive in the fenneled bark, something that kept the Lakashi women trudging back to the trees long after they were sick to death of babies, something that kept the doctors at their desks for years after they were ready to go home. Maybe Dr. Rapp had been correct in his original assessment that there was some mild connection between the mushrooms and trees, the smallest touch of narcotic in the bark that kept the women leashed to the forest.

As for herself, Marina dreamed of Martins. They were there, slim and stately, in front of her eyes before she opened them in the morning, and when she drifted off at night she was walking towards them. It was the thought that she could become addicted to anything in this place that first made her realize it was time to leave the Amazon, though everything was pointing towards departure. In one week she had sewn together the eyelid of a girl who had been bitten by the very monkey she had worn around her neck. It took both of her parents to hold the child down while Marina worked with too heavy a needle and too thick a thread to reassemble the delicate tissue. When she asked Dr. Swenson about getting some human rabies immunoglobulin, Dr. Swenson said she would first need to see a slide of the monkey's brain. She had removed a six-inch wedge of wood from between the third and fourth toes of a man who was cutting down trees to make boats to ride to Manaus. Three men had dragged him down to the lab without so much as a tourniquet, leaving Marina to do her best to piece together muscles and bones whose names she could no longer remember. The terror of the jungle was now redefined by the work it could dream up for her. While the other doctors, no doubt relieved that they had not been asked to perform the task themselves, praised her to the point of ridiculousness, the Lakashi peered over her porch railing at night and raised up on their toes to sniff her neck whenever they were close. It was clear to Marina that no good was going to come of this. She was tired of her two dresses, tired of waking up in the middle of the night trying to figure out how she could take Easter with her when she left. She was unnerved both by Dr. Swenson's repeated references to "our" delivery date and by the letters from her dead friend that she found waiting in her bed at night. She wanted out of all of it, but still, it was just now light in this beautiful, singular stand of trees and she cupped her hand around the slender trunk of one of them and leaned in.

Marina had never seen the rooms where the other doctors lived. There was a small circle of huts behind the lab but the lab was where they worked and ate and stayed to talk in the evenings. She had known for some time that one of the huts contained the mice that were forced into repeated pregnancies, their heavy bellies bumping against their exercise wheels, and now she knew that another hut was full of mosquitoes. Their larvae grew in tepid water inside of plastic trays that stacked into a tall rack of metal shelving. When they were ready to hatch they were transferred into large plastic buckets with a piece of pantyhose stretched across the top that was held in place by a rubber band. From there the mosquitoes were infected with malaria. It might have been because everyone felt so confident in the success of their vaccinations that they could afford to be so sloppy in their protocol, but when Alan Saturn first showed them to Marina she did not feel comfortable with the hundreds of flying insects per bucket banging their minuscule weight against a web of nylon.

"Feeding time at the zoo," Alan said, and soaked a large wad of cotton in a cup of sugar syrup. "Go on and give them a taste of what they really want. Breathe on them. Just lean over and exhale."

And so she did, and they flung themselves upward in one ineffectual black fist. Marina stepped back.

"Mammalian breath, that's what draws them. It's only the females that bite, you know. The males neither contract nor spread the protozoa." He dropped the cotton onto the hosiery and the mosquitoes went in like sharks for bloody chum. He watched them for a minute. "They always hold up their end of the bargain."

There were two plastic flyswatters tacked to the wall, their wire handles rusted. "How do you test yourself?" she asked, not entirely certain she wanted to know.

"We take five mosquitoes out of the infected bucket," he said, tapping the lip of the bucket she'd just breathed into. "When I first came here you should have seen what we went through. We'd put on hazmat suits, seriously, face masks, gloves. As if every tenth mosquito outside isn't carrying anyway. Now I just stick a net in there. I know what I'm doing. I put those five in a cup with a piece of nylon over the top, then I hold the cup on my arm, on my leg, it doesn't matter. When I have five bites I kill the mosquitoes and run them under the microscope on a slide to make sure they were all infected. That's pretty much it."

"That's it?"

"Well, then you wait. The malaria will present in ten days. But it doesn't present. It hasn't for any of us."

"So how can you be certain your mosquitoes are good?"

"The microscope tells us that, and then from time to time we infect one of the men in the tribe from the same batch. Ten days later, clockwork, he has malaria. We bring in some of the women and the same group of mosquitoes can bite them all day long and it's nothing." Alan was leaning over another bucket. He blew in before giving them the cotton.

"And this man who contracts malaria, how does he agree to this?"

He stood up and shrugged. "I suppose if this man had a lawyer it could be said that he hadn't agreed, or that he hadn't been made fully aware of what he was agreeing to. I've got some Cokes in here, I don't tell Annick that. They love them."

"You give them a Coke for getting malaria?"

"Don't make this out to be the Tuskegee Institute. Chances are excellent that these men have had malaria before, or that they would have had malaria eventually. The difference is that when they get it in this room we're also going to cure it. Curing malaria isn't the problem, you'll remember; the problem is figuring out a way to vaccinate against it. If they get sick for a couple of days in the name of developing a drug that could protect the entire tribe, the entire world, then I say so be it."

"Yes," Marina said, feeling a little uncomfortable with the argument. "But they don't say so be it."

Alan Saturn picked up his buckets and began to arrange them on the counter. "It's good to get out of the American medical system from time to time, Marina. It frees a person up, makes them think about what's possible." He took an empty plastic cup off the table and held it out in her direction. "Do you feel like trying it? At least you can count yourself as fully informed to all the risks, and you will have saved one unfortunate native from standing in your place. The best part is, all you'll wind up with in the end is five itchy bumps."

Marina considered her Lariam, long gone. She considered her father. She looked inside the cup and shook her head. "I think I'll wait."

"Research doesn't happen in a Petri dish, you know, and mice only go so far. It's the human trials that make the difference. Sometimes you have to be the one to roll up your sleeve."

But Marina didn't stay. She wanted more bark before she became part of the experiment.

Dear Jim,

I see how this could take years, how no amount of time would ever be enough to figure out everything that's going on here, but I'm going to begin the business of trying to get home. The first thing I'll have to figure out is the boat. Given Dr. Swenson's investment in keeping me I doubt she'll be quick to offer hers. But boats do go by and I know the direction of Manaus. Some days I think I'll see one and swim out to it, and if Easter swims with me then who would stop us?

Marina wrote more letters now. She wrote them every day. Dr. Budi left her pack of stationery open on her desk and Nancy Saturn was generous with her stamps. She would take Easter with her to the river and they would skip rocks from the shore or go for a swim. Boats did go by—a child in a canoe, a rare river taxi on its way to the Jinta—but then two or three days would pass with nothing. She made Easter keep watch when she was working, leaving him alone with the letters. It would never have occurred to her that it was possible for the system to work, except that it had worked, Anders had mailed letters, who knew how many letters, and some of them found their way to Karen. Yet as often as she wrote to Mr. Fox she hadn't really told him anything. She hadn't told him about the malaria or Dr. Swenson's pregnancy or Anders' burial. Those things she needed to say to him herself.

Easter and Marina liked the river best at six o'clock when the sun was spreading out long across the water and the birds had just begun to make their way home for the night. They sat on the damp banks, as far away as they could from the heat of the Lakashi's fire. It was too early to eat and still she wanted to leave the lab for a while, stretch her legs and roll her neck. Sometimes she would sit for twenty minutes, thirty minutes, and other nights she would stay until it was dark. She had never seen a boat go by once it was dark but it was such a pleasure to sit and watch the hot red ball of the sun sink fully down into the jungle that she made the excuse that one might come. Easter pointed out every fish that broke the river's surface and she pointed out the bats swimming through the purple evening sky. She had gotten very used to spending her time with someone who said nothing at all. She found that watching the coming on of night without feeling any need to comment on it brought about a sense of tranquility that she had rarely known.

It was in that tranquility a boat was spotted in the distance.

She heard it before she saw it, the sound of a well-maintained engine pushing effortlessly ahead. That was in itself worthy of notice as the boats she was familiar with here came in two varieties: the completely silent canoe/raft/floating bundle of logs, and anything with a grinding motor. She got to her feet with four letters in her hand, one for her mother and one for Karen and two for Mr. Fox. The boat was coming on fast, a small round dot of light fixed to the front that was pointing up river, and Easter, ever the thinker, jumped up and grabbed two long branches from the edge of the fire, one for Marina and one for himself, and they stepped into the water until it was up to their knees and they waved the branches overhead. A boat that fast was surely headed to Manaus eventually, even though it was going in the wrong direction for now. She wanted that boat. She swung the fire over her head and let out a high, bright sound, a sound she never would have guessed she had in her. She hoped it would encompass every language in which the words *Stop the boat* could be spoken. Whether the people on the boat heard her it would be impossible to say, sitting as they were just on the cusp between near and far, but the Lakashi heard her, and they ran through the jungle faster than any boat could travel and picked the fire apart and lit sticks from one another's sticks and then let out a giant howl, their own particular shibboleth, and all of this so Marina could send off her mail. Bless the Lakashi, and for this one night bless them for watching her too closely, because suddenly their shoreline was ablaze and the noise they made was deafening and the boat, which was almost on them now was certainly slowing out on the dark river though it wasn't slowing enough to give the impression of stopping, and Marina, buoyed up on the energy of the people, called out with the lungs of a soprano, "Stop the boat!"

All sound stopped, the Lakashi startled into a brief silence by the intensity in Marina's voice, even the frogs and insects for an instant held their breath. She wasn't used to it herself, the power of her own voice, and so in the new silence she called again, "Stop the boat!" And the boat, which was past them now, stopped. It turned and slowly came towards the dock, its spotlight sweeping the crowd on the shore slowly, left to right.

"Correspondência!" Marina called. She had been reading a Portuguese dictionary at night along with the Dickens. "Obrigado, obrigado." She came out of the water and ran down the planks of the dock, the letters in one hand, the burning branch in the other, and the light from the boat leapt across her and then returned. It hit her squarely in the face and froze her in mid-step. In her own defense she closed her eyes.

"Marina?" a voice asked.

"Yes?" she said. Why did this not seem strange, someone calling her name? It was because of the light she could not make sense of what was happening.

"Marina!" The voice was happy now. She did not know the voice, and then she did. The second it came to her he spoke his name. "It's Milton!"

The enormity of Marina's happiness was caught in that light. Of all the tributaries in all of the Amazon he had wandered onto hers. Milton her protector, Milton who would know exactly how to set everything to right. She threw her branch into the water and let out a scream of joy which took the shape of his name, "Milton!" But the scream that met hers was high and entirely female and there bounding over the edge of the boat and into her arms came Barbara Bovender wearing a short khaki colored dress with a stunning number of pockets. Milton was driving the boat for Barbara Bovender! The light of every Lakashi torch was caught in the reflective sheet of her wind-tangled hair. Marina embraced the narrow back of her friend who clung to her neck and whispered in her ear too softly to be heard above the cries of the Lakashi. She smelled of lime blossom perfume.

"How are you here?" Marina said. There was no sensible way to say it—how did you find us and why did you come and how long can you stay and will you take me with you when you leave? Easter bounded down the dock on a wave of childlike glee and straight into Barbara's arms, burying his face in her hair. Marina felt the smallest ping of something—jealousy? That couldn't be right. It was so much to take in and it was all too wonderful and confusing. The Lakashi were continuing to sing and the smoke from all the fires was as blinding as the spotlight from the boat. Marina was climbing over the edge of the boat to throw her arms around Milton, her feet bare, her dress torn at the left side seam, her hair neatly combed and braided because she had been sitting for a long time watching the sunset. She put out her arms to Milton and he took her hands, his arms out straight, and turned her entire body so that she could see there was in fact a third person there, and because that person was not catching the light it took her a moment to understand. It should have been Jackie and it was not Jackie.

"Marina," said Mr. Fox.

It was just that one word, her name, and suddenly she was certain of nothing. Could she embrace him? Did they kiss? In the torch light she could make out that all three of the visitors wore a similar expression, a look that was hollowed out and exhausted, possibly terrified, a look that Marina no doubt must have had on her own face that first night she came down the river to see the burning Lakashi torches. The other doctors would be walking down from the lab by now. They would have heard all the ruckus and come to see why this night was different from all other nights. Could she kiss Mr. Fox in front of Dr. Swenson? In front of Barbara Bovender? She had never mentioned that part to any of them, that Mr. Fox was the person in all the world she kissed. "I've been writing to you," she said, and held out the letters to him like a defense. He was wearing a white cotton shirt like Milton's and she wondered if he had come down in a wool suit. Had Milton taken him to Rodrigo's late at night to buy him clothes? "I was flagging down the boat to see if it would take my letters to you." He took the letters. He took her hand.

"I haven't had any letters," he said. His voice was hoarse. "I haven't heard from you." The time she had been gone had aged him, the boat trip had aged him. How long had he been in Brazil? How long had it taken him to wear the Bovenders down? "I didn't know what had happened to you. Are you hurt?"

"I'm fine," Marina said.

"There's blood all over your dress."

Marina looked down and sure enough there was, but she couldn't remember who it once belonged to or how much of it was just a stain she hadn't been able to scrub out. The Lakashi were coming on board now and they grinned as they slapped Mr. Fox who flinched at first and then raised his hand in what appeared to be self-defense. Marina pulled him back. They were slapping Milton and Barbara Bovender, pounding out their particular and aggressive form of welcome. Already two women had their hands deep in the white gold of Barbara's hair and she struggled hopelessly to get away. A suitcase was held aloft and then passed overhead and Marina leapt up to grab it. "Milton!" she called out, "don't let them take the bags!"

Milton managed to wrestle the remaining duffels and totes away from the natives. He waved to Easter, who came on board and gave Milton a hearty slap at the waist and then began to loop his arms through the various handles of bags.

Marina took Mr. Fox's hand and held it tightly. "We have to keep an eye on Barbara. She won't be able to manage this."

"I wouldn't worry about Mrs. Bovender," he said in a flat voice. This was not the reunion they were supposed to have. She wished he would have waited in the Minneapolis airport for her to come back. It wouldn't have been too much longer. Once they were on the dock he let go of her hand. Maybe it wasn't a good thing the boat had come at all. There was no aligning Minnesota to Amazonia. There was no explaining one world to the other. Dr. Swenson was walking towards them.

"Enough of that," she said, clapping her hands. "Leave her alone now." The two Lakashi women who fought over Barbara's hair had settled their differences, leaving her in under a minute with two long braids already tied off at the ends with pieces of thread pulled from their own dresses. Dr. Swenson walked by Barbara with barely a glance. "We'll be talking about this," she said as she passed, and Barbara dropped her head. When she got to the end of the dock her full attention turned to Milton. "Whose boat is this?"

"It belongs to a friend of Rodrigo's," Milton said.

"Rodrigo's friends don't have money like this."

"One of them does," Milton said. "The man who bottles Inca Cola. Rodrigo sells it in the store."

Dr. Swenson nodded. "Did you bring supplies or only guests?"

"Rodrigo put together a list of what you must need by now, plus some things you'll like. He had just gotten in a full case of oranges and he sent them all to you. I think he did a very good job."

Having dealt with two of the travelers, she turned to the third. "You no doubt moved heaven and earth for this, Mr. Fox."

Mr. Fox stood on the dock and stared at Dr. Swenson and stared at the entire flaming tableau that spread behind her. A bat spun down perilously close to the top of his head and he did not flinch. "We have had a difficult trip. There is clearly a great deal to discuss, including the heaven and earth I have moved, but for now you should tell us where we will be sleeping."

"I don't know where you'll be sleeping," Dr. Swenson said, making no concessions to civility. "We are working here, not running a Hyatt."

The Lakashi, sensing there was no further call for celebration, began stacking their burning sticks into a single raging bonfire that threatened to spread to the dock they were standing on. Thomas Nkomo stepped forward, waving his hand and bowing quickly to the guests. "Let us work this out away from the fire," he said calmly. "We will make sure everyone is accommodated." Once he had herded them gently to shore he told Barbara Bovender that she would follow Marina, and Mr. Fox would bunk with him, and Milton—

"I can sleep in the boat," Milton said.

Thomas shook his head. "There is a cot in the lab near Dr. Swenson's station. She will be happy to have you sleep there for tonight."

"Let's leave your assumptions of my happiness out of this," Dr. Swenson said. As she turned and walked back up the dock, Marina could see that Dr. Swenson was limping badly and wanted to go to her and lend her an arm, and she wanted to go with Mr. Fox because Thomas of all people would give them a moment together without asking questions, but instead she took Barbara Bovender's hand and led her through the jungle towards the storage shed.

"Do you know where we're going?" Barbara asked.

"I do," Marina said.

Jackie had left for Lima five days before, this being the season when the surf rose along the Peruvian coast with such ferocity that it cleared the lesser surfers from the beaches and brought forth the greater ones from other continents. The Bovenders had talked it over at length and decided this would be a good time for both of them. Barbara could work on her novel and he could spend a couple of weeks curled in the lip of a giant wave. "We went over everything that could possibly happen and decided there was nothing that I couldn't handle myself." She was sitting in the chair on top of Marina's extra dress. She closed her eyes and shook her head. "We didn't take Mr. Fox into account. I told him I didn't know where Annick was. That lasted about three minutes."

"He's better at it than I was."

Mrs. Bovender's blue eyes went round at the thought of it. "He's better at it than anyone. Vogel holds the lease on the apartment. He said I would be on the curb in an hour. He got Milton, Milton got the boat. I said, fine, good luck, and then he said I was coming with them. Milton's never been out here before and I'd only come with Jackie. Half the time I came with him I was asleep. Jackie gets seasick unless he's the one driving the boat. I was supposed to tell them how to get here? Oh God, it was awful, we'd pass one river and then I'd start to think a half an hour later that that was the river we were supposed to turn on."

"But you got them here," Marina said. She wasn't sure she could have done it.

"Marina, we left two *days* ago. All those rivers, all those trees. I get turned around in Manaus." Her hands were shaking and so she sat on them. "Do you have a cigarette? I would really love a cigarette."

"I'm sorry," Marina said.

"Thank God Milton was there. At first Mr. Fox asked me a lot of questions, mostly questions about you, but once he was convinced I really hadn't heard from you he stopped talking to me altogether." There was something about Barbara's hair, the two yellow braids hanging over her shoulders, that had robbed her of her considerable sophistication and left behind a fourteen year old girl. "I was staring out at the river bank every second. I felt like I was trying to intuit where you were, like it was my responsibility to know, and I didn't know. Mr. Fox wouldn't believe me when I told him I didn't remember. He thought I was still trying to throw him off Annick's trail, like it would be great fun for me to take us all out on the river and get us lost. And then I saw another river, a small one, and all of the sudden I was sure it was the right one. The opening would have been so easy to miss. If I had been looking on the other side of the boat for just a minute we would have kept going. Mr. Fox and Milton didn't see it at first, and they both perked up then because I was so sure. We went up that river for half the day and everything was quiet. Most of the time I was still thinking I'd gotten it right, and then I started to think we had gotten it wrong, and I was just about to say that, I was getting up my nerve, when we came around a bend and there were all these people on the shore in loincloths with their foreheads painted yellow. It was like they'd been standing there forever, waiting for us, and I didn't remember exactly what the Lakashi looked like. I was so tired by then and I was so confused by all the wrong choices I'd already made that I honestly didn't remember."

Marina leaned forward from the bed where she was sitting. She put her hands on Barbara Bovender's knees. All of the rivers in the Amazon and she knew which one this story had taken.

"So I said, 'There they are!' and Milton was slowing down the boat and he was whispering to me, 'Are you sure, are you sure?' He's met the Lakashi before. They come down to Manaus selling timber, sometimes they've come with Annick. He knows this isn't right, and then I know it isn't right, and the river is narrow there and they all raise up these bows and arrows and they're huge." She is crying now, and she takes her trembling hands out from beneath her legs and begins to wipe her eyes.

"You're okay," Marina said. "You found me. Milton got you out."

She nodded but her fingers could not get far enough ahead of the tears to wipe them all away, there were simply too many of them. "He did. He was so fast. Milton deserves some sort of medal. He'd never driven that boat before and he slammed it around so fast we nearly went over. When I looked back the air was full of arrows. Arrows! How can that be possible? And then I saw something. I thought I saw something."

"What?" Marina said.

She shook her head. "It was worse than anything, worse than Mr. Fox or us getting lost or those people shooting at us." She looked up at Marina and blinked her eyes and for a moment the crying stopped and a look of utter seriousness crossed her pretty face. She took Marina's hands. "I saw my father running through the trees," she whispered. "I don't know what you'd call it, a vision, a visitation? He was coming straight towards me, coming down to the water, and I threw myself on the bottom of the boat. There were arrows in the boat and Milton said not to touch them. I tried to look back for him but Milton said to keep down. Marina, my father is dead. He died in Australia when I was ten years old. I think about him all the time, I dream about him, but I've never seen him. He came there for me because he knew I was going to die."

"Did Milton see him, or Mr. Fox?"

She shook her head. "Mr. Fox was on the deck and Milton was driving. I don't think they would have been able to see him anyway. I think he was only there for me."

"Who would have known you were missing?" Dr. Swenson was saying to Mr. Fox when Barbara and Marina walked into the lab. Dr. Budi could not stop shaking her head and the two Drs. Saturn stayed very close together. The misery that comes from having a good imagination was writ large on Thomas Nkomo. "I suppose the Inca Cola man would have wanted his boat back at some point. When Jackie Bovender came home from his surfing expedition in two or three weeks they would have come here together. Don't you think so, Barbara? He would have come looking for you then."

Barbara Bovender, now the center of everyone's nervous attention, made the slightest gesture towards a nod.

Dr. Swenson held out a hand towards this confirmation. "One man missing a boat, one man missing a wife. What do you think I should have told them when they arrived? I wouldn't have had any idea where you were."

"If you had a telephone no one would have to risk their lives to find you," Mr. Fox said. How was it possible that Marina could not go to him? Why didn't he come to her now having survived a rain of poison arrows? How could he not take her in his arms regardless of who was in the room? He looked so out of place in his lightly embroidered white shirt and khaki pants, as if he had dressed up for a party whose theme was the Amazon.

"This is about my not having a telephone? Do you think Dr. Rapp came to the Amazon with a telephone? I am trying to finish my work. First you send a man down here who dies and when you decide to follow him it seems you are determined to die yourself and take two of my people with you. It is disruptive, Mr. Fox, can you understand that? You do not advance your own case by continuing to throw these tragedies in my path."

"I was looking for Dr. Singh," he said, tapping his glasses up the bridge of his nose with his index finger, a nervous tic Marina knew to be the slightest outward manifestation of simmering fury. "I hadn't had any word from her. I couldn't take the chance that another one of my employees was sick or in danger."

Another one of your employees, Marina thought. Well, there you have it.

"But you endanger them yourself!" Dr. Swenson said. "You throw a person in the river and then make a spectacle of jumping in to save them."

Before Mr. Fox had a chance to answer, Dr. Budi stepped between them. "I must ask that you stop this now," she said, her voice unexpectedly strong. "Dr. Swenson, this is not right for you. This argument has ended. You must sit."

The room fell suddenly silent and in the silence they could hear the unexpected sound of Dr. Swenson struggling to catch her breath. There was no ignoring Budi's advice. Dr. Swenson sunk down heavily in her chair and put her swollen feet up on a box in front of her. Nancy Saturn came over with a glass of water and Dr. Swenson waved her away. When she spoke again her voice was calmer. "Look at as much data as you need to reassure yourself, Mr. Fox. The two Drs. Saturn will help you. Tomorrow when it's light, Dr. Budi will take you to see the Martins, and after that you will get back on the Inca Cola and go to Manaus. That is all the hospitality I am capable of extending."

"Dr. Singh is coming with us." Mr. Fox said. It was not a romantic gesture but the first counteroffer in an ongoing negotiation.

Dr. Swenson shook her head. "That will not be possible. Dr. Singh has agreed to stay until I deliver my child." She put her swollen hands on either side of her belly. "The big reveal, Mr. Fox. Seventy-three years old and I am pregnant. If you trouble yourself to look around in the morning you will see that I am not alone in my condition. We are very close to being able to bring you what you want if you could only control your impulse for disruption. I'm keeping up my end of the bargain. I expect you to start keeping yours."

For a moment Mr. Fox was too far behind. He had missed the rodent trials, the studies in higher mammals. He had no knowledge of a first efficacious dose or the multidose safety studies. He had seen no reports on the probability of technical success, and then suddenly he was six months into the first human dose. First in Man, that's what it would always be no matter how inherently sexist the implications. Given all there was to absorb it took a moment for the news to settle in, but when it did the look on Mr. Fox's face was as tender and pleased and surprised as it had been on a night thirty-five years before when his own wife Mary had made a similar announcement. He took a few tentative steps towards Dr. Swenson. He softened his voice. "How far along?"

"Nearly seven months."

"I'm not qualified to do the section," Marina said to her. "I've told you that. You need to go to a hospital."

"I would feel more comfortable with Dr. Singh," Dr. Swenson said. "We can't afford any breaches in security at this point. I can't go to the city to have a child. I've seen her operate several times now. She does a brilliant job. I have no questions as to her complete competence."

While Marina had come far enough to contradict Dr. Swenson when they were alone, she still lacked the skills to do so publicly. There was no way to point out that these compliments were her road to perdition.

"We could bring in an obstetrician from Rio," Mr. Fox said. "We could bring one in from Johns Hopkins if you'd like." He had already forgotten about the trip from Manaus, about Mrs. Bovender, about the Hummocca. The drug worked, that was all he had ever needed to know. He didn't care about the paperwork, the trees, he didn't need to see Marina. He could get back on the boat tonight.

"What I would like is what I have already said. I trained Dr. Singh myself. You can spare her for a little while longer."

"I can," Mr. Fox said.

Marina started to say something but Dr. Swenson cut her off. "Dr. Budi is right, I am tired. Walk with me back to the hut now, Dr. Singh. I've done enough for tonight." She held up her hand and Marina took it. The skin between Dr. Swenson's fingers was cracked and bleeding. Mr. Fox touched Dr. Swenson's shoulder before they left the room and she nodded at him in return.

Once they were safely under the cover of darkness, the stars spreading their foam over the night sky, Marina started in. "I told you I wasn't going to stay," she whispered sharply over the grind of insects' wings, over the endless repetition of frogs croaking. "Did you think you could just lease me out from my employer?"

"Hold on to yourself for two more minutes," Dr. Swenson said.

Dr. Swenson's hut was the one closest to the lab. It was a small room with a single bed and a dresser, a folding table with two chairs. Dr. Swenson struggled up the four stairs, leaning her weight against Marina, and when she came inside she sat down heavily on the bed. "I'm going to have to lie down," she said, and with that she stretched over the bed, her stomach pointing up. She sent forth a low moan, though whether it was pain or the relief from pain Marina could not be sure. "Be a friend and pull off my sandals, Dr. Singh."

Marina struggled with the Birkenstocks but managed to get them loose. Dr. Swenson's toes were sunk halfway into her swollen feet which had an unnatural purple cast. "Don't make me feel sorry for you," Marina said. "The more I worry about you the more certain I am that you need to go to a hospital with doctors who know what they're doing."

"You know what you're doing," Dr. Swenson said, "and you will feel sorry for me because that is your nature. There's nothing I could do to prevent that."

Marina sat down on the edge of the single mattress. "Who's the man in the picture?" She took Dr. Swenson's wrist between her fingers. Her pulse was almost too rapid to count.

Dr. Swenson turned and looked at the frame on her bedside table. It was a black-and-white photograph of a tall, thin man with a very fine nose standing in the jungle. He was wearing a white shirt and seemed to be looking over the shoulder of whoever was holding the camera. "Never ask a question if you already know the answer. I find that the most irritating habit."

"He's very handsome," Marina said.

"He was," she said, closing her eyes.

"Where's the blood-pressure cuff?"

She pointed down to the red bag on the floor and Marina got the cuff and a stethoscope. "The baby is dead, Dr. Singh. It died yesterday, maybe the day before. I was going to tell you tonight but then the company arrived. You can go on and try to listen but nothing has moved. I'm not certain when it moved last. I haven't been able to find a heartbeat."

Marina put her hand on her teacher's arm but Dr. Swenson shook her off. "Go on," Dr. Swenson said. "Try."

Marina put the scope in her ears, ran the drum across Dr. Swenson's belly, trying one spot and then another and then another.

"There's nothing there," Dr. Swenson said.

"No," Marina said. She took her blood pressure then and then took it again to make sure her reading was correct. "One seventy-two over one fifteen."

Dr. Swenson nodded. "I have preeclampsia. There is no Pitocin. There is a syrup the locals use to bring about labor in these circumstances, a boiled-down extract of crickets or some such thing but for the time being I am finished with my own human experimentation. I don't think I'd survive labor anyway. So the bad news is you will have to do the section and the good news is you won't have to wait two months to do it. Mr. Fox will leave tomorrow with the proof he needs that the drug is viable, and that in itself will buy us a great deal of time. If you could stay here just a little while after the surgery to make sure there are no complications I would appreciate it. Later I'll have Easter and the Saturns take you back to Manaus in the pontoon. Can you do that?"

"I can put you on that boat in the morning and we can go to a real hospital with real medicine and a sterile surgical room and an anesthesiologist. I'm not going to operate on you with a syringe full of Ketamine."

Dr. Swenson waved her hand. "Don't be ridiculous. We have bags of Versed for special occasions."

There were things to say about that but Marina let them go. "These are serious circumstances. I know it isn't what you want but you have got to think like a medical doctor and not an ethnobotanist. If you go with Milton and Mr. Fox you'll be there in half the time. You could be there tonight, which, considering your blood pressure, is what you should be doing anyway. You'd never put this off if it were someone else."

"Listen to what I'm saying the first time, Dr. Singh. I don't have the energy to keep repeating myself. I'm not going anywhere tonight, so if I die before you have the chance to save me the onus will be completely my own. You can't have Mr. Fox take me to the hospital. Then all of his dreams will be shattered and subsequently my dreams will be shattered as well. I will not sacrifice a potential malaria vaccine for a hospital bed in Manaus. I am asking you to do this surgery as a way of saving myself from having Alan Saturn do it. I don't know that I have asked you for so much in the past that you would find this single request something you are unable to grant."

Marina waited, considering the horror of it all. In the end she could do no better than a nod of the head.

"There is of course every reason to think that this will kill me in the end." She opened her eyes and looked at Marina. "It's difficult to say if this is an outcome of the drug or the circumstances of age. Whether or not I am finished remains to be seen, but I want you to know that the drug is finished, at least the fertility aspect. Mr. Fox can go and cry in his cups. With a little luck we'll be able to keep that news from him for a few more years while he finances a malaria vaccine."

Marina shook her head. She wrote it off to the circumstances. In a couple of months when all of this was behind her Dr. Swenson would feel differently. "You shouldn't say that. You've worked on it for too many years to let it go."

"And how shall we test it further? I've been eating this bark for years. I've seen my own menstruation return at sixty. I've lived through the pimples and the cramps and I will tell you there was nothing there to enjoy. I did not need to see that aspect of my youth again."

"That's why they have NHV, normal healthy volunteers. No one expects that you should do all of this yourself."

"We would have to find a great many childless seventy-three-year-old women who were willing to be impregnated in order to evaluate safety. Chances are we would kill the lion's share of them in the course of the drug trials."

"Chances are," Marina said. She brushed down the insane wires of Dr. Swenson's hair with her hand.

"Don't be tender, Dr. Singh. We're fine the way we are. I only tell you this because I want you to know that if anything happens to me now, anything, it is not your fault. I've brought this on myself in the interest of science and I don't regret any of it. Do you understand that? This has all been to the positive. We are very close to securing a vaccine, and in addition to that we know what the body has told us all along, postmenopausal women aren't meant to be pregnant. That is what we had to learn."

"It might not work at seventy-three. That doesn't mean it couldn't work at fifty. This isn't the time to throw everything away."

"Let the fifty-year-olds console themselves with in vitro as they have in the past. I have no intention of unleashing this misery on the world because I trust women to stop trying at a sensible age." She shook her head. "So it's good then," she said, "it's good. I'm going to go to sleep now. I want you to get some sleep, too. We'll do this tomorrow in the afternoon when everyone has left and there's plenty of light. Do your best to get them off early. Milton and Barbara would swim out of here, I feel sure of it, but Mr. Fox may try to linger. Once you get them on the boat, go and ask Dr. Budi to assist you. There's no sense in telling her tonight."

"Alright," Marina said. She pulled the mosquito netting down over the bed. She turned down the flame in the lantern but she couldn't seem to make herself go.

"You're still here," Dr. Swenson said finally.

"I thought I'd wait until you fell asleep."

"I know how to sleep, Dr. Singh. I don't need you to watch me unless it is something you are trying to learn to do yourself."

When Marina got back to the lab, Dr. Nancy Saturn was explaining the relationship between the Martin trees and the purple martinets to Mr. Fox, and Thomas Nkomo was showing him the charts of pregnancies, birth weights, live births, and they were all lying to him in everything they chose not to tell. Milton and Barbara made sandwiches out of the store-bought bread they had brought with them. Everyone was helpful. Everyone was getting along.

"Have you seen all of this?" Mr. Fox said to Marina when she came over to them.

"I have," she said. "I've been here a long time."

"It's remarkable work. Truly remarkable work." He was smiling at her now without the slightest trace of collusion. He was simply happy. The drug would soon be in hand, the stock would exceed expectations, his risk would be lauded by generations of board members to come.

Dr. Budi handed her a sandwich on a plate, potted chicken after so many weeks of potted ham. "Dr. Swenson?" she asked.

"Her blood pressure is high," Marina said.

Mr. Fox looked up and Marina shook her head. "She's tired. She just needs rest, that's all. There should be as little stress as possible." It was a line of dialogue she remembered from meeting with patients years ago. It always comforted them. Anyone could embrace the idea that the answer was rest.

"We'll leave in the morning," Milton said.

"After we've seen the trees," Mr. Fox said.

Marina waited another minute for old time's sake. Mr. Fox bent back over the data and she wanted very much to put her hand on the crown of his head. It was probably better that he didn't look at her, that he didn't take her aside and whisper his true plan in her ear. If he loved her now, it would only be sadder later on when he realized that she had lied to him along with all the others. He would leave her once the whole thing fell apart. It might be years, but once he understood that he was holding a malaria vaccine instead of a drug for fertility and that she had known it and done nothing to stop it, nothing to save him, he would break with her in every possible way. That loss would be infinitely harder to take if he had ever loved her. "Let's go to bed now," she said quietly. Then he did raise his head, looking at her as if to say that surely he misunderstood.

"I'm with you," Barbara Bovender said, slipping the second half of her sandwich into one of the many pockets on her dress. The two of them took Easter with them while the rest of the group called good night, while Mr. Fox said good night.

"How does this work?" Barbara asked, looking again at the configuration of the sleeping porch.

"I have the cot and Easter has the hammock, but Easter sleeps with me so I guess that leaves you with the hammock. I'll grant you that it isn't much but it's better than winding up on the floor somewhere."

Easter was sitting on the floor wiping off the bottoms of his feet with a rag. It was the one bedtime ritual Marina had taught him.

"Look," Barbara said, twisting a fat yellow braid around her fingers. "I know this is your place, but if you wouldn't mind terribly could I sleep with Easter? It's just for tonight. I've been half out of my wits all day. Frankly, if he wasn't here I'd be asking to sleep with you, and I don't think the two of us would fit in that bed." She looked sadly at the child. "It's been a bad time for Jackie to be gone."

Marina nodded. She understood completely the calming powers of Easter. Still, as she shook the marmoset scat out of the hammock, she thought of how on this particular night she would have preferred not to sleep alone herself.

That night Marina dreamed not of her own father but of Barbara Bovender's father as he ran through the trees towards the river. When she woke up she had one leg and both of her arms hanging over the edges of the reeking hammock and her first thought was of the Martins. There was only the smallest bit of light coming onto the porch and Barbara and Easter were still sleeping, Easter in the nylon shorts he'd worn the day before and Barbara in a white cotton nightgown. For a moment Marina looked at them and marveled that such things as nightgowns had ever existed and that the people who owned them thought to wear them to bed. She took her flashlight and walked out into the jungle, keeping the beam pointed low to the ground as it was still so early the tarantulas would just now be making their slow crawl home. She wanted to get to the trees and back before anyone else was out. She was fairly certain there was some other quality in the bark that no one was talking about and she knew she wasn't going to make it through this particular day without it. She thought of how she would come out here on her last day and saw off a few branches from the trees on the farthest edge of the perimeter. She would saw them into smaller and smaller pieces and tie them together with twine and she would bring them back with her, a little something for herself. She pictured herself in her kitchen, a freezer full of twigs, taking them out only when she needed one, sitting alone in her living room scraping the bark down with her teeth, and while she was thinking about this she came perilously close to putting her foot into a nest of ants. She stopped and watched them cut a determined path through the leaf litter. She was walking too fast. She kept her eyes down for the rest of the way and when she finally looked up again it was to see the morning sun coming through the Martins at an easterly slant, the full illumination of the thin yellow trunks, the high crowns of pink flowers brushing the edges of the barely blue sky. Maybe she wasn't sorry not to be going back on the boat today. As she touched her mouth to an already soft opening in the bark, a feeling of peace and well-being spread through her veins. She wondered if in fact it was really time to go at all.

She saw the first three Lakashi women coming towards the trees in the same dresses they wore every day, the same dress she wore every day, and they raised their hands to wave to her. Marina waved back and moved quickly to the side of the stand. In the distance, she could hear the disembodied voice of Nancy Saturn lecturing on the purple martinet, the digestion and excrement versus the larval sack. Marina only knew one way out of the trees. One would think she could walk out in any direction and make a circle back around the edge but that wasn't the case. She needed a path. She had to leave the same way she came in or she would get lost. She had a distinct desire to run straight into the jungle, but why? What was there to run from? Mr. Fox was her lover, the Saturns were her friends. Either way she had already stood there too long.

"Marina!" Alan called.

She went to them. The Lakashi were busy at their trees and the gentle sound of their mastication was a comfort to her. One of the women patted her bottom as she walked past, her mouth firm to the bark. It was her nurse. Marina patted the back of her head.

"She's gone completely native," Alan said to Mr. Fox.

Like everything else around this place, Mr. Fox looked better in the light of day standing between the trunks of the Martins. He had on a blue shirt this morning and a darker pair of pants. She couldn't quite believe that in his rush to find her he had brought a change of clothes. "I was meaning to ask about the dress last night."

Marina brushed off the front of the coarse fabric. "It's the local uniform."

"What happened to your clothes?"

Marina shook her head. "A misunderstanding," she said. "Really, the dress has been fine."

"If my legs looked as good as yours I'd wear one too," Nancy Saturn said.

While Marina's legs were of sound basic construction they were also bruised, unshaven, scabbed, and covered in a fierce topography of insect bites. It struck Marina then that it wasn't only Mr. Fox she was lying to. She was lying to the other doctors, her friends, who would certainly have wanted to know that she had more than a professional relationship with the man they were trying to snow. A small Lakashi woman who had finished her requisite amount of bark came up behind Marina and gave her shoulder two hard taps and Marina sat down on the ground with thoughtless obedience. She didn't mind sitting down in the Martins. All of the insects save the purple martinets cut a wide berth around this part of the jungle. The woman untied the end of Marina's braid and combed out her hair with her fingers.

"Is this a service?" Mr. Fox asked.

"You can't stop them," Marina said. "There is absolutely no fighting this."

"I had long hair the first month I was here," Nancy said, nodding at Marina. "They were all over me. As soon as I cut it off I was invisible to them."

"They fix Budi's hair every morning," Alan said. "They come to her hut."

"So you've gotten used to the place?" Mr. Fox said, and for the first time he sounded as if he were speaking to Marina as if she were someone he had met before.

She nodded. "Finish your tour and then I'll take you back. You can catch me up on everything I've missed at work."

Mr. Fox agreed to this and went off with the Saturns. Marina listened to their voices—Martins and martinets and not a single mention of Rapps. She leaned forward from where she was sitting and picked one, the smallest, bluest mushroom that grew at the base of the tree. It was hardly bigger than her little finger. She brought it to her nose and sniffed it like a daisy and the woman who was braiding her hair began to laugh. She leaned over Marina's shoulder and sniffed the mushroom herself, then she put her arms around Marina from the back and hugged her, giggling into her neck until Marina had to laugh herself. When the woman finished Marina's hair she took the mushroom from her fingers and, giving a quick, furtive glance to either side, popped it in her mouth and walked away.

The Saturns stayed behind with their litmus paper and their cotton swabs while Marina walked Mr. Fox back to the lab. The Lakashi trickled past, raising their hands to her.

"You're popular here," he said.

She stopped and turned to him. She took his hands. They had gone to Chicago together once, gotten a fancy room at the Drake and stayed in bed until noon. "I wrote to you. Some of the letters will get there eventually. The second suitcase was lost and I didn't have the phone." Three more women came by. One of them reached down and slapped Marina's thighs and Mr. Fox let go of her hands. "Don't worry about them," she said. "They don't report back to anyone."

"Still," he said.

"It doesn't matter," Marina said. "No one cares what we're doing. It didn't matter before either." She kissed him then because she didn't know if there was ever going to be another chance. She remembered that she must smell horrible although she could no longer smell much of anything herself. The snake had burned it out of her.

He stayed with the kiss for only a second. There were too many women walking past and they were laughing quietly with each other. "You're fine," he said, pulling away. "You're going to be home soon and we'll have time to talk about everything. All of this is better than anything I could have imagined, and I have you to thank for much of that. It was very brave of you to come down here alone. I see that now." He turned away from her then and took a step forward and Marina saw the snake, his foot coming down right on top of it as she grabbed him and pulled him back, pulled him into her with a not inconsiderable strength. It was a little lancehead, small enough to be immature. She had seen the picture in one of Anders' books and she recognized it an instant before it darted away into the high grass.

"Marina!" he said sharply, but she had hold of him now so tightly he could not get away and she did not immediately let him go. Instead she put her lips very lightly to his ear.

"Snake," she said.

As soon as they were back Marina went to check on Dr. Swenson and found Barbara coming up the path. Her eyes were red and cheeks were flushed. Marina didn't know if she had just now been crying or if it was leftover from all the crying the night before. "She's alright," Barbara said, and stepped in front of Marina. "But you shouldn't go in there. She said she wanted to rest now."

"You're back to guarding the gate."

Barbara was wearing white linen pants and a tight navy top and Marina wondered if she had packed it thinking the outfit had a certain nautical look that was appropriate for river travel. "Maybe you could put in a good word for me then, tell her I'm still doing my job."

"Is she going to fire you for bringing out Mr. Fox?"

She looked back towards the door she had just come out of to make sure Dr. Swenson wasn't standing there watching. "I don't know. She may just be trying to scare me. She says she hasn't decided. I think she looks awful, by the way. I had thought the idea of waiting until later to have children was such a good one, and now I'm not so sure."

"It isn't a good one," Marina said.

Mrs. Bovender put her arm through her friend's arm and together they walked towards the water. "I don't know how you've lived out here. You were so miserable in Manaus but this is a thousand times worse. Maybe I'd be lucky if she fired us. I want to go back to Australia. I hate this entire country. Jackie hates it here."

"Then you should go." Marina found herself wanting to comb and braid the yellow hair which spread around Barbara's shoulders like a loose blanket. She was thinking that maybe the desire to groom was yet another component of the Martins that had yet to be traced.

"The thing is," Barbara said, "we'll never find a gig as easy as this one anyplace in the world."

Barbara Bovender gave Marina much of what was in her suitcase before she left: two pairs of lacy underpants and a matching bra and the white cotton nightgown and a jar of face cream that smelled like jasmine. Mr. Fox gave her the white shirt he had worn the day before and his extra pants which she planned to tie up with a piece of twine. Milton gave her his straw hat.

"But you wear this hat," she said.

He shrugged. "I can wear another hat."

She held it for a minute, looked at the thin red ribbon band. She put it on her head and immediately felt braver for it. "I'll bring it back to you," she said.

"Then it would be so valuable to me I could never wear it."

It occurred to Marina then that she should have run off with Milton that first moment she saw him in the airport. She should have begged him to take her to Rio where they could have vanished together into the crowds of dancing girls and handsome men. She and Easter went down to the dock and said goodbye to their three friends. She kissed all three of them and only Mr. Fox was embarrassed. Then she slapped each one on the waist. The Lakashi came down and stood with Marina and Easter and together they watched the beautiful Inca Cola boat pull away. Marina put her hand on Easter's head to comfort herself. Everyone waved. Long after the particular details of their features became small and blurred down the river she could still make out the gleam of Barbara Bovender's hair, which had turned into a great flaxen flag in the wind.

The future was a terrible weight and Marina stood on the dock for a long time after the boat was out of sight and felt it press down on her. Finally she went to the lab to look through the surgical supplies, and talk to Dr. Budi about assisting, and take whatever means were available to forestall the inevitable, but Dr. Swenson was there at her desk in front of a large spread of paper: file folders and typed reports and hand written notes pulled from spiral notebooks.

"You aren't really going to fire the Bovenders, are you?" Marina asked.

"Since when do you care about the Bovenders? They were the ones that kept you in Manaus for so long."

"You're the one who kept me in Manaus," Marina said. "They were just doing their job."

"So in the case of Mr. Fox they didn't do their job well, or I should say she didn't do it at all."

"But in the end it served your purpose, their coming here. It all turned out for the best."

"We are not in a rush, Dr. Singh, but neither is there an endless amount of time for what needs to be accomplished. You'll forgive me if I don't care to focus myself on the matter of the Bovenders' employment with the time that I have. There is so much to do here. I've been trying to organize some things, just in case." Her thick fingers cut and recut the stacks in front of her like a deck of oversized cards. "But I see now there's no doing it. It would take a solid three months of work to make them even passingly useful to anyone other than myself. I realize now I've been too cryptic, I've kept too much in my head. There are some things here I can hardly make sense of myself. I can see now I've been very optimistic. I should have taken failure into account."

"The failure of what?" Marina said. How far away was the boat now? Was it possible that one of them could have had a change of heart, if not Mr. Fox then Milton or Barbara? Couldn't they insist on turning around to go back for her?

Dr. Swenson looked over the top of her glasses. "I think it is safe to say we will be making surgical history today, though God knows we won't be getting credit. I can't imagine there have been any other women my age having cesareans."

Marina sat down heavily and put her elbows on the table and in doing so frightened a handful of small bats that nested inside the table's lip. Five or six of them went spinning around the room, lost in the bright light of day, until one by one they stuck to the walls and flattened out like thick daubs of mud.

"There could certainly be a problem with bleeding, but Dr. Nkomo has offered himself for a transfusion if we need one. He's A positive. That's a stroke of luck."

"Do you have a bag?" Marina asked. What they had and what they lacked was a source of great mystery.

"One line, two needles, gravity does the rest."

"You must be kidding me."

Dr. Swenson shook her head. "You would be amazed at all the things that are possible in a state of deprivation. It's only a matter of thinking things through. Just take your time, Dr. Singh. There's no reason to rush this. That was your downfall in Baltimore. Rushing is the greatest mistake."

Marina sat up, a sound like a bell ringing in her head. "Baltimore?"

Dr. Swenson looked at her without bemusement or compassion, two of the things that Marina might have hoped to see, then she glanced back at her papers. "You thought I didn't remember that."

"Because you *didn't* remember that. When I met you in Manaus at the opera you didn't know me."

"That's true, I didn't. It came to me later, not long after we were back, and by that point it didn't make any difference." She plucked a thick article out of the stack, scrawled a note across the top in illegible writing, and placed it in a blue cardboard file. "I only bring it up now because I don't want it weighing on you going into surgery. That's why I had you do that cesarean, you know, not just to see if you could do it. I wanted you to get your confidence up. You made a very common mistake that night at the General. You rushed, nothing more than that. Had it not been the eye you would have forgotten all about it in a week. Everyone at some point nicks a skull, nicks an ear. It was just your bad luck that the head wasn't positioned another centimeter in either direction. In retrospect the real loss was your quitting the program. If I had known you better then I would have stepped in. At the time though," she shrugged, "it was your decision. This will be easier for you. There isn't the pressure of a baby to save."

Marina sat down in a chair beside the desk, and there it went, the burden of her lifetime, taken. She wondered if she could have turned the Lakashi baby. She looked down at her hands. She wondered what they might have accomplished.

"It would have been remarkable if it had worked out, to have had a child at this age, to have had the chance to see myself in a child. I wouldn't have ever thought about it except for the fact that we came very close." She made another note, equally unreadable, and put it on the other side of the desk. "Be sure to freeze it, Dr. Singh. There are tests that I'll want to do later. I'll want to see what levels of the compound are in the tissues."

Marina nodded. She would have liked to know what any of it meant, especially the part that concerned her, but she was lost. Mr. Fox was speeding down the river now and she wanted him to come back. She would tell him everything. She would start with her internship and bring the story right up to today.

Dr. Swenson looked at her watch, and then she took it off her swollen wrist and laid it on the desk. When she stood up from her chair she struggled, the great and looming failure of her pregnancy going before her. "We should get to work now, don't you think? There's nothing else here that I can do."

Eleven

Many hours after the surgery, and well after dark, Easter and Thomas took the mattress off the cot on the sleeping porch and carried it to Dr. Swenson's hut. They had to take out the table and push the two chairs against the wall but in the end there was enough room for Easter and Marina to sleep. Not that Marina was sleeping, she was watching Dr. Swenson, watching the parade of every nocturnal creature in the Amazon as it wandered through the room. It seemed that they were all attracted to the light, which made her think of that first night in Manaus and Rodrigo's store. The next day she sent Benoit over for the cot frame and the mosquito netting. Easter brought his strongbox with him. For a moment Dr. Swenson opened her eyes and watched while they rearranged the furniture again. "I don't remember asking the two of you to move in," she said, but before Marina could launch her explanation Dr. Swenson had fallen back to sleep.

Aside from her quick morning trips to the Martins, Marina stayed close to her patient, watching her pass in and out of fevers. In her lucidity Dr. Swenson was demanding, wanting to talk to Alan Saturn about mosquitoes, wanting briefings on the data that had been collected since her surgery, wanting Marina to take her blood pressure. Then just as quickly the fever came back and she cried in her sleep, great flooding tears. She would ask for ice and Marina would go and get the small block she kept in the freezer where they stored the blood samples, chipping it into shards with a knife. It was the same freezer where she kept the child with the curving tail. Sirenomelia. It was two days before Marina remembered the name for it. The only time she had ever heard of it was in a lecture on birth abnormalities Dr. Swenson had given at Johns Hopkins. It flashed by in a single slide, *Sirenomelia, Mermaid Syndrome, the legs of the fetus are fused together into a single tail, no visible genitalia. It is nothing you're likely to see.* And there it went; with a click and a brief flash of blackness they were on to the next slide. The only person who ever stood to know what it would have been like to have Dr. Swenson for a mother had not lived to meet the experience. A life of such extraordinary beginnings had, in the end, amounted to little more than a science experiment. Marina had rested her hand on the tiny head for a moment when the whole thing was over, just before Budi covered it over to keep it from the insects and took it off to the lab.

In her fevered dreams, Dr. Swenson often gave bits and pieces of lectures, and sometimes it was a lecture Marina remembered, "Ectopic Pregnancy and the Damage to Fallopian Tubes." She fell into another broken sleep, the blood of Thomas Nkomo making a slow loop through her veins. Marina gave her fluids and tinkered with the antibiotics. For all that they lacked in the jungle their assortment of antibiotics was as comprehensive as any hospital pharmacy. She checked the incision, watched for excessive swelling. She sat in the small room with the door open and read the copious notes on malaria. As the days went by, Dr. Swenson's fevers would stop and then start again. Marina upped the dosages, beat them back. It was days before they could sit her up, and then stand her up. Marina worried about clots. With Easter on one side and Marina on the other, Dr. Swenson walked halfway down the path to the lab. When she was safely back in bed, too tired even to sleep, Marina read to her from *Great Expectations.* That became their new routine, and if the chapter was particularly good, or the day particularly dull, Dr. Swenson would ask Marina to read her some more. Easter sat on the floor with his paper and pad and practiced bending straight lines into the alphabet. Marina wrote out *Dr. Swenson* and put it on Dr. Swenson's chest. She wrote the word *Marina* and put it in her lap.

"Did you think I'd forget?" Dr. Swenson said, looking at the piece of paper when she woke.

"I'm trying to give him a few new words," Marina said.

Dr. Swenson put the piece of paper back on her chest and patted it there. "Good. Let him remember this. Dr. Eckman was always trying to teach him to write *Minnesota.* That was never going to do him any good."

"You never know," Marina said.

"I do know. I think about Dr. Eckman now. There is something very specific about having a fever in the tropics, very unlike having a fever at home. Here you feel the air burning into you, or you are burning into it. After a time one loses all parameters, even the parameter of skin. I think he couldn't possibly have understood what was happening to him."

"Probably not," Marina said. It had been almost a week since Easter had left one of Anders' letters in the bed. He must have run out of them. Easter was sitting shirtless by the door and the sun fell over exactly half of him, one leg and one arm, the left side of his face. The bruises had in time faded down to a dull green.

"How well do you think I am now?"

"You're through the worst of it but I wouldn't say you're well. That will take a long time. You know more about it than I do."

Dr. Swenson nodded. "That's what I've been thinking myself. Dr. Budi, Dr. Nkomo, even the botanist could look after me now."

In fact they came to visit every day. Just that morning Dr. Budi brought a bouquet of pink blossoms from the Martin trees in a drinking glass, who knows how she had managed to get them. They were there on the bedside table, the heavy blossoms crossing the face of Dr. Rapp. The Lakashi came too, the women keeping a silent vigil outside the window while they unbraided and rebraided one another's hair. Any one of them would have taken care of her if given the chance. Marina told her as much.

"None of them would do the job like you. I trained you myself, after all. You do your follow-up the way it's meant to be done. I would like to keep you on, Dr. Singh. You certainly could manage Vogel, keep them happy while everyone else did their work. The other doctors like you. The Lakashi have bonded to you in much the way they bonded to Dr. Rapp. Someone is going to need to look after them once I'm gone. I don't think any of the others could do that."

"The Lakashi can look after themselves."

Dr. Swenson shook her head. "Not if the world comes in to take the Martins, to take the Rapps. I will get over this surgery or I won't. Other people can take care of me but who can take care of them? The truth is, I could just keep thinking up reasons you had to stay. I understand you well enough for that."

"You've done a good job so far," Marina said, wringing out a cloth to wash Dr. Swenson's face and neck.

"Sit still for a minute," Dr. Swenson said, pushing her hand away. "Sit down. I'm trying to tell you something important. This is a conflict I am facing. I am telling you I want you to stay and at the same time giving you a reason to go."

"You aren't giving me any reason to go."

"That's because you won't be quiet. You won't stop moving all the time."

Marina sat down and held the wet cloth in her hands. It was cool. She'd let the extra ice melt in the bowl.

Dr. Swenson, small in her bed, looked up at the ceiling. There was a fly circling over her head and Marina disciplined herself not to shoo it away. "Barbara Bovender came to see me the morning that she left. She was worried that I was going to fire her, and because she was worried she told me the story of her visit to the Hummocca. It was a story that Milton had already told me, but she wanted to tell it again to show me how she had suffered for the cause. She sat in that chair where you are now and she cried. She told me she was so close to death that she had seen her father running through the jungle towards her, waving his hands, her father who had died when she was a child."

It was Barbara Bovender they were talking about? Not the child with the curling tail? Not Vogel? Not something that had happened thirteen years ago at Johns Hopkins? "She told me the same story," Marina said.

"She told you the same story? Then I would imagine you have come to a similar series of assumptions." Dr. Swenson looked at Easter sitting in the doorway. She kept her eyes on him for a long time. "I didn't realize she had told you."

"What assumptions?" Marina asked. It was a quiz of some sort and she had no idea what the answer was.

Dr. Swenson looked at her the way she always looked at her, as if everything was obvious. "Mrs. Bovender is a very tall, pale blonde. Wouldn't her father be the same? I can't help but think that what she saw was a white man in the jungle, a man who was not her father but from a distance, in her fear, might have looked something like him. He was running through the trees towards her, she was in a boat. She couldn't have seen him for more than a few seconds. I asked her if he had said anything, if he had spoken to her in English. She told me that her father had called for her to wait."

For the first time since she had left Manaus, that last morning when she had woken up standing in front of the air conditioner having dreamed about her father, Marina Singh was cold. She was so cold she thought her bones would break. She put the wet cloth back in the bowl. She felt as if there were ice around her heart. "He isn't dead."

"I would swear to you with everything I understand about this place that he was dead, but no, I did not see it for myself. Sometimes when Dr. Eckman was very sick he would wander off. He never went very far. We found him in the storage room once. Once he fell over the railing of the sleeping porch and hurt his shoulder. I left Easter there to watch him. Dr. Eckman would start to get up and Easter would put him back to bed. Easter was a very good steward of Dr. Eckman. The boy had grown attached to him, the way he's grown attached to you. Then one night he came into my hut well after midnight and he was frantic, frantic. He pulled me out of bed. I barely got my feet in my shoes and he was pulling me back to the storage hut. It was pouring rain that night, a blinding rain, and Easter was crying like it was the end of all the earth. I assumed that Dr. Eckman was dead. I remember feeling surprised, as sick as he was I had thought he would pull through. We came onto the porch and Easter had a flashlight. He showed me the bed, he showed me the room. Dr. Eckman was gone. While Easter was asleep in his hammock Dr. Eckman had wandered off in the night. I went to wake Benoit and he rounded up a group of Lakashi, but no one could find him. Not that night or all the next day. We never found him. You've been out there. It isn't so hard to imagine that a man who was very sick would last about twenty minutes in the jungle at night. He would step on a spider. He would crawl into the hollow of some rotting tree and never wake up. Something had eaten him, something had dragged him away. I didn't know what it was but he was gone, Dr. Singh, he was as gone as any man who had died, and so that's what I said. I told the other doctors the Lakashi take away their dead in the middle of the night. I wrote a letter saying we had buried him. And I believed I had handled the situation with as much humanity as was possible until Barbara Bovender turned up the wrong tributary and saw her father."

Marina had thought she understood this place. She had spotted the lancehead after all, she had cut apart the anaconda. She had performed surgeries she was neither licensed nor qualified to perform on a dirty floor and had eaten from the trees and swum in the river in a bloody dress only to find out that none of those things were on the test. There was in fact a circle of hell beneath this one that required an entirely different set of skills that she did not possess. She would have to go there anyway. She had been foolish enough to think that she had given up everything when in fact she could see now that she hadn't even started. Anders Eckman could still be alive. Anders her friend, Anders father of three, was down the river with the cannibals waiting for another boat to go by. "Is there any safe way for me to do this?" she said finally.

Dr. Swenson covered her eyes with the heels of her hands. "No. In fact, I imagine they'll kill you."

Anders took off his lab coat and put on his jacket that was hanging on the back of the door. He retied his tie, took his briefcase off the desk. "If I have to go to one more meeting it is going to kill me," he said to Marina.

Marina looked out the open door. Somehow it was still morning. It wasn't two hours ago that she had been eating the Martins. "I should go now," she said.

"After we've thought it through," Dr. Swenson said. "First there has to be a plan."

Marina shook her head, thinking of Karen Eckman and what she had said about Anders not being comfortable with the trees. She would have walked off the path at that moment. She would have gone straight into the jungle to find him. "I don't think tomorrow's going to be any better." And with that she left, Easter trailing behind her. She could hear Dr. Swenson calling her name as she went past the lab but she didn't go back. They could have talked it over for the rest of their lives. Marina only wanted to be on the boat, out on the water, heading towards Anders and her own fate. She was floating now, caught in a current that pulled her ahead and to her surprise she did not mind it. She was content to float, to be pulled under or tossed up. She would give herself over to the force of the river if the river took her to Anders. She would have gone straight to the dock but she needed to take something with her. She was trying to think of what she could offer the Hummocca in exchange for her friend. She looked around the storage room, opening boxes, and found ten oranges left in the bottom of the crate. She took them along with the peanut butter. She put the white nightgown Barbara Bovender had given her around her neck like a scarf, thinking if there was in fact a universal language of surrender it would at least give her the means to do so. She wished for buttons and beads, knives and paint. She wished for something other than syringes, litmus papers, glass tubes with rubber stoppers, bottles of acetone. She sat down on a box of fruit cocktail and closed her eyes. She saw Anders sitting on his desk looking through birding guides to the Amazon. She tried to think of something that was as valuable as Anders' life. And then Marina remembered the Rapps.

Easter stayed with her though he had never followed her out to the Martins before. The sun was high and hot though it was not yet nine in the morning. She carried a very large basket that she had found in the storage room, something the Lakashi had woven out of heavy grass. She had never come so late. In the two hours since she had last taken this trail the jungle had installed an entirely different set of birds screeching out an entirely different hue and cry. The mid-morning shift of insects replaced their early-morning brethren and clicked and vibrated a new and distinct set of messages. Marina kept her mind on the snakes that wrapped around trees and tangled themselves into vines and she placed her feet down carefully. She could not afford to make a mistake now. She stopped for a minute at the edge of the Martins, leaning forward to wipe the sweat off her face with the hem of her dress. The way the bright sunlight came into the field now turned the bark a softer yellow and she stood there, making a point to notice everything. She picked a Rapp and held it up to Easter, then she put it in the basket. She picked another and another and he followed her, going to other trees, taking just a few from every individual community of mushrooms, thinning them out while the basket rounded into a pile of pale blue jewels. No matter how many they picked the plants did not appear to be diminished. Maybe that was part of their secret. She had never realized how many of them there were. Protecting the Rapps meant protecting the Lakashi, and the Martins, and the fertility drug, and the malaria vaccine. No one could ever know where the Rapps had come from. But who had thought to protect Anders? If this is what was available to her then this is what she would use. When she picked up the basket it was scarcely heavier than it had been empty, and she covered the whole thing up with the nightgown and made her way back.

The mushrooms she knew were her best chance but she had Easter carry the peanut butter and the oranges just in case. She loaded all of it onto the boat. Thomas met her on the dock, Benoit was beside him. "I cannot believe what Dr. Swenson has told me," Thomas said, the panic rising in his voice, "What must Anders have thought, that in all this time we never came to look for him?"

Marina shook her head. "We didn't know."

Thomas took her hand. "I am going with you to find him." The Lakashi were there now, waiting to leap aboard.

It was all a set-up. Dr. Swenson would have called out for Thomas as soon as she was gone, telling him everything, telling him he had to go with Marina, and Thomas, guilt stricken in his ignorance, played right along. But it was not his destiny to see this thing through. "Anders was my friend," Marina said, and squeezed his thin fingers. "He's the reason I came here. I think I should be the one to go."

"I understand that," Thomas said. "But he was my friend as well and so it is equally my right. And you have no language with which to ask for him back."

"You don't speak Hummocca," Marina said.

"What Benoit and I have between us will be closer to Hummocca than your English. I will not wait on this dock and wonder what's become of you. I will not wait to see if Anders is alive." His face shone with such bright earnestness it was nearly unbearable. "I have already made a promise to Dr. Swenson. We are going along." Benoit nodded his head without understanding exactly what was being promised. Marina thought it was a nod of considerably less conviction.

"If you wait much longer to decide, Alan Saturn will hear about this," Thomas said. "He will insist on going. He has always been interested in the Hummocca. And Nancy would never let him go without her, you know this, so factor her in as well. I do not imagine Dr. Budi would agree to stay behind to watch Dr. Swenson but I could be wrong. If she insists on coming as well then we will need to put Dr. Swenson on the boat. We could make her a pallet on the deck out of some blankets."

If Anders were in fact alive in a tribe down river he had been there for more than three months. Marina would not have him there another night. "Alright," she said, finally. It only mattered that she left right away. It mattered less who was with her. "Alright."

Thomas nodded gratefully, glad that this part of the negotiations was complete. When he told her their next step was to find a gift she told him about the oranges and the peanut butter but didn't mention the mushrooms.

"I wish we had more," he said, looking at the ten lonely oranges with discouragement. "But we will make a good presentation. We will say to them, 'We have brought gifts' and 'Let us have the white man.'" Thomas said the two phrases to Benoit in Portuguese and Benoit gave back the closest approximation in Lakashi. Standing on the dock, the three of them repeated the words over and over again. Marina prayed the linguist was correct, that this was an uninteresting language that came off the same predictable root as the languages of all surrounding tribes, though it seemed doubtful the linguist had ever found the Hummocca. The Lakashi interrupted them as they practiced their lines. Benoit tried to explain that the gifts and the white man did not concern them. Marina's mind clamped down on every syllable, embedded them in her brain—*I have brought gifts. Let us have the white man.*

"We should go now," Thomas said. "Before the others arrive. We can practice when we're on our way."

"I need to get some water," she said, looking around the boat, "and a hat."

Thomas stepped onto the dock. "I will go," he said, and then he nodded towards the Lakashi. "You keep them off the boat." He turned back and raised his hand to her and at that moment Marina realized how easily she could lose Thomas on this trip. Suddenly she pictured him dead, an arrow in his chest, his body slipping over the side of the boat. She shuddered, blinked. How could she risk the life of Mrs. Nkomo's husband while going off to find Mrs. Eckman's husband? She tapped Easter hard on the shoulder, motioning for him to start the ignition while she untied the line. As they pulled back, Benoit yelled at her, pointing to the place where Thomas Nkomo had so recently stood, and with that she pushed Benoit backwards into the water. Easter seemed to think this was hysterical, Marina pushing his friend into the river, and he gunned the engine so the two of them could get away.

For hours they saw no one, no men on floating logs, no children in canoes. Occasionally a tree full of monkeys would scream at them or a silvered pack of sparrows would sweep past the bow, but other than that they were alone. Marina opened up one of the oranges and gave half of it to Easter. They had peanut butter and a bushel basket of hallucinogenic mushrooms. Marina kept her eyes trained to the right-hand side of the boat, trying to remember which slight parting of branches marked the turn they were supposed to take. "You see that river there?" Alan Saturn had said to her. "You follow that river to the Hummocca tribe." When finally she saw it, or saw her vaguest memory of it, she tapped Easter on the shoulder and pointed out the turn.

The river that went from the Lakashi tribe to the Jintas was itself a tributary of the Rio Negro. It was a modest river, half the width of the Negro and a fraction of the Amazon, but the tributary they had turned on was lesser still, a wide creek really, narrow and nameless. Marina had felt certain about leaving Thomas and Benoit behind until they made that turn and now she was wishing for all of them—the Saturns and Budi and even Dr. Swenson on the deck in a pile of blankets. She wished she had filled every available dugout with Lakashi and had them paddling along behind her. If there was safety in numbers she and Easter were perilously unsafe. The jungle closed over the entrance and after a few minutes she could no longer see the way out. In some places the trees touched leaves from either side and knit together a canopy, cutting the light into leaf-shaped shadows that covered over the water. Marina imagined Barbara Bovender and Mr. Fox standing silently in the back of the boat behind Milton, all three of them wondering if the turn they had taken could possibly have been the right one.

Easter took down the speed and the boat glided quietly ahead, the trail of purple smoke vanishing ten feet behind them. Marina couldn't understand how this part of the jungle could be so much worse: those were the same trees; this was the same water. They went along for an hour before the river widened, and then another hour before it narrowed again. Marina stayed close to Easter now. She kept a hand on his back. "I'd like to be out of here before dark," she said to him, because the sound of a voice, even her own voice, was a comfort, and that was when the arrows came raining down on either side of them, half of them making sharp clicks as they hit the deck while the others parted the water like knife blades and slipped inside. Easter leapt to push the boat ahead but Marina caught his hand. She pulled the throttle down to stop the engine and put her arms around the boy. This, she thought, was the outcome of the letter Mr. Fox had brought into the lab that she and Anders had shared: this moment, these arrows, this heat and jungle. Together she and Easter stared into the matted leaves. There were no more arrows. She opened her mouth and cried out in Lakashi, the series of pitches she sincerely hoped she had remembered correctly. She had a gift. She said it again as loud as she could. "We have brought gifts." It was ridiculous. They were not words, they were sounds. They were the only sounds she knew.

The wall of trees sat before her silently. She eased the throttle forward to counteract the current of the river that pulled them back. The arrows had fallen at least three feet away from them and Marina was willing to take this as a good sign. It wouldn't have been so difficult to hit the target had they meant to. She kept her hands on Easter's back and counted the seconds by the regular beat of his heart. Minutes passed. She called out to the jungle again, a sentence without meaning, and it echoed through the trees until the birds called back to her. She saw a movement in the leaves and then, slipping out from between the branches, a single man came forth, and then another. They were created wholly from the foliage, one and then one more stepping forward to watch her until a group of thirty or more were assembled on the bank of the river, loincloths and arrows, their foreheads as yellow as canaries. The women came behind the men, holding children, their faces unpainted. Marina thought of her father extolling the virtues of the pontoon boat but while it was steady in the water it was nothing more than a floating stage. She and Easter stood on an open hand offered to the Hummocca, and though she waited for her own fear it did not come. She was finally here. This was the place she had been trying to get to from the very beginning and here she would wait for the rest of her life. She tapped at the throttle to hold her place. They watched her and she watched them. Marina pushed Easter behind her and picked up the basket of Rapps. She tried to throw a few mushrooms as far as the shore but they fluttered into the water like a handful of blue feathers. She put down the basket and very slowly took an orange out of the box, holding it up first as an exhibit and then pretending to throw it and then throwing it so that it landed close to the middle of the group of them. They took a step back from it, making a wide half circle, and watched the orange where it lay in the mud until a man stepped forward from the back of the group and reached over for it. His hair was long and the color of sunlight, his beard ginger and gray. He looked to be thinner by half and yet he was there, still himself. Anders Eckman, just as his wife had speculated in the insanity of her grief, had only been missing. When Marina called his name he flinched as if someone had fired a gun.

"Who is it?" he called out.

"Marina," she said.

He stood there for a long time, the globe of the orange caught between his hands, his shirt filthy and torn, his pants torn. "Marina?"

"I've brought a gift," she said in English and then said it again in Lakashi.

There was a low murmuring on the shore and Anders seemed to be listening to it. "What is it?" Anders said.

"Rapps. I've got some peanut butter and some oranges and a very large basket of Rapps."

One of the men raised an arrow towards the boat and Anders walked over and stood in front of him until he lowered it again. He was saying something now, and then he pressed his thumbs into the orange and pulled it in half, taking out a piece for himself and holding it up to them before putting it in his mouth. Then he divided up the fruit into sections and handed it out to the men who were standing around him. "Do not under any circumstances give them the Rapps," he said calmly.

"It's what I've got," she said.

"You've got peanut butter. If these people find out about the Rapps they'll gut every last Lakashi by sundown and clean them out. How did you find me?" he called to her. One by one they cautiously laid the slices on their tongues and as they bit down they turned to Anders in their startled pleasure.

"I'll tell you some other time," she said. It was all she could do not to jump over the side of the boat, to swim to him.

Anders pointed back at the boat, and after further conference he called to Marina. "The orange is good. They want to know what you want in return."

She wondered if he was serious, if he really didn't know. "You," she said and then added to that the second sentence she knew, *Let us have the white man.* She wondered if a syllable of it made sense to them. She could feel Easter's breath through the fabric of her dress. His mouth was pressed against her back. She was an idiot to have brought him. She knew enough to leave Thomas and Benoit behind and then took Easter with her without a thought, like he was nothing more than her talisman, her good luck. No mother would have brought her child into this even if he was the one who understood the river and the boat.

On the shore Anders was pointing to his chest, he was pointing to the boat. A single heron skated down the river. After a long discussion he called again to Marina. "They want you to bring in the boat."

Once again Marina waited for her fear but somehow it held back. "Should I?"

"Do it," Anders said. "They have you anyway. Just give them a little bit, a jar of peanut butter to start."

Marina nodded and reached for the throttle, and when she did Easter came around from behind her. He put his hands back on the wheel. She put one hand on his head and pointed for him to go into shore and he nodded.

"Is that Easter?" Anders said. "I don't have my glasses anymore."

"I made a mistake," she said.

It was only fifteen feet and they came in slowly. The men waded out and the women kept to the shore behind them. Anders was very close now and she could see the hollow of his cheeks beneath his beard and she could see his eyes. When the Hummocca came to the boat Marina could see the shape of their heads was in fact slightly different from the Lakashi just as Dr. Swenson had said. They were not as tall as the Lakashi and Anders towered over them. She handed the one who looked like he was in charge the jar of peanut butter and for a moment he struggled with what to do with it, his hands squeezing the jar. He looked up at Marina, maybe he had meant for her to help him or maybe he meant to kill her, but what he saw there on the boat was Easter. The man with the yellow forehead stood there waist deep in the water, his chest against the pontoon, and the look on his face was the same look that had been on her own face a moment before when she first saw Anders, a cross of joy and disbelief, a look that was willing to accept that which was not possible. He turned and called to a woman on the shore who put the child she was holding on the ground and walked out into the water. Once she had seen Easter from a distance, she tried to move faster and the water held her back. She called to him, stretching out her arms, the trembling in her body sending out a ring of small waves into the water. And then she was there, pulling herself onto the boat and Easter shrank back behind Marina, his hands around her waist as tight as a snake.

Anders was out in the water, and then his hands were on the boat. He was calling out to the Hummocca with two sharp syllables. The woman scrambled up on the deck, her short legs muddied and wet. She knelt behind Easter, her wet arms covering his arms, encircling Marina's waist. She wailed a single word again and again while Easter stayed perfectly still, holding fiercely to Marina. The woman behind him was rocking. The man with the peanut butter jar was saying something to Anders that was not said in rage.

"They want Easter," Anders said. He was holding onto the side of the boat now, his hands on the deck. He was nodding at the other men in the water who were talking faster and faster now, one hand holding up an arrow, the other making circles in the air. Anders looked at Marina. For the first time she could see his eyes very plainly. "Give them Easter and we can go."

"No," she said. That could not be possible. She had brought gifts. She had come for Anders. She put her hands over the woman's hands, over Easter's hands. Their arms made a structure that held her up. She shook her head. "We'll give them the Rapps."

"This isn't a choice. They can keep all of us and the boat. Do it now while they're confused. We have no bargaining power at all here." Anders helped himself slowly onto the boat and, bending before Marina, he unlocked the layers of hands. Only then did Easter see him clearly and understand why they had come here at all. He reached for Anders' neck and made the sound he made in his sleep, a high trenchant cry that stood in place for the words *Not dead. You are not dead.* The Hummocca looked up from the water and were amazed to see their boy knew this white man and that clearly he loved him so well.

"Not this," Marina said. "If we stay with him we'll all be together."

"Go get the oranges and the peanut butter," he said, one hand on the back of Easter's head, his face in Easter's neck. Anders kissed the boy, his hair and ear and eye. They would have less than a minute together. The woman was standing now, her hands on Easter's back.

Marina got the fruit and the peanut butter and handed it over the edge, filling up every hand that was raised to her. Then Anders held Easter out by the waist. The boy's feet were bare and he was wearing dirty yellow shorts and a blue T-shirt that read "JazzFest 2003." Marina made a note of all of it, as if there was someone she could describe him to later on, an agency that went to look for missing children. Anders handed Easter to the up-reached hands of the man in the water and the woman slipped over the side of the boat to stand with him. The look on the boy's face as his eyes went from Marina and Anders and back to her again was one of terrified misunderstanding.

It was something worse than she had seen when the snake had him because the snake he had understood. He stretched out his hands to her and Marina closed her eyes. She left him there. She let him go.

The boat was turned around now and Anders was driving. In a minute they were full speed down the narrow turns of the river and Marina kept her eyes closed, one hand fixed to the pole that held the ragged cover over the center of the boat. She had accounted for her own death, and certainly she had accounted for Anders', but she had not been ready for this.

"They would have taken him," Anders said. "If they killed us, if they didn't kill us, Easter would have stayed with them."

He took a turn too fast and the basket of Rapps bounced twice and then sailed off the back of the boat and spread out over the water, an offering of little blue corks. Marina just caught the edge of the nightgown before it flew away and she tied it in a knot around her waist. She wished she had eaten a handful of the mushrooms herself. She would have been glad to have lost her mind. She would have been grateful to see God. There were so many things to say to Anders that she said none of them. She wanted to know what had happened to him all this time, and how he had gotten there, if he was still sick, but Easter stood in front of every question. She had not lost him or killed him. She had taken him into the jungle and given him away and there was nothing that anyone could say in the face of that. Once they were far enough away Marina drove the boat and Anders lay at the front of the deck with his eyes closed and his hands folded across his chest. When she looked at him sleeping she remembered that he had been dead for months now and that in order to bring him back she had given up everything she had known in the world. Anders who she had worked with every day, Anders who she knew very well and not at all, was once again alive. He slept as if he had stayed awake the entire time he had been gone and there were moments she wondered if he were dead again but she wouldn't stop the boat to see. From time to time it rained and when it didn't rain the light thinned in the tops of the trees and the bats began to loop out across the water. It wasn't hard to drive the boat. Why had she ever thought she needed Easter to come with her? Marina wrapped the nightgown around her head and face and squinted through the insects of early evening.

When Anders finally woke up hours later it was from a nightmare. His hands shot up into the air and he gave one short cry and then sat. It was pitch dark by then and Marina drove slowly, shining the light of the boat onto shore. She was worried she would drive past the Lakashi, that she would turn up some tributary and be lost all over again. Anders looked at the river and then the boat, he looked at Marina. From a distance they could just make out some small spots of fire down the river. "I had a lot of time to imagine my rescue," he said. "Army Rangers, soldiers of fortune, even the Lakashi. Mostly I thought it would be Karen."

"It should have been Karen. She wanted to be the one but I told her she had to stay home with the boys."

Anders closed his eyes so that he could see them more clearly. "How are the boys?"

"Everyone is fine."

"In all the times I dreamed of this, I never once saw you as the one coming to get me."

"I thought you were dead," she said to him.

"I was dead," Anders said.

It wasn't long before the voices of the Lakashi spread over the water and pulled them in. Marina was grateful for their fire, their enormous noise. For the first time in weeks she wondered what time it was. There were men swimming out to the boat and then men pulling themselves on board and as soon as they stood on the deck they were silent. Two unimaginable things had happened: Anders was with her and Easter was gone. Marina killed the engine, afraid she would run over someone in the dark, and the swimmers pulled the boat up to the dock. The men leaned in towards Anders, the burning branches high above their heads. They did not slap him but set their branches in the water where the fire hissed out. One by one slipped over the edge. Voice by voice the singing ceased. In the darkness Anders caught hold of Marina's hand.

Thomas Nkomo was standing on the dock with a flashlight as if he had been waiting there all day for Marina to remember him. Her first thought when she saw him was of the arrows that had fallen on the boat but she did not bother to tell him that she had saved his life as well. Thomas went to Anders and took him in his arms and the two tall thin men held one another. Dr. Budi came up behind him and then the Saturns and each one took their turn.

"Easter?" Nancy Saturn said, looking around her.

"We left him there," Marina said. The Lakashi were walking away from them and the lights from all those burning sticks trailed into the jungle in every direction while the doctors walked to the lab.

Marina took the path back to Dr. Swenson's. She didn't have a flashlight but the moon was bright. When she went inside she saw that her cot was gone.

"I had them move it this afternoon. I didn't think you were coming back." Dr. Swenson was lying in bed, a lantern burning on the table beside her.

"Anders is here," Marina said, standing by the door.

Dr. Swenson raised up her head. "Barbara Bovender was right?"

"He's in the lab."

"I don't know another story to match this," Dr. Swenson said, shaking her head. "I will be glad to see Dr. Eckman. Easter must be thrilled. I always thought he blamed himself for letting him get away. Dr. Eckman must have gone down to the river. I've been thinking about it all day and that's what I decided. One of the canoes was missing. He must have crawled inside and floated away. Then somewhere out there the Hummocca found him."

"Easter is gone."

"What do you mean, gone?"

"The Hummocca took him. That's how I got Anders back. A man and a woman took him off the boat. They seemed to think that Easter belonged to them. They were very definite about it."

There came across Dr. Swenson a wild look and she pushed herself up to sitting with her hands. Her nightgown was old and torn at the neck. "You have to go back there. You have to go and get him."

Marina shook her head. "I can't."

"I won't accept that you can't. Obviously you can. You got Dr. Eckman and you will get Easter. He's deaf. He doesn't understand what's happened. You can't just leave him there."

But Marina had already left him, and she understood that in life a person was only allowed one trip down to hell. There was no going back to that place, not for anyone. "Where did you get him?" she said.

"I told you."

"Tell me again," Marina said.

Dr. Swenson sank back into the pillows. She waited a long time before she spoke. "I didn't tell you because you wouldn't have liked the story. But that matters less now, doesn't it? No one tells the truth to people they don't actually know, and if they do it is a horrible trait. Everyone wants something smaller, something neater than the truth."

"Where did you get him?"

"They gave him to me. He came here. In the jungle one tribe knows what another tribe is doing, I told you that, tribes with which they have no obvious means of communication. One day the Hummocca sent for me. This was probably eight years ago, I'm not positive. Two men came in a canoe to get me but I wouldn't go with them. I knew who they were. Dr. Rapp had had some dealings with the Hummocca thirty years ago, nothing that was good. The next day the same two men came back with a child between them in the bottom of the boat. He was fantastically sick. There was pus and blood running out of both of his ears. Children die out here constantly, that's why so many of them are needed. I can only imagine this child belonged to someone who was very important because they had brought him to me. They got their point across without benefit of a mutual language, they wanted him saved, and after that they left him here. I certainly didn't ask them to. He had a fever of a hundred and six, a bilateral mastoiditis, probably meningitis. He was already deaf, there was nothing I could have done about that. Three days later the same two men were there again, wanting him back. He was on IV penicillin, fifty thousand units Q6H. It wasn't as if I could send him off in the canoe."

"So you kept him?"

"I told them the boy was dead. That would have been the case if it hadn't been for me. The fact of the matter is had they waited a few weeks I would have given him back, but they came too early, and he was too sick to go. I couldn't explain any of that, but I knew enough to tell them he was dead."

"You could have sent him back later."

"He was sick for a month, as sick as anything I've seen. By the time I brought him back they would have forgotten about him. A deaf child? They wouldn't have known what to do with him. Do you think you wouldn't have done the same thing? He was Easter even then, you know. After a month of feeding him and washing him and staying up all night with his fevers you really think you would have taken him back to the cannibals?"

"I wouldn't have taken someone else's child," Marina said.

"Of course you would," Dr. Swenson said. "You would take Easter from me now. You never had any intention of leaving here without him and I never had any intention of letting him go. He was mine. He was my boy and you gave him away."

Were he here she would have put him in a canoe tonight and rowed the boat herself in the dark all the way to the Amazon River. "I would have taken him," she said. "You're right. Except that now I don't have the chance. Why did you let me take him back there? Why didn't you tell me it wouldn't be safe?"

"He didn't belong to them," Dr. Swenson said. "He was mine."

Marina sat with this but there was nothing to say. She would have sworn that Easter was hers. "Anders and I are leaving in the morning."

"Take Dr. Eckman back to Manaus if you have to, or let someone else take him, but I still need you here."

"I'm going with him," Marina said.

Dr. Swenson shook her head. "It doesn't work like that. Trust me, you won't fit in there anymore. You've changed. You've betrayed your employer, and you'll keep on betraying him, and that won't sit well with someone like you. I changed myself once, it was a long time ago but I changed. I followed my teacher down here too. I thought I was coming for the summer. I know about this."

"It isn't the same."

"Of course it isn't the same. Nothing is ever the same. I wasn't like Dr. Rapp, and still I took his place. You're not like me but you wait, you'll go back there and nothing will make sense to you anymore."

Marina came and stood beside the bed. "Good night," she said.

"You'll come back," Dr. Swenson said. "But don't make me wait forever. There isn't an infinite amount of time to get this work done. Easter will come back, you know. He may even be back in the morning. He'll steal a canoe while they're sleeping. He knows how to get home. He won't hold it against you, what you've done to him. He's a child. He'll forgive us."

But Marina had seen the look on his face when Anders handed him over. She wasn't sure Dr. Swenson was right. "Good night," she said again, and closed the door.

When she went back to the lab to find Anders, Alan Saturn told her he had gone to take a shower. Thomas was off looking for the box where they had put his things, hoping that not all of his clothes had been taken. Nancy and Budi sat staring at the floor in front of them. "He says he still has intermittent fevers," Alan said finally. "Make sure he looks good when you get him on the plane. If they think he has malaria they won't let him back in the country."

"Could he have malaria?" Marina asked.

Dr. Budi looked up but she said nothing.

"It's the tropics," Nancy said. "Anyone could have malaria."

Dr. Budi shook her head. "Anyone but us," she said.

Marina went back to the sleeping porch. She washed herself standing in a basin and put on Mrs. Bovender's nightgown. It was no longer particularly clean but it was a veritable blossom of edelweiss compared to the dress she'd been wearing. She felt sick to be in this place without Easter. She opened his strongbox, which had been returned with the cot, and there beneath the feathers and the rock that looked like an eye was the letter from Anders announcing a reward for Easter's safe delivery. In that box she found not only Anders' passport but her own. He had had a picture of both of them. She also found her wallet, her plane ticket, and her phone. She sat with the phone in her hands for a long time before trying to turn it on and when she finally found her nerve to push the button nothing happened. The battery was dead. She put it back in the box.

"This was my room," Anders said.

Marina looked up and there he was. His beard was gone and he ran his hand over his face. It was the face she remembered. "Some Lakashi woman shaved it off for me. It seemed to make her inordinately happy. I never had a beard before," he said. "I hated it."

"You look like yourself," she said.

"I slept here." He pointed to the bed. "Easter was in the hammock."

"I know," she said. "I figured it out." She looked at the strongbox. "He slept with me. He had terrible nightmares after you were gone."

"So did I," Anders said. He turned off the two lanterns and put the strongbox on the floor. "Move over," he said.

Marina stretched out on one side of the cot and Anders lay down beside her. Their noses were touching and he put his arm over her shoulder. "I'm sorry," he said.

"No," she said. "It's better this way."

"Tomorrow we'll go home."

She leaned into him. She nodded into his neck. If they fell asleep they would have to fall asleep at the same minute. They would have to hold each other very close and stay very still until they woke up again. Until this point they had embraced every year when she came to his house for the Christmas party. He would open the door wearing a red sweater and she would be standing out in the snow, holding a bottle of wine, and he would give her a quick hug and then usher her inside.

"How was it you?" he said.

"I don't know. Karen wanted me to go, and Mr. Fox. I was supposed to find out what had happened to Dr. Swenson and find out how you died. I was so sorry when I heard you had died."

"No one thought I was missing?" he said. "No one thought it was strange that my body was gone?"

Marina shook her head very slightly against the pillow they shared. "Dr. Swenson said they'd buried you. She thought you were dead. She was sure you were dead."

"But you didn't think I was." He put his hand on her shoulder.

"I did," Marina said. "Karen didn't. She held out a lot of hope for you but I didn't believe her. I thought she just couldn't accept it."

"Then why did you come out there to find me?"

"Barbara Bovender," she said, and that was when she kissed him, because their mouths were so close, because he was in fact alive, because she could not explain any of it. She was in the Bovenders' living room and Barbara was asking her, did she love him? She loved him now, but only now. On this one night, after a day of the most extraordinary circumstances that either of them would see for the rest of their lives, she kissed him to prove to herself that all of this had happened, and he kissed her because it was true, he was here. And when they pulled their bodies closer still it felt like a necessity, trying to lie together in such a small space. When she cried it was because she saw the tributary again and she saw again how easy it would have been to miss it. Had she missed it, had Barbara Bovender missed it, Anders would never have been found, and Easter never would have been lost. Anders knew this, he said as much when he held her head in his hands. When they made love it was only to calm the fears they had endured. It was a physical act of kindness, a comfort, a sublime tenderness between friends. She would have made love to Mr. Fox if he had been there, and Anders would have made love to his wife, but for this night what they had was one another, and anyway, after all that had happened between them how could they not press themselves together, press through each other with their bodies to show how deeply, if only until the plane landed in Minneapolis, that they were intertwined. Without the scant weight of what was left of him to pin her down she might have gone to stand in the shallows of the river to see if Dr. Swenson was right about Easter rowing his way home to them in a stolen canoe, maybe the same canoe Anders had floated away in. Without the warmth of her he might not have believed the reversal of his fortunes. This would be the only part of the story that they would never speak of again, the part where he lifted her on top of him, his arms as thin as sapling trees, and she put her face down on his chest and she kissed him and cried.

In the morning, miraculously, they were both still balanced in the bed, two thin plates leaning against one another in a rack, Marina on her side, wearing Anders Eckman over her back like a blanket. She would have thought that she would go to the Martins one last time before leaving but now all she wanted was for this to be over. She was finished with the trees. The fact that she had ever considered bringing back a bag full of branches struck her now as ridiculous and slightly repulsive. The only thing to bring home was Anders. She was naked, in bed with her officemate, and in sliding out from under him she woke him up.

"Oh, Marina," he said, but she shook her head and leaned forward. For the last time in her life, she kissed him.

"Let's go home," she said.

And so they did, Marina wearing Mrs. Bovender's nightgown with a pair of her pants underneath it and one of Mr. Fox's shirts over it. She wore Milton's hat on her head and carried Easter's strongbox like a very small suitcase. The Saturns took them in the pontoon boat to Manaus. They were only an hour away from the Lakashi when an enormous eagle sailed over their heads low enough that they could see the expression on the face of the small monkey that dangled from its curving talons.

"That's a harpy eagle," Anders said loudly, tilting himself over the side of the boat to watch it pass. "Did you see that?"

"No one could miss that," Nancy Saturn said. The jungle was suddenly silent in the bird's wake, as if everything with eyes had the sense to hold its breath.

"That was the bird I most wanted to see when I came down here. They're almost impossible to find." Anders' body still strained forward in the direction of the raptor. "I can't believe I saw a harpy eagle."

When they arrived in Manaus they called Milton from the pay phone at the dock. Milton, forever resourceful, had a friend at the ticket counter at the airlines who was sympathetic to their case, and while they waited for him to arrange the details of two seats on the last flight out to Miami, connecting to the first flight out to Minneapolis, they went to see Barbara Bovender to tell her that it was not her father she had seen running through the trees and how in making that wrong turn on the river she had saved Anders' life. In telling the story to other people they told it to one another, about how they each had come to find Dr. Swenson, how Anders in his fever had wandered down to the river and gotten into a canoe, about the Hummocca who had found him half dead and floating in the bottom of his little boat though where he was he would never know for sure as all of those memories came from a place that was now fully under water, like a town that had been flooded into a lake, about the poultice they painted on him for weeks that smelled like horseradish and tar and how it blistered the skin on his chest. They became so good at talking that at one point Marina told Milton of her vision of Thomas Nkomo shot through with an arrow and Anders told Barbara about Easter being lifted from his hands though both Barbara and Marina had cried to hear it. By the time they boarded the plane, they had talked about everything except the thing they would never need to talk about. They drank Bloody Marys and watched as the Amazon grew farther and farther away on the in-flight map screen in front of them. In their reclining seats they both fell into a sleep that was deeper and more refreshing than any sleep either had had in months.

There was a good case to be made for calling Karen from the airport in Miami and a good case to be made for waiting, for going right to the house. Marina could see that there were equal parts of love and cruelty either way it was reasoned, and though she voted to go to the house she said the decision was of course unequivocally his to make. Anders stared at the clock and the rare bank of pay phones near the gate until finally the flight was called to board. Anders and Marina both agreed they had lost their skills on the telephone. Every mile they went backwards they felt themselves turning into the people they had been, two doctors who shared an office in a pharmaceutical company outside of Minneapolis.

Minnesota! It smelled like raspberries and sunlight and tender grass. It was summer, and everything was more beautiful than any picture she had carried with her. By the time they were in the taxi they still knew that something extraordinary had happened but they found themselves distracted, first by the tall buildings and then later by the trees that were fully leafed, by the wide stretches of prairie that let the eye sweep so easily in any direction, by the remarkable lightness of the air. Anders leaned over the seat and gave his directions to the Nigerian cab driver one turn at a time while Marina rolled down her window and let the wind press back her fingers and pull at her braided hair. For some reason she thought of driving with Milton and the Bovenders to that beach outside Manaus and the goat that Milton managed not to hit. There had never been a place in the world as beautiful as Minnesota.

When they got to the top of the cul-de-sac they passed a boy on a bicycle but Anders was looking in the other direction. He had by then caught sight of two boys in the front yard, boys who from a distance moved and played like Easter, and his hand was on the Nigerian's shoulder and was calling for him to stop the car, to stop. The door of the taxi opened like the door of a cage and Anders leapt out, calling their names. For a few moments the cab was stopped and Marina watched this world that had nothing to do with her even though she had made it herself. She saw the boy on the bike swing a wide, arcing turn and come careening back down the street towards his father. The front door opened at the sound of so much screaming, the boys were screaming like Lakashi, and the neighbors opened their doors. She didn't see Karen open her door but there she was, flying into his arms, her feet never touching the lawn. She was as small and golden as a child herself. It was as if they had waited for him every day he had been gone, holding their burning sticks above their heads, pouring their souls up to heaven in a single voice of ululation until he came back. And Marina brought him back, and without a thought that anyone should see her, she told the driver to go on.

Reading Group Questions

1. How would you describe Marina Singh? How has the past shaped her character? Discuss the anxieties that are manifested in her dreams.

2. "Marina was from Minnesota. No one ever believed that. At the point when she could have taken a job anywhere she came back because she loved it here. This landscape was the one she understood, all prairie and sky." What does this description say about the character?

3. Talk about Marina's relationship with her boss, Mr. Fox. Would you call what they share love? Do they have a future? Why does he want Marina to go to the Amazon? What propels her to agree?

4. What drew Marina to her old mentor, Annick Swenson? Compare and contrast the two women. How does Annick see Marina? Barbara Bovender, one of Annick's caretakers/gatekeepers tells Marina, "She's such a force of nature . . . a woman completely fearless, someone who sees the world without limitations." Is this a fair assessment of Annick? How would you describe her? How has the elderly doctor's past shaped the person she is and the choices she has made?

5. Describe the arc of Marina and Annick's relationship from the novel's beginning to its end. Do you like these women? Did your opinion of them change as the story unfolded? Why doesn't Marina ever tell anyone the full story of her early experience with Annick?

6. Consider Annick's research in the Amazon. Should women of any age be able to have children? What are the benefits and the downsides? Why does this ability seem to work in the Lakashi culture? What impact does this research ultimately have on Marina? Whether you are a man or woman, would you want to have a child in your fifties or sixties? How far should modern science go to "improve" on nature?

7. In talking about her experiences with the indigenous people, Annick explains, "The question is whether or not you choose to disturb the world around you; or if you choose to go on as if you had never arrived." How does Marina respond to this? Does Annick practice what she preached?

How do these women's early choices impact later events and decisions? How does Annick's statement extend beyond the Amazon to the wider world? Would you rather make a "disturbance" in life, or go along quietly?

8. Talk about the Lakashi people and the researchers. How do they get along? Though the scientists try not to interfere with the natives' way of life, how does their being there affect the Lakashi? What influence do the Lakashi have on the scientists?

9. Would you be able to live in the jungle as the researchers and natives do? Is there an appeal to going back to nature; from being removed from the Western constraints of time and our modern technological society?

10. What role does nature and the natural world—the jungle, the Amazon River—play in Marina's story? How does the environment influence the characters—Marina, Annick, Milton, Anders, Easter, and the others? Annick warns Marina, "It's difficult to trust yourself in the jungle. Some people gain their bearings over time but for others that adjustment never comes." Does Marina ultimately "gain her bearings"?

11. Marina travels into hell, into her own Conradian "heart of darkness." What keeps her in the jungle longer than she'd ever thought she'd stay? How does this journey transform her and her view of herself and the world? Will she ever return—and does she need to?

12. What is your opinion of the choices Marina makes regarding Easter? What role does the boy play in the story? Do you think Marina will ever have the child—one like Easter—that she wants?

13. What do you think happens to Marina after she returns home?

14. *State of Wonder* is rich in symbolism. Identify a few—for example, Eden Prairie (Marina's Minnesota home), Easter (the young deaf native boy), Milton (the Brazilian guide)—and talk about how Ann Patchett uses them to deepen the story.

15. *State of Wonder* raises questions of morality and principle, civilization, culture, love, and science. Choose a few events from the book to explore some of these themes.

16. What is the significance of the novel's title, *State of Wonder*?

P.S.

Insights,
Interviews
& More . . .

*

Meet Ann Patchett

© 2010 by Melissa Ann Pinney

ANN PATCHETT was born in Los Angeles in 1963 and raised in Nashville. She attended Sarah Lawrence College and the University of Iowa Writers' Workshop. In 1990, she won a residential fellowship to the Fine Arts Work Center in Provincetown, Massachusetts, where she wrote her first novel, *The Patron Saint of Liars*. It was named a *New York Times* Notable Book for 1992. In 1993, she received a fellowship from the Mary Ingraham Bunting Institute at Radcliffe College. Patchett's second novel, *Taft*, was awarded the Janet Heidinger Kafka Prize for Fiction in 1994. Her third novel, *The Magician's Assistant*, was shortlisted for England's Orange Prize and earned her a Guggenheim Fellowship. Her fourth novel, *Bel Canto*, won both the PEN/Faulkner Award and the Orange Prize in 2002, and was a finalist for the National Book Critics Circle Award. It was named the Book Sense Book of the Year. It sold more than a million copies in the United

States and has been translated into more than thirty languages. Her next novel, *Run*, was an instant *New York Times* bestseller. In 2004, Patchett published *Truth & Beauty*, a memoir of her friendship with the writer Lucy Grealy. It was named one of the Best Books of the Year by the *Chicago Tribune*, the *San Francisco Chronicle*, and *Entertainment Weekly*. *Truth & Beauty* was also a finalist for the Los Angeles Times Book Prize and won the Chicago Tribune Heartland Prize, the Harold D. Vursell Memorial Award from the American Academy of Arts and Letters, and the Alex Award from the American Library Association. In 2008 Patchett published *What now?* based on the lauded commencement address she gave at Sarah Lawrence College.

Patchett was the editor of *The Best American Short Stories 2006*. She has written for numerous publications, including the *New York Times Magazine*, *Harper's* magazine, the *Atlantic*, the *Washington Post*, *Gourmet*, and *Vogue*. She lives in Nashville, Tennessee, with her husband, and is the co-owner of Parnassus Books.

A Short Story Versus a Novel

Ann Patchett explains why she never writes short stories, with the exception of the one that follows.

WHEN I WAS IN COLLEGE, I wrote short stories. I wrote lots of them. I liked their compact size, the way you could manage the shift of a life in a matter of pages. When well told, a story captured the subtle moment of change. If a novel was a map of a country, a story was the bright silver pin that marked the crossroads. Because the story had less space to work with, a writer was more likely to rely on the readers' imagination. It gave the form a sense of interaction that I liked. What the story left unsaid carried as much weight as the words on the page. Also, stories were a pleasure to write. They were so portable, so accommodating. I could easily hold the entire plot of whatever I was working on in my head. I could be intimate with every character. If an idea looked to be a particularly good one, my schedule could be rearranged. I would cancel dinner plans to write a short story, stay up all night. It was a binge, dropping out of the world I lived in for a while to go stay in the world I'd made up. In a day or two or three, I'd have a draft, and then, disheveled and half asleep, I would come back to my real life to begin the process of revision. Of course, not all of the stories worked out, and I felt bad about the ones that didn't, but not very bad. I had lost only a handful of days, and inevitably something was learned. As soon as I had another idea, and hopefully a better idea, I jumped back in. In this way, writing stories was always a bit like falling in love with a stranger and running off to Marrakech for a long weekend. It didn't have to be successful to be thrilling.

With all the certainty of youth, I was convinced that I had found my form. Who would want to write a novel if the same effect could be achieved in the quick explosion of twenty pages? I went off to graduate school to continue my study of the craft. I read Cheever and mountains of Chekhov. I read and reread Grace Paley, who had once been my teacher. Magazines, books, anthologies, I read any story I could get my hands on. I was publishing stories too. As soon as one was finished, it was sold (though in many cases "sold" might be too strong a word—more often they were "placed"). Unlike other writers who used the story as a warm-up, a first act, I vowed to remain true to the form that I loved. The story was not a stepping-stone to something more important. As far as I was concerned, the story was the thing itself.

It was several years after I pledged undying loyalty that I wrote my first novel.

This is how it happened: by the age of twenty-five, I had made a mess of my life. I felt that I had fallen into a hole, and since writing was the only real skill I possessed, I figured I was going to have to use writing to get myself out. Given the depth and the darkness of this particular hole, I knew that it was going to take more than a short story. At the time, I kept a very literal picture of my circumstances in my head—standing on top of a short story, even several very good short stories, was not going to raise me up high enough to reach the ledge above me. A novel, on the other hand, was a bigger thing. It had the sort of heft and height a person would need to lift herself up. ▸

A Short Story Versus a Novel ***(continued)***

Assessing the situation, it was clear that this was a novel-sized hole I was in, and so I wrote a novel to get out.

The process of writing a novel bears very little resemblance to that of writing a story. The novel rarely gave any reason to cancel dinner. While a story can come in a bright burst of imagination that may require a lost night's sleep, a novel begs for food and regular rest. If a story can be a reckless affair, a novel is a long marriage, a regular job. Bit by bit, I learned how to stay still in my chair, how to show up day after day. The pages accumulated in a slow and regular way, by plodding rather than leaping. But as luck would have it, the plan worked exactly the way I had hoped: climbing on top of this novel allowed me to pull myself out of my misfortune and back into daylight. *The Patron Saint of Liars* was one of the best things that ever happened to me, but in the process of learning how to make something big, I carelessly lost my ability to make something small. After I was finished with my first novel, I stopped writing stories altogether.

When I was in my twenties I could pretty much fit everything I owned in my car. When I moved to a new town, I would buy a desk and a kitchen table at a thrift shop, and when I moved again, I left those things behind, knowing that they would be easy to replace. But at some point I started buying a few nice pieces of furniture, some paintings, and then eventually I bought a house to put them in. My life had changed, and there came a time that I could not begin to cram what I owned into a car. Writing a novel had caused a similar disruption in my life—it was as if I no longer fit inside a story. I had come to know the pleasures of space and time, of watching my characters make mistakes and then giving them the chance to try and rectify their circumstances. I had developed a fondness for describing things, for adding back story. I had let a reckless number of minor characters wander into the landscape, and now I didn't want to give them up. In short, I had become something very long.

There were a couple of times I gave the story another try. Once when I was teaching a graduate seminar at the University of California at Irvine, I gave my students an assignment that they told me was unnecessarily complicated, and in the spirit of camaraderie, I said I would give it a try myself. It turns out they were right, and, what's more, all of their stories were better than mine. When I was the guest editor for *The Best American Short Stories* series in 2006, I read so many wonderful stories I felt certain I could write one myself, but when I tried, I realized I was wrong. By now, so many years had passed that I had become a giant house with a basement and an in-ground swimming pool.

The fact that I didn't write short stories never stopped magazine editors from asking me for them. I would tell them I would write an essay instead. (Essays bear no relationship to fiction for me. They have always been easy.) One editor, David Rowell from the *Washington Post Magazine*, never would take no for an answer. Again and again, he asked me to write a short story for an upcoming issue. He told me it wouldn't be any problem for me. He said my essays were practically stories.

"They're not," I said. "I didn't make that stuff up."

He persisted, and after four years of turning him down, I finally told him I'd give it a try. The only reason I agreed was that I liked David and I disliked the feeling that I was continually disappointing him—that, and the knowledge that I was someone who never missed a deadline. I was curious to see if I might be able to write a story if I had to.

It was a holiday issue, and he told me I could have first pick: Thanksgiving, Christmas (or a religious or cultural Christmas equivalent), or New Year's. I jumped on New Year's, a festivity with which I have no baggage whatsoever because I have never been able to stay awake until midnight. I had an ocean of time, more than two months until it was due, and I regretted my decision before I'd hung up the phone.

I began to take long walks immediately, staring at the sidewalk as if looking for that part of my creative process I had lost in a different neighborhood more than twenty years before. I had written stories. I had written lots of stories. I knew how to do this.

But honestly, I didn't. Use it or lose it. Every plot I came up with fell apart like a dry leaf before I could type it up. What was worse, this very minor assignment (the story was to be 1,500 words) was eating up the time I should have been spending at work on my novel. I was a few months away from finishing *State of Wonder* and I wanted to give my full attention back to that. I became increasingly irritated with myself. Why couldn't I come up with anything? Why had I agreed to do this in the first place? And then, in the eleventh hour, it came to me, the only reasonable solution: I would cheat. I would borrow a couple of characters from the novel I was writing, and I would write about those characters years before the book took place. It was not a story line ►

A Short Story Versus a Novel ***(continued)***

that would have made it into *State of Wonder*, but it was a something I already knew, because the novelist knows all sorts of things that aren't meant to be included in the text. I would tell how Dr. Swenson met Dr. Rapp, and once I had decided on that, it was the easiest thing in the world. David Rowell thought I had done a wonderful job. "See," he said, "I was right. You write great short stories."

I told him the truth. He would have found out sooner or later. I really couldn't write a story anymore. All I could manage was an outtake from a novel. It isn't the same thing, but it can very nearly pass if no one looks too closely.

Studies in Modern Mycology

A version of this short story originally appeared in the Washington Post Magazine *in November 2010.*

THE YOUNG MAN used a digital voice recorder. As far as Dr. Swenson was concerned, the very moment he set it down on the table between them, the interview was as good as over. "You don't mind?" he asked. He was fumbling to find the on switch and did not look up to see the answer which was abundantly evident in her expression.

If he was incapable of listening with the facility of memory or, short of that, taking notes, if he lacked those basic skills essential to writing a book, it was not for her to correct. She simply chose to not answer his question, and since it appeared that the question had been rhetorical, they were able to proceed.

"You met Dr. Rapp in—"

"Cambridge."

"Year?"

"1960." She had been a sophomore. It was just before Thanksgiving break and the last of the flaming fall leaves that distinguished New England to its visitors had been raked and bagged and hauled away by the department of Buildings and Grounds. She had crossed Radcliffe's naked lawn and Harvard's desolate yard and then climbed the worn wooden stairs to the top of the Museum of Comparative Zoology, where she arrived at his office, utterly unflustered by the thought of knocking on the door of a great man. That was the power of youth. ▸

Studies in Modern Mycology ***(continued)***

"You were interested in studying mycology?" the interviewer asked.

Dr. Swenson made a mental note of the second strike against him: he dressed as if he were seventeen, khaki trousers and a blue T-shirt. Perhaps he was planning to visit the gym later in the afternoon and didn't want to be bothered to have to change all of his clothes. Even in New Guinea, Dr. Rapp had worn a jacket and tie. Then again, in New Guinea, Dr. Rapp had not used the crutch of a tape recorder. He waited until evening, until a lack of sunlight had separated him from his fieldwork for the night, and then opened his logbook and entered in the day's notes in his crisp and surprisingly delicate hand. "Mycology was not available to the women of Radcliffe," she said.

It was a Harvard boy who had first told her about the class. She could not remember the boy's name, only that he was tall and that when he leaned toward her over the little table in the coffeehouse she could see that his dark hair was just beginning to thin. Because this boy possessed enough self-awareness to know that nothing he had done in his own life could be of interest to her, he attempted seduction by reciting everything he could remember from Dr. Rapp's lectures. "He's identified new species of mushrooms on five continents," the boy said, and touched his fingers to the edge of her brown plaid kilt. She used her napkin to tap his hand from the vicinity of her lap. Dr. Swenson's interest had certainly been piqued, though not in the boy.

The interviewer was smiling at Dr. Swenson now in a way that struck her as overly familiar. "You must have made an impression. You were the first woman he ever allowed to audit his lectures."

Could this really be the book's author? The person Dr. Rapp had approved? Maybe not. It was possible that this was just an unpaid intern, a graduate student hired to conduct the interviews. Dr. Swenson silently admonished herself for not researching the details of this arrangement more thoroughly. "We're here to discuss Dr. Rapp's impact on the field, correct?" Martin Rapp at eighty-one lay dying in his bed at home of a melanoma metastasized to the liver. Overseeing his own biography would be the last act of his life. While Mrs. Rapp would not allow Dr. Swenson in the house to pay her respects (although at the age of sixty-two, Dr. Swenson would have run there gladly on a path of upturned nails), Dr. Rapp had sent word through an assistant that he wanted her to come to Cambridge to be interviewed for the book, to leave her research in the Amazon and fly to Cambridge to sit in front of this idiot and be asked the least important questions regarding his most important life.

"Correct," the interviewer said. "But this is a story about the man as well as the mushrooms. I want the readers to have a feeling for him, and that means getting to know you."

"How so?" She managed to pack an Arctic shelf of ice into those two words.

"I have the lists of everyone who went on his trips." For a moment he stopped and fumbled through his backpack as if he meant to produce the logs Dr. Rapp kept. He removed a sandwich in a plastic bag, a bruised apple, a plastic bottle containing a bright lavender beverage. After a considerable amount of rooting around, he seemed to resign himself to the fact that there were no notes. He decided to press ahead from memory. "The students change, the research assistants change, and yet you, Dr. Swenson, are always there: Indonesia, Africa, the entirety of South America. I have to wonder how you managed medical school."

"Dr. Rapp's records are meticulous, but I'm afraid your review of them is not. There were entire seasons of fieldwork I did not attend."

He shrugged, a single gesture that somehow managed to convey both stupidity and dismissiveness. "So you missed some trips. You're still the heir apparent to his legacy. You're the one continuing his work in Brazil."

Was Martin on that much pain medication that he would have hired this man, or hired another person who had incompetently hired him? Was Martin too sick to maintain oversight? It had been six years now since she had seen him. That was his last trip to the jungle. He had come without the usual cadre of students, and they rowed the canoe together, the two of them, in the bright light of morning. "With all due respect to Dr. Rapp and his enormous influence on my development as a scientist, the research I am conducting in the Amazon is my own." It was the thing she had learned as early as their first trip to South America: she had to have her own research. All the boys did was pander to Dr. Rapp and parrot back his ideas. But Dr. Rapp had never been looking for a partner in mycology. He had no interest in heirs. What he was looking for was intelligent conversation over brandy once the charts had been completed and the tarps had been secured for the night. What he was interested in was another scientific mind.

"You were an undergraduate when you began to travel together?"

"To Costa Rica," Dr. Swenson said. She pleased herself at the thought of that first night, the little tent she pitched by herself while the graduate students hovered around, begging to be of some ▸

Studies in Modern Mycology ***(continued)***

assistance, and how she hiked alone up a nearby cliff in the dark and spotted the orange glow of Dr. Rapp's pipe in the distance. The thrill she felt, when she realized what it was.

"Your parents thought nothing of you going off to Central America with your professor?"

That one at least made her blink, asking about her parents as if she were a schoolgirl, as if she would think of dredging up their memory for such nonsense. "I'm sure it's difficult for you to imagine that people could see, in this time before you were born, the value of an education for women."

"Not at all. But your relationship with Dr. Rapp—" He waited pointedly for her to help him finish his thought.

She leaned back in her chair, rolled a number-two pencil between her index finger and thumb. "Mr. . . ." she said finally. He had said his name when they came into the room, but she had disregarded it.

"Robinson," he said. "Please, call me Alec."

"Mr. Robinson, if there is something I can tell you about the discovery of a certain species, or if there is a particular event I may have been present for, I can help you. I'm sure you are interviewing people who have more insight than I do into the mushrooms themselves."

"When did your relationship with Dr. Rapp began?" Alec Robinson asked, leaning forward as if to show he would not be evaded. He was trying to be David Frost now, and that would make her Richard Nixon.

"Cambridge," she said. "1960."

"Your relationship," he repeated.

Everything ends. That's what medicine will teach you. No matter what the source of the suffering, sooner or later it would be over, taking the patient with it or not, and following that logic, this interview had now ended. Dr. Swenson picked up her satchel. It was with satisfaction that she thought of all the pictures and maps and carefully chosen journal entries she had brought with her, knowing that they could be useful for the project. All of that was hers again. She walked down the hallway and into the bright Cambridge autumn. She could hear Mr. Robinson trailing behind her, still talking, but she had ceased to listen. It had been three years since she had last come back to the States. To have left her work for this, well, Dr. Rapp would be mortified if he knew. But he wouldn't know. From what she understood of his condition, he would be dead long before the preliminary interviews for the book had been completed.

She turned in the direction of her hotel. Everything in Harvard Square had changed. All of these stores selling shoes and dresses, where had they come from? They should be bookstores, coffeeshops, places to buy cigarettes. No one should have to go back to the place where she had once been a girl. She could see herself everywhere on those streets, so serious and small, reading even while she walked.

It was New Year's Eve, or New Year's Day, close to midnight though she hadn't known the time. That was the answer to the question. They were in Peru, on a tributary off the Apurimac. The pummeling deluge of the late afternoon had given way to a lighter rain and the half dozen graduate students, all lazy boys, were sleeping in their various tents beneath the steady tapping of water. Annick Swenson had put on her poncho and gone out to sit on a soaking log to escape the particularly virulent band of mosquitoes that had been swarming around her sleeping bag. Not long after, Dr. Rapp came and stood beside her in the darkness. She could smell the tobacco in his pipe, which was somehow vaguely jasmine. One of the boys had told her he had it shipped in from Bali.

"Happy New Year, Miss Swenson," he said. His voice was clear and deep and it came from a place far above her head. He was so much taller than she was.

She wished him a happy New Year in return. It was her fifth trip with him in her third year of traveling. Contrary to Alec Robinson's report, she went on very few of the trips in those days. She was twenty-three years old. Dr. Rapp was forty-two.

"Do you have a resolution?" Dr. Rapp asked, sitting down beside her.

"A New Year's resolution?" She turned to look at him but it was very dark. She could only make out his outline, the place where he sat. "I've never believed in resolutions. I think it's better to have goals all year."

He seemed to think about this for some time and then, perhaps, he nodded. "I see."

"Do you have one?" she asked, concerned that she had answered his question incorrectly and that perhaps New Year's resolutions were a sign of good character.

Again he waited, and the rain came down on their heads and fell against the rubberized folds of their ponchos and spread across their shoulders as they sat side by side. "You, Miss Swenson," he said finally. "You are my resolution." And there in the darkness, in the rain, he took her hand.

Have You Read?
More by Ann Patchett

WHAT NOW?

What now? is an inspirational and thoughtful look at one of life's most important crossroads—graduation. With wit and candor, Patchett tells her own story of going to college, graduating, and answering the inevitable question, "What now?" But in a broader sense, this optimistic and feel-good book will appeal to anyone who finds him- or herself at a pivotal moment in life.

From waitress to line cook, from student to award-winning author, Patchett's own life has taken many twists and turns that make her exploration all the more genuine. Patchett understands that it's hard to know what's coming next, but she also highlights the pleasures of not knowing and not having everything nailed down. When you don't know what's coming next you can still believe that life is full of infinite possibilities, and she shows readers that there can be a great deal of excitement and joy in this state. Good for anyone looking for a little encouragement, this illustrated book will be the perfect gift for graduates and Ann Patchett fans alike who are contemplating their futures and seeking guidance or a few heartfelt words from one of our great contemporary authors.

RUN

Ann Patchett's fifth novel is the engrossing story of one Boston family on one fateful night during a harrowing blizzard.

Bernard Doyle didn't get the life he wanted. His beloved wife died when their children were young, and years later his oldest son, Sullivan, was a part of a scandal that ended Doyle's career as mayor. Now he has pinned his hopes on his two younger boys, his adopted sons, Tip and Teddy, both of whom are in college. He is certain that under his careful tutelage one of them will pick up the life of politics that he was forced to lay aside. The problem is that Tip is only interested in studying fish at Harvard, and Teddy sees his future in the Catholic Church. When the three of them step out of a Jesse Jackson lecture and into a blizzard on a Boston night, a violent turn of events forces each of them to reconsider not only what it is they've always wanted but who they really are.

At its center, *Run* is a novel about what defines family and the lengths we will go to protect our children. As she did in her bestselling novel *Bel Canto*, Ann Patchett beautifully weaves together seemingly disparate lives to bring our common humanity to light. Surprising and stunningly executed, *Run* is just the book to please her many fans while bringing her to the attention of an even larger audience.

Have You Read? ***(continued)***

TRUTH & BEAUTY: A FRIENDSHIP

Ann Patchett offers a startlingly honest look at her intense, chaotic friendship with the late poet Lucy Grealy, author of the bestselling memoir *Autobiography of a Face*. The two met in college in 1981, and, after enrolling in the Iowa Writers' Workshop, began a friendship that would be as defining to both of their lives as would be their work. This is a portrait of unwavering commitment that spans twenty years, from the long, cold winters of the Midwest to endless surgical wards, to the book parties of New York City. Through love, fame, drugs, and despair, this book shows us what it means to be part of two lives that are intertwined. Patchett's writing is frank, powerful, and utterly convincing, and the story of her life with Lucy is both tender and brutal. Beyond the tragedy of Lucy's death, this is a book about loyalty, and about being lifted up by the sheer effervescence of someone who knew how to live life to the fullest.

"A work every bit as entrancing, daring, and smart as her fiction—channels her grief [into] an electrifying portrait of Grealy, a bravura self-portrait, and a stunning and insightful interpretation of an epic friendship. . . . A generous and virtuoso performance."

—*Atlanta Journal-Constitution*

BEL CANTO

Somewhere in South America, at the home of the country's vice president, a lavish birthday party is being held in honor of the powerful businessman Mr. Hosokawa. Roxanne Cross, opera's most revered soprano, has mesmerized the international guests with her singing. It is a perfect evening—until a band of gun-wielding terrorists takes the entire party hostage. But what begins as a panicked, life-threatening scenario slowly evolves into something quite different, a moment of great beauty, as terrorists and hostages forge unexpected bonds, and people from different continents become compatriots, intimate friends, and lovers.

"*Bel Canto* is its own universe. A marvel of a book." —*Washington Post Book World*